My Lady Marzipan

Rare Confectionery Book Three

SYDNEY JANE BAILY

cat whisker press
Massachusetts

First Paperback Edition
ISBN 978-1-938732-34-8

Published by **cat whisker press**
Imprint of JAMES-YORK PRESS

Cover: Wicked Smart Designs
In conjunction with Philip Ré
Book Design: Cat Whisker Studio
Editor: Chloe Bearuski

DEDICATION

For Perry

The sweetest, nuttiest soul I know

OTHER WORKS
by
SYDNEY JANE BAILY

The RAKES ON THE RUN Series

Last Dance in London
Pursued in Paris
Banished to Brighton
Gretna Green by Sunset

The RARE CONFECTIONERY Series

The Duchess of Chocolate
The Toffee Heiress
My Lady Marzipan

The DEFIANT HEARTS Series

An Improper Situation
An Irresistible Temptation
An Inescapable Attraction
An Inconceivable Deception
An Intriguing Proposition
An Impassioned Redemption

The BEASTLY LORDS Series

Lord Despair
Lord Anguish
Lord Vile
Lord Darkness
Lord Misery
Lord Wrath
Eleanor

PRESENTING LADY GUS

A Georgian-Era Novella

ACKNOWLEDGMENTS

Thanks to the following beta readers: Toni Young, Philip Ré, Renee Sevelitte, and Victoria Piercey for doing their due diligence and having eagle eyes. And a big thank you to my mom, Beryl Baily, for always being supportive and loving.

PROLOGUE

London, 1879

Charlotte finished making small marzipan faux peaches, applying pistachio paste leaves to little clove stems before placing them on the plate in the display case.

"I am starting to think this is a magical confectionery," she said, thinking of the good fortune of her two older sisters. "You simply waited for the right man to come in, and he did."

"That's ridiculous," Beatrice said, leaning against the counter and stretching her back. "I worked hard even to like Greer before I loved him."

They all chuckled. Some considered the middle Rare-Foure sister to be prickly, and Beatrice and her husband had certainly traveled a bumpy road while falling in love.

"And I met Henry for the first time in a carriage," their eldest sister, Amity, pointed out, helping herself to a plain chocolate. "*Mm,*" she sighed happily.

"That may be true," Charlotte agreed, "but first, your beloved duke came in here, searching specifically for you."

"For *our* sister, of all people!" Beatrice quipped, earning an unduchess-like response from Amity, who stuck out her tongue.

They laughed again.

"In any case," Amity said, "I think you had best keep your eyes upon the door."

Charlotte shrugged. "I always do. After all, I've seen the men a London Season has to offer, and I wasn't impressed quite frankly. On the other hand, if I meet a man outside of the shop, I wouldn't discount him entirely."

Especially one in particular.

"What about the magic of Rare Confectionery?" Beatrice asked wryly.

Shrugging, Charlotte thought about Lionel Evans and how many times she'd invited him to come to the shop. "I cannot simply wait for lightning to strike thrice, as they say."

"Do they say that?" Amity asked, heading toward the curtain and the back room where she still had to clean up her work area.

"Something like that," Charlotte said.

Beatrice shook her head. "I believe the saying is more like 'lightning never strikes but once in the same place.'"

"But it did," Charlotte persisted, "for you two."

"Is love like lightning?" Amity wondered. The three of them stared at one another for a moment.

Then the shop bell tinkled. With wide eyes, they all turned expectantly to see an older man with a cane and an ancient top hat. This made them dissolve into a fit of giggles.

"Go on then," Beatrice told Charlotte as she pulled open the curtain to the back room. And before she and Amity disappeared, she added, "Wait on your Prince Charming."

CHAPTER ONE

The days leading up to Easter Sunday were bustling, and it seemed to Charlotte that every last Londoner had decided to buy their confectionery at the same time—and just before closing! As usual, she was offering samples and handling the counter sales, while her sisters made chocolates and trays of toffee in the back room. Amity's bunny-shaped chocolates and her chocolate eggs filled with creamy fondant, far larger than Mr. Cadbury's solid chocolate eggs, were selling well as were her own fruit-shaped marzipan creations.

All the past week and right through to Saturday evening when everything would grow as quiet as a fish, her mother, Felicity, was also in Rare Confectionery dealing with customers. To the youngest Rare-Foure sister, these were the best of times, when they were all together and the busy hours flew by. Moreover, she enjoyed how happy people became when they tasted a sweet for the first time and found it to be their favorite.

Charlotte didn't even mind when customers stayed to chat about their feast-day plans simply because, as her sisters often said, she was easy to talk to.

Today, however, when one chatty lady dawdled to offer her best wishes of the festive Easter week, those behind grew restless and grumpy. If Charlotte had her way, she would toss sweets over the heads of those pressing against the counter to reach everyone waiting in line. No one could be crabbed when eating confectionery. At least, that had been her experience in her nineteen years, thirteen of them spent in the confectionery, either watching and learning or serving.

Suddenly, in the midst of the already chaotic scene came three noblemen—her eldest sister's husband, the Duke of Pelham, and his two best friends, the oft-smirking Lord Waverly and the rather serious Lord Jeffcoat. Impeccably dressed and taller than their usual female customers, the men caused a stir and couldn't have picked a more hectic moment to pay a visit.

The last time she'd seen them all together had been at a costume ball for fourteen hundred revelers at Marlborough House the previous year. Even that had seemed less frenzied than their Bond Street shop with patrons demanding tins of this and bags of that.

With the dignity and authority of the highest rank of nobleman, the duke sliced through the crowd with evident purpose and slipped between the counters. After greeting his wife's mother and a nod to Charlotte, he disappeared behind the blue velvet curtain separating the front of the shop from the workroom. Apparently, he was there to visit with his wife who now carried their first child.

Charlotte's mother sent her a questioning look but continued to weigh toffee in the pan of their copper balance scale for the customer in front of her. For her part, Charlotte handed another woman a bag of chocolates, quickly took the payment, which she tossed willy-nilly into the cashbox, and turned to the next in line. As she did, she caught the observing glance of Lord Jeffcoat.

"Robin Hood," she greeted loudly over the noise. The dark-haired viscount had looked very fine at the ball in a tunic and long hose. Although her heart was engaged elsewhere, she had appreciated his shapely legs and arms. It hadn't been their first enjoyable encounter, either, as she'd once dined as his companion at the ducal residence on St. James's Place before the Duke of Pelham had married her sister.

While a tad solemn for her taste, Lord Jeffcoat's conversational skills had kept her amused all evening.

While Lord Waverly, who no one ever accused of being somber, winked outrageously at her, Lord Jeffcoat tipped his hat in greeting.

"Regards of the day, Turkish Princess."

She smiled at the memory of her colorful, silky costume that night. She'd been an exotic princess. Presently, feeling a little warm, with wisps of hair sticking to her temples, Charlotte didn't feel like a princess, Turkish or otherwise.

"I said I want a pound of toffee," an annoyed voice brought her attention back to her duty. "And I'm waiting."

With aplomb, as she'd asked a hundred times, she offered, "Plain or with nuts, madam?"

The woman's face puckered. "Of course, plain! Anything else is unnatural."

Charlotte couldn't help grinning. This remark tickled her, and as she packaged up a pound of Beatrice's buttery treacle toffee, she hoped she would remember to tell her. *How funny!*

"Are you laughing at me?" asked the woman with a face that would turn honey mead into vinegar.

"Merely thinking joyful thoughts," Charlotte answered swiftly. "Easy to do as we approach Easter. Would you care for a sample?" She nearly added, "Perhaps some of the unnatural toffee?" but kept that to herself.

"Only to have you charge me extra, no doubt," said the woman. She was obviously a brand-new customer and a sour one at that.

"Entirely free of charge, I assure you. Please, choose something." *And hurry*, Charlotte thought. The mob behind was growing increasingly impatient.

Looking suspicious nonetheless, the woman pointed to one of Charlotte's marzipan flowers dusted with cocoa powder. Using tongs to snag it, she set it quickly on a paper square. They eschewed their usual dainty china plates for samples that week, as the risk of them being broken was too great, not to mention constantly needing to wash them.

Snatching the treat as if the offer might be rescinded, the woman crammed it into her mouth in one bite. And then, as Charlotte knew it would, a miracle happened. The crabby customer chewed, and when the delicate sweetness burst upon her tongue, her eyes glazed over with a faraway look of happiness. And then, she smiled.

The rest of the transaction, exchanging the tin of toffee for coins, happened smoothly.

"Thank you, miss," the woman said, appearing entirely soothed. "I'll return soon." She moved away from the counter and seemed to float from the store.

Charlotte adored when that happened. Loud laughter caught her attention. Glancing up, she saw the viscounts in conversation with Lord Waverly gesticulating, doing most of the talking, and all of the laughing. Lord Jeffcoat, however, was clearly looking in her direction. When he caught her glance, he nodded. Not sure what to make of that, she nodded in return.

"Miss, please, miss," came a younger voice, and Charlotte had to lean farther over the counter to see a child, perhaps eight, with sandy-colored hair, shabbily dressed in a patched coat but clean-looking nonetheless.

"May I have a marzipan pig?" he asked.

"Why, yes, of course." It was her family's policy to accommodate the youngest citizens, even those who wanted only samples. Her parents had never forgotten that sweets were enjoyed most of all by children, and made sure their daughters didn't let London's youngsters go without.

Turning aside to the glass display case, she used the tongs to pluck one of the last of her swine creations with its cherry-juice blush skin. Not the usual Easter fare, but their sweet round bodies and carefully crafted swirl of a marzipan tail had made them popular. Placing this in a bleached-white paper bag with "Rare Confectionery" stamped upon it in sapphire-blue ink, she turned back to find her young customer had disappeared.

Her gaze first flew to the duke's friends, as standing in the customers' midst, they were the most obtrusive people in the shop.

Lord Jeffcoat raised a dark eyebrow as well as a hand before pointing toward the opposite wall. To her alarm, the lad was being lambasted by a woman dressed to the nines and to whom Charlotte had recently sold a pound of chocolates.

"You do not belong here," the woman raised her voice with derision, an elegantly gloved finger practically touching the boy's nose. "For all I know, you have fleas."

The boy took a step back, eyes wide, looking not angry as Charlotte would expect, but ashamed.

"You!" Charlotte called out from her post behind the counter, hoping to put a stop to such mean-spiritedness. The well-dressed lady ignored her.

"You, there," Charlotte tried again, but still, the woman had more to say to the boy.

"Imagine the likes of you being in this nice establishment. Do you know what that means, *establishment?* It means a place where street urchins do not belong."

Without thinking, Charlotte whistled, a skill her father taught her, which unnerved some folks for its shrill loudness but usually succeeded in getting someone's attention.

The entire shop fell silent, and every eye and head turned toward her, including her mother's. Felicity positively hated the sound.

In a flash, the duke, Beatrice, and Amity appeared from the back room, since they knew the sound of her forbidden whistle when customers were in the shop could only mean trouble.

Charlotte ignored everyone except the woman, now gawking at her, and the boy, who cringed against the shelves of shiny, empty tins awaiting to be filled by a customer's selection.

"I am speaking to you," Charlotte said into the silence.

The woman frowned, turned from the boy and took a step toward the counter although she couldn't get any closer through the crowd. "I already have my purchases."

"I know," Charlotte said, her tone as kind as ever but firm. "And now, I must ask you to leave as you are disturbing our other customers."

A collective gasp occurred at the intent of her words.

"Can you mean . . . ? Are you saying . . . ? Well, I never!" And the woman pushed her way toward the door.

Lord Jeffcoat beat her to it and held it open.

"She left more easily than I hoped," Charlotte said to her mother who regarded her silently.

Then Felicity sighed audibly, shook her head slightly, and returned her attention to the customers. "Who is next, please?" The hurly-burly recommenced in seconds.

The boy was about to leave, as well, but he darted a glance Charlotte's way. She smiled, crooked her finger at him, and held up the bag. He bit his lip but approached the counter, having to squeeze between other customers.

"There you go, poppet, one marzipan pig."

"I wasn't asking for nothing free, miss. I've saved up. It's for my mum." And he dug into his pocket and pulled out three farthings, and her heart clenched in her chest. Not even a whole penny.

Sensing the lad didn't want to be given a handout, Charlotte told him a small white lie, "You have quite a bit of change coming, unless you'd like to pick out something more. Also, every customer gets a sample at no charge." She avoided using the word *free*.

"Truly, miss?" His brown eyes looked delighted but doubtful.

"Truly. What do you fancy?"

"Well, I'd like a piece of toffee, miss, for my brother and sister. We can cut it in half. They'd be ever so pleased."

"Very well, but since the toffee might squish the pig, let me put it in a separate bag." Without him noticing, she shoveled in two pieces each of the plain, the one with nuts, and the chocolate-covered toffee." *The unnatural selections!*

"And for your sample, young sir?"

His cheeks turned pink at her form of address. "Will you put it in the bag, too, miss?"

She shook her head, knowing the boy intended to give it away. "Samples must be eaten here. That way, I can see if you like it."

"If that's the rule, miss," he said, again looking happy at her rules. She couldn't remember the last time she'd had to convince a child to take a sweet for himself.

"How about a chocolate?" she offered.

"Thank you, miss. Whatever you think best."

She managed to keep a straight face at his serious tone. Choosing a large bonbon of pure creamy chocolate fondant coated in plain chocolate, she decided to use one of their china saucer-sized plates instead of the paper and handed it to him.

When he saw the size of the confection, he swallowed, glanced at her, then back at the chocolate. She could practically see his mouth watering. Raising the bonbon, he examined it before biting into it.

Ah, she thought, *a boy who knows how to make something last.* By his broad smile as he savored it, she'd chosen well.

"What do you think?"

"I think it's the best thing I've ever tasted in my whole life, miss." He popped the rest between his lips.

She nodded, glad she hadn't given him marzipan instead simply out of pride of her own creation. Most children wrinkled their nose at the creamy almond paste when they could have chocolate or toffee.

"It seems like sorcery," he continued, "the way it melted on my tongue. The outside dissolved before the inside. I vow, miss, there wasn't merely one flavor but many."

She paused. They gave hundreds of samples a year, but she couldn't recall the last time she'd had a child in there who was as well-behaved and articulate as this one. Most children grabbed at anything she handed out and ate it without discretion.

But this lad . . . there was something about him.

"Charlotte," her mother caught her attention. The line of customers was out the door. Suddenly, she had an idea.

"Are you in school?" she asked.

"No, miss," he said, then shrugged.

She hoped he meant due to Easter week and not because he didn't attend, at the very least, one of London's so-called Ragged Schools, if not something better.

"Do you have a job?" she persisted, for even the youngest often were apprenticed to various skilled trades or were already factory workers, slaves to dark rooms and machines all day.

"No, miss. Nothing to be found nowhere because of the season. I'll be looking again after Easter Sunday."

The Elementary Education Act, which passed with much hullaballoo three years earlier, could cause a problem. "How old are you?" If he were under ten, as he appeared, then it was illegal to hire him anyway.

"I'm twelve, miss."

Goodness, he was small for his age. He clearly needed a few hearty meals and not merely sweets.

"Would you come again tomorrow, either at eight o'clock before we open or at six after we close?"

"What for, miss?"

"A job if you're willing."

His face lit with excitement. "Yes, miss. First thing in the morning, I'll be here. Thank you, miss. Thank you."

Thrilled, he nearly dashed out of the store without his purchases, but she managed to get both bags to him and ask his name.

"Percy, miss. It's Edward Percy."

Then Lord Jeffcoat, having remained stationed by the busy door, opened it and let the boy out and a cool April breeze in. Once more, the viscount's gaze caught hers. Charlotte wasn't sure if he could have heard her discourse with young Mr. Percy, but he eyed her with what she now realized were rather attractive, thoughtful eyes, almost as blue as her sister Bea's.

HAVING WORKED A QUARTER of an hour past closing, Charlotte was relieved when her mother finally announced they were done for the day. Felicity had already told Lord Jeffcoat to turn the sign as if he were an employee.

"And don't let anyone else in," she'd ordered, which caused Lord Waverly to ask, "Shall I start to sweep now, madam?"

Those remaining in the shop chuckled. The Duke of Pelham came from the back room with Amity, who was growing round with their first child, and Beatrice, both already wearing their cloaks, gloves, and hats.

While tending to the last customers, Felicity asked, "Where is my duchess of a daughter heading tonight?"

Charlotte couldn't help smiling. Her mother prized Amity's great fortune in marrying a duke and especially in doing so for love.

"We are going to the Dowager Duchess's home for supper," Amity said, referring to her mother-in-law. "All of us," she added, taking in the other two men.

"Not me," Beatrice said. "I'm heading home to my American, in case anyone's interested."

"Oh, we are," Lord Waverly promised, with an exaggerated tone, making them laugh. "And what about you, Miss Rare-Foure?"

Charlotte still found it amusing how she'd moved up in formal address after Beatrice married the previous autumn. She used to be simply *Miss Charlotte*.

"Perhaps you would care to accompany us," Lord Jeffcoat unexpectedly blurted, "if that's all right with Pelham, assuming there is room at the dowager's table."

Charlotte startled at the invitation from such an unexpected source. The viscount had now addressed her twice in the space of half an hour.

"My sister-in-law knows she is always welcome," the duke said. They all waited, looking at her.

Were Lord Jeffcoat and the rest of them feeling sorry for her? She was, after all, the last sister to be plucked from the vine of single womanhood.

She smiled at all of them. "Tonight is my art class at Burlington House, and I never miss it. But thank you for inviting me." She addressed that remark to both her brother-in-law and the two viscounts. "In fact, I must hurry."

Normally, she would have left Rare Confectionery in the capable hands of one of her family members and hurried off down the street. However, with the madding crowds of London seeking Easter sweets, Charlotte had needed to stay.

"Go, dear," her mother said. "I hope you're not too late."

Late or not, Charlotte intended to go to the academy. All she had to do was walk a little way until New Bond Street became Old Bond Street, and turn left at Burlington

Gardens. If the weather was poor or if it were dreadfully cold, she would go through the covered passage of shops known as the Burlington Arcade. If it were fine weather or if she were in a hurry as she was that evening, she would dart behind the arcade to more swiftly reach the Royal Academy of Art, housed in the main building at the northern end of the Burlington House courtyard.

Entering the esteemed academy and attending a painting class was the most exciting thing she did all week, twice a week. And not only because she often met painters in the lobby or got to see magnificent works of art newly displayed, sometimes before the public. No, it was because of a fellow student.

Over the last year, eight times a month, she had made moon eyes at Lionel Evans, while he sketched and painted, and while she half-heartedly and with great distraction did the same. Seeing him were the highpoints of her week, and she approached each class with great expectations. His sister, Viola, rather silly and spoiled but affable, was always ready to chat more than sketch, and when she did turn her attention to her drawing or canvas, she was even less talented than Charlotte.

Occasionally, Lionel joined in their conversation, and Charlotte always made a point to extend the invitation for them to visit the shop. He'd even agreed to do so. Nevertheless, when Viola had come in on two occasions, she'd been by herself.

Once, feeling a little shy, she'd brought a tin of her fruit-shaped marzipan to the class. The teacher and the other students had proclaimed them clever little works of art, but Lionel had not cared for the taste.

Still, after class, while Viola talked to their teacher, Lionel had struck up their first real private conversation.

"You have a talent for sculpture, Miss Rare-Foure. Why do you bother with painting?"

She supposed that meant he didn't think she had a talent for painting, which was perfectly true. But she could hardly tell him she bothered with it simply to be near him in class.

Instead, tongue-tied, she'd shrugged, but that night when alone, she was at least able to relish his having finally taken an interest in her. Twice a week since then, they'd chatted more. And then, one time, Viola had been absent due to a megrim, and Lionel had lingered after class while Charlotte gathered her things. In the hallowed halls of the academy, which were also quiet and shadowed by that time, he'd leaned close and kissed her—a furtive, splendid, terrifying kiss!

After that, she looked forward to each class with thrilling anticipation, usually ending with her hopes if not dashed, then definitely dimmed. Viola was always there between them, chatting, until a couple of months earlier, just after the new year. At that time, Viola stopped coming entirely without even saying goodbye. Lionel said she'd found another pastime in flute lessons.

Charlotte felt guilty for being pleased and knew it was wrong to be excited at no longer having Viola wedged firmly between them. And that evening, after class, Lionel took her in his arms and soundly kissed her for the first time. Their teeth clacked, and there was an unexpected exchange of spittle. But she was in Lionel's arms. *At last!* Surely, he would send an invitation by the morning post to escort her somewhere, such as a concert or play.

But he hadn't. A few nights later, when next their class met, it dragged on long enough for her to believe all the clocks had stopped in London.

"You know where I live, don't you?" she asked him with a degree of timidness that wasn't like her, but fearing if she pushed him, he would go back to the standoffish person he'd been for over a year.

"Yes," he said. *"Shh."* And he'd started to kiss her, backing her against the wall, which felt cool behind her back.

"Baker Street," she said when he lifted his head with his long pale hair unfashionably tied back in a thong as if he were from another century.

"And you know where I work," she reminded him.

"*Mm,*" he said, lowering his mouth to hers again. "At that sweet shop."

She'd given in to the sensations of a man's mouth searing her own. Or rather, warmly and moistly exploring her lips.

At the end of every class for the past month, he'd found a way for them to stay behind. The one time he hadn't, she'd had to go back for her "dropped" glove, finding Lionel in the upstairs hallway, looking annoyed. His irritation and his frown cleared as soon as he saw her.

"I thought you had left." His sulky tone demonstrated his feelings for her.

She nearly said, "Never!" In truth, however, she couldn't help wondering where this was going. If her parents knew of the liberties Lionel took, they would forbid Charlotte going to class. And for her own part, she wanted him to declare his intention to ask her out, to do something with him besides paint or kiss. Surely, he had an interest in seeing her in the daylight, in strolling through the park or even going to the theatre.

Perhaps he would declare himself her suitor that night!

Hurrying into the back room under the many watchful eyes, she thought her cheeks were going to be red as strawberries with guilt over her inappropriate thoughts. Putting on her springtime, pale-gray cloak, she pinned her hat in place and tugged on her gloves. After snatching up her satchel with her art supplies, she emerged to find everyone still there, talking to Felicity.

Charlotte would speak with her mother later when she had time about the offer she'd made to Edward Percy. Bidding everyone good day, she walked toward the door.

Lord Jeffcoat remained at attendance and held it open for her. Their eyes locked, and he gave her a friendly nod.

"Be well, Miss Rare-Foure."

"And you, my lord," she returned, aware of having to brush past him. She even caught scent of his cologne, turning her face toward him for the briefest moment before strolling out into the dimming light.

As she hurried toward the academy, wishing she were already there and not missing a minute of Lionel's company, strangely instead of anticipating the evening ahead as usual, she was recalling the incredibly intoxicating aroma of Lord Jeffcoat, a smoky gingerbread scent with a hint of rum. Her father, who had made a good living trading in sugar, often had West Indies rum in his study, and naturally, Charlotte had tasted it with a squeeze of lime.

Most unusual and delicious, she mused, then shook her head to clear it of the image of the viscount. *What on earth had got into her?*

CHAPTER TWO

Lord Charles Jeffcoat knew he was in trouble. Although he'd been in the company of Charlotte Rare-Foure on numerous occasions and even partnered with her at Pelham's dinner table when his friend was still chasing that shallow earl's daughter two years earlier, he wasn't sure he'd ever really seen her before.

At the fancy dress ball at Marlborough House seven months prior, she'd looked pretty, of course, in colorful Turkish garb, with a mid-length blue skirt putting on display her brightly colored yellow and green silk pantaloons, along with allowing a hint of her ankles. Along with every man in the room, he'd also noticed her low-cut scarlet bodice— apropos to the costume, of course—showing off her shapely bosom. He hadn't been able to forget the vision of her.

Beyond her looks, however, every time they'd met, he'd considered her to be a little light between the ears, wide-eyed at everything, elated by the duke's dining room, thrilled at her sister's wedding reception, and even spinning like a top to show off her silks at the costume ball. He'd considered her practically a child, except for her distinctly feminine attributes, and also a tad vain.

Today, watching her handle difficult customers and witnessing her extreme kindness to the boy, he realized Charlotte was a grown woman with something quite special about her. He could hardly credit himself inviting her spontaneously to the dowager duchess's party the night before, but he hadn't wanted to say goodbye.

Waverly would never let him live it down. Charles had tried to ignore his friend's ribbing all evening and his muttering under his breath, "Come to dinner, saucy shopgirl, oh, do, please!" Charles nearly stabbed him with a fork by the end of the *relevés* course.

Now, in the light of day, seated at a table in the library at Lincoln's Inn of which he was a member and had received his training, Charles had trouble keeping his mind on the law and off the impressive Charlotte. Taking off his spectacles, he rubbed the bridge of his nose.

She was not his usual cup of tea, to be sure. He had escorted a few women over the past few years, a head-strong granddaughter of a duke, a tart-tongued baronet's sister, and, once, a Spanish princess to whom he'd almost given his heart, but she'd longed for home and he was an Englishman through and through.

Last Season, he'd avoided the debutante events and been mostly occupied with studying the law and the baronet's sister. Her sharp tongue eventually sliced him one time too many, and he found he preferred the quiet of his own company, the solitude of his law books, or the irreverent and jolly fun of Waverly. Moreover, he'd been called to the Bar at Michaelmas and could now practice the profession.

Drawing a new pen from his pocket, he turned the page on his tablet of paper, put on his glasses, and went back to scrawling notes about his latest case. Unlike Pelham and Waverly, Charles knew his future was not in Parliament but in the courts. If his friends passed the bills, then Charles wanted to see the laws of the land upheld by arguing each case and demonstrating the right of it. Eventually, perhaps he might even become a judge.

"Why not?" he asked himself as long as he didn't let a distraction like the tempting Miss Rare-Foure get in his way. At that moment, he realized he had sketched a pair of long-lashed eyes and a set of full lips on the top of a page that should already be filled with notes.

On the other hand, a man had to have balance in his life. She might have been busy the night before, but she might be open to him escorting her to a concert or a play. He supposed the only way to know was to ask her.

CHARLOTTE COULD BARELY DRAG herself into work, walking with sluggish feet down New Bond Street. She would have begged off work due to an aching head, which was the truth, and stayed home if she hadn't loved her family so much. She simply couldn't leave her mother and sisters short-handed on yet another busy day of Easter week.

In fact, she'd left for the shop earlier than usual to avoid any discussion over breakfast. Nevertheless, she walked reluctantly, not eager to be anywhere in particular. Her head down, staring at the pavement, Charlotte noted for the first time how gray it was. Everything in London was gray in fact. The buildings, the sky overhead, her reflection in the windows, the other people coming toward her or passing her by. Moreover, she seemed to have gained an enormous amount of weight overnight. Not only were her limbs leaden, her heart felt like a massive stone in her chest. Beyond all that, her eyes were the consistency of overcooked coddled eggs as she'd spent more of the night crying than sleeping.

Again, as countless times over the last few hours, her thoughts turned to Viola's stricken visage when Charlotte had entered the art studio five minutes late.

Instead of being shocked that Viola had returned to class, she glanced past her to look for Lionel. Last night, however, he'd been absent from his spot, just an empty stool and easel. Then she'd really taken note of Viola. Something awful had happened, and her heart had tightened. *Was Lionel hurt? Taken ill?*

"What's wrong?" she'd asked, scarcely able to breathe, not sure she wanted to hear.

"It's my brother. He's gone." A tear had slid down Viola's cheek.

Ignoring the fact that their teacher and all the other students were listening in, Charlotte gasped.

"Gone? Where? For how long?"

"To the Continent. Forever, I think." Viola dabbed at her eyes with a handkerchief. "He ran off with the model."

"*My* model," their teacher had interrupted, derision in his tone.

Charlotte brought to mind the woman who often sat in the middle of their easels, her blonde hair over one shoulder in a cascade of riotous curls or up in an imitation of a Grecian style, and her attractive body draped in any manner of materials, sometimes velvet, sometimes silk. At times, their teacher gave her a vase to hold, or a mirror or even a piece of fruit.

In all the hours Charlotte had spent observing Lionel, she'd never noticed him paying special attention to the model. Not once. She, herself, didn't even know the woman's name.

"Miss Rare-Foure," the teacher had said to Charlotte, his tone remaining irritated, "would you model for us tonight?"

She'd reared back, still shocked by the suddenness of Lionel's departure. The enormity of his betrayal rained down upon her like a sudden London shower. *Why had he kissed her if not to start something wonderful?*

"Miss Rare-Foure," the teacher prompted again.

Even if she hadn't been on the brink of tears to match Viola's, she had no intention of displaying herself in the center of the art students. Her mother would never forgive such vulgarity.

"No, thank you," she'd said. "I am not staying."

The teacher sighed, and asked another female student on the other side of the room, and all the focus turned away.

"Are *you* staying?" she'd asked Viola.

"No, I came only to tell you," she said, gesturing with her hands to show that she had no supplies with her. "When you weren't here on time, I thought perhaps you had gone with him and I'd been mistaken about the model."

Charlotte shuddered again at the notion. She would never do something that rash!

As she put the key in the lock of Rare Confectionery, Charlotte's heart ached at the thought of Lionel and his blonde model taking the train from Charing Cross station and then the ferry across the Channel to start a new life. Viola said he'd left their parents a note stating he wanted to practice his art amongst the old masters and ancient ruins of Europe.

Pushing open the door, she stepped inside and instantly the walls closed around her, leaving her feeling trapped and . . . abandoned. Lionel could have simply gone to one of their London museums and set up his easel among their grand collections of Dutch and Flemish oils, not to mention the Elgin marbles for inspiration.

She would never see him again! That terrible thought stopped her in the middle of the wooden floor, tears pricking her eyes as they'd done all night. *How would she bear the loss of him and his kisses?* She thought of Viola's momentary concern that Charlotte had been the one to go with him.

Despite hearing the bell tinkle behind her, lost in a fanciful game of *what-if*, she didn't turn. Deep down in her bones, Charlotte knew she never would have done such a selfish thing to her family. Not even for Lionel.

"Miss, excuse me, miss?"

"We're not open yet," she said, her voice choked with emotion.

"I know, miss. You said to come back."

All at once, she remembered—Edward Percy. Taking a deep breath, collecting herself, she turned to face the boy who'd touched her heart. In that instant, seeing him, hat-in-hand, wearing the same clothes as the day before, with his hair combed under his worn cap, his face obviously scrubbed clean, she recalled life was far bigger than her obsession with Lionel Evans.

"Hello, Edward," she began, trying to put her thoughts in order. "You are certainly prompt."

"Yes, miss. I wouldn't take lightly the offer of work."

Ah, yes. Her offer of a job. After the heartbreaking debacle at the academy, Charlotte had gone home and directly up to her room. She hadn't asked her mother's permission about employing young Edward. Indeed, she'd forgotten all about him. However, it was decidedly Felicity's shop, not hers nor her sisters' and not even their father's. What her mother said was law at Rare Confectionery, and it had always been that way.

But things had been changing, and quickly. Her mother had left the running of the shop to her grown daughters for the past few years, coming in for a few hours as it suited her. Amity wasn't there as often since becoming—of all incredible things—a duchess in February of the prior year. And Beatrice, who had married Mr. Carson just last autumn, sometimes kept shorter hours. Only Charlotte's role had remained the same.

The truth of the night's heartbreak crashed in upon her once more. To think, she had brought it upon herself—believing he cared for her when she hadn't meant a thing to him. It had been all on her side, in her own head. Through the entire Season the year before, she hadn't truly considered anyone with whom she'd met and danced, because Lionel had taken up all the space in her heart and her mind. All for naught. Just wishful thinking.

And then he'd started to kiss her . . .

Not only that, ever since The Langham, London's most opulent hotel, had contracted with them the previous summer to provide all their confectionery, others had taken notice. Rare Confectionery now had weekly deliveries to The Grosvenor Hotel at Victoria Station and The Great-Western Hotel at Paddington, as well as at The Albion, a restaurant in Covent Garden, and the Gaiety Restaurant on the Strand.

Charlotte, her mother, and her sisters hadn't had a discussion yet, but they would soon need help to fill the orders as the demand was more than the three of them could produce, especially while also keeping the shop stocked—and if they wanted to continue to expand their business.

Did they? Perhaps her family was moving on to other interests. With Amity due to have a child in a few months, everything would change drastically again. While her sister pledged her continued support of Rare Confectionery and her desire to be their chocolatier, she'd already cut back on her hours. *What would they do if she couldn't make chocolates for an extended period of time?*

And Bea and her husband had found time to go to their country home in Scotland just once since their marriage, and Charlotte knew they were dying to go back and work on the farmhouse.

If both her sisters moved on with their lives, how would the confectionery continue? One thing Charlotte was certain of—she ought to dust off her skills making both chocolates and toffee. Anyone could run the front counter, but the lessons and recipes they'd learned from their mother to make delicious confectionery were special.

At that particular moment though, all Charlotte wanted to do was close the shop entirely, go home, and bury her head under her pillow. But here she was, faced with the eager Edward.

"Do you have a certificate of standard saying you don't have to be in school?" she asked.

He hesitated, either because he hadn't expected such a question or because he was about to lie to her.

"Yes, miss, at home. Anyways, I'll be thirteen in six months and then they can't make me go back."

Good enough, she supposed. It wasn't as if she were trying to force a six-year-old to be a chimney sweep. Charlotte couldn't contain a small shudder at the dreadful notion. What an awful existence those children had endured before the Chimney Sweepers' Act passed a mere four years earlier. While many youngsters still worked dangerous jobs in mines, mills, and factories, at least she could offer Edward something better.

"Very well. At first, I thought you were younger and could only tidy and sweep, but since you're twelve, I hope I can count on you to handle deliveries. Our confectionery goes to hotels and restaurants around the area. Can you handle that?"

"Oh, yes, miss. I know London as well as any cabbie."

"Good. You might be given tips by any of those establishments, and you're free to accept them. Plus, I'll pay you—" With no idea what she ought to give him, she almost said *thruppence,* then doubled it at the last second. "Six pence a day."

His eyes grew wide. "A tanner, miss! That's a pound, every forty days!" His tone was one of awe.

"Maybe sooner. We'll see how you get on, Edward. Shall we?" Plus, she had to ask her mother, and maybe Felicity would say it ought to be a shilling a day, in which case the boy's eyes might fall out of his head altogether. It also depended on how many hours he put in and what use they could make of him.

"We'll have to make you a small apron like I used to have when I was a youngster, but for now, come in the back."

Leading him between the counters and into the workroom, she showed him where he could hang his coat and put his scruffy cap on a shelf. Then she hung her own coat beside his, before untying her bonnet, having been unable to care about pinning a stylish hat in place that morning.

From the drawer where they stored aprons, she pulled out a clean one and tried tying it high up under his arms. It did no good. He would still trip.

"Never mind, I'll figure out your apron by tomorrow." Charlotte pinned and tied her own on. He nodded, staring around the room at the big iron stove and copper counters and across from it, the marble slab where Amity tempered chocolate.

"Tell me, how did your family like the sweets?" she asked, taking up the bottle of vinegar from another cupboard and a few old newspapers.

His gaze snapped back to her. "Those are for Easter Sunday, miss, and not before."

Restraint—another good trait in the boy, not often seen in children.

"Let's have you start by cleaning the glass display cases out front with this vinegar and rub them down with the newspapers." If they got the opening chores done, and if a large enough crowd gathered, Charlotte might turn the sign around early.

"Take that pail, put in some water from the sink, and then pour in about two tablespoons of vinegar."

He looked instantly anxious.

"Here, let's do it together today. Put the pail under the tap."

She let him fill it half full and place it on the floor. "Now, as I pour, I shall count, one . . . two. There, that's about enough."

Edward carried the bucket through to the front.

"Now, scrunch up some newspaper and dip it in. Don't touch your eyes until you've had a chance to wash your hands or it will sting like the devil. Right then, wipe the glass and the fingerprints and smears shall disappear."

"They do," he said wondrously.

She went back and snatched up the small bristle broom.

"We do the display cases every day, sometimes twice if children have come in and pressed against them. Or anyone without gloves," she added, starting to sweep the front floor, working around Edward. "And we do the inside of the front windows a couple times a week. My mother has a man who comes around and does the outside, along with the stores on either side of us."

While she spoke, she finished sweeping any debris into the dustpan, which she dumped into the rubbish bin in the back. Edward finished a moment later, standing back to observe his efforts, before darting forward to clean one spot again.

"You can dump that in the sink, slowly and carefully please so as not to splash. There's a rubbish bin in the corner for the newsprint, and then wash your hands thoroughly."

"Yes, miss." He disappeared behind the curtain, and Charlotte pulled the cashbox out from under the counter, confirming she had plenty of coins to make change for any early customers.

"Now, we make the display shelves look attractive," she told him. "As you can see, after yesterday, they're nearly empty."

They had two confectionery cupboards with trays of sweets and a coldbox with ice at the top and bottom, keeping such items as their butter and milk. Amity also used it to quickly cool fondant or chocolate when she was making bonbons. While Beatrice's toffee hardly ever needed its help to harden, in the hottest weeks of the London summer, Charlotte found the coldbox useful to keep her small marzipan confections from becoming unappealing blobs. Luckily, that wasn't a problem at their busiest times of year, Valentine's Day, Easter, and Christmas.

Hearing the door's bell tinkle, she snatched up a tray and gave another to Edward before hurrying to the front.

"Good morning," Amity said, stopping in her tracks at the sight of Edward.

"Our new helper," Charlotte said and introduced them. "Mr. Edward Percy, this is my sister, the Duchess of Pelham."

The boy looked as if he might fall to the floor in supplication and drop the confectionery. Luckily, Amity was good at setting ordinary people at ease since she'd been one of them all her life, until the previous year's February wedding.

"I'm pleased to meet you, Edward. I make the chocolates here, and you may call me Mrs. Westbrook," Amity said, giving the boy her husband's family name.

"Yes, missus," but he sent Charlotte a look of alarm.

"Have you tasted one of my chocolates?" Amity asked.

"Yes, missus. It was delicious. It melted in my mouth."

"Perfect," Amity said. "I had best get started."

Then Charlotte set him to work filling the display cases, telling him what went where, while her eldest sister began immediately to make chocolates in every shape and size and flavor, plain and milk, some with fruit and nuts. And Charlotte set up her own station behind the counter making marzipan sweets, which she did all day long in between serving customers.

When Edward had finished stocking the shelves, he wandered into the back and Charlotte could hear Amity explaining what she was doing as she worked. The boy's natural curiosity, hopefully, would turn him into a confectioner's apprentice, which would be a most useful thing.

Beatrice and their mother entered at the same time.

"If we can get the display glass cleaned quickly, and the shelves stocked," Felicity began, "then maybe we can open early." However, she trailed off to see the glass sparkling and the cases filled.

"How early did you get here?" her mother asked.

"Now I feel lazy," Beatrice said, but she smiled. "And relieved. I honestly hate the vinegar job and am unsure how I ever got saddled with it."

"Consider yourself unsaddled," Charlotte said. Then she looked at her mother. There was no point in prevaricating or dawdling. "I haven't been here too long, but I did hire some help and forgot to mention it to you. Naturally, if you don't think he's a good fit for us, then I will send him on his way." The thought was a terrible one. *How would she bear Edward's disappointment?*

"He!" Felicity repeated. "Hired help! We've never had anyone in here who wasn't family." She didn't look pleased.

"Edward," Charlotte called out. A moment later, he came through the parted curtain.

"Yes, miss." His face was impossibly earnest.

"This is my mother, Mrs. Rare-Foure. She owns this shop, and she taught me everything I know about making sweets. She taught all of us, in fact."

His eyes had grown rounder looking at Charlotte's pretty mother.

"Mother, this is Mr. Edward Percy, a capable young man."

"Missus," he said, giving an awkward bow, before walking forward and fearlessly shaking her hand.

Felicity gave him a good long look, taking time to stare him in the eye.

"You can work hard, young man?"

"Yes, missus."

"And you don't mind taking orders from females?"

"No, missus."

"And your parents know you are here?"

Perhaps only Charlotte sensed the slight hesitation.

"Yes, missus. I told my mum last night."

Then, Felicity nodded. "He shall need an apron by tomorrow," she proclaimed and sailed past him into the back room to hang up her coat and don her apron. Charlotte would speak to her later, in private, about his wages. Meanwhile, Beatrice still stood there, already removing her coat.

"And this is my sister, Mrs. Carson. She makes the toffee."

"Truly, miss?" he said, shaking her hand. "I haven't tasted yours, but toffee is an excellent sweet."

Charlotte hoped Beatrice wouldn't laugh at the boy and his serious ways.

"Thank you, Mr. Percy," she said. "I wholeheartedly agree."

"Please, missus, call me Edward."

"All right. First of all, let's remedy your terrible lack of experience. Charlotte, please," she said, holding out her hand. "A piece of plain toffee."

She handed her sister a piece on a square of paper, which Beatrice held in front of the boy. "Take it, suck it a minute, don't try to bite it right away. Then tell me what you think, Edward. I can trust you to tell me the truth, I'm sure of it.

"Yes, missus." He popped in the whole piece and worked it around his mouth. He closed his eyes and sucked hard, then worked it some more, before tucking it into his cheek.

"It's delicious, missus. The best toffee I've ever had."

"It's the treacle," Beatrice said, not able to keep from gloating. "If you are a cautious sort of person, then I will teach you how to create it." She paused. "But make no mistake, it is a dangerous business, making toffee." She winked at Charlotte. "Like working with molten fire. One needs the constitution of a dragon-slayer to make toffee."

"Really, missus?" Edward said in a thin voice. Then he coughed and said more firmly, "I would like to try."

"We shall see." Beatrice passed him by, ruffling his hair as she made her way into the back.

"You've tasted both my sisters' confectionery, but not yet mine," Charlotte said. "Would you like to try marzipan?"

He nodded, and she fetched a sculpted leaf, waiting until he'd swallowed the last of Bea's toffee.

"Marzipan, some call it *marchpane*, is made from ground almonds, and honestly, it's not to everyone's taste. I shan't be at all offended if you don't like it." With that, she handed him the leaf.

"It's cleverly done, miss," he said, examining her artistry. "It looks almost real." With that, he popped it in his mouth, worked it around on his tongue and swallowed.

"It's good," he said.

"But not as good as chocolate or toffee," she amended.

His cheeks turned pink.

She laughed. "It's fine. Most of the customers who adore it are older than you. I can make it in a variety of ways, and I can bake it, too. Sometimes Amity puts it inside her chocolate, and sometimes I put her chocolate inside my marzipan."

He took it all in with thoughtful eyes. "It tasted a bit like a flower, miss."

"That leaf had a little rose-water in it, a recipe from the late-sixteenth century, if you can believe it. Now, let's see if Mrs. Rare-Foure will allow you to make our deliveries today."

She sent Edward to the back room to speak with her mother, but, as soon as she was alone again, Lionel's face popped into her thoughts. Her heart squeezed with pain. *Was he even then in sunny France, planning his grand art tour?* They'd had a discussion about the museums on the Continent once, since her family had been abroad thrice. However, as the Evans never had, Lionel had been envious, she recalled, and a little sullen with her. She'd never brought it up again.

Suddenly, a tap on the door snagged her attention. Looking up, she was surprised to see Lord Jeffcoat's visage pressed against the glass.

"Robin Hood," she muttered, going around the counter to let him in.

CHAPTER THREE

Charles was pleased to see Miss Rare-Foure in the front of the shop. He knew he was there early. The streets were practically deserted except for delivery men and the gangs of sweepers. And he had planned on simply walking by if he hadn't seen her.

But as if fate were assisting his pursuit, Miss Charlotte was not only there, she came to the door and opened it.

"Lord Jeffcoat, you cannot possibly want sweets this early," she said by way of greeting.

She did not accompany this with her usual smile, one he'd thought inviting from the first time they'd met. With her full lips, often bowed, she seemed in a continuous state of happiness, something he'd noticed about her whenever they were near.

As the day before, her chestnut brown hair was up in a tidy bun. Perhaps because it was morning, before the hordes of customers had descended upon New Bond Street and run this pretty miss off her feet, none of her soft curls had yet escaped the pins.

A shame. Yesterday, she'd looked like the subject of an Italian pastoral painting, if he were a man to make such poetic associations. Usually, he was not. Today, she was far too tidy, and he had a visceral image of sinking his fingers into her silky hair and sending the pins flying in order to release her locks. Perhaps when he was about to kiss her.

His cheeks heated at the wayward—and completely unexpected—thoughts. What's more, he knew she'd seen something in his gaze because she blinked slowly and raised a dark eyebrow. He realized he'd said nothing yet, merely standing like an idiot, more bewitched by her at each encounter.

"Good day, Miss Rare-Foure. You are correct. I am not here for confectionery."

Before he could say more, an entire army of confectioners came out of the back room, or so it seemed. Leading the charge was Mrs. Rare-Foure, the family's matriarch. It was hard not to admire the woman who had built this successful establishment on the expensive shopping street, where the rent must be high. And she had done it selling sweets! At the same time, she'd born three lovely girls and taught them to make confectionery.

Pelham's duchess, an impressive young woman who'd made his friend blissfully happy, appeared by her mother's side. She was holding tins of chocolates and speaking to a young boy. If Charles wasn't mistaken, it was the same lad from the day before. The boy held a sack in each hand, staring up at the duchess, hanging on her every word.

Last came the *snapdragon,* as he thought of the middle sister, Beatrice. A bit tart for his liking, despite being lovely. In any case, she'd managed to snag herself a husband the year before, and Charles remembered the man showing up half-naked at Marlborough House, as if a costume was any excuse to go shirtless. Pelham said the snapdragon's husband was a good brother-in-law, nonetheless.

All talking stopped when they saw Charles standing in the doorway with Miss Rare-Foure.

"Lord Jeffcoat, what can you be doing here this early?" Mrs. Rare-Foure asked.

He was absolutely determined not to tell them. That much was certain.

"Just passing by when I saw Miss Rare-Foure through the window"—that he'd pressed his face against like a child—"and I thought I would say hello."

He couldn't help noticing her sisters glance at one another.

"I can see you are busy. Thus, I shall take my leave at once."

"Nonsense, do come in and close the door," the mother said. "We don't want flies, do we? I would offer tea or chocolate, but as soon as we get the kettle going, it will be time to open. How is your father? Would you like to take him something for Easter? I couldn't ask yesterday as it was mobbed when you arrived."

No one ever mentioned his disloyal, wanton of a mother, and he hoped it was because she was long-forgotten by respectable society.

"Indeed," he began, "I noticed yesterday your business is doing very—"

"Business, yes! I must get back to it. Charlotte, please help Lord Jeffcoat with whatever he wishes while I prepare our new employee to make his first deliveries."

The boy appeared awfully young to be given such an important task. He wasn't even holding all the confectionery yet, as the duchess was trying to give him more tins.

"I don't need anything really," he said to Charlotte who was still standing beside him, watching her bustling family.

"Edward needs another sack," Beatrice said. "Or perhaps we should get him a pushcart."

The females were overwhelming the lad.

"I thought having Edward would make it so none of us had to leave the shop, but maybe I should go with him," Charlotte said softly, clearly thinking out loud more than discussing it with him. "Otherwise, he may have to make two trips."

"Perhaps, if it's the boy's first day, I could accompany him wherever he needs to go." Charles was surprised to hear himself make the offer. He had a long day of writs and briefs, but when she glanced up at him as if he were a hero, he was pleased he had made it.

Strangely, tough, her usual bright smile was not in evidence.

"That is most thoughtful and kind of you, my lord," she said. "I cannot imagine any other gentleman in your position offering to do such a thing."

He was no saint, but he also wasn't going to accomplish his task of privately asking her out. Thus, he might as well make himself useful before he went to the Inns of Court.

"Edward," Miss Charlotte said, cutting through the noise of her mother and sisters, "come meet Lord Jeffcoat, a friend of the family."

That startling introduction gave Charles pause. *Was that how she saw him?* He wasn't sure if that was promising or if she considered him to be like an old familiar pair of slippers.

The boy approached. "Lord Jeffcoat," Charlotte said, "this is Edward Percy."

"Good day, my lord." Edward bowed before sticking out a hand that entirely disappeared when Charles engulfed it for a simple handshake.

How old could he be? Ten perhaps?

"Good day, Mr. Percy. I bet you know London well. Would you mind if I accompanied you to see where your deliveries are?"

"Are you new here, my lord?"

Charles smiled at him. "No, but perhaps I can lend a hand. I shall be cooped up the rest of the day, and it would be nice to have a stroll first, assuming you were planning on walking."

"I was, my lord."

Charles looked up to see the other ladies watching their exchange. "You had best load us up," he told them. "With Mr. Percy's strong arms and my assistance, we shall have no trouble."

Finally, Miss Charlotte gave him a watery version of her former smile, and he wished he knew her well enough to ask her about her troubles.

"WHAT DO YOU MAKE of that?" Beatrice asked after the viscount and the boy had left.

"Surprising," Charlotte said, watching them saunter down the sidewalk, "but nice. Lord Jeffcoat seems a bit serious. Being with a child might do him good, and I'm sure Edward has never walked beside a viscount before."

When she turned around, her family, all three women, were staring at her. "What is it?"

"Did that young man go in the back room?" her mother asked.

Charlotte wondered at her mother's question. "Of course, he did. You were back there with him."

"No, dear girl, the *other* young man. Did Lord Jeffcoat go into the back room? With you?"

"Mother! Of course not. Why would you ask such a thing?"

"No reason," Felicity said, but Beatrice grinned.

"Because our dear mother thinks any man who goes into the back room with you is destined to be your husband." Bea laughed a moment. Then abruptly stopped. "Actually, she was right." Turning to their mother, she asked, "How on earth could you have been right about that?"

Amity added, "Yes, Mother *was* right. Therefore, take care with whom you go into the workroom."

Charlotte gasped, raising her hand. "Oh, no! Too late!"

"What do you mean?" Amity asked, and Bea and her mother stared with interest.

"It's fate. Irrevocable destiny. I was in the back with Edward Percy this morning." She let them all think on that. "At least he's off of leading strings." Then she tried to laugh, but the rock where her heart used to be wouldn't let her do more than shrug at her own jesting words.

"Silly girl," said Bea, returning to the back to make toffee, followed by Amity.

"I like the young man," her mother said.

"Which one do you mean now?" Charlotte asked, glancing around the shop to make sure everything was ready.

"Our new employee. I recall he was in here yesterday," she said.

"Yes, he was. Something about him touched me," Charlotte confessed. "I'm glad you let him stay."

"We certainly have plenty for him to do. Speaking of which, don't you have marzipan to make?"

Someone tapped on the glass behind her. "And you might as well turn the sign around," her mother added. "Maybe it won't be such pandemonium in here if we let the customers start early."

Her mother was wrong about that. As soon as Charlotte indicated they were open, a steady stream of people came in all morning. She fit in making marzipan bunnies and eggs with chocolate centers when there were lulls that her mother could handle by herself. At some point mid-morning, Edward returned, and when Charlotte glanced up, Lord Jeffcoat raised a hand in farewell outside the shop window but didn't enter.

"How did it go?" she asked the boy.

"Well, miss. Everyone was ever so nice, although it could be because of the company I kept."

Smart lad! It was hardly surprising he'd been treated well when strolling into a hotel or restaurant with a viscount. It had been a grand idea of Lord Jeffcoat's. When Edward made his next deliveries, they would recall the likes of whom he associated and act accordingly.

"Why don't you ask my daughters in the back if they need anything?" her mother said. "Supplies and whatnot, and then we'll see what else you can do."

"Yes, missus. One thing I wondered," Edward added. "Since the deliveries are in two different directions, perhaps I could go one way, then come back for the rest of the sweets and go in the other. Also, the manager of The Albion—oh, miss, what a place to have a bang-up meal!—he said he would like a dozen more marzipan swans tomorrow and a dozen more rabbits, as he's putting them atop his raspberry sponge-cakes."

Then Edward darted between the counters and disappeared through the heavy, blue velvet curtain.

"That was well done," Charlotte's mother said. "He did the job and remembered an order." Turning her attention, she asked, "May I help you?" to the first customer who approached the counter.

Charlotte was pleased with Edward but couldn't help frowning as the next wave of customers washed over the threshold. When was she supposed to make twenty-four more marzipan sculptures? Maybe they should have hired an experienced confectioner, not a delivery boy.

"Now that he's made his deliveries," Charlotte mused at the same time as making change for the customer in front of her, "what more can Edward do until closing?" Suddenly, she doubted her actions. "I should have asked you first."

Felicity glanced at her. "He'll do fine. He can fit back here with us to restock the shelves in the mid-afternoon, and at closing, he'll help clean. And perhaps, if he's the right sort of person, he can learn how to be a confectioner. Isn't that really what you saw in him?"

Charlotte recalled the moment Edward ate the chocolate the day before. "I suppose I thought he had the patience and the . . . ,'" she trailed off. *What made Rare Confectionery sweets extraordinary?*

"The spark," her mother finished. "I do see that in the boy, too."

At least Charlotte's judgment hadn't been as disastrous in hiring as it had with where she placed her affections.

After that, the shop became too busy for Charlotte to think about Lionel, which was a good thing, but also kept her from making any marzipan sculptures, which was not good at all. Edward restocked the display shelves and the tins on the shelves on the other side of the room, and occasionally, he opened the door for a customer. In the late afternoon when they could see the day's end in sight, Charlotte went into the back room to make tea and found Edward standing beside Amity, watching her stir the fondant.

Taking a cup of tea out to her mother, Charlotte waited for the next lull and said, "You know, ever since we started supplying confectionery to The Langham, we have been growing."

"True," Felicity said. "Which means you'd best make more marzipan before we run out, and the swans and bunnies, too."

Charlotte took up her position behind the counter where she had a sturdy cast iron grinder for grinding almonds and a cool marble slab for creating her little sculptures.

"I was thinking," she said casually, "that we might want to expand the shop."

"Expand the shop?" Felicity exclaimed, her tone shocked. "How on earth would we do that? Cheaper and easier to add another case if we had time to fill it." She pointed to the opposite wall. "And then move those tins into the back."

Charlotte frowned. That was simply more of the same. "How about a little café?"

Her mother sipped her tea then shook her head as if already dismissing the idea.

Charlotte persisted, "Something like Gunter's." Often their parents had taken her and her sisters for ices at

Berkeley Square before wandering over to Hyde Park for a stroll by the Serpentine. As an adult, she still thought the café with nothing but sweet treats, custards, cream ice, and frozen mousses to be absolutely magical. "I love that place, don't you?"

In response, her mother tapped the book on the shelf behind them. *Gunter's Modern Confectioner* sat alongside *Le Confiturier Royal* and *The Art of Spinning and Casting Sugar*.

"Yes, I do, but *they* are not on New Bond Street," Felicity pointed out, "and we don't know anything about running a café or providing anything other than confectionery. We would have to have servers and a pastry chef and whatnot. I cannot even think about how much work that would be, not to mention the cost."

Nevertheless, Charlotte thought she saw excitement in her mother's eyes.

"You always wanted one of us to learn the art of patisserie."

That induced a smile. "True," Felicity said, "mostly so I could eat such desserts right here for free, rather than having to go all the way to Maison Bertaux."

Charlotte giggled. "All the way?" It was a mere fifteen-minute walk to Greek Street and one of the few London bakeries selling the authentic French pastries her mother adored. If they went as a family, her father would skip the patisserie and pop in next door to The Coach and Horses pub for a pint.

"Truthfully, dear one," her mother continued, "I have considered, even dreamed about, a small establishment selling the highest quality of a very limited offering. Tea from the freshest leaves, the richest coffee beans offering their heavenly aroma, our confectionery, and the addition of some decadent pastries. A place for women to gather and chat in style and comfort." Her expression took on a faraway look.

Charlotte could easily imagine it, too. Then her mother dashed it away with her next words. "But I don't want to move from New Bond Street and risk losing our current customers, and I don't want two separate places to run. What a nightmare! No, we must be satisfied with the best confectionery in Mayfair, and on the best street, too. Nothing to quibble about. We are blessed."

Her mother was right on all points. Besides, as it was, her sisters had no interest in running the shop, and that task was going to fall further upon Charlotte's shoulders. She would remain behind the counter in the same spot for the rest of her life. The thought had never bothered her before because she loved everything about Rare Confectionery— the look of it, the aroma, the customers.

Now, all because Lionel Evans was gone, and she'd been left behind—and because his twice-a-week kisses had been exciting—that insidious notion of dissatisfaction had worked its way inside her, as inextricably as when she pressed fine sugar into ground almonds to make her marzipan paste. *She had become restless paste!*

Sighing sadly as the bell tinkled over the door, she let her thoughts become occupied with work. Customers streamed in all afternoon until the shelves were practically empty again. Her sisters had stayed all day making confectionery with Amity coming out twice to take first their mother's place and then Charlotte's, giving each a few minutes to eat cheese, bread, and their cook Lydia's cold sliced beef in the back of the shop. They'd even brought in another chair during their busy week to amend the normal singular stool that only Beatrice favored.

After that week, things would return to normal, and they would bake a meat pie or, at the least, warm up Lydia's food from the night before. Sometimes it was a cheap and cheerful treat to buy ham sandwiches from one of the sandwich boys who sold up and down the street.

At last, it was time to turn the sign to "Closed." Edward began to sweep at once, while the rest of them stared at one another in mutual exhaustion. Charlotte could put her head down on the counter and sleep right there.

"Your sister is right," Felicity said to Bea and Amity. "We are growing, and we do need help. I think we shall start by training this boy on whichever confectionery he would be most apt, maybe all three so he can help out with anything at a pinch."

They all looked at Edward who blinked back at them. It seemed like a lot to put on a twelve-year-old's shoulders, but it might be his best chance for a lucrative future if he had no other prospects. He smiled and nodded reassuringly.

"I would like to learn, missus."

Their mother nodded. "That's settled then. When you're not cleaning or delivering or stocking shelves, you'll be learning the trade from each of my daughters." She sighed. "And whenever I can get away from the counter, I shall teach you myself."

Charlotte sent a knowing look to Amity, who sent it on to Bea. Felicity might sigh over instructing, but she'd been a wonderful teacher and had always said she enjoyed it.

"All my girls can make every confection in this shop, don't let them fool you with how they've divided their chores. But it's true that some have a special talent for one thing over the other. No one can blend flavors into chocolate fondant like our duchess, nor curl a marzipan pig's tail like Miss Charlotte, and no one can take the toffee off the stove at precisely the right moment like Mrs. Carson."

Edward nodded solemnly, looking daunted.

"But if you can do any of those things passingly well," Felicity added, "then you will be a tremendous help to us." She clapped her hands, then brushed them off. "Today is done and dusted. Are we all ready to go home?"

However, after Charlotte and her mother had said goodbye to everyone, including Edward, locked up, and began the short walk home, Felicity surprised her.

"I think you should be in charge of Edward. He was a grand find, and I'm pleased you hired him. You have a good head on your shoulders."

Before Charlotte could thank her, there was a noise behind them of a window breaking and a crash, both unfamiliar sounds on New Bond Street. They whirled in their tracks.

42

CHAPTER FOUR

"Gracious!" Charlotte's mother exclaimed.

In front of their shop door, where a moment earlier they'd been standing, a brass table lamp lay on its side surrounded by broken shards of glass, glazing, and pieces of the window frame.

"And that's that!" yelled a female voice from above.

Looking up, Charlotte saw the window that had broken when the lamp went through it. A six-over-eight sash was hanging dangerously askew.

"Extraordinary," Felicity said.

It was exactly that. For above their shop was a pillow maker. That was all the woman had done Charlotte's entire life. She took the finest goose down, stuffed it in the most luxurious silk and satin cases, and made pillows that were sold in various shops on Bond Street, in the Burlington Arcade around the corner, and on Oxford Street. Moreover, the pillow woman, as Charlotte thought of her, was nearly always silent. At that instant, she couldn't think of her real name.

"What should we do?" she asked her mother.

A moment later, the door that sheltered the staircase to the second floor flew open and a man exited in a hurry. With a grim expression, he looked at the mess on the pavement and at Charlotte and Felicity, and then he hurried off.

"I suppose we should look in on her," Charlotte's mother stated and marched toward the open door.

In all her years, Charlotte had been upstairs only once, when she was about six, to be introduced to the tenant above their heads. Everything had been clean and tidy in the spacious suite of rooms, one containing massive boxes of down and shelves of beautiful fabric, and one containing the pillow woman, who was also the sole seamstress. She'd seemed old to Charlotte back then and hadn't been too friendly. While being calm and quiet, focused on her work, she'd told the six-year-old not to touch anything in case she had sugar or chocolate on her hands.

At the top of the stairs, they encountered another open door and entered.

"Hello, Mrs. Hafflen, are you well?" Felicity called out.

"Who is that?" came the voice, not soft as Charlotte recalled but sharp. And when they went in farther, nothing was as it had been years ago. It was plainly chaos. The bins were in disarray and goose down was everywhere. In fact, some tiny feathers were floating in the air since the man had recently walked through and disturbed them.

"Careful not to breathe it in," her mother said, putting her gloved hand to her mouth and nose. Charlotte did the same until they'd passed through the room into the front one that overlooked the street. Amazingly, in the middle of more muddle, Mrs. Hafflen sat by the broken window sewing on her whisper-quiet Singer machine, her foot pumping the treadle under her skirts.

She looked up while continuing to sew at a slow, constant rate.

"Mrs. Hafflen," Felicity persisted. "I am Mrs. Rare-Foure from the confectionery downstairs. Are you well?" she repeated.

The woman's eyes appeared glassy, unable to look directly at them. Then she turned back to her work at hand where she was stitching two different colors of satin together, an odd and ugly combination, the fabric not lining up properly to make a pillow case.

They waited in silence a moment until the seamstress yanked the fabric from the machine and held it up, close to her face, before she clucked angrily. Then she tossed it to the floor where there were others already strewn in disarray.

"Damn it all!" she swore. "I've sewn it closed again. Did you see? There's no opening for the feathers."

Charlotte looked at her mother, who winced.

"Who was that man?" Felicity tried again to get the old woman to tell her what was happening.

"My son. The fool wants me to stop. If only I'd had daughters. Do you have daughters?" she asked.

Charlotte felt her mother startle beside her. *How sad!*

"Yes," Felicity said. "Three."

Mrs. Hafflen sighed. "He said I had made enough pillows for all of England and had piles of money, to boot. He said I had to go live with him. What if I don't want to? And who will make the pillows? I threw my lamp at him, and the bloody fool ducked! He should have caught it."

Charlotte and her mother took another few steps closer. Beside the pillow woman and her untidy pile of cases, there were empty teacups and the remains of a pie. *How long had she been sitting there no longer able to ply her craft properly?*

"Can we do anything?" Felicity asked. "It's closing time, after all, and growing dark."

"Closing time?" the woman repeated before shaking her head. "No, he's coming back. The dunce!" Then she peered at them. "Who are you, and how did you get in here?"

Charlotte had been silent up until then but drew from her pocket the bag of confectionery she always carried with her in case they met with any children on the walk home, which happened almost every night.

"We came to give you some sweets."

"Truly?" The woman's eyes focused for the first time on the bright white bag with the blue shop name. "I haven't had anything sweet in a donkey's age."

Charlotte held it out to her. The woman took it slowly, opened it, and reached in for a chocolate. After inhaling the aroma with closed eyes, Mrs. Hafflen stuffed it into her mouth.

"Oh, that's good. Very good, indeed! Must be careful not to get any on the fabric," she muttered, helping herself to another one.

"Do you think her son is really coming back tonight?" Charlotte asked her mother in a whispered voice.

Her mother shrugged. "I hope so. I suppose we shall wait and see."

"How long?" Charlotte asked.

"At least for a while," Felicity said. "After all, her son looked to be a determined man. He will return. If not, I suppose she shall come home to dine with us."

Looking around, Charlotte's mother spied a small cast iron stove, a kettle perched atop. "Let's see if she has some coal," Felicity said. "We might as well make a pot of tea."

JEFFCOAT COULDN'T GET OUT of Lincoln's Inn fast enough. His thoughts were far from the dry books that made the law seem boring. When he was in court, even as a student in the moot court, observing, taking notes, it was anything but that.

It had been over a week since he'd last seen Charlotte Rare-Foure, deciding after dropping off Edward Percy that he'd better let the busy Easter week finish before approaching her again.

Charles wished he had a reason to go into the shop besides wanting to see her. He didn't want Waverly to catch wind of it until a favorable reception from the young woman was assured. And that was the worst of it—Miss Charlotte had given him no inclination of any interest.

Charles was no coward, however. He'd never shied away from approaching a woman to whom he felt an attraction. And he'd never been turned down yet. Why then had he waited another entire week before sauntering along Old Bond Street until it turned into New Bond Street?

Moreover, why had he been into two shops next door to Rare Confectionery but not yet made it inside where he hoped Charlotte to be?

Actually, he knew from chatting with Pelham's wife that Charlotte often opened the store and then left mid-afternoon, letting the snapdragon sister close up shop. Since they were no longer run off their feet with Easter custom, he'd hoped their routine had returned to normal. If it had, he ought to be able to intercept her smoothly as she strolled out of the shop.

Except she hadn't. And he was becoming fidgety. Not only that, he knew he looked suspicious. For the past few minutes, he'd loitered in Finnigans, the luxury luggage and trunk maker, staring out their front windows in case Charlotte went by. He hadn't even realized he'd picked up a leather satchel until a shop clerk came over to stare at him. Hard. With frowning eyebrows.

Slowly, he set it down, glanced at the stack of wicker picnic baskets, imagining taking Charlotte on a picnic someday soon, and then left the shop. With determination, he walked steadfastly down to the confectionery, not pausing to see who or what was inside. He simply entered, hearing the bell tinkle as he pushed open the door.

To his relief, Charlotte seemed to be alone, bent over the counter working on something.

Thus, he startled when a second head appeared. *Edward.* Before Charles could recover, the boy spoke.

"Good day, my lord," Edward said, sounding supremely happy. "I'm learning to make marzipan, not the little sculptures. Not yet. But grinding almonds and sugar together with a drop of water. Do you want to see?"

With a glance at Charlotte to make sure it was acceptable, Charles approached the counter to see they had two bowls on a marble slab. Edward tilted his forward so Charles could look into it.

"It looks good," Charles agreed. "Or at least, I think it does."

Charlotte, who still hadn't spoken, tipped hers forward. It seemed to contain an identical substance.

"Yes, I can see you're doing excellent work," Charles added. "You've managed to match Miss Rare-Foure's precisely." He turned his attention to her. "Good day. How is the confectionery business?"

Charlotte appeared unexpectedly dour, greeting him with neither a smile nor her usual exuberance. "Good day, Lord Jeffcoat. It goes well, I suppose. We're relieved to have a little quiet time."

He paused. *Was she indicating her displeasure at his unexpected arrival?* Her heretofore placid face had a gravity to it of a person with problems.

At that moment, the bell tinkled again, and they all turned to see a duo of customers. Charlotte frowned, pursing her lips in displeasure, and that surprised him more than anything.

Two women wandered along the display case, looking at the offerings.

Without moving from her spot, Charlotte called out to them, "May I help you?"

Charles backed away from the counter to give the ladies more space and took up a place on the opposite side of the room where tins, waiting to be chosen and filled, lined the wall.

One of the women pointed at something. "What is this exactly?"

With an audible sigh, making Charles cringe at her rudeness, Charlotte went to the back side of the display, bent down, identified the confection, and then said, "That's a chocolate with raspberry essence."

He knew she would offer a sample next. He'd seen her do it during the time he'd stood there with Waverly, to every single customer. And yet, she didn't. She waited in silence.

"Is it possible to taste it?" the woman persisted.

"When you go to the fishmonger," Charlotte said, "do you taste his wares ahead of time? Or at the green grocer's, do you ask to eat one of his apples or pears before you buy?"

"No, but—" the customer began.

"Have you had chocolate before?" Charlotte asked.

"Why, yes, of course," the woman answered.

"And raspberries?" Charlotte continued. "Have you ever had a raspberry in all your life?"

"Yes, but—"

"Well, that particular confection tastes just like that—chocolate and raspberries."

Charles would have taken the point that Charlotte was in a horrendous mood, but these customers didn't. The other female asked, "What about the marzipan?"

"What about it?" Charlotte asked, folding her arms across her generous bosom, at which he presently found himself to be staring. He averted his eyes immediately.

"Is it all the same?" the woman asked.

"The same as what?" Charlotte responded, being difficult.

"I mean, does it have flavors and centers?"

"Yes," Charlotte answered with another sigh.

Charles glanced at Edward, who caught his eye with a grown-up expression of chagrin.

"What are the flavors and the fillings?" the customer asked. "It would help if the confectionery was labeled."

"It has never needed to be labeled before," Charlotte pointed out, as if these customers were particularly obtuse.

Charles nearly put a hand to his forehead. It had never needed labeling, he would wager, because a helpful shopgirl had always explained the confectionery and given samples.

An unpleasant scrabbling noise overhead, followed by a woman's cry, caused the hair on his head to stand up, or so it felt. The customers looked up, too. Charlotte and Edward ignored it.

The whole encounter was unpleasant and unnerving, and the three turned for the door without purchasing anything.

"Would you like a sample?" young Edward called after them, but they left, one of the women muttering about Chatman's Chocolates on Regent Street.

Charlotte returned to the bowl of marzipan. When Edward settled in beside her, he said, "You used to always give out samples."

She shrugged noncommittally and said nothing. Charles dreaded the entrance of any more customers as it was painful to watch her treatment of them.

"Would you like to taste the marzipan, my lord?" Edward asked.

"Hm." He glanced at Charlotte, wishing she would offer him the smile he found immensely captivating, but she didn't. As serious as a gravedigger, she fixed him with her deep-brown gaze.

"Some people don't like marzipan," she said softly.

"I like it," Edward said, looking from Charles to Miss Rare-Foure, but she merely shrugged.

Where was the young woman who'd exclaimed in delight over swan-shaped pastry filled with meat at her sister's reception dinner? Or the happy female who'd excitedly twirled to show off her Turkish costume at the fancy-dress ball? This Miss Rare-Foure seemed as bland and uninteresting as cheese.

Nonetheless, she reached beside her to the display case, withdrew a cream-colored leaf, and handed it to him. *With her bare hand!*

"My hands are clean for making confectionery," she said when she caught him staring.

Taking off his gloves, he let her drop it onto his palm. Bringing this to his nose, he sniffed it.

"The scent makes my mouth water," he confessed. And then he bit the leaf in half. "Sweet," he said, "and with such a delicate flavor. Oranges, I think?" He said it as a question, hoping she would appreciate his effort.

She nodded without enthusiasm, nor did she look particularly pleased.

"Sometimes, Miss Charlotte adds rose-water and sometimes orange-water," Edward explained. "You can buy marzipan paste already made, but she grinds the almonds herself and mixes in the sugar. Now I know how to do it."

She nodded at the boy's words.

Charles looked in the display case at the various shapes of her marzipan. "You're truly an artist," he said.

She stiffened. "If you'll excuse me."

With that, she disappeared swiftly into the back room through a heavy drape of blue velvet.

"Did I say something wrong?" he asked so softly she wouldn't hear, then realized the inappropriateness of querying a child.

"Miss Charlotte is moody sometimes," the boy responded.

Suddenly, there was a loud thump from upstairs, and then another.

"They're moving out all the seamstress's things today. Poor old lady. She gave me a pillow."

"Did she?" Charles was starting to think the confectionery was a bit like Bedlam. On the other hand, he thought of how lovely Charlotte's smile used to be and how sparkling her eyes and enthusiastic her temperament—the opposite of the law clerks at Lincoln's Inn.

How desperately he wanted her happiness in his life! That startling realization was followed quickly by a question only he could answer: *Was there a better time than the present?*

"Carry on," he said to the boy, with a nod at the bowl, and then deciding to beard the lioness in her den, he passed through the space between the counters and followed Miss Rare-Foure through the velvet curtain.

52

CHAPTER FIVE

Charlotte whirled around upon hearing the footsteps, knowing as she did that they didn't belong to Edward and instantly wishing she'd kept her back to the curtain.

Too late, she faced Lord Jeffcoat while she was still wiping at her tears. His surprised, discomfited expression probably mirrored her own.

"I apologize," she said, knowing it marked her as an emotional female to be found crying in the workroom. What's more, people didn't come to a confectionery to encounter sadness, and she'd tried desperately to tamp down her sentimental feelings over the past two weeks. In most cases, holding her misery at bay had caused her to be dispirited and uncharacteristically crabbed, as she felt that day.

"My fault entirely," the viscount said, not taking another step closer. "You have nothing for which to apologize. I said something to upset you out there." He gestured behind him to the front of the shop. "And then I barged in here when you were indisposed. I am extraordinarily sorry. My actions are unforgivable."

He probably thought her a mawkish ninny. She could hardly tell him that any mention of her being an artist felt like an arrow to her heart.

"Truly, my lord, I'm glad you liked the marzipan, and it was good of you to notice the subtle hint of orange blossom."

"But neither of those things were what upset you," he pointed out.

She considered his intelligent face and decided to tell him something of the truth.

"I'm afraid I have a bit of a bruised heart at present, and try as I might to ignore it, it causes pangs at the most inconvenient times. Sometimes, I wish I had no heart to speak of."

His expression flickered with surprise again, but then, against all expectation, he smiled slightly. It was a nicely symmetrical curving of his lips, reminiscent of a Renaissance portrait. And the pain returned as her thoughts went to Lionel painting somewhere on the Continent.

"Don't say that," Lord Jeffcoat ordered. "I've seen your warm heart in action, and it was splendid."

Charlotte gasped softly. "What do you mean?" She had a terrible vision of him having seen her kissing Lionel in the dark hallway of the academy's upper floor.

"Before Easter," Lord Jeffcoat explained, "the way you defended Edward to that female customer, it was truly heartwarming, and here he is, working for you."

She felt her cheeks grow warm.

"I'm sorry about your bruised heart," he continued, sounding sincere. Then, rather abruptly, the viscount added, "Perchance, would it feel better after a night on the town?"

Lord Jeffcoat was full of surprises. If anyone had told her he would ever ask her out for the evening, she would have said they were a lunatic. Ever since she'd first met him at the duke's home, he'd been polite but distant, during each of their previous encounters. Staring at him, she recalled the moment when he'd held the door for her and she'd caught a whiff of his appealing scent. It had given her pause, and she'd flirted with the notion of being attracted to him, but only because she thought Lionel was waiting at class. She'd been giddy with anticipation.

When everything seemed possible, before she'd found out Lionel had left.

His lordship's cheeks grew a little red, too, as the long moments of silence stretched on.

"That was presumptuous of me," he muttered. "I had best leave you to your work."

Drat it all! She had embarrassed him. As the counter clerk for Rare Confectionery, she'd helped hundreds of customers over the years and tried to do so with the graciousness taught by her mother, something that had entirely eluded Beatrice.

Now, Charlotte could sympathize with her sister's short-tempered disgruntlement. Being pleasant and cheerful lately seemed a tremendous chore for her. She'd failed at both all day, and she had even offended the duke's good friend.

He certainly didn't deserve it after demonstrating such kindness.

"My lord, I would very much enjoy a night on the town, as you call it. It sounds most inviting. I was simply shocked into silence."

His slight smile returned. "Shocked into silence? I didn't realize my asking you out would be considered outrageous. After your Season, with all the young bucks who were buzzing around you, I thought I would be standing in line for the chance."

And now he was bolstering her spirits and her confidence. He was being a prince.

Regaining a little spirit, Charlotte asked, "Except for the Marlborough House ball, you and I weren't at any of the same events last Season. How would you know about bucks, young or otherwise, doing any buzzing?"

"You have got me to rights, Miss Rare-Foure, but I can imagine them. Am I right?"

Her cheeks grew even warmer. She was probably blushing profusely.

"I suppose I had my share of dance partners," she admitted.

"*Ah-ha.*" He raised a finger as if he'd proved a point.

That did make her smile. "Where shall we go?"

"What do you like?" he asked. "The ballet, a concert, a play?"

No one had ever asked her before. *What could she say?* She had been to each of those with her family, and perfectly content to do so, but never with a man.

"What would *you* prefer?" she asked, wanting to be amiable.

"I would prefer your honest answer as to what *you* wish to do."

Gracious! They could go on being polite forever and never get anywhere.

"A play, then," she decided. "I like seeing the actors pretend to be other people so convincingly that I just about believe it. My sister, Beatrice, is very gifted at recitation. It takes an astonishing memory, don't you think?"

"Agreed. Then we shall see a play. Naturally, we shall need a chaperone."

"Naturally," she said. In truth, she hadn't thought about that for a second. Having served as the chaperone to Beatrice and Mr. Carson before their marriage, it seemed strange that she would need one herself. Nevertheless, he was right.

"Would our maid, Delia, do?"

"Fine by me but entirely up to you," he said. "Shall we say tomorrow night?"

Truly? She'd barely had a chance to get used to the idea. "Very well. I look forward to it." And strangely enough, she did.

HER PARENTS SEEMED AS surprised as she'd been when Charlotte told them about the arrangement to go out with the Viscount Jeffcoat.

"That's a peach stone in the plum jam," Felicity said. "Most unexpected. I thought that dashing Lord Waverly might come to show an interest in either you or Beatrice, but then the American snapped up your sister quick as a whip, and now the more serious Lord Jeffcoat has come calling."

"In any case," her father added, "our girls attract them like bees to flowers. And rightly so."

Normally, that would make Charlotte chuckle, but it seemed an effort to laugh when somewhere in the middle of her chest, she felt a tightness all the time.

"I didn't know you were thinking of either of these men," she said, "for me or for Bea."

For her own part, Charlotte regretted how much time she'd wasted thinking of one man. And she was fair sick of her own sadness, which lingered despite each passing day since Lionel had left. Moreover, having given up her twice weekly art class, unable to bear the reminder of having spent hours merely watching the way his long fingers held a paintbrush, she had little to occupy her evenings.

Losing the class didn't bother her as she'd never had a passion for painting, but she'd also lost the excitement in her life. She'd even lost the remaining tattered friendship she'd shared with Viola. They had exchanged a few missives since Lionel's departure, and even met for tea and scones, but Charlotte had found it too distressing. Viola's incessant talk about the pain of losing her brother, not knowing about Charlotte's own heartache, left her feeling ragged.

And then Viola had begun to receive letters. While at first, with almost morbid fascination Charlotte had wanted to hear them, after a few weeks, the narration of his new life abroad, happy and carefree, utterly mindless of any responsibilities to his parents and to what he'd left behind—including her—had become too painful. Even after she'd learned he and the artist's model had parted company somewhere in Rome.

Besides, he had never once asked after Charlotte. And while her first feelings were those of betrayal and having been duped, eventually, she was glad he didn't mention her. Her humiliation had Viola ever discovered she'd let him kiss her would have been unbearable.

While Charlotte didn't expect her heartache to heal overnight, she did hope to enjoy an evening at the theatre and was looking forward to Lord Jeffcoat's distraction.

Thus, she and her parents were in the parlor, her parents seated while Charlotte stood by the fireplace, dressed in one of her favorite gowns from the prior Season, keeping it from getting creased.

While awaiting Lord Jeffcoat's arrival, she felt strangely calm, an entirely different sensation than the unsettling anticipation she used to feel before each art class.

"You look very pretty tonight, dear daughter," her father said. Then finished with the conversation, Armand picked up the book he'd been reading on sugar manufacturing in the West Indies and buried his nose in it.

Charlotte smiled at her father's words and smoothed her gown yet again—a pale-green color with black lace trim. She had dressed with care, hoping Lord Jeffcoat thought her pretty, too, for she thought him a decidedly attractive man, in or out of his Robin Hood hose. Not in a dazzlingly swank way, like the famed Beau Brummel, or even like Lionel, with his overly long hair and tendency to flamboyant clothing. No, the viscount was more the dark, brooding, but elegant type. She felt her cheeks warm, thinking of him.

"He *has* been in the back room!" her mother suddenly declared, echoing the question she'd asked her days earlier.

With astonishment that somehow her mother knew—and the realization that Lord Jeffcoat had, in fact, been in the back—Charlotte burst out laughing. It felt good, despite knowing her mother thought there was some connection between men going into the back room and marrying her daughters.

Armand Foure snapped his book closed and leaned back with his pipe in his hand.

"That's the first time I've heard you laugh in a long time, my girl. I suppose he must be the right one."

"Father, it's our first time going out together." *Her parents weren't going to become pushy, were they?*

"He's lightened your mood, at any rate," her father insisted. "And that makes him a good chap."

"Oh, I know he is a good man," Felicity agreed. "Recall when he helped Edward on his first day."

Charlotte nodded. "He's working out well."

"Lord Jeffcoat!" her father exclaimed.

"Father, I meant Edward Percy."

"No, I mean, here is Lord Jeffcoat." And her father stood to greet him.

Charlotte turned, and sure enough, there was her escort for the evening, standing in the open doorway.

"It seems Mr. Finley has gone missing again," her mother said, standing to welcome their guest. "I don't know why we even pay him."

Her father laughed, never bothered by their butler's periods of absence or inattention to detail.

"Good evening, young man," Armand Foure said, not even addressing him correctly.

Charlotte rolled her eyes, but she knew Lord Jeffcoat wasn't the type to take offense.

His lordship shook her father's hand first, then bowed over her mother's before turning to her. He was impeccably dressed in black with a white vest, shirt, and ascot. His dark brown hair was brushed back, although a few tendrils were springing forth over his forehead, belying her earlier thoughts that he was too elegant to ever have a hair out of place. In fact, he looked a little rakish.

"Good evening, Miss Rare-Foure. Are you ready to go to the theatre?" His blue eyes flickered in the firelight.

"I am." A little drop of joy tried to trickle through her—and succeeded. "Mother, have you seen Delia? I asked her to accompany us tonight."

As if on cue, their middle-aged maid-of-all-work appeared in the doorway. "I'm ready miss, and I have your cloak. It's a little chilly tonight."

"Never fear," the viscount said. "My carriage has warming bricks and is quite comfortable."

"Then off you go," Felicity said. "I wonder if you will see either of your sisters there."

She had no idea what Bea and her husband did in the evenings, but Charlotte knew what her eldest sister would be doing.

"Amity is determined to stay home every evening with her feet up until she's delivered of her baby."

Charlotte steered them quickly out the door before her parents decided to join them, and before her mother could tell Lord Jeffcoat her theory of men in the back room marrying her daughters. Felicity would scare him off, and all Charlotte wanted was a diverting evening. She couldn't possibly see a future with the viscount, simply because he was not Lionel. Having nursed that fantasy so long, all other outcomes seemed inferior.

WHEN THEY GOT INTO his carriage, and the close, warm air encircled them, Charles could smell Miss Rare-Foure's delightful perfume—lemon and lime, yet soft, not tangy, with a floral aspect that made the scent seem creamy, too. He was mesmerized. He wanted to ask her about it, but he always found chaperones impeded personal discussion until one reached the safety of the private theatre box. Then, he could seat the maid behind them and be at liberty to lean in close and ask her questions.

"What are we going to see?" Miss Rare-Foure asked, smoothing the skirts of her green gown, which he could see where her cloak fell open. As he'd noticed in the parlor, it had a fashionably low-cut décolletage and small cap sleeves. The bodice and sleeves were trim with black lace drawing his eyes where they shouldn't go, at least not while he was still with her parents.

On the other hand, if a woman had such a pretty physique, small-waisted and big busted, as Miss Rare-Foure, and if she wore such a gown, then obviously, she expected to be observed and admired. Again, both would be easier to do once they were at the theatre *sans* cloak—and, he hoped, *sans* maid.

"In keeping with the spirit of lightening your heart, we are going to the Haymarket to see a comedy."

"In truth, my lord, I'm relieved it's not the Lyceum Theatre. While I admire greatly Mr. Irving and Miss Terry, they are often at their best with a Shakespearian tragedy."

"Agreed. Tonight, there shall be no tragedy, I assure you. A rather farcical comedy called *Engaged*."

"Oh yes, by Mr. Gilbert." She looked like she was about to clap her hands. "His *Sorcerer* and *H.M.S. Pinafore* were very witty. I am looking forward to the evening's entertainment."

He was glad her spirits had perked up. By the time they'd passed through the impressive columns at the entrance to the newly renovated Royal Haymarket Theatre, he hoped she might warm to him as well. He very much wanted to be the cause of her next beautiful smile.

The theatre's gaudy pink marble had been removed and a magnificent proscenium arch gilded in gold surrounded the stage. He knew there'd been somewhat of an uproar over the installation of stalls and the removal of the pit, but it didn't affect him or his guest in the box directly overlooking the stage on the right-hand side.

With her maid seated a polite distance behind, they had a few minutes to settle in and observe those below them and to their left where the theatre stretched back and up into the circle seats.

Uninterested in anyone but her, Charles leaned in close to sniff Charlotte's intoxicating fragrance, opening his mouth to ask her about it. She chose that precise moment to lean forward and push aside the red-and-gold drapery that framed each box, in order to better see more of the audience.

"I think I spy my sister and Mr. Carson. Do you see them? They're in the front of the balcony."

He peered around, but in all the people milling about and getting seated, he couldn't make out the snapdragon and her American husband.

Charlotte waved, stood up, and leaned out.

"Careful, Miss Rare-Foure. You don't want to take a tumble and become part of the evening's performance."

"I'll be careful," she said, not looking at him, although he had a glorious view of her midsection, the way her waist nipped in and then blossomed out above with her generous curves.

He sighed. *Was he a superficial man?* He didn't believe so. After all, he wasn't with her for her looks, or at least, not her looks alone—albeit they were certainly pleasing. He'd become interested in her for her personality and good humor. When he'd realized what he'd first thought of as her childishness was actually *joie de vivre*, then—

A piercing whistle split the bustling sound of the noisy auditorium, and he knew at once who'd caused it. *Dear God!*

He felt as though every eye in the Haymarket turned in their direction, to their box by the stage. Behind him, the Rare-Foure's maid muttered to herself, "Oh, no, oh no, what is she doing?"

In front of him was only shocked silence, and then, against all odds, Miss Rare-Foure waved grandly before taking her seat.

"Beatrice saw me," she said with satisfaction. Then she blinked into the drawn-out silence, looking out over the theatre as people started to whisper. In the next instant, the theatre-goers began to speak more loudly, returning to normal until the gas lamps dimmed.

"Is something wrong?" she asked when he didn't speak.

He groaned. In a flash, he imagined her as his wife, performing her duties as his viscountess and playing hostess to some ministers of Parliament or a group of stodgy judges. And Charlotte in the middle of it—whistling to announce dinner or appearing in her garish Turkish silks. That would never work. She simply wouldn't do!

What on earth was he doing with her?

"Nothing," he said tightly. "Nothing is wrong." There was no point in telling her she'd behaved outrageously. Moreover, the last thing he wanted was her sister gawking across the theatre at them or the American making his jokes as Pelham said the man was wont to do.

And then, while Charles was starting to regret the whole evening, at last, Charlotte turned to him and smiled. It was perfectly exquisite, transforming her face to radiant.

"Beatrice will find us at the intermission. Have you met her husband? Of course you have, at one of the duke's gatherings and at the Marlborough House ball," she chattered on.

"He is an amusing man, worthy of my sister's intelligence and interesting mind. My family, all of them, are each different, but they somehow are also the same. All perfectly delightful, the kindest, most generous people you will ever know. Except for Beatrice sometimes. I know she can be crabby, everyone has seen it, but lately, I've understood her impatience with people a little better."

She paused, then added, "One never knows, does one?"

He had no idea what she meant, but he did know she loved her family tremendously, and he thought that made her a special woman, indeed. While he was fond of his father, he hadn't seen his mother in a decade and a half, nor cared if he ever saw her again. And he had no siblings, although Waverly and Pelham felt as close to brothers as he could imagine.

Still, he was a little awed by the depth of her feelings.

The lights flickered and dimmed again, and they settled down for the first of three acts, opening in a Scottish cottage, near Gretna. To his pleasure, Charlotte was laughing almost at once.

After the second act, there was an intermission, and she jumped up, a smile on her face. "May we go find my sister? Won't they think it's funny? I remember Lord Pelham telling Mr. Carson not to mention Scotland to young ladies at the balls last year in case they thought he was inferring a trip to Gretna Green and a hasty marriage."

Charles nodded and found himself swept along by her good humor to the lobby, her maid trailing behind. As Charlotte had predicted, her sister quickly found them. The women hugged, and Mr. Carson stuck out his hand for a solid shake.

"Are you enjoying it?" Charlotte asked, not pausing for an answer. "I knew you would. What a clever premise, and how fun the two of you coming. Did you know it was set in Scotland? Mr. Carson, did it make you think you should have stolen my sister away?" And then, she did clap her hands in glee. "I think the two of you should join us in the box for the end of it. You do have to crane your neck a little, but there is oodles of room."

She turned to Charles who'd never heard such a tide of words, as if a dam had broken. "That's fine with you, isn't it? The more the merrier. Oh my goodness! Where is Delia? Did we lose her? Bea, Delia is with us as my chaperone. Can you believe it? As if I needed a chaperone, and with Lord Jeffcoat?"

Charles felt as if he'd been slapped in the face and emasculated at the same time.

The snapdragon recognized the slight at once, and said, "Dear one, you recall last year. We all need a chaperone for propriety's sake." Then she glanced at her husband. "And any man may turn out to be a danger to one's heart, if not to one's person."

Charles watched the two of them exchange a long look before Mrs. Carson looked at him again, cocked her head a little jauntily and added, "Lord Jeffcoat seems as likely a suitor as any I've ever seen."

Well! He appreciated that, to be sure. Charlotte paused, gave him a long appraisal, and said, "Of course. I didn't mean he wasn't as dangerous as any man. But I trust him more than any other I know because he is the duke's good friend. It's like having another brother-in-law."

Charles breathed in deeply. *Worse and worse.* Now he was like a brother! He had greatly miscalculated his own appeal, to be sure.

"Shall we all have some champagne before it is too late?" Charlotte continued, unaware of how her honest words cut him.

Only then did the snapdragon take her sister in hand with the mildest of reprimands.

"You really should not have used that abominable whistle of yours. Imagine Mother's face." She fell silent with a shake of her head.

Incredibly, instead of looking chagrinned, Charlotte began to snicker, and her sister joined in, probably together picturing their mother.

"Miss Charlotte did succeed in getting our attention," Mr. Carson added, and then they put the matter behind them as if humiliation on such a grand scale were nothing.

Charles was stunned, even though he knew it was pointless to dwell as there was no redress for it, no taking back the wretched sound.

After the refreshments, they headed back into the auditorium, and as Charlotte had insisted, the Carsons joined them in his box. With the maid, there were five of them enjoying the performance. All hope of sniffing Charlotte's neck and asking what perfume she wore or telling her how much he appreciated her smile vanished like the artful stage smoke. What's more, she spent all her time whispering to her sister when she wasn't laughing uproariously at the play's events.

Despite thinking Charlotte's laughter to be delightful, so genuine and spontaneous, Charles had come to an irrevocable conclusion by the play's end. The evening—and asking out Miss Rare-Foure—had been a mistake from start to finish.

CHAPTER SIX

"I'm so sorry to leave you like this," Felicity said over dinner a week later while Charlotte anxiously absorbed the startling news of her father's sudden ill-health.

"It's just indigestion," Armand Foure grumbled. "Interfering physician."

"My love," Felicity said, "he is a good doctor, you know that. And it may be merely indigestion, but you've not been yourself and he said the sea air is what you need. It's warm enough now, we won't freeze in Newquay. We'll even be able to swim."

"Newquay," Charlotte mused, recalling a visit to the Cornish coast a few years back with her parents and her sisters. She wished she could go, too, but as her mother was making clear, the shop was hers to run.

It was the first time she would live alone on Baker Street with only the servants. Moreover, she would be working practically alone, too. She had Edward, but Bea never came in early when it wasn't a busy time of year, especially now that Edward could do the cleaning. And Amity hardly came in at all anymore. Instead, her sister made chocolates from home, and Edward retrieved them for the shop. Fortunately, he had taken to confectionery like a duck to water and could actually make smooth fondant, temper chocolate, and create bonbons by himself. He didn't have the skill to blend flavors, but he carefully followed recipes that Amity gave him.

When Charlotte opened the shop the next day, for the first time in her life, a tendril of fear unfurled inside her. This was their family's livelihood, after all. Then she realized, that wasn't the case for Amity and Beatrice anymore, and the fear eased off slightly. Nevertheless, without her mother there, Charlotte would have to stay all day, every day.

Daunted for a moment, she reminded herself it was temporary, and her father would be well soon. Even then, her parents were already on a train on their way to Cornwall. Everyone knew good salty air and seawater would make Armand Foure right as rain in no time. Still, she had a small lump of worry in her throat that she couldn't quite swallow away.

Edward arrived, right on time as usual. They tidied and cleaned anything that hadn't been done the night before, and then, while he stocked the cases, she prepared the delivery orders.

"We're like a well-greased machine, Edward."

"What do you mean, miss?" he asked, adjusting his apron, of which he now had three that all fit him well and made him look more his age.

"Meaning we work well together, you and I."

"Oh, I see," he said. "The greased parts of machinery don't grind against one another."

"Precisely, although I never thought about it so deeply."

He chuckled. Charlotte had come to enjoy that sound. At first, he had been the most serious child, but after weeks of making steady money, learning the trade, and feeling more confident, he was becoming lighter in manner and humor.

When she explained about her parents going away, his expression became grown-up in an instant. "I will do anything I can to help you, Miss Charlotte."

"I know you will, and I appreciate it. Get the deliveries done and when Bea arrives, you can try making another batch of toffee with her."

He'd burned the last one, but Charlotte wasn't sure she would have done any better. Toffee-making seemed the most persnickety thing in the world, and she'd decided to ask Bea about getting an hourglass timer and marking it to the precise moment so both she and Edward could be assured of success when her sister wasn't around.

After turning the sign to "Open," with Edward not yet returned, Charlotte began working quietly making marzipan sweets, interrupted every few minutes by a customer's arrival. After the excursion with Lord Jeffcoat the previous week, she had regained some of her former good humor, realizing she was missing the friendly interactions with her customers by being churlish and melancholy.

An hour passed pleasantly with her handing out samples and selling more than she had in days. When the door opened, Charlotte looked up at the bell with a welcoming smile to see not a customer but their landlord.

"Mr. Richardson," she said with surprise, for she'd only seen him half a dozen times in as many years. Nothing changed about him except his moustache grew thicker and grayer each year. "What brings you in? Some sweets for Mrs. Richardson?"

She had no idea if there even was a missus, but it was always good to ask. Most men didn't think about it until the idea was put into their heads that confection was a welcome present, especially for no occasion at all.

"Why, yes," he said, looking around as if only just realizing what they sold. "I'll take a tin of that toffee everyone's always raving about."

Glad to hear of it, she was more determined than ever that Bea teach her and Edward how to time it properly.

"But I came to speak to your mother. Is she here?"

"No, sir." And then the realization hit here. "She is away indefinitely, but I'm in charge. I am running the shop."

"Really." He peered at her over his spectacles. His bushy moustache moved up and down as if he were chewing the air while pondering that fact. "I was going to say you seem young to manage a shop, but then, you've been here all your life, haven't you?"

"Yes, sir. Is something the matter?"

"The contrary actually. I am wondering if your mother would like to expand the shop to have the second-floor suite. It's vacant now. Mrs. Hafflen has retired to the country. It's been all cleaned out. Before I start showing it to possible tenants, I wanted to offer it to your family. A more convenient thing, I can't imagine, than suddenly doubling your space without having to move."

Charlotte could scarcely breathe. *Was it fate?* It was exactly what she'd hoped for when she'd spoken to her mother about expanding weeks ago. Felicity's answer had been definitely no, but only because she didn't want to leave New Bond Street or have two locations. *This was a miracle offering!*

"How long do we have to consider this offer?" Charlotte's hands were trembling, and absently, she reached for a chocolate and popped it in her mouth. She would send a letter to her parents at once and—

"Just until tomorrow I'm afraid."

Charlotte swallowed too quickly and choked. Grabbing a paper napkin, she coughed until she'd regained her composure. Mr. Richardson's moustache moved up and down more rapidly, but he waited patiently, saying nothing.

"Excuse me," she said when she could speak. "I do wish I had more time."

"Word got out quickly after Mrs. Hafflen moved out, and all sorts of people have been asking. Everyone wants to be on New Bond Street, as you know. I'm being mindful that you don't want a dance hall above your head." He laughed ruefully as if that were a possibility.

In truth, Charlotte didn't want anything above her head except the quiet pillow woman unless it was more Rare Confectionery.

"Do you have a lease I can read over? And the rent? Is it the same as for this floor?"

He eyed her a minute. "Actually, it's a little less because there aren't street-front windows."

She nodded, feeling a thrill of potential dance down her spine. Glancing around the shop, she thought about customers being told they could go upstairs for a rich beverage and to eat confectionery. Or maybe the dining room would be down here and the counter service upstairs. The possibilities spread out before her.

"We would have to decorate upstairs to resemble the shop," she mused. Her mother liked as much white and sapphire blue as possible, although Charlotte adored the myriad rich jewel tones of the popular Aesthetic mode.

"You could do that. You could even build a staircase in here." The landlord glanced around. "I suppose over in that corner. Then your customers wouldn't have to go outside to get upstairs."

"Could we?" Charlotte asked, feeling even more excited. In her mind, she could already see the rooms above filled with small, cloth-covered tables and customers enjoying steaming mugs of chocolate or coffee and plates of sweets. They had so much extra income from the hotel and restaurant contracts, she couldn't see any problem with paying more rent. And with Amity and Beatrice no long living off the store's profits, expansion seemed perfectly reasonable.

All at once, despite standing alone in the shop with all the responsibility of Rare Confectionery having fallen to her, she couldn't think of a single reason not to do it.

"Will you return tomorrow? I promise to have an answer for you then."

He nodded and drew some papers from his satchel. "Here are the terms, the rent, and the square footage. All that."

Taking it, she tucked it on the shelf behind her and grabbed a pound tin of toffee, sliding it across the counter to him.

"How much?" he asked.

"With my compliments," she said.

"Hm. If you want to be a woman of business, Miss Rare-Foure, then you must charge me."

She smiled. "All right, I will. But first, please choose a sample. As a business woman, I want you to try something else, and maybe you'll wish to buy it as well."

He laughed. She gave him one of Amity's coffee-flavored chocolates, the distinctive taste of which made his eyebrows raise.

"I'll take half a pound of those," he said, drawing out his wallet as soon as he'd swallowed, "along with the toffee. You *are* a fine business woman. I shall see you about the same time tomorrow. I hope you take my offer. Otherwise, I believe it will be a photographer above your head having clients marching up those side stairs from morning till night, or the other interested party was a well-heeled boot maker—" he paused to laugh at his own little pun.

"That one hoped you would close soon so he might open a shop right here below. In any case, that might be quite a bit of hammering overhead. Both those two fellows were chomping at the bit."

IT WAS INSANITY—CHARLOTTE knew that, but time was fleeting. Heading straight to Park Lane after work, she knocked on Lord Jeffcoat's townhouse door all by herself.

Without a chaperone! It was unquestionably no longer polite visiting hours, which ended about three o'clock for the aristocratic set. After that, a visitor might expect an invitation to a meal, and most people didn't want that imposition laid at their doorstep or upon their kitchen staff at short notice.

An older man, nearly as tall as Lord Jeffcoat, answered the door, clearly a butler of the quality of Amity and the duke's efficient butler. Nothing like their own dear man-servant Mr. Finley, who was labelled a *butler* only by the most generous interpretation of the term.

The butler looked over her head for a moment, and Charlotte wished she had Beatrice's height. In any case, when he looked down at her, his rather severe face softened.

"Yes, miss?"

In her gloved hand was a Rare Confectionery business card. It didn't have her name, but she said, "I am Miss Rare-Foure. If his lordship is home, would you mind giving him my card? I shall wait."

Handing it to him, she tucked her hands behind her back and almost started to whistle. Not the whistle that seemed to make everyone uneasy, but a little tuneful song. However, she stopped herself when he looked at the card and turned it over, then over again. Perhaps he had no intention of letting her in. It was out of the ordinary, to be sure. Probably no unexpected or uninvited visitor had turned up at the viscount's home all week if not all year.

"Lord Jeffcoat and I are already acquainted," she assured him. Perhaps the butler thought her a woman of ill-repute, wanting to be caught in a compromising situation in order to blackmail the viscount. Maybe he feared she were some poor servant whom his master had ill-used, who was there to declare she carried his child.

With her thoughts running wild—from reading too many of Delia's penny-dreadfuls to keep her mind busy in the evenings—Charlotte could do nothing but look directly into the man's eyes while smiling encouragingly. *After all, she was a woman of business!*

Something worked on the butler, for he stepped back and invited her in. "If you will wait here, please, miss, I shall ask his lordship if he is seeing visitors."

"Thank you," she said, delighted to wander the foyer. The man went up the stairs, leaving her to examine a marble bust that seemed to be someone ancient, a Greek, she supposed. Then she moved on to a gorgeous red vase that she knew to be Venetian glass, having seen the like in Italy. Very pretty, with gold overlay seeming to drip symmetrically down the sides. She had to clench her fists behind her back. Her mother had always said the safest thing to do was not to touch, but she sorely wanted to.

Lastly, on the far wall next to a closed door, there was a landscape. Charlotte's heart clenched when she saw it was similar to one they'd attempted to copy from a print in art class, probably the same painter. Lionel's copy had been the best, without doubt.

Footsteps drew her out of her thoughts spiraling into sadness. When she turned, Lord Jeffcoat was arriving on the bottom step, looking as though he'd galloped down them. He ran a hand through his hair combing it back, and then tugged at his coat as if he'd just donned it. She'd apparently caught him in a state of dishabille.

"My apologies, Miss Rare-Foure, for keeping you waiting. I was not expecting any visitors tonight."

"It is I who must apologize for barging in here uninvited, but I knew of no other lawyer, and I have only until early tomorrow." Surprised to learn the previous year that Lord Jeffcoat was studying the law, as she'd assumed no titled gentleman did anything so taxing, the other evening he'd informed her he'd been called to the Bar. Charlotte couldn't be more relieved to have a legal mind close at hand within her circle of acquaintance.

He hesitated, but then said, "That's quite all right. You are always welcome as the sister-in-law of my very good friend."

She thought that kind of him, although she also realized they'd taken a step back. She noted with curiosity that she wasn't welcome simply as the woman he wanted to escort around town, which she was no longer confident to be the case.

Lord Jeffcoat had seemed to enjoy her company at the Haymarket Theatre, as well as that of her sister and Mr. Carson. Nevertheless, after bringing her directly home, he'd seen her to her door, and with a curt bow, left her and Delia on the front step. Moreover, he had not returned to the shop after that, nor had he invited her out again.

In truth, she was a little interested at the reason for his inattention, taking it to mean he'd found her unsatisfactory in some way. Distracted with running the shop in her mother's absence, though, Charlotte had been unable to rise to the level of being miffed and could barely claim herself even to be bothered—simply curious.

Seeing him as a nobleman at home, surrounded by his fine things—*and she hadn't even made it out of the foyer yet!*—Charlotte assumed Lord Jeffcoat had thought her provincial or too middle-class for him. Perhaps she'd laughed too loudly at the play.

"You are aware I am a barrister and not a solicitor. That means—"

She waved her hand. "I know what that means, my lord. You're more comfortable arguing before a judge than dealing with legal contracts. That's fine. I simply need someone to read over a document and make sure I'm not missing something or being ill-used."

He frowned. "What kind of document?"

"A lease. I want to expand Rare Confectionery."

Looking startled at the import of her visit, he said, "Well, then, I had best take a look." He peered past her to the butler, who had returned to await any orders.

Lord Jeffcoat's frown etched deeper into his forehead. "Are you here without a chaperone?" His tone was incredulous.

"Yes," she admitted. "I came straight from closing up the shop."

He shook his head while muttering under his breath. She heard the words *rash* and *ruin*.

"Phelps, please bring tea into the . . . ," he hesitated and looked around his house as if he wasn't quite sure where he was.

"The drawing room, sir," said Mr. Phelps. Charlotte stifled a giggle before the capable man servant turned to her. "May I take your cloak, miss?"

There was a chill in the air and in the foyer—and she was not an invited guest—thus, she declined.

Lord Jeffcoat nodded at his butler, then gestured for her to precede him across the foyer and through the double doors beside the painting that had irked her.

"Do you live alone here?" she asked, glancing around what could best be described as a forlorn room. It hardly helped when he turned up the lamps. Signs of neglect were everywhere. Not in cleanliness, of course. There wasn't a trace of dust or a cobweb to be seen, but it was cheerless, nonetheless.

And it was cold. It seemed Lord Jeffcoat had not updated his home with the modern convenience of steam or gas heat, and the coal fire was unlit, appearing as if it hadn't been used for ages.

"My father, the Earl of Bentley, resides here, too. He keeps to himself mostly."

Charlotte supposed that was the answer. No female presence. No fresh flowers, nor a book on the table. In fact all the surfaces were bare, and the sofa and chairs had no pillows or warming blankets draped over the back. There wasn't even a fern or a potted palm. She would vow the room was never used, but only cleaned by the staff.

"Will you sit?" he offered.

She did, on the hard sofa. When he went to sit in the chair farthest from her, she sighed.

"My lord, perhaps you could sit closer so we can go over the lease together. I don't want you to scan it and say *aye* or *nay*. I want you to show me anything that might be considered dodgy or any language in it that might harm me and my family to the benefit of the landlord. I do think him to be an honest man, but it never hurts to investigate."

Again, he hesitated but remained standing. "After Mr. Phelps brings in the tea, then I shall sit beside you."

"Very well." She could imagine how Lionel would have taken advantage of the situation to press her back against the sofa and kiss her. She realized it seemed cowardly and shifty to her now, that he had never once seen her in the light of day!

Silently, she observed the calm reserve of the viscount, even though he was standing before her a little awkwardly. For his part, he was staring resolutely at the door as if willing the butler to hurry. Apparently, not only wasn't he going to sit until after Mr. Phelps' reappearance, he wasn't going to speak either. It was up to her to relieve the tension.

"I am sorry, my lord, to have put you in this position."

"It is not I who is in a position," he said a little sharply. "It is you. A position to lose your reputation, the likes of which could not be easily repaired."

Charlotte couldn't help an unladylike shrug. "I fail to see the harm."

"Yes, that is exactly the *failing* on your part, that you do not see a potential problem."

"Perhaps." She nearly smiled, then realized he wasn't teasing. He was finding fault with her, which she didn't care for. Not one bit. "Again, I apologize for coming here directly. I should have stopped home for Delia."

"This is most inappropriate," he added.

Before she could defend herself again, the door opened.

Mr. Phelps had undoubtedly instructed tea to be made in record time. Luckily, with the large modern stoves kept on most of the day, water was always simmering in the kitchen.

"There we are," the viscount said, as the butler placed the tray upon the low table in front of the sofa. Also, nestled between the cups and saucers and the teapot was a pretty china plate with some biscuits and wafers, which Charlotte appreciated as she had skipped lunch and was growing peckish.

"Shall I pour, sir?"

"No, Phelps. I'll handle it," the viscount said.

Removing her gloves and taking a biscuit, Charlotte munched it while the butler left and his lordship finally took a seat beside her. When he did, she caught his interesting scent of spice and rum again. As she'd discovered, there was something appealing about a man who smelled a little like gingerbread.

Admittedly, at that moment, alone in the room with him, seated close together, she felt a new awareness. Recalling the furtive kisses with Lionel, always hurried and fraught with danger of discovery, she realized how simple it would be for two people given the time and place—such as the next hour in a private drawing room—to utterly break the boundaries of acceptability and respectability. *Hm!*

The lease was folded on her lap, and she now handed the two sheets of paper to Lord Jeffcoat. He drew from his coat pocket a pair of blued-steel wire spectacles, which he slipped on his face, making sure they hooked upon his ears before he opened the folded sheets. She'd never seen him wearing glasses before. While he began to read, she observed him.

His face was an attractive one, to be sure. His mouth was different than Lionel's. Much as she hated to admit it, Lionel had a smug way of pursing his lips while he was lost in his painting or sketching, and his mouth gave way to an air of petulance when the teacher gave the slightest criticism.

Lord Jeffcoat's mouth had nothing petulant or puckering about it, merely determined, as if he were going to suss out any possible problem in the lease by hook or by crook. She ate another biscuit while he looked at the next page.

He had nice eyebrows, she decided, dark and finely shaped. And from the side, she could see his long lashes practically touching the oval glass in his spectacles. Most becoming. Then, while she was staring at his flat earlobe and his strong jawline, his head turned. He looked directly into her eyes with his cerulean blue ones, and something inside her shifted.

"You're staring at me," he said, "and I'm finding it hard to concentrate."

"Am I?" She wiped her hands together to remove any crumbs. "My apologies, but there is nothing else to do." The room held no books or newspapers. Besides she wanted to know at once, by the look upon his face, if he found anything untoward. "Shall I pour the tea?"

"Fine. Yes, please do. I like a teaspoon of sugar." Then he added, "Perhaps everybody does."

"I don't think they do," she said, and glanced to see if he'd been joking. He had a well-shaped nose, not too sharp. And while his cheekbones weren't ridiculously protruding, they cast a slight shadow upon his cheeks.

"You're still staring," he pointed out. "Would you like *me* to pour?"

"No." She put a splash of milk in the bottom of each cup and then dispensed the tea on top, added the sugar, and even stirred both cups before handing him his.

"Your tea would stay hotter in the pot with a knitted cozy," she told him.

"You're distracting me, Miss Rare-Foure. I'm nearly done."

She sat back with her tea and a wafer. After sipping as quietly as possible, she spoke again without thinking. "Plants bring a room to life, don't you think?"

He didn't answer.

"And with a silver candlestick on either end of that sideboard, maybe with a bowl of fruit in the middle or a large china figurine, it would look much more inviting."

He turned his head toward her again.

"Even the red vase from the foyer would look good, right there." She pointed. "It would bring in a dash of color."

He blinked.

She sighed. "Your tea is growing cold."

Setting the pages down on the table, he removed his spectacles, picked up his tea and drank it down quickly. "I don't need a cozy on my teapot because I don't sip and dawdle. I drink it before it gets cold."

"What about brandy?"

"What about it?" he asked, both eyebrows raised.

"Do you sip it, or do you tip your head back and swallow it so quickly you barely taste it."

"I sip it," he confessed, "but brandy is not tea. Brandy is to be savored slowly. Like a kiss." Those words froze all the thoughts in her brain, and she gaped at him.

Was he flirting with her?

CHAPTER SEVEN

"Oh," Charlotte said after a pause, knowing the viscount had caused her to blush. None of the kisses she'd had with Lionel had been slow. Quite the opposite. They had been hurried and sometimes a little rough as he ground his mouth upon hers, always with both of them listening for footfalls.

Imagining how it would have been if she and Lionel had time at their disposal—she tried, but she couldn't picture Lionel or his mouth when seated next to Lord Jeffcoat and his unfathomable blue eyes.

"My apologies," he said, his gaze remaining locked on hers. "I should not have made reference to an intimate act when we are without a chaperone. That was poorly done of me."

She swallowed, her glance dropping to his mouth. *What would it be like to have a slow kiss with the viscount?* They would undoubtedly savor the moment instead of grasping at one another and then breaking apart just as the excitement was building.

"That's quite all right," she assured him, lifting her glance to his again. "We're not bashful debutantes. Or at least, I'm not. Of course, you're not, either. Not that you could be. You're a man." She started to laugh, hearing the nervousness in her voice. She coughed. "What I mean is, I've had a Season, after all."

Now it was his gaze that had dropped. While she was speaking, he studied her mouth—or seemed to be—before his glance flickered back to her eyes. He was also ever-so-slightly smiling. Hopefully, he wasn't laughing on the inside at her addle-headed babble.

Regain your composure, Charlotte ordered herself, and she did.

"Besides, those of us who enjoy the taste of tea and don't drink it merely to quench our thirst want to savor it, just as you do your brandy. And we like to savor it hot."

Looking thoughtful, he nodded, then he smiled more broadly for the first time, and to her surprise, a single dimple appeared. It was quite attractive, and she had the odd desire to touch it.

"You are correct, Miss Rare-Foure," he said, making her quickly look into his eyes. He was *not* talking about his dimple.

"Am I?" she asked.

"You are. If you like to sip your tea, who am I to judge you?" Leaning forward, he tapped the contract with the arm of his spectacles. "As to this lease, I am not an expert in English land law or even real property law, but this lease is straightforward. He is already your current landlord, correct?

"Yes, ever since my parents opened the shop. And suddenly, the upstairs has become vacant for the first time."

"From what I see, it doesn't quite double your rent, but close." He pointed to the final clause on the second page where the monthly payment was stipulated. "Why aren't you speaking with your parents?"

That made her sound like a child, but she supposed he had the right to ask. With a lifting of her chin, she told him, "My parents are away, and I've been left in charge. I spend more time in the shop than anyone in my family." She hoped she didn't sound defensive.

He nodded. "Nonetheless, do you think you ought to discuss this with your sisters?"

"May I pour myself another cup of tea?" she asked, wanting to consider her answer.

"Yes, of course," he said.

Milk, sugar, tea, stir. Sitting back, Charlotte finally told him, "You may know that your friend the duke is soon to be a father. My eldest sister, without saying anything personal, needs to spend more time with her feet up. I wouldn't want to worry her about the confectionery right now. And, in any case, she will be even less involved in the coming months. Not that I'm saying the decision isn't hers to make," she added, "although actually, that is exactly what I am saying."

"And what about the snap—?" he stopped abruptly.

"The what?" she asked, leaning forward.

"What about your other sister?"

"I'm sure she would have something to say about it," Charlotte agreed, "but she has always spent the least time in the shop, and as little as possible with the customers. Undoubtedly, she would leave it to me and to my mother to make a decision."

Truthfully, Charlotte was fairly certain Bea's opinion would be not to expand if it meant she might have to serve upstairs. Moreover, the last thing her sister wanted at that moment, with a new husband and a home in Scotland to renovate, was a larger confectionery. But Charlotte had been left in charge, not Bea.

Lord Jeffcoat sighed, poured himself another cup of tea and took a biscuit. "Miss Rare-Foure, this clause here," and he pointed to another higher up on the page, "says this is absolutely binding between the signer—meaning you—and

Mr. Richardson. If you change your mind, he won't excuse the fact that it's you and not your father signing the document."

"Or my mother," she said.

He raised an eyebrow. "As it turns out, you have the power to sign but not your mother."

"I beg your pardon."

The viscount leaned back, not looking comfortable, but that was undoubtedly due to the stiff sofa. "Under traditional English common law, you are a *feme sole*, or a single adult woman."

"Yes." She wasn't sure what he was getting at.

"Strange as it might seem, you can own property and make contracts in your own name. However, your mother, as a wife, is considered a *feme covert*, a covered woman. Of course, you're aware that she cannot hold property in her own right or enter into a contract."

"I suppose I knew it, but since she has always been in charge of Rare Confectionery, I never thought about the ramifications."

"She is considered to be the same entity as your father. At least, that's the nicest way I can put it. They are one person under the law."

"But that one person is my father, not my mother."

"Precisely."

"It seems . . . antiquated at best and ridiculous at the very least. My mother has built the shop up to what it is," Charlotte pointed out.

"To be fair, the law of coverture also protected women at a time when they were considered feeble-minded or weak-willed." He held up a hand when she started to protest.

"It ensured that a wife could perform all manner of heinous acts or even drive a couple into bankruptcy," he further explained, "with no consequences to herself while her husband would be held accountable."

"Don't you think many husbands behaved abominably because of that," she asked, "treating women like children, being cruelly strict with them, not allowing their wives any freedom, and then punishing them for any infractions?"

"Most assuredly. Fortunately, the Married Women's Property Act of 1870 and the Matrimonial Causes Act last year have addressed some of these issues."

"Last year!" Charlotte thought about Amity and Bea, both marrying and giving up their legal status as people. *How strange!* And they had done so willingly, for love. They each must trust their husband beyond anything.

"In any case," he continued, "if you have indeed been given the power to run the shop, then you can sign the contract of lease. I see nothing untoward in the document. However, I expect if you do something your mother doesn't want you to do, then the force of the law is the least of your worries. Is that correct?"

She smiled at his unerring supposition. "True. I would rather a stint in Newgate jail than to draw upon me my mother's displeasure."

At his concerned expression, she added, "I speak in jest, my lord. My mother, while formidable and exacting, has always been fair and kind. She said she would like to expand if we could stay on New Bond Street."

"Then this seems to be the perfect solution." Then he cocked his head. "And you're quite correct about the tea. My second cup is cold."

CHARLES WAS IMPRESSED BY Miss Rare-Foure all over again. The next thing he knew, he'd invited her to stay to dinner after determining she had no plans and was going home to an empty house. He'd even agreed to send a footman to her home to stave off the inevitable worry of the family's long-time staff, who might be concerned, having already expected her arrival.

Lastly, he had the coal fire lit in the dining room, thinking not for the first time how modern Pelham's home was with gas lighting and heat. With only himself and his father, two bachelors, they had never seen the need to renovate, except putting in a new kitchen stove at their cook's request. Nonetheless, he now saw the benefit since it had been difficult as the deuce to get Miss Rare-Foure to remove her cloak.

During the meal, his father did not put in an appearance, and Charles thought that was for the best. The earl was often cantankerous. On the other hand, the way she handled customers, her delightful personality might have done him the world of good.

Charles was secretly pleased to see she had regained her good humor and pleasant countenance, both of which had been blatantly absent the last time he was in her shop, watching her chase out customers. Perhaps it was the possibility of expanding Rare Confectionery that had put her in such a happy mood, but he could practically see her excitement in her sparkling eyes and bowed lips.

Who would have ever guessed inside the young woman who crafted marzipan and loved pretty things, there beat the heart of a woman of business?

He hoped it all worked out for the best. He also wished he'd invited her out a second time. It had been narrow-minded of him not to, but he was decidedly on the fence whether they were well-matched at all. While the attraction grew each time he was with her, if she were entirely unsuitable to become a viscountess, there was no point in leading her on. After all, he wasn't a scoundrel to dally with a woman's feelings, especially not the sister of his friend's wife.

Without hesitation, she accepted his offer to dine together alone as if it were the most natural thing in the world for a single female to dine at a single gentleman's home. He couldn't help rolling his eyes at the precariousness of it and hoped Pelham, as her brother-in-law, didn't look unkindly upon him.

As it turned out, over a creamy vegetable pottage followed by roast chicken with sliced potatoes, Miss Rare-Foure further enchanted him with her knowledge of art as well as the broadness of her thoughts. She'd traveled extensively on the Continent but didn't put on airs about it. Instead, she seemed to have developed a keen insight into the differences among cultures while appreciating the sameness of people's responses to such basic things as good food, wine, and music.

In literature, she was not extremely well read, apparently preferring gossip rags and sentimental novels to anything philosophical. But then during dessert, she mentioned William Harrison Ainsworth.

"I'm working my way through the three volumes of Mr. Ainsworth's latest publication, *Beau Nash*. And I understand he is still writing at age 74."

Charles almost spit out his wine. "That's remarkable."

"Is it?" She looked at him over a forkful of the strawberry tart Cook had made for the pudding course. "People do many things into their seventies."

"No, I didn't mean because of his age. I meant because I greatly admire him as well. I've read nearly all of his works," Charles declared, "*except* that one. I just haven't had time as yet."

"Do you read him because he is also a lawyer?" she asked.

What a delight, he thought, *to have someone else with whom he could discuss an author he greatly admired.*

"Precisely, although not a satisfied one. He has the heart of a poet, I think." Charles admired the man who could bring a bit of dash to the law profession, which many viewed as dull. "Have you read *The Star-Chamber*?"

"No, I haven't," she admitted. "But I read his *Windsor Castle* and thoroughly enjoyed it."

"I, as well. I have *The Star-Chamber* if you wish to borrow it. Two volumes." He jumped up from the table. "Come along, bring your wine." He'd never known a woman who'd read William Ainsworth before. He felt as if he'd found a fast friend, but he caught himself a second later. "That is, if you've finished with your tart."

For answer, she popped the last bite between her full lips, distracting him for a second and making him forget to immediately draw out her chair. When she started to push it back, he sprang into action recalling his manners. Then he led her from the dining room and up the main staircase to his study.

"You must have read *The Miser's Daughter*," he said, holding the door for her to enter. Normally, it was his sanctum, breached only by his father, Pelham, or Waverly. Still, he didn't think twice about inviting Miss Rare-Foure inside. "And *The Flitch of*—"

"*Of Bacon*," she finished, naming Ainsworth's novel that explored the old tradition of awarding married couples a side of bacon if they could swear to having no regrets a year and a day after their marriage. "A bit sappy but strange enough to hold my interest."

When they entered the room, with him leaving the door open for propriety's sake, she started to laugh. The sound unexpectedly sparked his desire, giving him pause. *What the devil had got into him?* He was not a randy youth. Yet, looking at Charlotte, with her rich brown eyes glittering in the lamplight, the bow of her upper lip curved with mirth, she was a delightful sprite. A few hours ago, he could never have imagined such a sweet creature in his study.

She set her glass down on the edge of his crowded desk and twirled in a circle. "Just look!" She gestured with her delicate hands.

"What am I looking at?"

She laughed again, then said, "It is as if all the inviting bibelots and whatnots have been placed in here. The drawing room was very plain, one would think you had just moved in, and your dining room could best be described as stark. But here, you have attractive paintings and all these beautiful books, and that pretty silver candlestick. Anyone would proclaim the Persian rug under my feet to be most welcoming. Why, you even have a plant, looking healthy, if I may say."

"I think you've insulted most of my home," Charles told her without rancor. In fact, he found it amusing she would be so frank. "But I'm glad you like my study. Here is where I spend most of my time."

"I can see why." She wandered around the entire room, running her hand across the back of his leather chair, looking at his desk, even the papers strewn across it, which most would consider an insolent invasion of privacy. But when she did it, Charles didn't mind. Eventually, she stopped in front of his bookcase where she began to peruse the titles. The entire occurrence gave him an odd but pleasurable feeling of familiarity.

He had an upholstered chair by the glowing fire, only one since it was his private domain, and beside this a lamp table. He took her wine glass from the edge of his desk and set it on the table next to his, then he stood beside her to find the particular books.

Her intoxicating fragrance filled his head as he bent to a lower shelf and withdrew the two-volume set of *The Star-Chamber*. He handed her one of the books.

"It has everything," he proclaimed, tapping the cover with his glasses before putting them on and flipping through the pages. "History, a thrilling story, that Gothic aspect everyone seems to love, and court scenes, too."

She laughed again. "And court scenes."

Charles wanted to kiss her at that moment more than he wanted to take his next breath. But he was a gentleman. He handed her the other volume and stepped away to put some distance between them. Picking up his wine glass, he took a quick sip and watched her while she opened the book.

"Your name is Charles!" She stared at him from across the room, having read the bookplate on the inside cover. "Is it really?"

"Yes," he said, knowing instantly that the coincidence of their names would also make her laugh, and it did, a sweet bubbling sound.

"How strange I never knew it. No one told me, although I suppose I never asked. Charles Jeffcoat," she mused.

"Charles Jeffrey Jeffcoat," he said, just to tickle her funny bone again.

"It's not!" And she clutched the books to her while she chuckled.

"You've found a good-humored doxy," came his father's voice from the hallway, and Charlotte went absolutely silent.

They both turned to the Earl of Bentley. His father stood in the doorway, his gray-streaked hair still predominantly brown and, at that moment, uncombed and in frightful disarray. He wore a dressing gown over his clothes in lieu of a coat. Charles could see he had on neither tie nor cravat of any kind, and his shirt under the robe was open at the throat. Naturally, he also wore his favorite slippers.

Charles couldn't help rolling his eyes. His father spoke without malice, simply stating what he thought was the truth and in no uncertain terms. Evidence would have one believe there was a light-skirt in the study, for what other kind of woman would be alone with a man, drinking wine and behaving in such a relaxed fashion?

"Father, she is not a doxy." He glanced at Charlotte to gauge her reaction. She looked more curious than anything and, thankfully, not insulted. "Miss Rare-Foure, allow me to introduce to you the Earl of Bentley." Then he turned back to his father. "Miss Rare-Foure is a family friend."

"What family? Not ours," his father pointed out, slipping his hands into the pockets of his housecoat.

"My sister is the Duchess of Pelham," Charlotte spoke up, ignoring his unfriendly tone.

"*Ah*, Pelham!" the earl exclaimed. "Known him since he was wet behind the ears. Goes on about nothing except coffee, but a good sort, I suppose. And *he* is a man with a superior mother."

Charlotte glanced questioningly at Charles, but this wasn't the time to discuss his own mother's numerous flaws. He merely shrugged, hoping that imparted everything and nothing.

Charlotte seemed to catch on. "Yes, the Dowager Duchess is a wonderful woman who treats my sister very well indeed."

"*Hmph,*" his father said. "Did I miss dinner?"

"Yes, sir. Wasn't a tray brought up to your room?" Charles reminded him of his usual custom.

His father shrugged. "I suppose it was, but I had intended to visit with you."

At these words, Charlotte stepped forward. "My lord, why don't you come in and have some wine with us. Or do you prefer brandy? It's much more pleasant in here than downstairs anyway. Perhaps you would care for some dessert."

She looked to Charles for confirmation, and he realized her shopgirl skills of making customers at ease was, as he'd suspected, the same as those of a good hostess.

"Yes," he agreed. "Father, come sit down by the fire. We were just discussing books."

His father was still frankly studying Charlotte, who handled his impolite stare with aplomb.

"What was for pudding?" he demanded of her.

"Strawberry tart," Charlotte responded. "It was delicious."

Not looking at him, his father said, "Get me some, will you, Charlie?"

Wishing the familiar nickname didn't make him sound like a little boy, Charles pressed the bell by the door to summon a servant.

At last, his father came farther into the room and took the winged chair by the fire.

"Actually we were discussing family names," Charlotte said.

"So I heard. And Charlie was lying to you. He isn't Charles Jeffrey Jeffcoat. How absurd!"

"Oh!" Charlotte turned her big brown eyes upon Charles wonderingly. She probably thought him a bald-faced liar.

"I was only trying to be funny," he confessed, feeling foolish. "Our family name is Lambeth." There was nothing amusing about that.

"Charles Jeffrey Lambeth, The Viscount Jeffcoat," she said, putting it all together.

Oddly, Charles hoped she liked his long designation. He flicked her a smile, which she returned.

"One day—probably sooner rather than later—to be the Earl of Bentley," his father added, "but, of course, you knew that."

Charles rolled his eyes at the slight insult, practically calling her a title hunter, but Charlotte didn't appear to take offense. Instead, she walked around the chair to stand by the glowing coals and face his father.

"Do you admire the writing of Mr. Ainsworth?" Charlotte asked.

Charles expected his father to jump up at once at realizing his own atrocious discourtesy. Instead, he leaned his head back and laid blame elsewhere.

"I'm terribly sorry. My son is remiss in having just the one comfortable chair, and I took it like a dunce. We are unused to visitors." He rounded on his son. "Charlie, bring your desk chair around here for me. Then the young lady can have this comfy one."

"That's quite all right, my lord," Charlotte began, but stopped when Charles did as his father commanded and got the two of them settled. He was left to ask a footman for dessert as well as for another chair, deciding to remedy the lack and place another wingback chair by the fireplace soon. Perhaps that would bring his father in more often for a chat.

In any case, he was astounded to hear Charlotte and his father fall into an easy conversation. Every time the earl became prickly, she said something to soothe him until the dessert arrived, which his father tucked into with glee. Naturally, the earl confessed a preference for older works from Homer to Shakespeare, barely allowing Voltaire and Goethe as worth reading.

"Everything else is just drivel, including that Ainsworth," he nodded toward the books she held.

"Oh, I enjoy them tremendously," Charlotte said good naturedly, retrieving her wine glass from the small table. "I also like Swift or Defoe for a diverting adventure."

"Bah," his father said, but his tone was pleasant. Then he glanced at his son and back at Charlotte. "If you're not a doxy, why are you here?"

"Father!" Charles was ready to trounce him. It was beyond the pale to make a guest feel unwelcome. His father who could act with all due decorum in Parliament was undoubtedly being rude for sport.

Before he could say more, the earl added, "I suspect you didn't come over merely to eat our food and borrow some books, but to secure yourself a titled husband as your sister did."

CHAPTER EIGHT

Charles watched Charlotte's cheeks turn pink with embarrassment. He felt her mortification down to his own toes.

"Father, that was rude. Miss Rare-Foure came to ask my legal advice, and you owe her an apology."

"Do I?" the earl asked, taking the dessert plate off the table where he'd set it aside. Saying nothing more, instead he took the last bite of tart and chewed happily.

Clearly, he knew he'd said something inflammatory and was enjoying himself anyway. Sometimes lately, his father descended into a childlike state of willfulness, but Charles thought it was more likely due to increased isolation, and thus a lack of need for the practice of civility, than due to any loss of his mental faculties.

"No, it's all right," Charlotte said. "Naturally, your father is confused."

Charles nearly laughed out loud as her words had mirrored his thoughts, coming up with the opposite conclusion—or, at least, pretending to, in order to excuse the earl's outrageous behavior.

His father lowered the fork, his brows drawing together. "Confused? Why would you say such a thing?"

Charlotte fixed him with her chocolate-brown gaze. "I assume you're a little befuddled, my lord. Why else would you walk around here in your housecoat, with no idea if you've had your dinner, eschewing good manners for impolite words and wearing your slippers in mixed company. And all the while able to speak cleverly about great literature."

Charles's mouth dropped open. She had managed to insult the earl every which way while putting him in his place and sounding like a charming guest at the same time. Not to mention finishing with her warm smile and practically a compliment. Then she sipped her wine.

He wanted to say, "Brava!" but held his tongue.

His father looked put out. "I am neither confused nor befuddled, young lady."

"Then how do you explain your behavior?" she asked, tilting her head in a pretty fashion.

All of a sudden, this had become interesting, Charles mused.

The earl opened his mouth, then shut it. He would have to confess either to being a rude old codger or a befuddled one.

"I suppose I owe you an apology," he muttered at last. "In my defense, we never have guests and this one," he jerked a thumb in Charles's direction, "never has a female 'friend' over. The only people who ever come in here are Pelham and Waverly. And you were right, the strawberry tart is delicious." He turned to Charles. "You forgot to order me a glass of wine. Hurry, I'm parched. Now, what was this legal matter?"

To Charles's amazement, the three of them had a brief but civil discussion about Rare Confectionery, and his father thought any expansion on New Bond Street to be "a capital idea." Basically, although unasked, he gave Charlotte his blessing.

In another hour, with more wine having been drunk, Charles offered to take her home.

"It was my pleasure to meet you, Miss Rare-Foure," his father said, standing to see them out.

"It was a pleasure to meet you as well, my lord," she returned.

"Of course it was," Charles muttered in her ear as they descended the staircase.

CHARLOTTE LAUGHED AND HUGGED the books to her chest. "It *was* a pleasure," she insisted. "Your father is delightful."

Lord Jeffcoat draped her cloak around her shoulders. Behind her, she felt him shake his head. "He was not," he said close to her ear.

His breath tickled, but she didn't move away as a frisson of excitement snaked down her spine.

"Not at first," she clarified, "but after."

"After you turned on your charm," he insisted.

She couldn't hold back her laugh. "I am known for it," she confessed, hoping she didn't sound boastful.

His lordship's butler appeared. "Your carriage is ready, sir."

"Thank you, Phelps."

Charlotte abruptly realized how far she was stretching the bounds of hospitality. Whirling to face the viscount, she had to protest his next act of kindness.

"You mustn't take me home. I showed up here uninvited, and yet you helped me with my legal concerns, you fed me, and you even lent me some books." She patted the top volume. "I can easily hail a hackney."

"As my best friend's sister-in-law, I do consider you a friend," Lord Jeffcoat told her, his blue eyes holding her gaze. "Besides, Pelham would throttle me if I let you go off into the darkness alone. Or the duchess would. Come along. It's a short jaunt to Baker Street."

"Precisely," she protested, "and thus, it's hardly worth you harnessing your horses."

"Already done, and not by me, I assure you."

The butler opened the door, and Lord Jeffcoat—*Charles, as she now knew him to be*—held out his arm to her. She placed hers through his and let him escort her down the two steps and along the short path to the awaiting carriage.

"After all," he continued, "it's not as if I went out to the mews to harness the mounts and put bits in their mouths."

She hoped she hadn't offended the viscount by inferring he had to do any menial work, but when he helped her into his clarence, which was lit inside and out, she could see that wasn't the case.

He gave her his slight smile and added, "Although I do love riding and everything about horses. I am as happy in the stables as in the courtroom. More so, in fact. We have an estate in Wiltshire where I raise them. It's a joy. And I don't mind brushing them or cleaning their hoofs or any of that, by the way."

He had surprised her. "We have a country house, too," she told him. "But we don't raise anything there except flowers and some chickens."

They both chuckled. Then, as the carriage started to roll, he said, "I'm going to pull down the shades, because with the interior lamps lit, we are on display like actors on the stage."

"Of course." She wasn't alarmed in the least. "I don't want to be taken as a doxy again, do I?" Charlotte meant it in jest, but his expression turned serious.

"I am an idiot," he said. "I should have brought one of the maids with us. Again, we are risking your reputation."

She shrugged. "No matter, my lord. I will put my hood up when I get out. Will that help?"

His eyes widened. "You take your reputation too lightly, Miss Rare-Foure. And I became complacent because, in truth, you are easy to talk to and such a good companion, even with my father, that I felt as if I were in fact taking a friend home. Not a woman."

Not a woman! She sat back in her seat feeling a little deflated.

He shook his head, looking chagrinned. "That did not come out as intended at all. Obviously, you are a woman. And a lovely one. And I did invite you out before," he reminded her.

"But not twice," she said quietly, deciding in the security of the carriage when they could talk privately to determine the reason. After all, if she had made a bad impression on a man, making it easy for him to forget about her, as had now occurred with both Lionel and Charles, then she had best find out why.

"I had a splendid time," she confessed, "and then I never saw you afterward. You must not have had such a good evening."

"I did," he said quickly, then sighed, "Except . . . ."

When he left her hanging, Charlotte leaned forward, the edges of the two volumes pushing into her ribs. *What was the exception?* Her laughter? The way she drank her champagne too quickly at the intermission? Perhaps how she'd clapped too long at the end of the play?

"You whistled before the play started," Lord Jeffcoat said. "It was . . . unsettling. And it wasn't the first time I've heard it. You did it that day in your shop, the day you hired young Edward."

"I whistled," she repeated, recalling how many times her mother had warned her not to do so in public. Felicity Rare-Foure was always right.

"Everyone in the theatre heard it," Lord Jeffcoat continued, "and looked at us."

"Oh," she said, her glance falling to her lap. She'd humiliated the viscount, and now she was mortified. Charlotte blinked, sitting back against the squabs and feeling close to tears.

"And then you invited your sister and her husband to join us. First, at the intermission and then into my box. If Mr. Carson hadn't had his own carriage, I'm certain you would have had them drive back with us, too."

Her gaze snapped up to his when she realized the import of his words. "You don't like my sister?"

"No!" he exclaimed.

She recoiled from the man who didn't appreciate a member of her family.

He waved his hands at her expression. "I mean, no, you are *incorrect*. It is not that at all. Although, to be fair, of the three of you, she is by far and away the most direct in manner, some might even say short-tempered."

Her anger started to boil. "Beatrice is the smartest person I know, and a good judge of character, which you, apparently, are not! She simply has a low tolerance for fools. And while you are reading Ainsworth," she plopped the books onto the leather seat beside her, no longer interested in borrowing them, "my sister is reading the works of Homer in the original Greek, and the *History of Britain* in . . . in Anglo-Saxon dialect, or whatever it is."

"Probably Latin," he provided.

Undaunted by his helpful interruption, she added, "Your father would surely approve of her!"

"Miss Rare-Foure," Lord Jeffcoat began. This time, he was the one to lean forward since she was still angling away from him. "I believe you misunderstood me. I do not know your sister well enough to dislike her, nor was I meaning to cast aspersions upon her character. She does seem bright, indeed, and beloved by you and the duchess each time I've seen you all together."

Suddenly, he reached out and took her hand in his. "However, on the night in question, I was hoping to get to know you better and to have time alone with you, despite the presence of your maid. Yet you seemed to have no interest in doing the same with me. Thus, I decided, if I did not merit your curiosity, nor your attention, then I would not put you through another evening with me."

"Oh!" She blinked at him, and he slowly drew her forward again, her hand clasped in his.

"Tonight, was enjoyable. I would say it was fun," he added, as the mood between them shifted. "Both before my father interrupted us and even, surprisingly, afterward."

She nodded. Charlotte couldn't deny she'd enjoyed her time alone with him at dinner and also in conversation with the earl. She'd been at ease the entire time. More than that, she'd been interested . . . and attracted, each time Charles gave her a thoughtful look or his not-quite-there smile.

His thumb stroked the bare section of her wrist, just above her glove, making her shiver. Their gazes locked again.

"Are you interested in me, Miss Rare-Foure?"

She didn't hesitate, not when faced with Charles Jeffrey Jeffcoat gazing into her eyes. Nor was she one to prevaricate. "Yes."

He pulled her another inch or two closer and closed the space between them by scooting to the edge of his seat. In the next instant, he claimed her lips. Releasing her hands, he placed his upon her shoulders, holding her in place, while he cocked his head and fitted his mouth against hers.

His warm lips tasted faintly of strawberries and wine. His broad hands on her shoulders branded her through the fabric of her cloak and gown. His mouth covered hers, pressing gently but firmly.

She thought it would end as soon as it began, but it didn't. To her delight, Charles began a slow examination of her lips, nibbling on her lower one, dropping kisses on the left corner, and then the right. Then she felt his tongue touch her upper lip, and she opened her mouth.

His body shifted closer, and she could feel his legs widen to encompass her skirts, his thighs pressing along the outside of hers.

When she gasped softly, unable to stop the trembling in her limbs and the flutter in her stomach, he slid his tongue inside her mouth.

With her lungs burning, she took a quick breath through her nose. A languorous kiss was, she decided, the perfect type of kiss once one got used to it. Then she could form no other coherent thought, aware only of how her body sizzled and her tongue wickedly stroked his in return, and how the man before her smelled divinely of rum and spice.

Heaven help her!

She heard the driver call to the horses just before the carriage stopped, continuing to rock for a few moments. Charles released her, not hastily, but gently, easing back and allowing her to do the same.

Oh my!

They stared at one another, both breathing heavily.

"I would like to ask you out again, Miss Rare-Foure."

"I would like you to," she responded, unable to keep herself from putting her gloved hand to her lips, which felt as if they were pulsing with heat.

"I also think we should have a chaperone in the future," he added, watching her movements. "I believe now you can see why one is deemed necessary."

She nodded, but she couldn't help smiling. "Honestly, I'm glad we didn't have one tonight."

His mouth spread in a delightful grin, and his dimple appeared. "I must agree with you on that point."

He tapped on the roof, and the next instant, the door opened and the footman pulled down the step. Charles climbed out first, then turned back to offer her his hand.

"Don't forget the books."

Scooping them up with her free hand, Charlotte alighted from the carriage, landing on the pavement beside him, the length of her body swaying momentarily against his. She sighed. *What a magical evening!*

"You forgot to put up your hood," he reminded her.

"Oh!" Charlotte started to fumble, since she didn't have a free hand.

"Never mind," he said, sounding half-exasperated, half-amused. "Let's get you inside." Lord Jeffcoat walked her to the door, which didn't open at their approach. He looked surprised by such an insubordinate infraction, something she was certain never happened with his capable Mr. Phelps.

"Undoubtedly it's unlocked," Charlotte told him and tried the handle. Sure enough, the door pushed open.

The viscount frowned, his dark brows drawing together. "Will you lock it as soon as you enter?"

"I shall," she promised. "Thank you for reading over the lease." It was safely tucked in her bag, ready for her to sign.

"My pleasure. The entire evening was a pleasure, in fact, and I will not be remiss this time in sending you an invitation for another outing. That is, if you're willing."

"I am. That would be lovely. And thank you for the books. If I don't fall asleep right away, I'll start one tonight."

He nodded, looking hesitant to leave her, and if they weren't standing on her doorstep in plain view of the windows across the street, she could imagine rolling up onto the tips of her toes and planting a kiss on his attractive mouth.

"Good night," she said before stepping indoors to keep from doing anything stupid.

"Good night," he said and departed to his waiting carriage.

She hadn't expected such a turn of events. And then it dawned on her. She hadn't thought of Lionel, not once, when she was kissing the viscount. *What a blessing!*

Shrugging out of her mantle and leaving it in the front hall, she dashed up the stairs, got halfway up, and ran back down to lock the front door, rolling her eyes at her own forgetfulness. Then she climbed the stairs more slowly, still clutching the two volumes with Charles's name scrawled on their bookplates. Such an intimate thing, to have his own handwriting in her hands.

Their few servants had all gone to bed, which was a relief as she feared Delia might want to help her undress. Normally, that was an extraordinary circumstance, done only if she were trussed up in a fussy ballgown.

However, their long-time maid would think nothing of offering to brush her hair in order to wheedle tidbits of gossip out of her. And with neither of her sisters around in whom she could confide, Charlotte feared she would tell Delia something indecorous or embarrassing.

In another minute, Charlotte had gained the solitude of her bedroom, where the fire had been lit earlier and the lamps turned on.

Glancing at herself in the mirror as she removed the pins from her hair, Charlotte thought her face plainly revealed that she'd had a long and satisfying kiss. At least to her eyes, it was obvious by her happy expression and her lips being a little redder than usual. She wouldn't want Delia to see the same.

And soon, maybe even tomorrow, she was going to receive another invitation for an evening with the viscount.

Picking up her boar-bristle brush, she started smoothing her hair, reminding herself the viscount wasn't supposed to be the thought uppermost in her mind. After all, the very next day, she was expanding Rare Confectionery for the first time in twenty years!

Everything would be perfect!

CHAPTER NINE

Why did it seem nothing was going smoothly? From the moment Charlotte entered the shop, feeling a little tired from her exciting evening and having read Ainsworth's *The Star Chamber* for half the night, little things began to go wrong.

Edward, who was always punctual if not early, was late. Since Bea was back to coming in at noon, Charlotte had to quickly clean and then start packaging up the delivery orders. As she was turning the sign to open, Edward appeared looking as grim as the rain clouds that had blown in, but refusing to say anything more than an abject apology. She had no right to pry.

"If you need my help with anything, please know you can always ask," she assured him.

With a grown-up nod of his head, he went in the back to don his apron and grab trays to restock the display case, which he was still doing when the first customer entered.

Charlotte thought she'd had plenty of small change to start the day, but didn't have the right amount for the first customer, and ended up having to give some of the confectionery away.

"I must run to the bank," she told the boy, "or we shall go broke. I should have done it yesterday or first thing. My head is not screwed on correctly today."

"What about the customers?" he asked, eyes wide.

For a second, she considered turning the sign to "Closed." Then thought better of it. "If you know them, then tell them we're putting their purchases on their account for today. Just make note of their name and the cost. All right? Unless they have the exact coinage, and then . . . well, you know, you can handle it. I shall be back as soon as possible."

She ripped off her apron and ran out the door before recalling the landlord.

"Edward," she said, re-entering on a chilly gust of air that was blowing the tree branches and sending raindrops skittering across the sky in a horizontal direction. "If Mr. Richardson shows up, a man with a bushy moustache, please keep him here and tell him I'll be back as soon as I can. It's important. Don't let him leave."

"Yes, miss."

The boy looked terrified, which spurred Charlotte to run without any decorum along the street through the downpour. Luckily, she didn't have to go any farther than Lothbury Street at the end of Old Bond Street. If it had been any other time, she would have continued on to Amity's as she was a mere few streets away from St. James's Place.

There was no line at one clerk's window at The Imperial Bank, and within five minutes, Charlotte was lifting her skirts with one hand so she could sprint back up the street to the shop, clutching her purse and the leather satchel in which they kept money for transport. In her panic, she'd neglected her cloak with its protective hood and her umbrella.

Pushing open the door, feeling like a drowned rat, she didn't see an impatient landlord waiting for her as she'd feared, but four customers and one frazzled boy.

"Excuse me, please," she said, pushing through them to get to the gap between the counters. "I'm happy to help whoever is next."

For the next few minutes, she served the customers, dismissing Edward to the back. And then, even though another came into the shop, Charlotte had to ask her to wait in order to get Edward out the door with the deliveries. It took her a few minutes to load him up with the proper sweets before he hurried out with bags bursting.

"Go easy," Charlotte told him. "Don't drop anything." Closing the door behind her, she took in the smartly dressed customer. "My apologies for keeping you waiting," she said to the woman who'd been circling the shop, picking up tins, looking at everything in both display cases.

"Do you normally have more help?" she asked.

It was an annoying question. Charlotte prided herself on how well she ran the front of the shop, usually with everything under tight control. At the same time, she always felt relaxed and able to brush off little problems, even able to make her marzipan at the same time. In any case, she didn't think the brief delay in getting the deliveries out the door warranted her explaining about a pregnant sister or another one who didn't like to come in before noon, or her mother being away. It was none of this woman's business.

"I apologize about the wait," Charlotte repeated. "May I help you?"

"Is it common practice to serve without an apron?" the customer demanded.

Charlotte looked down, having forgotten she'd removed it. Before she could answer, the woman continued.

"And with your hair dripping onto your shoulders? You would make a better impression if you were tidier and wearing a clean white apron. Also, did you know the floor is particularly filthy? Most unappealing in a confectionery."

Charlotte had come in trailing dirty water from the street. Normally, on such a day with rain falling, she or Edward would kick a towel around between customers to keep the floor looking presentable and not slippery. Today, neither had had a chance.

"Would you like to wait while I don an apron, dry my hair, and wash the floors?" Charlotte asked and then bit her tongue on her sour remark, much more suited to Beatrice than to herself. She needed to begin again.

Offering a pleasant smile, she said, "I apologize. That was ill-said of me. To tell you the truth, our confectionery is normally spotless and well-staffed, but today—"

"Where *is* your staff?" the woman asked. "I heard you have a duchess working here. May I speak with her?"

Charlotte hesitated. For the first time, she saw a hint of malice flickering in the customer's eyes. "Not today, no."

"Not today. Of course not. Maybe not any day," the woman said. "It hardly seems like a place for nobility. It seems like the type of rumor a shop would put out to increase its patronage."

"Would you like to buy something?" Charlotte asked, attempting to keep her tone neutral rather than sharp as she wanted, ready as she was to toss this woman out into the rain.

"Yes, I would like a variety so I can taste what you offer, and hopefully, you have time to explain what's in them."

"Of course. Would you like to sample anything first?"

"That seems like bribery. A free chocolate will taste better than one I've paid for."

"Will it?" Charlotte asked, trying to follow the woman's logic. *What on earth did she mean?* "You don't have to have a sample if you don't wish it. We offer one to everyone who enters."

"Do you? *Hm.* That's a nice policy. What do you suggest?"

Charlotte wanted to suggest she leave and go elsewhere. Instead, she said, "Everyone likes chocolate. Unless you have a particular hankering for toffee or marzipan, then please, let me give you a chocolate to sample."

"Very well." The woman waited, as Charlotte took a small saucer off the shelf behind her and chose a chocolate with the silver pincers, placing it on the plate before handing it to her. "That has a hint of orange in it. Delicious and refreshing."

Just then, a couple entered, the man clearly doting on the woman, barely watching where he was going for gazing at her, and the young lady equally distracted. Newlyweds, Charlotte would hazard a guess.

"Would you like a sample?" she asked them, while the woman in front of her ate the chocolate. "Or do you know what you want?"

"You don't want this," the woman said.

"I beg your pardon," Charlotte's attention snapped back to the difficult customer. Even the distracted pair looked up at her tone.

"If they want chocolate and orange, I mean, for there isn't a hint of orange in it."

Frowning, Charlotte retrieved the plate the woman held out to her and reached for another chocolate. She sniffed it and then bit it in half before placing it on the counter behind her.

"You're correct," came the words she wished she didn't have to say. "Apparently, those are plain chocolate, put on the wrong shelf. How about raspberry and chocolate?"

"Since you don't know what's in your chocolates and since I can't tell until I've eaten them, which might take all day, I think I would like to try the toffee."

Ignoring the insult, Charlotte nodded and handed her a piece of Bea's treacle toffee on the plate.

Then she turned to the couple. "Would you like a sample, perhaps chocolate with raspberry essence?"

"If you can believe it," the woman muttered.

"No, thank you," the man said. "We'll take a half-pound tin of the chocolate-covered toffee, right, my love?"

His lady-love nodded. "And two marzipan pigs," she added. "They're adorable."

Even as she was speaking, Charlotte had already gathered up a tin and filled it with the chocolate treacle toffee, and was just reaching for the pigs, when she was interrupted.

"Are you ignoring me?" the woman asked. "I was here first, but you're serving them."

Charlotte looked from her to the newlyweds at the other end of the counter.

"They know what they want," she said "I can serve them while you're tasting the toffee."

"I've tasted the toffee," she said, "and it is burnt. My Aunt Jenny makes better." She looked at the two newlyweds. "I wouldn't get it if I were you."

"We've had it before," the man said. "It's delicious."

The woman shrugged. "To each his own." She pointed to the plate. "But that was burnt. In any case, I was here first, and I had to wait before that."

"We can wait," the young woman said, sounding less than enthusiastic.

"But not for long," the man added. "My wife's parents are outside."

Charlotte felt like huffing with frustration with the way one customer had taken over the situation when she had almost got the other two out the door, which now seemed imperative with this testy female maligning everything.

However, hoping to disavow the woman's judgment, Charlotte picked up a piece of toffee and tucked it into her mouth to suck on. *Scorched!* She couldn't help coughing. It had definitely cooked too long. She had no way of knowing if the chocolate-covered toffee was the same, and she wasn't sure whether to give the young couple a taste or not.

She'd never had a moment's doubt about their confectionery before, yet now . . . *What an odd predicament!*

Hoping for the best, Charlotte put two pieces of the chocolate-smothered toffee onto a clean plate and handed it to the man. "Please, I insist. While you wait." They took it gratefully and she turned her attention back to the first.

"Would you like me to put together a variety of confectionery, chocolate, marzipan, and toffee?"

"I suppose, although what I just ate makes me doubtful. Still, how bad can it all be?" The woman said that with a casual shrug as if she hadn't just insulted all of Rare Confectionery.

Charlotte tamped back her irritation. Out of the corner of her eye, she saw the couple each take a piece of toffee.

"And the tins are pretty," the woman continued. "I would like to have my order in one of those. I'll have one of the chocolates from each of those shelves and the chocolate toffee—it can't be any worse—and a piece with nuts. And I'll take those two marzipan pigs."

"Those are the only two I have left," Charlotte said, glancing again at the young couple who seemed to be making faces at each other. *Oh dear! Was that toffee scorched, too?*

"That's not my problem, is it?" the woman remarked. "Whoever makes the marzipan should have made more. I understand this shop has been here for many years. It certainly looks old, with this dirty floor and your shabby appearance. Someone here should know how many marzipan pigs to make for a day."

Charlotte felt her face flame. She'd never been told off like this before. Her heart was pounding in her chest. In truth, she should have made more marzipan sculptures the night before, but instead, she'd run off to Lord Jeffcoat's with the lease.

"I'm sorry, but this couple has already reserved the pigs."

"But I was here first," the woman protested.

Charlotte had never been at such a loss. She'd already started filling a tin with chocolates and toffee, but now she felt like dumping the tin's contents onto the customer's head. Smartly dressed with a jaunty hat, a well-fitted paletot, and no-nonsense wool skirt, the woman looked, in a word, professional. Yet against all reason, she was behaving like a shrew.

"The marzipan leaves taste the same as the pigs," Charlotte told them. "Or the fruit shapes, with some additional flavorings."

"I want the pigs," she declared.

"That's all right," said the newlywed bride. "She may have the pigs."

"Thank you," Charlotte said.

"In any case, we can't wait any longer," the young man said. "We'll return another time."

Before Charlotte could rescue the sale, the door opened again. The couple slipped out as Mr. Richardson walked in.

"I'll be with you shortly," she told him, quickly putting the pigs into the tin and jamming on the lid.

"Shouldn't you have weighed each of those separately?" the woman asked.

In truth, Charlotte would have, except she charged for the pigs by the piece not the pound, and she knew how much the chocolates and the toffee weighed approximately. She'd been doing this for so long, she'd already added it all in her head.

"I know what the cost is," she said stubbornly, and told her the price.

"How do I know that's the cost? I ought to see it weighed."

Charlotte sighed, removing the two pigs while stating, "These are thruppence a piece, as the sign says, or 2 shillings per pound." Then she put the toffee on the scale. "This chocolate-covered toffee is 1 shilling, 6 pence per pound. More expensive than the plain toffee." Then she put the chocolates on the scale. "And this assortment of chocolates, made in the French style, are two shillings, six pence per pound."

Again, she gave the woman a total cost.

"You said less before."

She stared the woman down. "I was off by tuppence in *your* favor, and since you were buying a large quantity, I charged half price for the tin, which should be another six pence. The tin is reusable and thus very good value."

The woman shrugged. "It could as easily have gone the other way."

Charlotte took her money, and the woman still didn't leave. "Will there be anything else?"

"No."

They stared at one another.

"You may help this gentleman now," she said as if giving Charlotte permission. "I want to see how you treat other customers."

What on earth?

"He and I have private business to attend."

"Really?" the woman dragged the word out and raised her perfectly sculpted eyebrows.

"For pity's sake," Charlotte exclaimed. "I'm going to have to ask you to leave."

After a knowing glance at Mr. Richardson and then a slow look back at Charlotte, the woman sauntered out with her tin.

"How are you, Miss Rare-Foure?" he asked, approaching the counter.

"Bewildered, Mr. Richardson. She was one of the strangest customers I've ever had the misfortune to wait upon. And everything seemed to be a bit off, including our confectionery."

"Yes, about that," he said. "My wife and I tucked into the toffee after dinner. It . . . well, it had an odd flavor. The coffee chocolates were superb however. But the toffee . . . Anyway, I am not complaining, but I thought you might want to know."

Her heart sunk into her shoes. "Thank you for telling me. I would give you a different batch today, but I fear we are having a bit of a problem with our apprentice." She sighed, but then recalled why he was there.

"Meanwhile, I have an answer for you. I am pleased to say Rare Confectionery would like to take over the second floor. I will sign the lease, but we'll need a notary public." She was glad she could use the unfamiliar term that Lord Jeffcoat had mentioned to make sure everything was legal and authorized.

Mr. Richardson nodded. "Yes, certainly. We need two copies anyway. I'll get this one copied at the printer's, and for a notary public, we can go to Cheeswrights. It's across from Billingsgate Market."

Charlotte drew back, astounded. "I cannot possibly go all the way to the docks today." In any case, her parents would definitely not approve of her going to the Canary Wharf by herself. "I have a business to run."

"All right. John Venn and Sons is closer, on Aldwych Street. I'll meet you there later. Will four o'clock work, just before they close?"

She didn't see how she possibly get there when she would have an open shop, customers at the counter, and questionable confectionery. Nevertheless, she nodded.

"Yes, that's fine. I'll see you there."

CHARLES WAS CONFLICTED, AND he didn't care for the feeling. Leaving the Inns of Court, he went home and saddled his favorite gelding. A ride through Hyde Park in the afternoon would clear his head. What he saw everywhere were husbands and wives riding together. Or, at least, he imagined he did. He didn't know how Waverly felt about marriage—or even if the rogue had feelings—but watching Pelham experience marital bliss and now approach fatherhood, Charles felt he, too, was ready to take a wife.

After all, he had passed the halfway mark of his twenties and could see the great age of thirty on the horizon. And lucky him, he happened to have found a young woman who piqued his interest.

Why was he conflicted? An easy answer.

He didn't yet know if Charlotte Rare-Foure were truly a suitable wife, even though he'd been thinking about her to the detriment of his cases and any useful thoughts, ever since dropping her home. The memory of their astounding kiss haunted him, if such a thoroughly delightful occurrence could be considered in such terms. But haunting seemed correct, for her face appeared before his eyes as he tried to write notes and the feel of her lips, the taste of them, too, had him longing for more.

At his age, he thought it a pleasant revelation to learn how kissing could be a new experience. He'd kissed his moderate share of women, but when his lips had touched Charlotte's . . . he shook his head. All he knew was he could have continued kissing her for hours, feeling at the time as though they were forming some singularly deep bond.

Directing his horse along Rotten Row, he nodded to those who greeted him, although he seemed to recognize no one while absently pondering the confectioner. Her sisters had both found husbands, and Pelham's wife made an acceptable duchess by all accounts, seeming calm and gracious. *But Charlotte as a viscountess and one day a countess?* Charles wasn't sure.

Undoubtedly, she could easily handle the task of being an excellent hostess, as well as handle household accounts since she could run a shop and seemed to have a good head on her shoulders. But there was more to a mate than that. She must be a nurturing mother, a dependable helper, and if he needed a good ear, she ought to be like the pulpit sounding board, so he could discern his clearest ideas from her returning them to him.

Moreover, if thousands of evenings together stretched before them, perhaps seated in his study, he wanted a wife who would enjoy reading and discussing the stories.

Strangely, the middle-class shopgirl seemed suited to all that and more.

As to the other talents of ladies of his class, he knew they ought to be able to sketch, play the piano, and even sing, but he didn't care one way or the other if she had any of those dubious skills.

There was, in fact, only one thing that truly mattered to him—*faithfulness*.

CHAPTER TEN

Waverly was going to tease him whether he learned of it sooner or later, and therefore, Charles might as well get the worst of it over. He sat at White's club with Pelham and Waverly, partly enjoying a mid-day meal, partly not enjoying it, since his thoughts were racing.

Pelham vowed not to spend every moment talking about siring an heir, but as it was the single thing on his mind, he did just that anyway. The duke predicted when he thought his child was going to arrive, explained in detail what strange things his wife was asking to eat, and listed the names they were considering for their offspring. However, when he started to describe the colors they'd chosen for the nursery, Waverly sighed loudly, drowning out Pelham entirely.

"I'm sorry," Waverly said, "were you still talking? I thought I could hear flies buzzing in my ears. What about you, Jeffcoat?"

He set down his wine glass. "Bees droning, I believe."

"All right," Pelham said, but his smile was no less bright. "I am going to be a father."

"Really?" Waverly quipped. "One would never know it. Why don't you tell us all about it?"

The three of them laughed.

"Well, what other news then?" Pelham asked. "What about you, Waverly? Any sweet young lady in your capable sights?"

Waverly shrugged. "I am not attending anything this Season, unless the two of you want to make asses of yourself again at a costume ball."

"I think not," Pelham said. "Once you've been to a royal fancy-dress ball hailed as the event of the decade, it seems as if there is little point in going to another."

Waverly shrugged, as if that said it all. But Charles wondered if Pelham realized their friend had dodged and deflected the question about a woman of interest. Apparently he did not, for Pelham was busy humming a lullaby they all knew from childhood.

"Are you practicing?" he asked the duke.

"What?" Pelham exclaimed.

Charles smiled. "You seem to be humming a little song meant for children. I must assume you are practicing."

Waverly chortled as Pelham's face went red.

"I hadn't realized I was doing so. My duchess and I, that is, she gave me a book."

"What book?" Waverly pressed.

"*Tommy Thumb's—*" Pelham began.

"God, no!" Waverly exclaimed, looking horrified.

"*Pretty Song Book,*" the duke finished.

"*Tommy Thumb's Pretty Song Book,*" Waverly echoed, torn between being aghast and thoroughly amused. In the end, he grinned and shook his head.

"Yes," Pelham said, lifting his chin, "we have both been memorizing the songs."

Charles didn't have the heart to make fun of him. "I think that's wonderful. You will make a good father, and your duchess will make a fine mother."

The three fell silent. His good friends knew how his own mother had turned out—not the best, to be exact—and had made an even worse wife to his father. After a moment, Pelham asked, "What about you?"

Charles frowned. "What about me?"

"Come along, Jeffcoat, isn't it time you leaped into the marital abyss?" the duke asked.

Since that was extremely close to his own thoughts, he couldn't dismiss the question or laugh it off, and Waverly caught the scent of a juicy tale immediately.

"Why, I believe our Jeffcoat does in fact have someone in mind with whom he wishes to leap into that infernal abyss. Look at him, Pelham," Waverly insisted. "He can hardly concentrate on his food for fawning over some miss."

Charles blinked at them both, gathering his thoughts, ready to tell them.

"I do believe you are right," Pelham said, his tone not in jest like their friend's.

"He is right," Charles confessed. "There is a female whom I fancy. I'm not sure . . . ," he trailed off. *What part of his doubts should he disclose?*

"No one is ever sure," Pelham said, and his simple words made Charles feel better.

"That's true," Waverly joined in. "I remember Pelham here thinking his duchess might love another man, then he thought her in love with her chocolate or some such nonsense. In the end, we all knew they were perfect for one another. What about you, Jeffcoat?"

Charles sipped his wine again. Once he told them, there would be no retrieving it. He fixed Pelham with his gaze. "I fancy myself attracted to your sister-in-law, as it turns out."

But it was Waverly who barked out a laugh. "That ship has sailed. She's been taken!"

"What do you mean?" Suddenly, Charles wondered if they were aware of Miss Rare-Foure's having already entered into an arrangement of which he hadn't heard.

"Well, she married that American in case you missed it."

"No," Pelham said. "I believe he means my other sister-in-law."

"Oh," Waverly said. Then he grinned. "The buxom one?"

Charles wanted to wipe the smile off his friend's face, but there was no denying Charlotte was well-endowed. He nodded.

"Isn't she a bit young?" Pelham asked.

"I don't think so." Charles frowned. "You do know she's about to turn twenty."

The duke's visage brightened. "Is she? Good lord, I thought her to be about sixteen. Well, that's all right, then. Otherwise, I was going to have to step in on behalf of her absent father."

Waverly continued smiling. "How long has your flame been burning for our saucy shopgirl?"

Charles shrugged, ignoring the ridiculous moniker. "I've admired her appearance since the first time we met, I suppose. That must have been a couple years ago, you know, at Pelham's party. But lately, I have come to appreciate her many fine qualities."

Waverly laughed. "At least a couple of them."

"Here now!" Pelham warned him. "She's my family now."

Charles knew there was no point in trying to tame their rakish friend. Thus, he ignored him.

"Miss Rare-Foure is friendly," he began. "You can tell how she likes people by the way she treats the customers. Not a sharp barb to her tongue." Except for that day when he'd witnessed her unusual behavior, not her normal self at all. Even then her tone had been more listless than harsh. "And she seems to have a way about her. You should have seen how she tamed my father's irascibility—"

"Your father?" Pelham interrupted. "How did she run into your father?"

Charles had no intention of damaging her reputation. "Father and I were walking along Bond Street. Anyway, it's no matter."

"Go on about her many fine qualities," Waverly prodded. "After that baronet's sister, I can easily understand why you want a smooth tongue to your woman."

Charles rolled his eyes. Waverly could turn the most benign remark into a sinful insinuation. Pelham glared at him, still playing the protective brother-in-law.

"Miss Rare-Foure is extraordinarily loyal to her family, which I greatly appreciate, and she runs the confectionery mostly by herself at present, demonstrating her capability and intelligence," Charles continued. "And I admire her aplomb."

Waverly grinned. "I think you admire her—"

"Waverly!" Pelham warned.

Their friend sighed. "I shall stop. So you fancy this young woman, and then what? Are you seriously considering her for your wife?"

Why did he make it sound like a frivolous idea? Charles shrugged again.

"Why not?" Pelham asked. "Mr. Foure and Mrs. Rare-Foure raised three splendid daughters. It's a shame you missed out on the middle one," he said to Waverly.

"I missed out on nothing. She is more like Jeffcoat's baronet's sister, I think." Then he smiled at Charles. "I suppose I could turn my attention to the youngest daughter if she's the paragon you make her out to be. We could compete for her attention."

Charles knew his feelings for Charlotte were genuine and deeper than he'd suspected when Waverly's proposal lanced him with jealousy. He wondered whether to protest, which might make his friend even more intent on pursuing Charlotte for sport, or if he should feign indifference to put him off.

In the end, Pelham said, "We're friends first, aren't we Waverly? When we both had our eye on Lady Madeleine a few years back, you abandoned the field of battle."

Waverly's expression tightened. "Because all other things being equal, you are a duke, and I am not. Thus, I knew which way the earl's daughter would run."

"But we are both viscounts," Charles said. "Would you trounce upon our friendship and go after a female in whom I've expressed an interest? Would prefer to win—or in this case, lose—rather than maintain our bond?"

Waverly tried to stare him down, then he rolled his dark eyes, and finally, a smile appeared. "Of course not, Jeffcoat. You are like a brother to me, and I wouldn't endanger that for any haybag, no matter how curvy."

"Haybag! I say!"

Waverly held up his hands. "I mean for any woman whomsoever. If you like her, not only will she become instantly like a sister to me, but I shall assist you in any way possible, as I did for Pelham here, both when he pursued Lady Madeleine and his current duchess."

"Was he helpful?" Charles asked the duke.

Pelham shrugged. "Moderately. At least, he didn't get in the way."

Waverly folded his arms across his chest and cocked his head at the duke.

"All right," Pelham conceded. "He actually gave me some sound advice on more than one occasion. How he can see clearly about anything to do with women when he's such a confirmed bachelor, I'll never understand."

"Let's drink to that," Waverly said.

They all lifted their wine glasses. "To what?" Charles asked. "To your being a bachelor for the rest of your life or for your offering me some sound advice if needed?"

"Either, both. It's no matter," Waverly said and drained his wine glass.

Charles couldn't imagine asking or needing either of his friends for help, but he was relieved neither of them had tried to dissuade him from his pursuit, if that was what it was. If either had heard anything about her being flighty or fickle, knowing his distaste for females who were unfaithful, they would have told him.

"I have been out on the town with her once and I have invited her to go out again. To a concert."

He wondered if he should tell the duke about Charlotte's intent to expand the shop, seeing as the duchess might have a strong opinion, but that seemed to be breaking a confidence, and thus, he held his tongue.

Instead, he let Waverly expound on the most romantic venues in London and kept his thoughts to himself.

CHARLOTTE HAD TASTED SO many sweets by the time Edward returned from deliveries, she had to let him watch the front and go have a cup of fortifying tea in the back. Not everything was wrong, but some of the confectionery was "off." Some of the chocolates had a strange herbal flavor she couldn't put her finger on, the toffee as already discovered had been cooked too long, and a few of Amity's bonbons seemed to be filled with brick instead of smooth, creamy fondant. The worst part was, she couldn't tell what was good by looking at it.

One thing she knew for certain, she had sold that smartly dressed saucebox some bad tasting confectionery. She wouldn't be surprised if the woman returned to rage about it.

Sipping the tea, feeling a little sick to her stomach, Charlotte wondered whether to close the shop until she could sort the mess out when she heard the bell. Feeling heartsick, not to mention weary from poor sleep, she nearly stayed where she was and let Edward handle it alone. However, hearing him ask if he could help the customer, his young voice sounding as much like a girl as a boy, she rose to her feet.

"Two pounds of toffee," was the reply as Charlotte pushed open the curtain. "One plain, one smothered in chocolate."

Oh, sweet mother! It was a footman from the palace, wearing the royal livery. It happened only a couple of times a year that the queen sent someone. The other times, they received a notice asking for confectionery to be delivered. She must want to eat some immediately if she'd sent a servant.

Now Charlotte really did think she was going to be ill.

"Good day," she began, watching Edward start to open the display. She ought to have pulled out every last piece of toffee and dumped it into the rubbish, but the task had seemed monumental, not to mention wasteful. Still, she was in charge and ought to have been decisive.

"You're from the palace, aren't you?" she asked.

"Yes, miss," replied the footman.

"I assume, then, that this toffee is for Her Majesty?"

"Yes, miss, and the queen's guests."

Edward promptly dropped the tongs he'd been using, luckily onto the counter and not the floor.

"Does she need the toffee this very moment?" Charlotte persisted, trying not to become flustered at the notion of sending the servant on his way with two pounds of inedible toffee.

"I beg your pardon, miss, but I was sent here because Her Majesty wants it today."

Where was Beatrice? That question popped into her mind first. Followed by a rash hope that the chocolate smothered toffee was perfectly fine.

"Would you care for a sample?" Then she frowned. Maybe having the footman try it wasn't the best course of action, but she and Edward couldn't start munching on it as if unsure of its quality. Besides, footman or not, he would know good toffee.

"I beg your pardon, miss," he said again, "but I am not sure I am allowed."

"Everyone who comes in gets a sample," said Edward. "Even I did."

The liveried servant looked bemused. "But you work here," he pointed out.

"I didn't at the time. Go on. What would you like to try? Miss Charlotte's marzipan is ever so good."

"No," Charlotte interrupted, practically with a yell. She already knew there was nothing wrong with her own confectionery, but the rest was dodgy at best.

"I mean, I hope you will try the same as you are taking to Her Majesty. Please, have a chocolate-smothered toffee."

She looked at Edward, who picked up the tongs and blew on them. Charlotte made a mental note to tell him later that wasn't the way to clean a utensil in front of a customer. Then he put a piece of the toffee on a plate and handed it to the footman.

With a nod of thanks, he removed his glove, tucking it under his arm, picked up the sweet, and popped it into his mouth. For a moment, Charlotte thought all was well. Then the man's placid smile altered. He frowned slightly, which turned into a puckered expression of distaste.

Then to her dismay, Edward proudly proclaimed, "I made that myself!"

Dear Lord! The mystery was solved, but at such a cost. The footman was chewing manfully but not with delight. The texture was probably correct and even the chocolate might have been tasty, but the toffee! Their renowned delectable treacle toffee!

Charlotte had tasted the burned, bitter flavor, like stale coffee, twice already while trying to determine if each batch was bad. It had been a nasty experience.

"We will not be able to sell you any toffee, as you have determined," she told the man.

"What?" asked Edward, clearly stunned.

She would explain to him after they got rid of the queen's servant.

"I apologize. Please tell Her Majesty—" she broke off at the footman's expression.

Obviously, he was in no position to tell the queen anything. He was to deliver it to some lowly kitchen maid who would deliver it to the cook or housekeeper who would probably deliver it to the butler or whoever waited on the queen.

Perhaps she could ask the footman to tell everyone at the palace that they were sold out. *Would he lie for her?*

"I wonder if Her Majesty can wait," Charlotte couldn't believe she was saying such a disrespectful thing, "until early evening. By then Rare Confectionery will have our usual highest-quality chocolate-smothered toffee." Or they would lose the favor of the palace, and her mother's disappointment would be crushing.

"What time shall I return?" the footman asked.

Grateful that the man was willing to go along with her idea, she was just calculating how long it would take to make a good batch when the shop bell tinkled and Beatrice strolled in. Charlotte sagged with relief, sending a thank you up to Heaven. Bea would still need time to cook and cool the toffee, then to melt the chocolate so it was pourable, and it, too, would need time to set. They would have to stay open late.

"About six o'clock," she said, if they started immediately.

"Very good, miss. I'll be back then."

"I am terribly sorry for the inconvenience."

He gave a shallow bow and left.

"What's going on?" Beatrice asked.

Charlotte took a breath. "We have a few issues with some of our confectionery," she began, not wanting to hurt Edward's feelings, but this couldn't happen again. *If that toffee had gone to the palace!* Charlotte shuddered to think.

"I don't understand," Edward said.

"Taste it," Charlotte told him.

His eyes wide, he took a piece from the display tray and ate it. Looking crestfallen, his gaze went from Charlotte to Beatrice.

"Is it burnt?" Bea asked.

"Yes," Charlotte told her. "And some of the chocolates don't have the right flavoring or none at all. Now that you're here, you can make the toffee for the palace and extra, of course, and I'll work on the chocolates."

Beatrice didn't jump to it as Charlotte had hoped. Instead, she hesitated.

"Is something wrong?"

Bea opened her mouth, but the bell tinkled and more customers entered.

"Edward, remove all the toffee from the display, and quickly."

"What about the chocolates?" he asked.

"No, leave them. I have to have something to sell." She looked at Bea who was frowning. "Please, Bea, get started."

Her older sister sighed and went into the back room while Charlotte served the customers. Inspiration struck as soon as she considered how to sell the mysterious chocolates.

"May I help you?" she asked, praying they wanted marzipan, which they were woefully low on, too.

"I would like two of the marzipan pears," one of the women said. "And some of the raspberry chocolates."

Charlotte packaged up the pears and tried out her plan. "We have a little fun going on in the shop today. The chocolates are half price, and they are all mixed up, so you won't know exactly what you're getting. Like a sweet surprise for your mouth."

At first the woman blinked, seeming about to protest.

"Half off?" repeated her friend. "That's an excellent deal. Every chocolate I've ever had from here has been delicious. How can one go wrong? I'll take a pound."

Charlotte hoped to recoup some of her loss. "Would you like a pretty tin? They can be used for other things later, like holding gloves or hatpins. Small ones are thruppence, bigger ones are six."

"Oh, no, thank you. If these were a gift, I might, but they're just for my family."

Charlotte nodded, weighed out a pound of assorted chocolates, and poured the measuring bowl from the scale into a white bag, before tying the top with a blue ribbon, just the way her mother liked.

"Well, I still want the raspberry chocolates," came the other woman's voice.

Turning to her, Charlotte did the only thing she could think of. "I'm sorry, but we're all out."

For the rest of the day, Charlotte made marzipan sculptures, sold chocolates at half price, and told lies about what they had run out of if a customer insisted since she had no way of knowing what if anything was in a particular chocolate. It was beyond draining. Edward stayed in the back with Beatrice, presumably learning to do better.

Just in case, however, she stuck her head through the curtain and eyed the two of them. "You're keeping an eye on the cooking time, Bea?" she asked.

Edward glanced away, his cheeks turning red.

"Yes, sister, don't worry."

Charlotte turned around at the sound of the bell again. That was easy for Bea to say. She hadn't been humiliated by trying to sell burned toffee, and to the palace of all places!

They would have words later in private, without Edward. *How could her sister have left him unsupervised to do something that important?*

And it wasn't merely Bea's reputation at stake, it was all of Rare Confectionery's. Moreover, he must have been allowed to make chocolates unsupervised when he went to Amity's house recently to train and had returned with box upon box. It seemed both her sisters had taken leave of their senses.

When she realized the time, it was almost four o'clock. *Mr. Richardson!* She hadn't even had a chance to tell Beatrice. In fact, expanding the shop had been the farthest thing from her mind all day. And if she gave it more thought, after discovering how quickly things could go wrong, Charlotte might find her feet had grown roots to the floor.

Hurrying into the back room, she announced, "I have to go out. I forgot I had an appointment." Quickly, she removed her apron as Bea looked up, a frown on her face.

"You can't be serious. You've been worried all day about my getting the toffee finished, and now you're going to leave us."

"It's all done, isn't it?" Charlotte asked, slipping on her fitted jacket and reaching for her satin hat. Luckily, it tied under her chin and she wouldn't need pins. "The chocolate just needs to set on the toffee. And it would have been finished earlier if you'd come in before one."

Her sister looked surprised by her tone, as did Edward, who'd avoided her for hours and could scarcely look her in the eye.

"Sorry, Bea," Charlotte said, tugging on her gloves. "I know you've got other things on your mind now you're a married woman."

Bea shook her head. "About that—"

"I have to run," Charlotte interrupted her. "I have somewhere I ought to be by four, and obviously I'm already late. You heard what I told the customers about the chocolates. Half off and all a surprise!"

Without waiting another instant, she rushed toward the front. "I should be back well before the queen's footman." *A sentence she never thought she would utter!*

CHAPTER ELEVEN

Charlotte didn't mind her parents being gone, but she appreciated having the family's small staff at hand. She liked hearing noise when she was puttering about in the morning, even though she ate breakfast alone. The following morning, Finley appeared beside her with two missives.

"Thank you," she said, assuming one was from Charles and the other from her parents. Instead, the first one she scanned had Viola's name scrawled along the bottom. Seeing it brought everything back. She didn't want to think of the Evans at all.

"Lionel needs funds desperately," Viola wrote with little preamble. "From the days when you still counted us among your friends, I hope you will find it in your heart to . . . ."

Charlotte stopped reading, picked up her tea, and drained it, before resuming the presumptuous message of how Lionel had already exhausted every other avenue, including begging his parents. *Of all the gall!* Truly, it wasn't Viola's fault except for extremely bad judgment. Charlotte would help anyone in need, but Lionel had brought it all upon himself and used her sorely. She was not going to fund his self-indulgent lark through Europe.

Should she even respond? Ultimately, she didn't. Anything she wrote would make her seem mean and miserly unless she told Viola about the special attention Lionel had paid her, leading her to believe his intentions were for a future together.

The second, a crisp envelope with Lord Jeffcoat's seal, made her stomach twitch with excitement. He'd invited her to a concert the following evening. By the time she'd finished reading it, she'd tamped down her effrontery over Viola's bold request, and realized the ache resurrected at seeing Lionel's name had already dissipated. It had been a mere ghost of the sadness she had previously felt. Nothing more. And her heart seemed to be her own again.

She looked forward to what was to come. Even the difficult day before had ended better than it had begun. Although Beatrice had already left the confectionery when Charlotte returned from the notary public, she'd rushed in to find Edward manning the counter. After the last customers left, the queen's footman had returned, and they were able to sell him the freshly hardened toffee and close up the shop.

Edward had said nothing more about the part he'd played in the disastrous day, but when they started to clean, he spoke up, "I know it was my fault, miss. If I've lost my position, I understand."

Her heart had gone out to him. "No, of course not, but your confectionery should not have been on the shelves until it was perfected."

He'd hung his head, and Charlotte had dropped the matter.

Twenty-four hours later, she focused on being grateful she had Delia at her disposal as a chaperone. While everyone in the upper class would look down upon a maid as suitable and insist upon a married woman of the same class,

Charlotte couldn't imagine how she could go out with Lord Jeffcoat elsewise. She could hardly ask Amity who rarely left home anymore or Beatrice . . . who knew what she was up to?

"You look lovely, my girl," Delia said in her familiar way. Since she'd been with the family for nearly fifteen years, she felt more like a trusted aunt than a maid.

"Thank you." Charlotte wore another gown from the previous Season that she'd attended with Beatrice. Her only Season, one she hadn't thought she'd needed as she'd had her heart set on Lionel. "I hope you don't mind being kept out late for the concert."

"Not at all. I'm looking forward to a bit of music, though not as much as you are, I'm sure. Your Lord Jeffcoat seems a good sort."

"I think so, too. It's strange though, not knowing his past. When you're in a ballroom, you need but lean over and ask the female next to you, and they all are willing to tell the entire story of every single man there, especially a viscount. I suppose his peers know whom he's escorted around town before, and whether he's ever been engaged. It's not as if one begins life the moment someone else meets them."

Delia stopped fussing with Charlotte's hair and looked at her in the mirror until their eyes met.

"What's troubling you?"

"He's about five or six years older than I am. He's a viscount, and a handsome one. Why isn't he attached to some appropriately upper-class lady? And why is he interested in me?"

"You're a pretty young woman," Delia said.

Charlotte dismissed her words with a shrug. "He can have many a pretty face, I'm sure. London is filled with them, either in the nobility, fluttering around Amity's parties, or even some actress on the stage. But why me suddenly, do you think? I hope I'm not being led down the garden path." Her judgment was obviously terrible, after all.

"Led down the—?" Delia repeated, her cheeks going pink. "Oh, no, he doesn't seem the type."

"I don't know *the type*, Delia. What if he's a rogue?" Charlotte recalled Amity's husband once warning her about such a fellow, yet despite such a warning, she'd let Lionel kiss her twice a week.

"For one thing, your parents wouldn't have let you go out with him before they went away. And for another, he's a good friend of the Duke of Pelham's, isn't he? That fine gentleman wouldn't be friendly with a rogue."

"That's true." Charlotte considered a moment. "I suppose I could simply ask Lord Jeffcoat why he wants to be with me? Is that too forward and strange? Maybe even ask him about his previous lady friends."

"I don't know, Miss Charlotte. He's a member of the nobility, and they are not for the likes of me to understand."

Delia finished setting her hair, then stepped back to admire the coiled braids and soft ringlets. "Honestly, my girl, I don't think it's proper for you to pry into his past. Men don't like to talk of such things."

Charlotte sighed. "Which is probably all the more reason women want to know." They smiled at each other.

"You look lovely tonight, too," she told Delia, who was wearing a demure gray gown with pale cream trim to act as chaperone.

Again, the maid's cheeks pinkened. "Oh, go on with you! I don't, but you're a sweetie for saying so."

Charlotte stood up. "Let's wait in the parlor. Who knows where Mr. Finley is, and we might not hear the door."

CHARLES COULDN'T RECALL THE last time he had butterflies in his stomach when going to pick up a woman. It felt good to be excited at the notion of seeing her. Even better when he knocked on the door and she answered. He almost laughed at the refreshing absurdity of going to a home where the person he wanted to see actually opened the door.

She didn't have a chance to prepare her features into a polite expression while a butler or maid showed him into a drawing room. Nor was she busy posing on a sofa, nor arranging her hair over her shoulder for the best possible impression. Charlotte simply welcomed him into the foyer, her deep-brown eyes sparkling and a generous smile on her soft lips. She looked genuinely happy to see him. He was enchanted.

Taking her ungloved hand—which in itself, seemed shockingly sensual—he lifted it to his lips and kissed the back of it. It was an impulsive, formal gesture, but it felt right. He felt the urge to make some kind of contact with her as soon as he saw her.

After he released her, she looked at her own knuckles a moment, then back at him. He nearly blurted how pretty her hands were. And they were! Not limp and useless, pale and overly soft. They were delicate and clean, to be sure, but he knew them to be capable and artistic hands, too. Moreover, he had the insane desire to feel them roaming his bare skin, in the same way as he wanted to run his fingers over her body.

"Good evening, my lord," she said, and he realized his gaze had been roaming her, head to toe. She looked to be perfection in a silvery blue gown that fit her like the glove she ought to have on for propriety's sake.

Cautioning himself to tamp down his sudden longing for more, he removed his hat and bowed slightly. "Good evening, Miss Rare-Foure. Are you ready?"

"I am." And she gave two quick claps of her hands, startling him. "My apologies," she muttered, turning away to reveal her maid behind her holding an evening mantle. "I am simply excited."

He liked her enthusiasm and her honesty. And he wanted to take the black cloak from the maid—Delia, he recalled—and drape it over Charlotte's shoulders himself, merely for the excuse to touch her again. Instead, he kept his hands by his sides.

Belatedly, she drew on black satin gloves and retrieved a small blue reticule from the hallstand while her maid donned her own cloak and gloves.

With all three of them settled in his carriage, and Delia tucked in the corner looking out the window, Charles could finally talk to her.

"How did it go with your landlord?"

He was practically scorched by the brilliance of her smile and happy visage.

"It went well," she said unnecessarily for he could see that. "And it was on the heels of a particularly trying day. I nearly sent burned toffee to the queen!"

"Perish the thought," he said.

"You're teasing, but consider our reputation. If Her Majesty withdrew her favor, our sales from the hundreds of nobility in Mayfair would plummet."

"Understood." He shouldn't take anything she said regarding confectionery lightly, as it was her family's livelihood. "You managed to get it sorted out?"

"I did. Young Edward, you remember my worker? He had made toffee with my sister, and rather thoughtlessly, she'd let him put it out for sale. Likewise, he went to my other sister's to have chocolate training, and when he returned a few days ago with boxes of sweets, I didn't realize he'd made the lion's share of them. Nothing dreadful, mind you, but not up to our standards. Worse, I couldn't tell what was what." She shook her head in wonder.

"After all, you cannot sell something if you don't know what it is, and how could I know without tasting each chocolate?" she asked, raising her hands in a gesture of helpless dismay.

He shook his head, fascinated by her. "You couldn't."

"And I could hardly bite into each one to discover its secrets."

Watching her perfect mouth discussing biting and secrets made his own abruptly go dry.

"No, of course you couldn't," he agreed. "I doubt anyone would buy chocolates you'd already bitten into." Except him. Charles would lick one right off her lips if he could.

What had got into him? He was well and truly captivated, and he couldn't remember ever feeling struck by such fervent interest before.

She explained how she'd sold them as surprises, which seemed like a smartly creative solution to her bewildering problem.

"Pity you had to drop the price," he said.

"It was a pity," she agreed. "Especially with adding an entire floor to the shop. I need to keep the revenue coming in."

He watched the maid startle and then slowly turn to her.

"Excuse me, miss. Did you say you'd added a floor?"

"Yes, Delia. I am expanding Rare Confectionery."

The middle-aged servant paled. "Without your mother here? She's ever so particular, as you know."

Charlotte nodded but looked undaunted. "I am certain she'll be pleased."

"Very well, miss." But the woman looked doubtful nonetheless.

Charles felt a frisson of unease. It did seem like a large step to take, especially without her parents' permission.

"Is it a *fait accompli?*"

"It is." Her tone became high pitched with excitement. "Tomorrow, I shall start looking for a carpenter to build a staircase inside our shop."

"If you need any assistance," he offered, although he knew nothing about builders or securing a carpenter. But he assumed neither did she.

"If you would like to come by the confectionery tomorrow after closing, I'll show you the upstairs." She grinned like a fiend. "Mr. Richardson gave me the key."

Again, Delia turned to her. "Shall I arrive then, too?"

Charlotte frowned. "Whyever for?" Then she slanted her maid a smile. "Oh, I see. My reputation again is in extreme danger from Lord Jeffcoat," she teased.

Charles wondered at her innocence, and in someone of her years, too! It was a miracle no man had managed to get her alone during the Season the prior year, in an alcove or an empty gazebo or even behind a garden hedge. Or maybe someone had!

"I believe Beatrice will be there, Delia, and Edward, too," Charlotte promised. "Will they suffice?"

The maid hesitated, her glance flickering over to Charles. "Yes, miss."

For his part, he was relieved Charlotte had those around her who loved her, but he wanted to change the topic of their conversation, since it was all about how to protect her from the likes of him, as if she were a lamb and he, a slobbering wolf.

"I shall come by tomorrow," he promised, honored she'd invited him to see the shop's second floor before anyone else.

"Where are your glasses?" she asked suddenly, leaning forward, taking him off guard as her mantle parted and her shapely bosom nearly defied the confines of her satin décolletage.

And at that moment, he did feel more like a wolf than he ever had.

"Pardon?" he asked foolishly, then her question penetrated his distracted brain. "Oh, right. My spectacles. I only need them for reading. Not for seeing you"—*thank God!*—"or for listening to music." They both chuckled. "And with any luck, it will be a few years before I need a hearing horn."

"But for reading tonight's program," she pointed out.

"Yes, then out my specs shall come." He patted his pocket, but it felt empty. He reached inside. Nothing. Then he tried the other pocket, also empty. Opening his coat, he slid his fingers into his interior pocket to no avail.

"I never forget them," he vowed. "Until tonight." He wasn't going to tell Charlotte in front of her maid how the anticipation of seeing her had caused him to rush out his front door without his glasses, a singular occurrence.

"Never mind," she said. "I shall read anything you wish. Besides, I can better see your blue eyes without them."

He paused. Her flirtatious remark sent a shard of excitement through him. Moreover, she'd noticed his eye color. *How wonderful!* She'd even offered to be his eyes, proving him right about her sweet nature.

St. James's Hall, designed by the same architect who'd styled the interior of the Crystal Palace, was packed. The popular young pianist and singer George Henschel was the main performer whom everyone was there to hear, along with the prestigious Philharmonic Society orchestra.

Even with such a performance ahead of them, it was hard not to be equally impressed with the Florentine beauty of the concert hall, imitating a Moorish palace in which two thousand Londoners could enjoy music. Three galleries lined the room, all with a wonderful view of the domed stage and its organ. The tall windows, each in its own massive pointed bay, and the soaring ceiling gave one the impression of being in a cathedral.

"We are certainly not at the Oxford Music Hall tonight," Delia quipped, which Charles plainly overheard. He doubted Charlotte had ever been to such a place as that or any of the other tawdry music halls. The worst was probably in Islington where men more often brought their mistresses instead of their wives or sweethearts. The audience often joined in the performance, loudly singing along with whatever was happening on the stage while drinking the worst grog. He'd been to a few as a student and vowed, after a particularly unpleasant vulgar display of comic songs, grotesque dancing, and ridiculous tumbling never to go again.

A music hall was definitely not his preference for amusement.

At St. James's Hall, one of his favorite venues, Charles liked the gallery that faced the stage directly, and had obtained seats in its front row. He was grateful that Delia had agreed to let him sit beside Charlotte and even chose the seat on her far side. At least they could spend the evening side by side.

With his former lady-love right behind them!

Miss Virginia Stadden, the sharp-tongued baronet's sister, gave him her frostiest stare as he ushered first the maid and then Charlotte into the row before taking his seat.

What an idiot on at least two counts! He should never have brought Charlotte to the same place he used to frequent with Virginia, and if he were going to commit such a stupidity, then he ought to have at least chosen a different part of the two-thousand seat hall.

Shaking his head at his own folly, Charles would have to attribute it to not having escorted that many women around London, and thus, he usually never had to worry about one meeting another—or that other looking annoyed. Waverly probably knew every way from Sunday how to avoid one's previous paramours. And as expected, almost immediately, he felt a tap on his right shoulder, causing him to turn in the opposite direction from Charlotte.

"How nice to see you again, Lord Jeffcoat?" Her icy tone was like the hissing of a snake.

"And you, Miss Stadden. Quite the coincidence," he added.

"Is it?" she asked, her voice rising. "Did you think I wouldn't come here any longer? Was I supposed to hide myself away from all of Mayfair's society because the elusive Jeffcoat no longer wished to be seen with me?"

"Um . . . ." He felt Charlotte stir with interest beside him. He really didn't want her involved in an ugly scene. And sadly, he knew it was going to deteriorate rather quickly. For his part, he thought their parting had been easily

accomplished, but in retrospective recollection, Virginia hadn't wanted their association to end. And now, their first meeting was extremely public.

Was it his imagination or had it grown quiet around him as every nosey-poke listened in?

Turning farther in his seat until his back was facing Charlotte entirely, he hoped to make Virginia see the futility of going at each other. His eyes flickered over her to her companion—*Dear God!* It was her mother, a bear of a woman who had thought for certain her daughter was going to become a viscountess. Her expression was as withering as her daughter's.

The lights dimmed in the hall. Charles sighed. "If you wish to speak to me privately at some other time, then I will be amenable to such."

Virginia raised her voice. "Are you trying to arrange an assignation with me while you are escorting another woman?"

And thus began the unfortunate scene, obviously more interesting to those around him than Mr. Henschel and the Philharmonic could ever hope to be.

"Please, Miss Stadden, this is not the time."

"And now he's *begging* me," she proclaimed with glee.

Meanwhile, her mother looked as if she might hit him with her opera glasses.

Rescue came from an unexpected quarter. Miss Rare-Foure herself.

CHAPTER TWELVE

Charlotte could see what was happening. A jealous woman from Lord Jeffcoat's past—probably an old flame—sought to ruin their evening. Naturally she would like to know more about the pretty creature, fine-boned, fair-haired, and bejeweled as she was. But not at that moment. She wanted to hear the concert.

Turning awkwardly in her seat, she managed to get her head close to the viscount's and look back at the woman, who seemed to be accompanied by a fire-breathing dragon, or her dear mama!

"The concert is about to start," Charlotte whispered loudly. "According to the program, there will be an intermission when you can go into the lobby and gabble to your heart's content. But right now, you are disturbing those around you. It's rather rude."

Stunned silence met her proclamation. *Good!* She had their attention. Then she rummaged in her reticule and drew out her ever-present white paper bag, glad it had softened over the past day into a less loud and crinkly version.

Opening it, she turned down the edges to reveal what was left.

"Would you care for a sweet? If you tuck it into your cheek and let it melt, it will keep at bay the desire to talk when you shouldn't. At least, it works well on children. Will you try it?"

And she held out the bag to the woman who was about her own age. Her offering was met with a stony-face, pursed lips, and a clenched jaw. Then, as if a match had been lit beneath her, she exploded out of her seat, standing with a great deal of gestures and inarticulate noises, and then she said, "Come along, Mother. This place has become far too common!"

Her mother stood with some difficulty as she'd been wedged between the velvet-covered wooden arms of her chair. Charlotte thought a little butter over her hips might help to release her. Eventually, the woman stood, huffed loudly, glared at everyone around her, and exited the row, followed by her daughter.

At the last moment, the pretty blonde whirled around and addressed Charlotte.

"I wouldn't be too smug if I were you. It's obvious why he's with you." With that, she turned and left, just as the orchestra played their first notes.

Puzzled, Charlotte turned around. Lord Jeffcoat was fidgeting beside her, smoothing his coat and keeping his face averted.

"Are you very fond of confectionery?" she asked. "Is that what that lady meant?"

"We'll talk after," he promised.

Nodding, she held out the bag to him. He hesitated, his thoughts impossible to discern in the darkened auditorium. Then he reached in and took a piece.

"Thank you," he whispered, against her ear, making her shiver.

Inappropriately, she wanted to lean her head on his shoulder and breathe in his fragrance. Luckily, she could catch it anyway. *Would she ever smell gingerbread or rum and not think of this man? Or want to be kissed by him?*

WHEN BEATRICE WANDERED IN at one o'clock the following day, Charlotte was fit to be tied.

"Why are you coming in later and later?" she asked her older sister, trying to keep from sounding peevish, but feeling a little desperate. She and Edward were working hard from opening until closing, but they were barely keeping up. And she hadn't let Edward make any more toffee, not without Beatrice there to supervise.

"Good day to you, too, sister dear," Beatrice said.

Charlotte noticed she wasn't wearing her regular day gown, but a . . . traveling outfit! Nor did she take off her coat or head into the back room.

"What's going on?" Charlotte asked, feeling a little leaf of dread unfurl inside her. Plainly, Beatrice was not there to work.

"I have spent all morning packing up our home. Mr. Carson and I are going to Scotland. There is some emergency with the flock and the well water."

Charlotte knew her mouth had dropped open but was at a loss how to clamp down on her burgeoning panic. "You're leaving town?"

"Yes. I was going to discuss it with you yesterday, but with the royal request and then your abrupt departure to who knows where, I didn't get around to it."

"But with Amity out . . . ," Charlotte trailed off.

"I know, and I'm sorry." But she shrugged, as if this were a matter of a being out of a stick of butter or a pound of almonds.

"Can't Mr. Carson go alone?" Charlotte wished she could take the words back since Beatrice was still considered a newlywed.

Her sister looked chagrinned. "It might be weeks, and I can't be parted from him that long. I know it's selfish of me."

"No, I understand." Charlotte's thoughts flitted to Lord Jeffcoat. If he were her husband—*what a presumptuous thought!*—then she wouldn't want to let him go away for weeks, either.

"But I'm not simply walking out and leaving you without toffee."

"You're not?"

"I spent all day with Edward yesterday. He has got the hang of it, I promise you. I even told him about another flavor I wanted to test, and he made it perfectly."

"A new flavor?" Charlotte asked with trepidation. It didn't seem a good time for experimenting.

"Yes, our new toffee is based on the Everton brand. We're going to add some ginger essence."

"Ginger," Charlotte repeated, startled at how many times she'd been musing about that spice recently. But everyone knew the famous Everton was popular. "And Edward is going to launch this new toffee without you here?"

Beatrice grinned. "I told you, he made it perfectly. I even gave him *The Frugal Cook* to keep in the back, which has the recipe right in it. Where is he, by the way? I brought him something."

"I just sent him out to do an extra delivery. The Langham didn't have enough chocolates to get through the week, which makes little sense since the order has been the same since—"

"I can't stay," Beatrice interrupted, indicating there was no point in Charlotte's next tactic, to drop to her knees and begin pleading.

"But I don't have Amity either, nor Mother."

"Mother should be home soon. How long can they possibly stay at the seaside?" Beatrice asked.

Charlotte had no idea, but then, she felt as if she had little control over anything anymore. *Was there a point in telling her sister about the expansion of their shop if she wasn't even going to be there?*

Charlotte didn't think she could stomach it if Bea said something unkind about the notion, especially as it was now too late.

"When Amity's little one comes along, things will get back to some semblance of normalcy," Beatrice said.

They looked at one another, neither one of them believing that.

Then her sister came closer, passed through the space between the counters, and wrapped her arms around Charlotte. It was an unexpected but comforting gesture.

"I'll come home as soon as I can," her sister promised. "And then things will return to how they were with my being insufferably peevish and barking at you from the back room."

Charlotte tried to smile but failed.

"And we shall have Edward so everything will be less work."

Yesterday had been more work along with a loss of income, but she didn't say that.

"Are you going to see Amity before you leave?"

Beatrice nodded. "Yes. I'm going there now."

"Please tell her I'll send Edward tomorrow as soon as he's helped me open. He'll take supplies with him. Not only must they make more, they must label everything. And tell her—"

"Oh, my," Beatrice said. "I don't think her thoughts are focused on chocolate-making."

"I know they're not, but she's still our chocolatier. I'll remind Edward to have her write down what everything is *supposed* to be. But I was going to add she must watch him and make certain he doesn't change the recipe."

"I'll remind her, but she seems as apt to start singing a silly nursery lullaby as to pay attention." Beatrice tilted her head and fixed her with her serious gaze, a brighter blue than Jeffcoat's but reminding her of him anyway. "You may have to start making the chocolates, too. You were good at it, I recall."

"When would I do that?" Charlotte asked dully, feeling like Cinderella in Perrault's fairy tale, but with no godmother in sight.

"You are in charge," Beatrice reminded her. "Better than any of us, you know the financial state of Rare Confectionery. Perhaps until Amity's child arrives, you should hire someone to work the counter, freeing you to make chocolates, unless Edward turns out to be as good at that as he is at toffee-making."

"I've tasted only his burnt batches," Charlotte muttered.

"Oh, that reminds me," Bea said. "Here's what I bought for our apprentice. A little expensive, but I'm sure he'll be careful with it." She drew a thermometer out of her satchel.

"He already understands what to look for while cooking the toffee," she assured Charlotte, "and I showed him the cold water trick to test it, but this will help him." Beatrice handed the instrument to Charlotte, who stared at the mercury-filled glass tube.

"Just stick this end in and read the scale. About 280 degrees should do the trick," Beatrice said, a bit too casually. "Also, yesterday, I gave him an hourglass and marked it for the right time when he should start to test the consistency."

Thank you," Charlotte said. Her sister had done all she could. They hugged again, and then Bea was gone. Swallowing the lump in her throat, she used the rest of the lull in customers to make as many marzipan sculptures as she could.

CHARLOTTE WAS THRILLED TO turn over the shop's sign at the end of the day, feeling merely the tiniest twinge of guilt when she made eye contact with a man about to push the door open. Offering him a regretful smile, she turned her back. With her luck, he was probably the wealthiest man in England and had wanted to buy every last sweet.

That wouldn't be hard for inventory was woefully low. She hadn't even allowed Bea to take any to Scotland, as her sister could make toffee when she got there if her new staff was clamoring for it.

Her staff!

Charlotte needed a staff, too. Down one and a half confectioners, because Amity was definitely not producing her usual amount, she had but one young boy to assist her. And Bea was probably correct about hiring counter help, except Charlotte had always enjoyed that part of her job.

Edward had returned from deliveries and gone directly into the back room to make confection. He exclaimed with joy over the thermometer. When customers were in the shop, they couldn't talk, but when he heard the bell tinkle, knowing they were alone, he occasionally called out a question.

That made Charlotte smile, recalling when she and her sisters were younger how they would ask their mother for instructions from the back room. Felicity, like Charlotte, preferred to chat with customers.

How strange to be the only one of her family remaining in the confectionery!

Edward had completed all his closing tasks and hung up his apron. Donning his coat, he looked weary. Charlotte hoped he didn't regret working for her. Surely, it was better than a workhouse, at any rate.

He was at the door when she recalled Lord Jeffcoat's imminent arrival. Hating to ask, but with no Beatrice there, she had no choice.

"Edward, can you stay any longer?"

He turned around. "Sorry, miss. I promised my mother I would go straight home. I have my two younger bantlings to look after while she takes in piecework. She finishes gentlemen's shirts."

Charlotte felt guilty for having asked him. In comparison to him looking after his family and his mother still facing hours of work, what right had she to try to use him as a chaperone? Besides, she was a grown woman, not a child who needed watching over, as if she or the viscount couldn't be trusted. It was absurd.

In the moment her thoughts were churning, Edward's expression had fallen. "I am sorry to let you down, miss."

"Oh, no," she reassured him, "you haven't. Don't give it another thought. Everything is fine. I'll see you tomorrow morning. Please give your mother my regards. I hope to meet her someday."

He nodded, albeit without enthusiasm. He'd told Charlotte in the past that his home was not for the likes of her to visit, but he would bring his mother in if ever she could spare the time.

The boy had scarcely disappeared from the shop when she heard a rapping on the glass. And there he was, her new friend, the viscount.

IN A FEW MINUTES, Charles found himself exiting Rare Confectionery and entering through a doorway between it and the shop next door. Truthfully, he'd never even noticed the door, and now, as Charlotte had not procured a chaperone, he followed her quickly inside. The less time anyone saw them alone together, the better.

Shutting it firmly behind her, she locked it. Then, in the tight confines of the narrow utilitarian stairwell, she passed him, her light citrus and floral fragrance instantly entering his head. As she proceeded him to the next floor, she gave him a splendid view of her ankles.

Charles sighed. He had to stop thinking of her in those terms particularly at that moment when she needed a friend. She'd already explained how Bea had left London for her husband's country estate and that Edward had needed to go home.

Upon hearing of their impending inappropriate seclusion, Charles had nearly begged off the favor. He ought to tell her they would go upstairs another time when she had a companion. Except Charlotte seemed a little sad, and the only thing that brought a smile to her face was the notion of showing him the new space for Rare Confectionery's café.

After she unlocked a door at the top of the stairs, he followed her into an empty room with dull floors in need of polish. The walls, though, were freshly painted, and the windows at the back, overlooking the mews, were sparkling. Not a cobweb in sight on the plaster ceiling either. In the center of the empty room, Charlotte turned to face him.

Somewhat shyly, she asked, "What do you think?"

He chose his words carefully. "It is a good, clean room with plenty of space."

She nodded, satisfied by his declaration. "Come see the front room overlooking the street. I can practically imagine it furnished, although I'm torn between faux bamboo tables or something with inlay and a hint of gilt accent."

"Why not both?" he asked, engendering an odd look from her. Obviously, he had betrayed his ignorance in all matters of decoration and furnishings.

Following her toward the front, he passed through a wide arch. "It's a good thing there isn't a wall and door here. I like how this whole floor seems almost to be one space."

"Exactly my thoughts," she agreed, and he regained some pride. "Though depending what we end up serving," she added, "we might need to build a little kitchen in the back."

He swallowed. *Did she have any idea how much it would cost to put in plumbing up here if there were no pipes for taps and a drain?*

He had no notion of the cost, either, but it was probably considerable.

"Perhaps you should use the kitchen downstairs in the back room until you start to show a profit."

"I am rethinking this," she said, giving him a start. After all, she'd signed a contract. "We should have soft cushioned chairs in here so ladies will stay longer, drink more chocolate, and eat more confectionery."

He smiled at the image of her customers growing larger as they lingered in the dining area eating sweets. But it was no joking matter that she was focusing on the details of decoration and not the great expense of putting in a sink and an oven.

"With your current revenue from the shop, will you be able to do everything you wish to do up here?"

She was staring toward the front windows, lost in thought, and he could admire everything about her in silence for a long moment. At last, she turned.

"Wool gathering," she said with an apologetic tone. "I was imagining those three-tiered serving dishes, not silver but porcelain, with our confectionery and some biscuits on all three plates. I wonder if we ought to hire a pastry chef, a *pâtissier* if I am to be specific, to make proper desserts or if Mother will think that strays too far from our primary purpose. Would people expect to buy the pastries in the shop downstairs the way they do our confectionery after they eat them up here?"

He thought she was asking a rhetorical question as happened often in the courtroom, but by her attentive expression, he realized she was awaiting his response.

"I suppose you could offer in your dining area more than what you sell downstairs. If I am in a restaurant or café, I never expect to be able to buy anything on the menu to take home with me."

"That's true. Our shop could remain as it is below, with perhaps another sales counter up here."

She turned around and went through the arched opening. "I think the stairs from below will come out somewhere about there." She gestured to the right-hand wall, then she clapped her hands. "It is so exciting." In the next instant, she looked practically distraught.

"What's the matter?" he asked, taking a step closer.

"To think, not one of my family even knows about this yet. Only you." She glanced at him. "I know it's not your place to say," she hesitated, "but you don't think I've made a mistake, do you?"

His heart sank. *God, he hoped not!*

"I think you have a good head upon your shoulders, and if you think your shop has the necessary funds to expand, then it probably has."

Probably. He took another step toward her. She ought to back up. When she didn't, he veered away to pace the length of the room and come to a stop where she'd indicted the stairs would be.

"It's a very good idea to have a staircase put in, not simply for the ease of your customers in the shop below, but also in case of fire."

"Yes, I hadn't thought of that." This time, she seemed to be drawing nearer. Irrationally, Charles flattened himself against the wall.

"What on earth are you doing, my lord?" she asked, a small smile on her face.

"Doing? Why, nothing?"

"You look as though you're in some distress," she said. By the glimmer in her eye, she was doing it on purpose. He relaxed.

"You know as well as I do we should *not* be up here alone."

She nodded. "But we are."

"Then we should keep a few feet apart," he suggested.

This statement was met with her laughter, bubbling and contagious. He laughed, too, although he wasn't sure why.

After a moment, he asked her that exact question. "Why are we laughing?"

"Because I find it ridiculous that adults cannot be trusted. I know if we were discovered, it would *look* bad. I understand about appearances. Yet to suggest we need to stand apart when no one is watching as if you truly think you might be overcome and pounce upon me," she began, then shook her head, dislodging a soft brown tendril that he itched to tuck behind her ear.

"It's not for *your* protection alone," Charles pointed out.

Her beautiful eyes widened as did her smile. "Oh, I see! You are concerned I might be unable to help myself." She moved even closer. "I might be utterly overcome by your extraordinary magnetism until I cannot be held responsible for pressing myself against you."

And she did precisely that, brushing her shapely frame against him, while he gritted his teeth.

For pity's sake!

CHAPTER THIRTEEN

Charlotte's warmth was seeping into him. And Charles could feel her softness against his arm and then his chest. A moment later, she was laughing once more and walking past him toward the back windows.

He swallowed, and even the nothingness of air stuck in his parched throat.

The infuriating woman had no idea how splendid she was or how much he wanted to snatch her to him and taste her lips again. Doing so would strip him of any claim to being a gentleman, especially since she'd invited him as a friend.

He was quickly discovering there was such a thing as too much friendliness where Charlotte was concerned.

"Oh, look there," she exclaimed, and he had no choice but to follow her and venture within the circle of her attraction. *Too close.* But she was correct—he was not an animal who couldn't be trusted.

Striding to the *other* rear window, he peered out to see what she was looking at. It wasn't much of a view actually.

Neither was the front of the confectionery, which despite facing St. Paul's in the distance, offered nothing but an intimate look into the shops across the street. And at the back, he could see only the alley and more buildings. *What had drawn her interest?*

In a heartbeat, she moved to stand beside him. He felt like growling, not like an animal, but merely a man meeting with too much temptation.

"I've never seen the view from up here. I can see Hyde Park, or at least its treetops, and Green Park." She opened the window and leaned out. "And if I stretch my neck," she added, "I can even see the Thames in the distance."

Leaning out farther, her feet suddenly left the floor and her body teetered on the window sill. Charles grabbed for her as she yelped with surprise. Tugging her back inside, he held onto her tightly.

"What on earth! Miss Rare-Foure, if I hadn't been here, you would have plunged to your death in the alley below."

She looked sideways down at the mews. It was clean as far as alleys went, but still, it contained the trash from the various Bond Street establishments, along with dropped chunks of coal from deliveries that missed their mark through the chutes on the bottom floor. He shuddered to imagine her lying broken on the cobblestones.

"That would have been an ignominious end," she agreed, seemingly entirely undisturbed. "However, I don't think I would have made it through the opening without catching myself with my hands against the frame."

He begged to disagree. Not only was she on the shorter side, she was what he would describe as top-heavy. The laws of gravity would have ensured she toppled out and had a quick descent.

He pulled her closer as he imagined it. Wrapping his arms around her, he closed his eyes and rested his chin upon her . . . her prickly hat. It was uncomfortable at best. Moreover, she was resisting his embrace, as she should, pushing against his chest.

Quickly, he dropped his arms from around her and stepped back.

"My apologies," he said. "I was briefly overcome with a picture in my head of what would surely have happened. Promise me you won't do anything so foolish again."

Charlotte had frozen in place, staring up at him. "That was the sweetest thing," she announced. "Your rescuing me and then embracing me. I am sorry for worrying you."

Again, she was drawing closer. Before he could react, she threw her arms around his waist and hugged him in return.

The whole situation had got out of hand, and now, they were in an untenable position. Clasping him to her, she gazed up, and he knew what it meant to fall deeply into a woman's eyes. For that was what he did, her deep-brown eyes welcoming him into her soul. His stomach lurched with the sensation.

Without thinking, he lowered his head and claimed her lips.

CHARLOTTE GASPED AGAINST LORD Jeffcoat's mouth, and then relaxed. Her entire body had been tingling since they'd entered the suite of rooms, and she knew she'd been teasing him to distraction. Although nearly falling out of the window, possibly to her death, had been an accident.

Nevertheless, it had achieved her goal. He was finally kissing her again with a long, blissful kiss.

"*Mm,*" she said against his lips, and felt his response in the way his fingers squeezed her waist and how he deepened the kiss, his mouth seeming to caress hers. After a long while, he drew back.

She opened her eyes and watched his own gaze go from faraway into sharp focus, and then his features tightened.

"Blast it all!" he swore and strode away from her, down to the end of the room and through the archway to the other set of windows.

After recovering from his surprisingly sharp reaction, she hurried after him.

"Lord Jeffcoat, is something amiss?"

He wasn't looking at her, but staring out the window. Daring his displeasure, for he was radiating annoyance, she stood beside him.

"This view is more familiar, but it's still hard to see over the rooftops across the street."

He didn't say anything.

"Lord Jeffcoat, are you going to remain silent until we part?"

"Maybe," he muttered.

"Whyever for?"

"Because I have behaved abominably and should be whipped."

She felt the urge to giggle at his serious tone after their pleasant kiss, but then she imagined him stripped bare for a lashing and sobered at the thought of seeing his torso.

"I . . . I am sorry if I have caused you distress," she offered.

"You!" he exclaimed. "You are not the one to be sorry. I am the one who is supposed to be reasonable and rational and cautious and . . . and protect your innocence. Instead, I mauled you and stole a kiss."

This time, Charlotte could not contain her good humor. She tried to press her lips together, but her laughter spilled out.

"Oh, my lord. You know as well as I that I threw my arms around you."

"*After* I had already embraced you," he pointed out.

They stared at one another.

"Is it really so terrible?" Charlotte couldn't refrain from asking.

He sighed. "You have asked such before, and you know the answer."

"I know," she conceded, "my reputation is at stake, but perhaps not if we come to an understanding."

He looked shocked, actually paling.

What had she said to alarm him? she wondered.

"Miss Rare-Foure, there can be no *understanding* that allows for a single man and a single woman to make light of the restraints of civil society. We ignore decorum and tear apart those restraints at our own peril."

Lord Jeffcoat paced, and she imagined him doing precisely that, back and forth, before the bench of some lofty judge as he made his case.

"If discovered, you would be labeled a light-skirt at worse or a loose woman at best. I know all too well that I would be forgiven in society's eyes as being tempted beyond reason by your charms."

"And are you?" Charlotte knew she ought to stop prodding him, but she couldn't. He was too proper with his perfect cravat and his gray gloves.

"Am I what?" he snapped.

"Tempted beyond reason?" she asked.

"Argh!" he exclaimed and walked away from her again. But then he turned and walked back.

"Miss Rare-Foure—"

"You could call me Charlotte," she pointed out, "when we are alone, seeing as we have kissed. Twice."

He clenched his jaw.

"And I could call you Charles. Only, as I said, when we are alone."

"We will not be alone again," he vowed. "We mustn't."

She sighed. "The arrangement I referred to was the kind couples make when they like each other and have an understanding."

He narrowed his eyes. "Do you mean an engagement?"

After all that, hearing him say it—when she'd had to spell it out for him—was mortifying in the extreme. If he wanted to spend time alone with her and had such intense feelings, then an engagement ought to have been upper most in his mind. Not hers. Or at least, not hers alone.

"No," she countered to save face. "I suppose I meant . . . ," she trailed off.

"Well?" he asked, as if he were a barrister interrogating a witness.

"My sister, Mrs. Carson, before she was such, had an arrangement with Mr. Carson. They were . . . partners . . . in a scheme to find him a titled lady as his spouse."

Lord Jeffcoat rolled his eyes. "And how did that work out for them?"

"Perfectly," Charlotte told him. "They fell in love, and obviously, they belong together."

"*Hm.*"

That told her nothing of his thoughts.

"If we had an arrangement, something we were doing," she persisted, "then we could be together without suspicion."

"No, Miss Rare-Foure, we could not. Besides, what would we be doing together? I am not an estate lawyer. Nor can I build your much-needed staircase."

She sighed. "Never mind. Why don't you tell me about that lady at the concert hall?"

He looked shocked again. "An inappropriate topic," he said.

"I think not. Why won't you tell me? If you can ask me out and then take me somewhere that I may run into your past paramours—"

"Miss Rare-Foure!"

"Your past lady-friends, is that a better, more civilized term?" she asked. "If you put me in their path, then I believe I have a right to ask. After all, she besmirched me."

"Besmirched you?" he repeated, frowning slightly.

"She did," Charlotte reminded him. "I am not so naïve that I don't know what she meant about why you might be keeping company with me."

His face flushed a rosy color and his glance slid away from her face. She'd embarrassed him.

"It's all right. I am quite aware of certain of my traits that draw men's attention."

Since Lord Jeffcoat looked as if he might run, she ceased her outrageous discussion of her own body.

Developing beyond both her sisters, Charlotte had been on the receiving end of many a man's gawking stare. Nonetheless, a woman, particularly Lord Jeffcoat's lady-friend, snidely mentioning her figure had been a new and uncomfortable occurrence.

As if she were nothing more than a large bosom and pretty lips!

"Why *did* you ask me out again?" she asked him. "I believe it wasn't solely due to what your lady-friend mentioned."

"She is no longer that," he corrected stiffly. "In fact, she is of no consequence whatsoever."

"Regardless, she was rude."

"She was," he agreed. "And she was wrong. I like you because you're interesting."

Interesting? A shopgirl who made marzipan was interesting? Yet she believed him, and his declaration warmed her.

"If she is unimportant, then you can tell me who she is."

"You would make a good barrister, Miss Rare-Foure. Or at least a persistent one." He folded his arms. "She is Miss Virginia Stadden. I escorted her around town and to some parties for a couple months. However, she is unkind, and after a while, I couldn't stomach it."

"I see." She supposed that answered all her questions. As long as the woman was no longer in his mind or heart, she mattered nothing, exactly as he said.

"You are the opposite. You are kind," Lord Jeffcoat offered.

Charlotte couldn't help smiling. "I am," she agreed, making him bark out a laugh.

"And modest," he teased, after a moment.

"Does it seem boastful to agree that my nature is basically kind?"

"Not really, not when *you* say it," he agreed. "I've seen the evidence."

She shrugged. "It's easy to be kind and to make people happy, especially with confectionery."

"Most of the people I work with are unsmiling," he said. "Perhaps even unhappy."

"Something as grave as the law can drain the happiness away," she mused. "But you are not a sad man, albeit a little serious sometimes."

"I've been told that before."

"You take after your father, perhaps," she mused, although the earl seemed more cranky than serious. But if Charles's lifelong role model for being a man was the grumpy earl, then she supposed he had turned out very well indeed.

"Better my father than my mother," he quipped, then looked as though he wished he could suck the words right out of the air and swallow them back down.

"Your mother has passed away?" Charlotte asked him, fearing the worst.

He said nothing for a long moment. "If you don't mind, I would rather not speak of her." His tone had become reticent and off-putting.

It was probably too painful for him. "Of course. I am sorry to have pried. In any case, I have taken up too much of your time."

Suddenly, she recollected that all this space belonged to her—and Rare Confectionery—and her joy bubbled up once more. Returning to the center of the room, she twirled in a circle.

"Can't you just imagine it?" she crowed. "Everything appealing down to the finest detail, the floors and paint and wallpaper and furnishings. And it will smell divinely of Amity's chocolates and Beatrice's buttery toffee. And coffee, too. It will be grand."

"I can imagine it. I'm sure your marzipan will be here, too," he added.

How sweet of him to mention it. "It doesn't have a warm, delicious scent. It is undoubtedly the least popular confectionery in the shop."

With that, realizing she still had work to do down below, she began to walk toward the door.

"And that doesn't bother you?" he asked, sounding surprised.

"Not at all. My marzipan is part of the success of Rare Confectionery, after all." She glanced at him. "As a family, we fail or succeed together, I believe."

He stopped in his tracks. "You have amazed me again, Miss Rare-Foure. What's more, you have done so more than anyone I know."

Charlotte didn't know what to make of that. "Most families are similar, are they not?"

"I wish it were the truth," Charles said, making her understand he had not the same experience in his life.

She recalled how Lionel had left without any indication of when he would see Viola or their parents again. *Pure selfishness!* But surely, Lionel was an aberration of an artistic mind! She hoped no such thing had happened to the viscount within his own family.

"May I escort you somewhere again this week?" he asked.

His question drew her out of thoughts of a man she might never see again, one she'd finally put behind her.

"Yes," she answered. "We shall need Delia, obviously, because we cannot keep our hands off one another."

Charlotte meant it in jest, but he stiffened. His lordship was a tad too serious for his own good. Why, she almost leaned over to kiss him just to ruffle his feathers once more, but restrained herself. That would most certainly end with him berating himself again.

"I am speaking in jest. I shall be on my best behavior," she assured him, "and I'm certain you will, too."

That made him smile, if only slightly. "I enjoy riding. I think I may have mentioned that before. But you work every day, do you not?"

"Except Sundays."

"I shall plan an outing for some evening this week," he proposed, "but also, I would like to take you riding on Sunday."

She would have to confess the truth.

"My lord, I am a middle-class shopkeeper's daughter. Our family does not ride in the park because we do not keep mounts or have suitable riding clothing."

Nevertheless, Charlotte thought she would look fetching in a green velvet habit. *Could she obtain such a thing from a ready-made clothing store and on such short notice?*

But she would also need a horse, and not one of the sturdy mares that pulled her father's carriage around town.

Lord Jeffcoat was undeterred. "Have you ridden before?"

Should she confess to riding bareback at their country home? Once or twice, just for fun, she'd ridden astride along the River Blackwater since they didn't have a side saddle. The fat mare had moved as slowly as treacle on a cold day.

"A few times, yes, but not in Town," she admitted.

"Perfect. You will enjoy yourself, I promise. And any gown will do, I'm sure, as long as it has a full skirt to go over the pommel. I'll give you a well-mannered mount and a comfortable saddle. We'll ride early while the rest of London is still abed. Say yes, Miss Rare-Foure."

She could think of no impediment, given that he was providing her with a horse.

"All right. My answer is yes."

Then she remembered. "What about Delia?"

He frowned. "I cannot be responsible for your maid if she has never ridden. I will bring a footman." After a pause, he added, "Maybe two."

Charlotte fixed him with a smile, raising her eyebrows. "Are you positive *two* chaperones will be enough?"

With an uncharacteristically broad grin that brought out his gorgeous dimple, he shook his head and gestured for her to lead the way downstairs.

"No, Miss Rare-Foure, I am not at all sure."

CHAPTER FOURTEEN

"Edward, we need to find a carpenter to make us a staircase, cheaply and with as little fuss as possible. I suppose also as swiftly as possible, for we shall have to close the shop when the building begins."

The boy's eyes were like saucers.

"Don't worry," Charlotte said, making fruit shapes as quickly as Edward made the marzipan for her. "I won't ask you to get to work with a saw and hammer."

They were not behind, yet nor were they ahead. Amity was producing some chocolates at home, and Charlotte had dusted off her skills to make more in the shop. Edward, with the help of the candy thermometer and the sand timer, was making excellent toffee using Bea's recipes.

"I'm just wondering how one goes about finding a reputable person. I have never needed anything built before. I know there is a carpenter's guild because they demolished their meeting hall a couple years ago, and they won't open their new one until next year." She chuckled. "All those carpenters and it's taking them over half a decade!"

"I live down that way, miss. Within spitting distance of the Aldgate Pump."

She knew of it. It marked the start of the shadier East End of London, but Edward puffed up his chest slightly and added, "You know they moved the pump a little to the west."

She supposed that somehow made his neighborhood seem less shabby. She was about to ask him about his living situation when he returned to the point of their discussion.

"The guild hall is already a beautiful building, miss, even though it's not finished. Right on the London Wall Road. Just below Finsbury Circus."

Charlotte shrugged. "I've hardly ever been to that area. Occasionally, I've gone to the docks with my father and my sisters, to source out sugar or cocoa beans or my almonds."

"That's all right, miss." He wrinkled his nose. "It gets ugly anyway the farther east you go."

And not very safe, either, from what Charlotte knew of the slums of Whitechapel. She hadn't liked the wharf area either, but had felt safe with her father.

"I could ask one of the carpenter's when I come past in the morning," Edward offered.

Frowning, she attached a small clove to the top of her faux marzipan peach. It wasn't the job for a boy, yet nor did she have time to go all the way across town, although it would take her past the Inns of Court. She shook her head. She didn't have time for dropping in and visiting with Barrister Charles Jeffrey Lambeth, if that were even allowed. There must be somewhere closer that one could hire a builder. Perhaps the business on Cavendish Square near The Langham, that made stained glass and vestments for churches. She'd passed it whenever she made deliveries to the hotel. Then she realized the answer.

"I am a cloth-headed ninny! The newspaper is the answer. I will look through the papers tonight with my dinner and come up with some prospects."

Edward looked disappointed so she relented.

"If you wish to stop by the guild hall and see what you can suss out," Charlotte told him, "I would be most obliged. Between the two of us, we shall discover the right man for the job of building our staircase."

WHILE CHARLOTTE HAD WRITTEN down the names of two builders from advertisements in the newspapers and brought them to the shop the following morning, when Edward came in, he not only had the name of a builder, he had the man himself.

"Miss, this is my uncle, Mr. Tufts. He says he can do the job."

Charlotte walked around from behind the counter, coming to a stop in the middle of the floor. While she felt a little peculiar meeting with a tradesman, and wished she had an inch or two more on her height to give her an air of authority, she was nonetheless in charge. The man had neither the same sandy-colored hair as his nephew, nor any hint of the boy's open-faced earnestness about him.

Instead, his gaze darted up and down her figure, then flickered around the shop, giving Charlotte a moment of discomfort. Yet, when the man met her eye again, he nodded in a friendly fashion.

"A tidy shop you have here, miss, and that's no mistake. My nephew told me you need stairs built, and I can help with that."

"Are you a master carpenter, Mr. Tufts? Or a journeyman?" Obviously, he was too old to be an apprentice.

"A builder, I am, miss. I can do a little of this, a little of that. Roofs, walls, stairs. It makes no matter what, I can do it."

She glanced at Edward who remained quiet.

"I'll get started working, miss," he said and disappeared in the back to get his apron.

"His mother's as pleased as Punch you've given the boy work to do."

"He's a hard worker, and capable, too."

"Takes after me," the man said, puffing up his chest.

A swaggerer, Charlotte thought, but if he was good at his job, then that was no matter.

"Where would you be wanting the stairs?" he asked, starting to stroll around.

"In that back corner. We're expanding to the second floor and the current staircase is outside."

"Expanding your sweet shop, are you? You must be doing quite well, and on this street, too. A lot of rich folk buying from you, are they?" He didn't pause for answers but went to the shelves where they kept their pretty tins for larger orders. Next, he banged on the wall a bit with the flat of his hand.

Charlotte frowned. *What could that tell him?*

"Good construction here," Mr. Tufts said when he saw her looking at him. Then he looked up. "Gots to cut a hole right there."

"Undoubtedly," Charlotte said. And then, into the silence, she asked, "Would you like to have a sample of confectionery?"

"Free?" he asked.

"Yes, of course."

"But I ain't buying nothing."

Charlotte smiled. "That's all right."

"A piece of toffee, then, lass. I need to go upstairs and see the lay of the land."

Charlotte thought about what had happened with Charles Jeffcoat upstairs. "I'll get Edward to take you up. I've got too much work to do to open. I wasn't expecting to see a builder this morning."

She called Edward out of the back room and gave him the key before giving his uncle a piece of toffee. The boy seemed oddly sullen, not meeting her eyes, but she would talk to him in private after his uncle left.

Before they went out, she asked, "Mr. Tufts, do you have references?"

The word she had never used before sounded strange and demanding. She'd never hired a maid or an employee, except Edward. But she knew one asked for such to determine a person's character and ability.

"Oh, yes, miss. Only the best. Edward, here, for one." He reached out and mussed the boy's hair, which he didn't seem to enjoy, for he ducked away.

Charlotte smiled. "I'm sure Edward will vouch for you, but I would like the names of some of your previous employers and the addresses of some residences or businesses where you built something."

He nodded. "That's fine, then. I'll send that along with Edward tomorrow. And I'll give you a price as soon as I see the upstairs."

"Thank you."

Whey they'd left, Charlotte felt as if she were getting somewhere. Maybe she wouldn't need to pursue any of the other builders from the newspapers, as it would be nice to work with Edward's family.

However, when the boy returned a few minutes later alone, he didn't look happy.

"What's wrong?" she asked him as he handed her the keys.

"Bit of an upset stomach, miss," he said. "I'd best get the display cases wiped down."

They were running a little behind, but she wasn't ready to let the matter drop.

"Do you think your uncle can do the job?"

"I believe so, miss. Why else would he have asked to come?"

Indeed!

"I assume he lives with you and you mentioned the stairs."

"Yes, miss."

"And do you want me to give him the work?" Frankly, it appeared to her as if Edward would rather she kept his uncle at bay, but she couldn't be sure.

The boy sighed and rubbed his stomach. "Yes, miss. It would help my mum."

Charlotte supposed the uncle was his mother's brother and would give a little of the money to support the family. From what she could tell, there was no father at home.

"Where is your father?" she asked him, having never pried before.

"Dead," Edward said and disappeared into the back.

AFTER AN EVENING AT the theatre—*without* the snapdragon and her husband—Charles was more firmly convinced that Charlotte was the woman he'd been searching for.

Not for all his life! He couldn't say anything as romantically silly as that. Yet now that he was considering taking a wife, she seemed to suit his needs. He wanted to touch her and kiss her and sniff her hair whenever they were close. That was a good thing. Moreover, he enjoyed conversing with her, and he especially liked her humor. She seemed the perfect mate.

And then, in the midst of enjoying her company, he recalled his father saying how Charles's mother had seemed the perfect companion, too. Fair of face but also charming, easy to converse with, attentive. Wifely. She'd also been strong-willed, intelligent, and terribly, crushingly fickle.

Watching Charlotte decide between the sparkling champagne and the wine during a ballet intermission, he hoped he didn't detect a thread of such fickleness in her. If he ever did, it would be the end of their blossoming relationship.

After he dropped Charlotte and Delia on Baker Street, Charles found himself missing her by the time he reached home, wanting her there, drinking a late-night brandy, warming his bed. All of that and more. *Did she want the same?* He had no way to know whether she was ready for such a responsibility. Nor could he tell if she would be true to him for the rest of their lives. *Was any woman capable of such?*

"She seemed a nice young lady," his father said, coming upon him carrying brandy up the stairs to his study.

Hesitating mid-step, Charles turned to where the earl stood at the bottom, in his housecoat as usual. "Who do you mean?"

"Don't play coy," his father said, ascending with one hand on the railing, looking older than his years. He needed a good haircut and to have his valet get him into some presentable clothing. "The pretty one who was here the other night," his father continued. "With the lovely laughter."

It wasn't the first time he'd mentioned her. "What makes you think I was thinking of her? Why are *you* still thinking and talking about her?"

"You've been out with her, haven't you?" The earl leaned over rudely and sniffed his son. "I can smell her fragrance."

Charles flinched. "Stop it. Yes, I escorted Miss Rare-Foure to the ballet this evening."

His father shrugged and passed him on the stairs. "As I said, a nice young woman."

Charles considered the back of his father as the earl headed along the hallway, shuffling in his slippers.

"Then you approve of her?" he called after him.

His father turned, scowling as he did. "Approve? Are you truly asking me that? You're not a green youth, nor is she your first paramour."

"I am not asking you to pass judgment upon a lover, of which she is definitely not one." Charles thought for an instant. *In fact, what was he asking?* He supposed he wanted help in not making the same mistake his father had. "One day, the woman I marry will be the Countess of Bentley."

"I suppose your wife can be no worse than the last countess, can she?" his father said.

They blinked at one another in shared misery over Charles's mother.

"Since I made such a poor choice" the earl continued, "blind to all the flaws that were plain as the nose upon my face, I cannot possibly counsel you on your choice. Nor am I positive any woman can be any better than . . . ," he trailed off as they never spoke her name. "They may all be disloyal, capricious vixens for all I know."

"That's not true," Charles protested. He knew Pelham's wife to be none of those things.

Again, the earl shrugged. "So you say." He turned and started down the hall again, then paused without looking back. "Your Rare girl, whatever her confounding name is, may be rare indeed, or as commonly deceitful as the rest of them. Only time will tell, I suppose."

With that, his father continued to bed, and Charles entered his study. She'd been in it just once, but he could imagine Charlotte there by the bookcase, laughing, looking breathtakingly beautiful.

His mother, what he could recall of her, had also been beautiful and joyful, laughing a lot, sunny and spirited. And then, in the blink of an eye, she'd left. He vaguely recalled she brushed a quick kiss across his forehead, touched his hair, then dashed out the front door. He had never imagined in his child's brain that it was the last time he would lay eyes upon her. That she would never even write to him.

How could a mother do such a thing to her child?

Charles sat down calmly even though, ridiculously, the old pain welled up in him. The memory remained strong of finding his father on his knees in the drawing room, holding a letter penned in the countess's scrawl, which the earl could barely read through his tears.

Charles sipped his brandy and wished he could erase the image of his strong, capable father, sobbing as he learned of his wife's betrayal and duplicity. After that, after putting his arms around him for a moment, knowing the earl didn't want his son there to witness his shame and grief, Charles had slipped out of the room quietly, a little afraid of the adult pain he'd encountered. He'd gone to bed, never to shed a tear for his horrid mother, and he'd never brought up the incident to his father.

Moreover, neither of them had ever forgiven her!

CHAPTER FIFTEEN

After she'd opened the shop and an hour had passed with no customers, Charlotte felt a prickle of alarm. Late afternoon the day before, it had also been slower than usual, as they often had a rush of people taking sweets home to enjoy after dinner. When that hadn't happened, she and Edward had easily cleaned up and turned the sign precisely at closing time.

After sending him home, Charlotte had spent another hour sketching what she wanted the upstairs to look like and making lists of things they would need.

The notion of a brand-new Rare Confectionery was thrilling, the most exciting thing she'd done since she'd shared the prior Season with Beatrice. And now, she was getting to use her gowns to go out with Lord Jeffcoat, a man who was effortlessly taking up all the space in her heart.

No longer did she experience pangs of sorrow at the notion of Lionel. Instead, she enjoyed the way her heartbeat sped up when she was about to see Charles.

She sighed, leaning against the counter, listening to the sound of . . . nothing except Edward working in the back room. An empty store and no bell tinkling. *What was going on?*

Suddenly, as if in answer to her prayers, the door opened. But it wasn't a customer. It was the Duke of Pelham, and upon his face was an expression of consternation. Immediately, her thoughts flew to her sister and the unborn baby.

Charlotte rushed around the counter. "What's wrong? Is it Amity? Is everything all right?"

"What?" He looked flummoxed. "Oh goodness! Yes, she's fine. She just misses you. You must stop by. How about having dinner with us tonight?"

"Yes, of course. But you didn't come here to invite me to your home."

"No, I wondered if you'd seen the *Evening Mail* last night?"

"Father doesn't care for their editor, so we don't subscribe. Why?"

"There was a story about Rare Confectionery in it yesterday. It will be out again today in the *Times*, too, which owns the *Mail*." He squared his shoulders. "To put it bluntly, it isn't favorable."

Charlotte was surprised into silence. The shop had never had a bad word written about it that she was aware. "Did you bring it, Your Grace?"

"Yes." He drew a piece of newsprint out of his pocket. It had been read and rolled as her father liked to say. "Amity insisted I bring it directly."

She took it but didn't look at it. "Tell me more about my sister."

Henry relaxed. "Larger, but good. She enjoys the time with that Percy boy when he comes over. It distracts her from her discomfort and boredom."

Charlotte nodded. "Edward has learned a lot from her." Unexpectedly, she realized she wished to speak to her brother-in-law about the viscount. After all, when would she ever have a chance to speak with Henry alone again?

"You probably know that your friend Lord Jeffcoat has been escorting me around town," she began.

The duke blushed slightly as if they were discussing something personal.

"I was aware, yes." Then he grimaced. "Not that Jeffcoat is gabbing like an old woman with a pot of gossip-water, you understand."

"No, I didn't think that. Anyway, I enjoy his company. I merely thought I would tell you that." She hesitated. This was a little awkward. "I wanted to make sure I had your blessing, I suppose. In any case, if you didn't want us to keep company, you would have said something to him, but you can also talk to me."

The duke's cheeks grew ruddier. "I think he is a fine man. What's more, I know you to be a wonderful young woman. I see no impediment to your keeping company."

She nodded. "Thank you. I had wondered if he suffered from some great lost love. There is something about him, a little cautious and sometimes sad."

Henry was silent a moment. "Jeffcoat did suffer severe heartbreak when he was younger. It affected him greatly, although he won't admit it. I hope he tells you about it as it is not for me to do. Do you understand?"

Nodding, at least she'd had her concerns confirmed, even if all the duke had done was pique her curiosity further. Then she rattled the paper in her hand. "Why is Amity overly concerned about an article in the paper? Even a bad one can hardly be that bad."

His face froze.

"Can it?" she asked, fear clutching at her stomach.

"You had best read it. Amity thinks you may have to start some new advertisements to counteract the effects. Anyway, do not worry. The article is rather bleak and could hurt sales in the foreseeable future, but you have a tidy, economical business here, and even a short downturn in profits won't hurt too much." He tipped his hat, nodded, and turned to the door. "We'll see you tonight for dinner. Come at seven o'clock. You can visit with your sister beforehand. Maybe I'll have a surprise for you."

Scarcely listening when the bell signaled his departure, she noticed the paper was folded to reveal the offending story, written by a Miss J. Whittaker. She had never heard of her.

"While the shopgirl tried to help, she clearly hadn't a clue what was in the confectionery being sold . . . . There was a great variation in quality between one sweet and another, particularly the chocolates, which were a mystery of good and not good at all . . . . The treacle toffee, heralded by many as superb, may have, indeed, been so in the past, but this writer found it to be sadly below anyone's notion of what is tasty. Its flavor could best be described as distinctly *unpleasant*. In a word, it was *inedible* . . . ."

When she finished disparaging the sweets, the writer went on to malign the shop: "It was not as clean as one would wish. Granted, the day was a rainy one, but then with our London weather nearly always containing a few raindrops, that cannot be used as an excuse for a grimy, slippery floor . . . . Understaffing was the reason given for the shop's appearance . . . . The shopgirl, while attentive at first, seemed to lack focus, unable to keep track of which customer she was helping."

That last sentence stung as much as any of them, and they all, in fact, hurt Charlotte's pride. And the reporter's conclusion, stated in the paper for all to read, was plainly the reason for the sudden lack of customers: "While Rare Confectionery has been relied upon in the past for quality treats, it has clearly fallen into disorder and ignominy. For the same cost of their sweets, or even cheaper, delicious Cadbury's and Fry's confections can be found conveniently in many a shop in the form of fancy boxes and bars, without having to take a special trip to New Bond Street to be sold overpriced, inferior confectionery."

For goodness sake! Even Charlotte wanted to rush out and get a Cadbury bar to take the nasty taste of the article out of her mouth.

Overpriced, inferior confectionery!

The duke had said they had an economical business and thought they would weather this little downturn easily. But Charlotte had just doubled the size of their space—and their monthly rent. And the shop's bell hadn't tinkled all morning. Tonight, she would finally tell him and Amity what she'd done.

Sending Edward out on the deliveries, she had time on her hands to get ahead by making fresh marzipan and starting to create the pigs people enjoyed with cherry juice blush to their skin.

By noon, they'd had a few customers, people who hadn't read the paper and a couple regular patrons, but it hadn't been their usual flow. Edward had been busy making toffee, which Charlotte tasted at every stage. It was satisfactory. She wasn't even certain she could tell the difference if pushed between his and Beatrice's. He was following her sister's recipe to the letter. If that awful woman returned—and naturally, Charlotte now knew precisely who had written the article—the reporter would find it not merely edible but delicious.

She shook her head at the realization that one scathing review in a popular paper could do such dreadful damage. Then she had a thought. That certainly meant a good review could *restore* their reputation. The best thing would be to entice Miss Whittaker to return, stuff her smug cake-hole with delicious sweets, and make her recant.

However, that seemed unlikely. Not to mention dangerous. If something went wrong—and Charlotte had learned literally anything could go wrong at any moment— that might mean disaster. And it would be writ in the *Evening Mail* for all to see.

Perhaps she could entice another reporter into the shop. She supposed if she went to place an advertisement, she could ask to speak with the paper's editor and determine if he would send out someone to review the shop. On the other hand, she was about to cut a hole in the ceiling and would have to close for a few days. She had to hold off until that was finished before she invited anyone in.

Perhaps a simple written rebuttal was in order. Wandering back around the other side of the counter, she looked through the paper again. As expected, there were letters from the public printed for everyone to read. Most were grievances and criticisms—about the water pressure in the East End, trash blowing into shops on Oxford Street, even a horse carcass left to rot north of Hyde Park, as well as the ever-present complaints about the stench of the Thames. A letter protesting a bad day at a confectioner's shop seemed futile. Irksome as it was to let the article go unchallenged, writing a letter to the paper's editor would be a watery defense.

With the hours stretching endlessly and passing slowly, Charlotte welcomed the return of Edward's uncle.

"Here I am, miss, ready to do an honest job for honest pay."

He slid a piece of paper across the counter toward her. Poor penmanship made the words hard to make out, and she realized they were mostly misspelled once she recognized them as street names. Below these were what she assumed were people's surnames, all jumbled together.

"All them's work I've done and done well. Now, about the price." And he went on to discuss the cost of lumber and nails, balusters and a handrail, posts and newels, risers and—

"Perhaps if you could write all that down," she asked.

His face soured. "I already wrote all of that," he protested, pointing to the single sheet. "I haven't got time to compose a novel for you."

Fair enough. "What's the final cost, Mr. Tufts?"

"Not too dear, not too cheap, you'll find it perfectly reasonable."

"What is it?" she asked again.

He named his price, and she did think it fair since she had no idea what the price of a set of stairs should be, but his cost wouldn't empty their account.

"How long will it take? I'll have to close the shop, and I want to do that for as brief a time as possible."

"Yes, miss, of course. I'll need the money up front to buy the supplies, and I can start as soon as I have them and finish as soon as I'm done."

She stared hard at him. *Was he giving her any real answers?*

"An estimate of how long once you start, please, Mr. Tufts."

"Shouldn't take longer than three days."

She nodded. That was quicker than she had hoped. "Do you work alone?"

He hesitated. "Yes. If I had another man with me, I'd have to charge you more."

"Of course." That made sense. "Give me a little time to think about this," she told him. After all, she needed to follow up with some of the places he'd given her, and she needed to gather the funds. The only thing that gave her some assurance in this new endeavor was that the man was Edward's uncle. Since she'd given his nephew a job, he would do right by her.

"Can't wait too long," he interjected quickly. "I've got other work to do. Getting busy, you know. If you don't hire me now, you may have to wait longer, and I don't know when I will be able to fit you in. I was doing this quickly and cheaply as a favor, being as how you hired Edward."

"I appreciate that, Mr. Tufts." But she wouldn't be rushed. "I'll let you know," she added firmly.

"I'll come back tomorrow for your answer," he said, just as firmly, turned, and left, without even asking to say hello to his nephew.

Well!

"Edward, do you feel comfortable handling the front while I run out on some errands?"

He appeared through the blue curtain. "Yes, miss. It doesn't seem as if I'll be run off my feet."

No, it certainly didn't. Grabbing her jacket, hat, and gloves, Charlotte set off in a hackney to see some of the places Mr. Tufts had listed, and hopefully, speak to some of his previous employers. Also, as she was no ninny, she would drop into the offices of two of the builders she'd gleaned from the newspapers.

After all, she wasn't trying to get a mansion built, just a simple staircase. *How hard could it be?* She and Edward could probably manage it themselves. That made her giggle as she directed the driver to the first address.

CHARLOTE WAS A LITTLE early to arrive at her sister's house on St. James's Place. Amity had turned the massive antiquated home into a modern and welcoming one over the past year with bright, cheerful wallpaper and soothing paint, new rugs, and some soft furnishings.

"There's my lovely girl," Amity said, not getting up but dropping her knitting project onto her lap and holding out her hands.

Charlotte ran over, grasped her sister's hands, and took the space beside her on the pretty rose-colored sofa.

"You look wonderful," she told Amity, whose cheeks had filled out along with the rest of her. "The picture of health."

"Thank you. I do feel good except for being tired. Anyway, I'm glad you came."

"Where is your dashing duke?" Charlotte asked.

"Around somewhere. He'll be in shortly. What do you think?" Amity held up the knitting needles with cream-colored yarn and a mass of tangled wool.

Charlotte couldn't help it. She burst out laughing. "What is it?"

Amity didn't bother to look miffed. "First, I thought I would knit the baby a bonnet, but rather quickly, I decided it had best be something straight, like a blanket."

"What changed your mind to making a spider's web?" Charlotte asked, lifting one edge of the disaster. They laughed together.

"I shall buy you a soft, beautiful bonnet and a blanket for the baby," Charlotte promised. "Please don't inflict this disaster on my little lambkin, be it a boy or a girl."

Picking up the knitting, needles and all, Amity tossed it into the chair across from her as the door to the drawing room opened. The duke entered followed by Lord Jeffcoat.

At once, Charlotte knew the viscount was the surprise her brother-in-law had mentioned.

"Have you given up on the knitting?" the duke asked. "But you had me buy you a cart load of wool for that bonnet."

"It was a *blanket*," Amity corrected, as Lord Jeffcoat nodded in greeting and moved forward to lift the snarled wool from the chair before sitting.

"Was it truly?" he asked. "I think you're both wrong. I think it's a . . . ," he paused and lifted it up, then held it out, then shook his head. "I'm sorry, it is like nothing I've ever seen."

Charlotte smiled at the viscount's attempt to placate. He looked particularly handsome in dark gray, with a cream cravat.

"You are all having fun at my expense," Amity said. "And I don't mind a bit! Give the wool away to someone who has more patience."

"Don't give up, dear sister." Charlotte patted Amity's hand. "Many find knitting to be entertaining. Why don't I find you an easy pattern to try? You have loads of time on your hands now that young Edward is nearly as good a chocolatier as you are."

"*Whoa!*" Both of the men exclaimed at once, as if reining in a wayward horse.

Charlotte chuckled. "My sister knows two things, gentlemen. One, that I think the world of her and believe her to be the best chocolatier ever, no matter that we tease each other. And two, she knows we need Edward to become as good as he possibly can so we don't offer our customers inferior confectionery."

"Which brings us to the newspaper article," Amity said. "It sounds as though you had a particularly bad day."

"What article?" Charles asked, and the duke filled him in before either of the ladies had a chance to.

"In my defense," Charlotte said, "I was unaware that the confectionery I was selling that day had been made almost exclusively by Edward. Bea never said a word."

Amity shook her head. "Nor did I. I am truly sorry. I had him here for a couple days of experimenting. I had no idea what he made would end up on the shelves. I should have paid more attention."

"My duchess is a little scatter-brained of late," the duke said, looking fondly at her. "I find it utterly charming." He crouched down beside her, lifted her hand to his lips, and kissed it.

Charlotte and the viscount exchanged a glance and a bemused smile until the duke took his seat.

"Be that as it may," Charlotte said, "the reporter was not in the least bit charmed by anything at Rare Confectionery. I really cannot blame her. And I must hope I can find another reporter to give us a glowing review and undo the damage." She took a deep breath. "But that will have to wait until after the construction starts."

Three faces turned to her, although the viscount knew about everything.

Amity placed her hands upon her burgeoning stomach, and repeated, "Construction?"

CHAPTER SIXTEEN

"Yes," Charlotte declared. It was time to tell her. "I am expanding Rare Confectionery."

"You are expanding . . . ," Amity began and trailed off. "But I don't see how that's possible. Where are you expanding it to?"

"The only thing we need is a staircase," Charlotte assured her. "I've signed a lease for the second floor."

"You've signed a lease," her sister repeated, and Charlotte wished Amity would stop doing that.

"I don't think it's an optimal time," the duke pointed out. "I believe you said your business was down already."

Amity looked alarmed, but Charlotte didn't want her sister getting the least bit upset.

"As I said, another article, favorable this time, can bring it back up again, and all the problems that the reporter encountered have been solved. Except for being a little short-staffed."

"Your staff is rather short," Lord Jeffcoat pointed out. They all looked at him. Charlotte believed it was the first jest she'd ever heard him speak. While she appreciated the attempt at levity, her sister still looked concerned.

"Edward may be short, but he does the work of a full-grown man, and he's picked up on making confectionery like a duck takes to water."

"But . . . but . . . what will we do with the upstairs?" Amity asked. "How many more chocolates and trays of toffee and marzipan pears will we need? And what happened to the pillow maker."

"Her son took her away," Charlotte said. "I thought he was harsh at first, but he was a good man looking after his mother. Just as any of us would do. The duke for the dowager, us for our mother, and," she paused and looked at Lord Jeffcoat, who was frowning. The duke shook his head.

She continued, "And now we have all that room to create a café."

"A café!" Amity exclaimed.

"Will there be coffee?" the duke asked, a well-known lover of the rich brew.

"Yes, naturally," Charlotte said, "and our confectionery and pots of chocolate served just the way Amity likes and tea." She decided to keep talking until someone said what a good idea it was. "I was thinking it would be lovely to hire a *pâtissier*, but he or she would need a place to work. There is a kit and cargo worth of space upstairs, but as Lord Jeffcoat reminded me, we shall need plumbing and an oven if we are to have a kitchen. A pity the pillow woman never put one in. All she had was the tiniest coal stove for making her tea."

"In a pinch, that small stove is all you need to make coffee," the duke mused. Then he turned to his friend. "Hold on. Jeffcoat, you knew about this?"

The viscount nodded. "It was not my news to tell, Pelham, so don't become huffish with me. You're like a brother to me, but a woman's secrets are her own to disclose, or not."

Charlotte liked him all the more for saying that.

"Plumbing and an oven," Amity echoed. "And Mother is pleased with all this?"

Charlotte pursed her lips.

"Oh," Amity said. "I thought it was only me who didn't know."

Shaking her head, Charlotte explained, "Beatrice doesn't know either, because she left for Scotland and the lease had to be signed immediately. Elsewise, our landlord might have put any type of business above our heads."

"But now sales are down," Amity said.

"That won't last. And we have money in savings to create a beautiful space upstairs."

"You and young Mr. Percy won't be able to handle all that."

"That's true. We will have to hire more employees. At least one. A server to take the orders to the tables."

"Look at her," the viscount said. "Miss Rare-Foure, you have grown radiant with excitement."

She put her hands to her cheeks. "I admit, I find the challenge of creating a new experience for our customers at Rare Confectionery to be beyond thrilling. Maybe we'll even have ices like—"

"Gunter's," Amity filled in. "You always loved that place. We all did, but you the most." Then she tilted her head. "But do you know anything about hiring a server?"

"No," Charlotte said, "nor a builder." She made a decision to put her sister's mind at ease, even though, until that second, she hadn't made her mind up about Mr. Tufts. "But I managed it. We now have a builder with references who gave us a good price, and he can start immediately. I think he will treat us well because he is related to Edward."

As she'd hoped, that information caused both the duke and Amity to relax. After all, they all had acknowledged she'd done well to hire the boy. There was no need to mention she'd been unable to speak with anyone whom Mr. Tufts had worked for. She'd seen some impressive residences but had no idea what work he had done at any of them. She could hardly knock on doors—yet, in fact, she had done that at one townhouse, and the housekeeper said she thought she recognized the builder's name. The woman had been unable to say for sure, nor did she know the scope of the work.

Every address she'd had time to investigate was tidy and well-kept. Any work he'd done must have been good if it had been accepted by those people. Then she'd stopped in at a builder's office whose address was in an advertisement in the newspaper. His clerk had been rude as if he couldn't believe Charlotte was in a position to hire anyone. When she'd insisted on being given a price for a staircase, he'd told her an exorbitant sum and that nothing could be done for a month.

Edward's uncle had suddenly seemed like the best choice, all things considered. Moreover, Charlotte was pleased to be able to tell Amity she had things well in hand.

"I think we should toast to Miss Rare-Foure for what she's accomplished," Charles said.

"That may be a bit premature," Charlotte protested, while feeling warm and happy.

"No," Amity said, "I agree with Lord Jeffcoat. We are lucky to have you running the shop." Then she added, "I am sure Mother will be pleased."

If only her sister had said that more convincingly.

When the Pelham's butler, Mr. Giles, announced dinner was ready and the four of them, with Amity decidedly waddling, went into the dining room, Charlotte was on Charles's arm. As he drew out her chair, it reminded her of the first time they met and dined together at that same table a couple years earlier.

It had been a momentous night when she'd accompanied Amity to a party at the Pelham residence before her sister became engaged to the duke. In fact, it was the night Henry was supposed to propose to another. Instead, as Charlotte learned later, it had been the night that ended his previous relationship. She'd been partnered with

Charles at dinner and recalled making the viscount laugh when she'd exclaimed over the fancy dishes being presented.

Glancing at him now, across the table, she wondered if he'd thought her half a fool when she'd simply been trying to be entertaining. Later that night, standing up for her sister, she'd told off a room full of nobility and not regretted it. *Would her previous behavior—some had called it rude and outrageous—make him think twice about her suitability?*

CHARLES COULD IMAGINE HAVING many gatherings like this, entertaining and relaxing, with good friends and good food. And Charlotte. He glanced at her across the Pelham's dining table. *Even better if she became his wife.*

He had made his decision, and simply had to bring it to fruition. The notion of waiting until her parents returned so he could ask her father properly for permission was appealing However, it seemed the duration of their time away from London was unknown. Over the pottage, Charlotte and the duchess discussed letters received from their mother, filled with vagaries and lack of detail. If he read between the lines, he would guess their father had taken a downturn in his health and their mother didn't wish to worry the sisters.

Besides, it wasn't as if these were the dark ages, or even the time of Prinny and his ilk. Charles knew many a man who had secured the woman's consent *before* asking her father. Far less humiliating that way as far as he could see. Not much could be worse than having Mr. Foure give him permission, only to have Charlotte then say no, thank you.

He considered what else his peers did before becoming engaged. He would relinquish the age-old right to study her family's bank account or inspect her ancestral lineage. He didn't even particularly care about her family's political connections or leanings, although a shopkeeper's politics were generally known.

Moreover, Pelham had smoothed the path in their inner circle for taking as wife a girl not of their class, and elevating her to the nobility. It was still uncommon, to be sure, but was less extraordinary than it was in yesteryear. And Charles didn't mind in the least if his wife ran a shop, any more than he thought it strange to be a barrister who was also a viscount.

As for his own father, the earl wouldn't stop him or say anything to gainsay the arrangement. On the other hand, it was unlikely he would give his blessing, disgusted as he was by his own marital disaster.

Charles sighed, thinking how that had defined much of his father's life, and in some ways, his own.

"That was a deep sigh, Lord Jeffcoat," Charlotte said. "I hope not one of discontent when this roast is perfectly delicious."

He smiled at her. "Certainly not one of discontent. There are potatoes smothered in cream on my plate. What could ever possibly be wrong?"

"And I believe dessert will even outshine the potatoes," the duchess promised.

"Truly?"

Pelham grinned at the other end of the table. "My wife enjoys her sweets. It will probably be something with chocolate."

"Perfect," Charles said.

What a contrast to a few years back when Pelham and Waverly were his dining companions, often at a greasy chophouse if not at their club. How much nicer with lovely ladies who smelled floral and citrusy! And instead of Waverly's often sarcastic or even cynical wit, they were treated to the Rare-Foure sisters' charm and clear thinking. But thinking of the devil . . .

"What is Waverly up to?"

The duchess looked chagrinned. "I confess, he was not on my guest list tonight for I couldn't come up with a suitable dining partner for him on short notice."

The duke laughed. "My dear wife has taken to heart the rules of our set. Better to cut someone out than to have an odd number at the table."

"*Oh,*" the duchess moaned. "You're right. I was a ninny. I should have simply invited him. Who cares about the symmetry when I might have hurt his feelings!"

Pelham looked at Charles, and they both laughed.

"Really, my love," the duke assured her, "Waverly isn't going to care one whit about missing a dinner, not even with potatoes. He's off doing something he finds exciting, I know it."

"And what would that be? What does a gentleman of your standing find exciting?" Charlotte asked, looking at her brother-in-law.

Charles looked at him, too, watching the man squirm. "Yes, tell us, Duke," he commanded, adding to his friend's discomfit.

It was the duchess who laughed and rescued her husband. "Don't tease him, Lord Jeffcoat. First of all, there is no one of his standing," she insisted, looking only at Pelham, her gaze full of love.

Charles didn't think of himself as a soppy sentimentalist, but he would vow he could feel the duchess's love go from one end of the table to the other. His glance shot to Charlotte, who seemed to sense the same thing. Her beautiful brown eyes widened, and then her lips broke into a sweet smile. At that moment, he very much wanted her to look at him the way the duchess was gazing at Pelham.

"Second of all," the duchess continued. "I know you two would be at your club, playing billiards or cards, and drinking too much brandy if you weren't here being tamed by the gentler sex."

"Tamed?" Charles repeated. *Is that what happened to a man when he married?*

The duke found his tongue. "Thank you, my love. I admire how well you know me. I also have appreciated how you've never stopped me going to White's to spend time with my friends."

They looked at each other again as if they were alone. This time, Charlotte cleared her throat.

"Enough of that moon-gazing at one another. I recall in Godey's *Lady's Book* that the host and hostess are not supposed to make their guests feel as if they are spoiled pudding, to be ignored."

"I would never ignore spoiled pudding," the duke said. "I would make sure my footman came in and swept it into the rubbish bin."

"Henry!" the duchess exclaimed. "My sister is right. We can make moon eyes at each other later. Or at least, you can do so straight into the looking-glass, for I shall be asleep directly after dessert."

Charlotte shook her head. "Honestly, sister, you are also not supposed to make your guests feel as if they've stayed too long and are keeping you up." She sipped her wine and added, "Sometimes, I think I would make a better duchess."

"Or a viscountess." Charles realized he'd said the words aloud when they all turned to him. His head swiveled as he looked from his best friend's amused expression to the duchess's with her raised eyebrows, before finally, his glance landed on Charlotte.

Her lips were parted, the full lower one caught between open and closed. She was surprised at him voicing such a thing, almost as much as he was, and her cheeks had turned a pretty shade of pink. He assumed his own had, too.

"Or a baroness or a . . . princess," he stumbled on, trying to make them believe he hadn't meant anything by his remark.

"Why don't we have dessert in the drawing room? This dining room is too large for four," Amity said, proving she was a good hostess after all, breaking the tension-laden moment. Before she could do aught but set down her napkin beside her plate, the duke was sprinting around the table, there like a flash of lightning to pull out his wife's chair and assist her from her seat.

Charlotte waited for Charles to do the same, although he did it at a less frenetic pace. "I'm sorry if I embarrassed you," he murmured close to her ear.

He felt a little shiver go through her, but she placed her arm on his, letting him escort her in their hosts' wake.

"This was rather different than the first time we dined as partners in this room," she reminded him.

"At least that night, we were seated next to each other and not five feet across a table. It was easier to converse. Tonight, every word seemed to echo around the room."

"Every word," she agreed.

And he knew she referred to only one: *viscountess*. It still echoed in his own head. But he would not say anything more about that tonight. This was hardly the romantic setting he'd envisioned for proposing.

As they entered Pelham's drawing room—vastly different from his own in that it had cushions and soft flickering candlelight and attractive things—Charles had to confess to himself he had never envisioned how or when to propose. Except he knew they should be alone. *How on earth could he be alone with her?*

"You're frowning, Jeffcoat," his friend observed, pouring brandy as the ladies took their seats.

Charles shook it off and took the proffered glass as a footman brought in a tray with cake slathered in chocolate sauce. The duchess clapped her hands with delight. Obviously, the duke was right about his wife's love of dessert.

Then he wondered precisely how one was supposed to keep a young woman's reputation from being marred yet find a way to get her alone to ask for her hand. If he showed up at her home on Baker Street, he supposed he could ask for a moment without the ever-present Delia sitting close by.

He watched Charlotte, as she lifted a forkful of cake to her mouth, ate it, and savored it, her tongue appearing to lick her lips before she recalled where she was. Quick as lightning her tongue disappeared, and she lifted a napkin to her mouth. At the same time, her glance fell upon him.

Charles decided he had best be quick about asking her, lest she start to think him rude for staring whenever he was in her presence. And then it dawned on him the best place to get her alone.

Should he write up a persuasive argument as he would for the judge? Hopefully, he wouldn't need flowery, romantic words—simply the truth.

CHAPTER SEVENTEEN

"Before your uncle begins the stairs, we shall have to sell all the confectionery we have and not make any more," Charlotte told Edward when he returned from making deliveries. "Stop making toffee. I'm going to put it on sale as I did the day I had no idea what was in the chocolates."

She returned to the front, then strode back through the curtain. "Except not a half-price sale. Something smaller but will yet pique their interest."

He nodded.

"I think 10 percent is too small. Perhaps 25 percent off."

He nodded again, so she turned and left him. Speaking with Edward was not the same as having her sisters there to discuss issues. They would certainly have had an opinion.

Then a thought dawned on her, and she called out to him, "However, we need to have confectionery for our deliveries. I fear if we don't continue them uninterrupted, those establishments might seek their sweets elsewhere."

Edward didn't respond.

"Can you tally up how much we need for five days?" she requested. "I'll go over the amounts later and make certain. But five days will give your uncle plenty of time, and then we'll do nothing but deliveries until the dust clears. Once the sawing and hammering has ceased, we shall begin again to sell down here and, at the same time, we'll start to decorate upstairs."

Still, Edward said nothing.

"I've already ordered tables," she persisted. "Six of them. I saw one in the window of Chunley's Emporium with a square marble top and black lacquered legs that have the sweetest gilt decoration. I think they're perfect."

Only silence met her remarks.

"Edward, are you there?"

"Yes, miss."

Charlotte sighed. She had to work this out herself. She must continue to supply the hotels and restaurants but close the shop to regular customers. Perhaps she should put a sign on the door saying where one could find their chocolates.

She frowned. Customers would not stay at The Langham in order to eat Rare Confectionery, but they might go to one of the restaurants.

There was much to think about. Not just with the shop but also with Lord Jeffcoat. When she was alone with a few minutes to examine her emotions, she could honestly say she now had a *tendre* for the man. More than that. Her heart leaped when she saw him and beat a little faster when he was near. Or when he spoke to her. Or when he gave her a certain look and smiled crookedly. Moreover, she was desperate for him to kiss her again.

She knew she shouldn't let him take liberties with her person, but it was such a nice liberty.

With the tinkling of the bell, her thoughts were wrenched from such pleasant thoughts to the matters at hand. Mr. Tufts stopped by as promised.

"I would like to hire you," she said, "but I shall pay you half the total cost at the start, and the rest after the work is completed." The duke had suggested such a compromise, and when Mr. Tufts agreed, Charlotte shook his hand firmly, feeling as though she'd driven a hard bargain.

"I'll be back tomorrow to begin," he said and left with a bank cheque.

"Edward," she called out. "You just missed your uncle."

After a moment, his face appeared at the velvet curtain.

"He's starting tomorrow."

The boy nodded. While she wouldn't say he was grim-faced, he'd definitely been quiet recently, even a tad sullen.

"Is there anything you wish to speak to me about?"

His eyes widened. "No, miss. I must get home."

"Very well. I'll see you in the morning."

"Yes, miss."

After he left, Charlotte turned the sign, locked the door, and began to write out a notice to put in the window explaining about their temporary closure. She ought to have built time into her schedule to have one printed, but it would have to do.

When her stomach started to growl, realizing she'd skipped lunch, she sucked on a large piece of toffee, hoping Lydia would have something hot and delicious for dinner. At that thought, she put another piece into her mouth and then heard a knock on the glass.

Lord Jeffcoat!

Waving to him, she rushed around the counter, then slowed her steps. He would think her a silly goose, indeed, if she went running to the door. With dignity, she let him in, smiled, and drooled golden brown toffee onto her apron.

"Rajb!" she tried to exclaim with her teeth partly stuck together. *Double drats!*

"Miss Rare-Foure, are you well?"

Pointing to her mouth while fishing a handkerchief from her pocket, she wiped her chin, dabbed at her otherwise white apron, and said, "Offee."

"Toffee," he agreed, looking at her bulging cheeks, and then he started to laugh.

So much for her dignity! Charlotte couldn't even join in his merriment. Instead, she hollowed her cheeks and sucked hard, then tried to masticate the wad of solidified treacle.

Holding up her index finger to grab his attention, she gestured for him to shut and lock the door before she turned away. *Good Lord!* She had dribbled in front of the viscount!

Sweet mother! Would he ever think her desirable again? She hurried into the back room, put the kettle on, and lit the flame beneath it. A quick cup of tea would do the trick.

When she turned around, Charles was behind her.

"Are you all right?" he asked.

She nodded, not trusting herself to try and speak yet. She'd been a greedy guts, and no doubt about it.

Pointing to the kettle, she asked, "Eee?"

He shook his head. "I came to speak with you. It's just as well that you are indisposed to talking at present."

Glancing around, he spied Beatrice's blue stool, now often used by Edward, and drew it over toward her. "Sit," he ordered.

Their eyes locked, and she knew something important was coming. Swiftly, she did as he requested.

"I have reached a certain stage of my life when I find myself ready to have a helpmate, a partner in the day-to-day events, a good friend living under my roof."

Gracious! He was going to propose. She considered his words thus far. There was nothing particularly loving about them. A helpmate could be the nursery nanny or a chamber maid. A partner belonged at work. And as for a good friend, he ought to buy himself a dog, which would not only be under his roof but also under his bed at night.

While making smacking noises with her lips, she swallowed a chunk of the toffee, and it promptly stuck in her throat. Good thing there was no reporter there to witness the dangers of Rare Confectionery's treacle toffee.

"In short, Miss Rare-Foure, I have not been on the hunt for a wife, but since knowing you, I find myself thinking about such a position more than I ever have."

Such a position? It sounded as though she had been auditioning for the role of viscountess without knowing it. Perhaps his kisses hadn't been driven by passion or desire to taste her lips but simply to see if she was good enough at the act to become his spouse.

Abruptly, she rose and went to the stove, where she quickly prepared the brown-Betty teapot with loose leaves and then poured in the boiling water.

Charles began to speak again, but she held up her hand to halt him. Not bothering with their blue, knitted tea cozy for she wasn't going to let the tea steep hardly at all, she opened the cold box and splashed milk into her mug. Snatching for the sugar container, she grabbed up a dash with her fingers, then froze. He would think her a barbarian, but it was too late.

Reaching for a spoon—it was a large unwieldly tablespoon and not a delicately appropriate teaspoon to her chagrin—she stirred while she poured the tea, then waited a moment to let any leaves settle.

"Miss Rare-Foure, if I may continue, I have much to recommend the union—"

Again, she held up her hand. If Charles couldn't even call her by her first name, they were not at a place in which he ought to be asking for her hand. She wanted to stop him before he did. Once he made the offer, for apparently all the wrong reasons as far as she was concerned, then she would have to say no. His manly pride would be hurt, and they would have to stop keeping company, which would destroy any chance they had of growing closer.

Sipping the tea, she tilted her head back slightly, keeping her gaze on his startled face, while she let the hot beverage melt the toffee that was stuck to her back teeth. *Using tea as a gargling liquid—another barbaric moment.*

If he still wanted to marry her, she ought to grab onto him with both hands. But she wouldn't do that. She wanted him to be absolutely head-over-heels in love with her the way the duke was with Amity and Mr. Carson was with Bea. The way she was starting to feel over him, if she could just stop thinking herself somewhat unsuitable.

In any case, having seen such love, she could settle for no less. Perhaps all they needed was a little more time.

"Lord Jeffcoat," she said at last. "You caught me at an unfortunate moment. I let my hunger get the best of me and thought two pieces of toffee would be wise. Obviously, it wasn't."

"That's quite all right," he said. "As I mentioned I came to speak to you and wasn't expecting you to do too much talking back."

"Really?" *What a strange thing to say.* Then again, she supposed lawyers liked to persuade to their satisfaction and not hear a lengthy argument in return.

"There is only one word I want to hear after I ask my question," he said. "Will you sit again?"

"Are you sure you don't want a cup of tea?" she asked, stalling as she considered how to stop him.

"No, really, I don't. If this goes well, I'll have a celebratory glass of champagne at my club. If it doesn't, I'll have a soothing glass of brandy in my study."

She couldn't help rolling her eyes. The man was a dolt of the first order.

"Lord Jeffcoat, if my answer were satisfactory, I would assume you would have champagne with me, not with your friends at your gentlemen's club. But I believe you will find yourself in your study."

He paused, apparently considering the ramifications of her words.

"Are you turning me down?" he asked, his tone incredulous.

"No," she said quickly. "I am not letting you ask."

Silence met her response, and then, "Why not?"

"Because I don't wish to turn you down, but you are asking me prematurely, don't you think?"

He frowned and reached for her mug. Surprised, she released it to him and watched him take a sip, then drain it completely. All the while, he continued to look concerned.

Handing the empty cup back to her, he sat upon the stool, something a gentleman in his right mind would never do, not while she remained standing. Clearly, she had bewildered him into discourteous behavior.

Running a hand through his hair, he stared at her, his deep blue eyes puzzled. "I thought it was the goal of all young women to be asked for their hand."

She smiled wryly, setting the cup aside. "You believe our goal is merely to be asked, not even the loftier goal of getting married?"

"Well, first the proposal, of course," he said.

"You think a young woman wants simply to be asked by *anyone*," she mused.

His cheeks flushed a ruddy color. "I am *not* just anyone."

Ah. The viscount had his pride, as she suspected. The nobility was a different breed of horse altogether. Not that she didn't think every man had a dose of conceit, but these titled men would naturally consider themselves to be the choicest supplicants for a woman's hand. And they would be right. Nevertheless, they couldn't expect the instant devotion of every female, nor a positive response in every case.

"No, you are not just anyone. To me, you have been a good friend."

He winced.

"And more than that," she added quickly, thinking of the way he'd touched her and the exquisite sensation of his lips upon hers. "We have had many pleasant hours together, and I hope more to come." That was as honest as she could be without asking him if he thought he might fall hopelessly in love with her.

"I see," he said.

Did he?

"Miss Rare-Foure—"

"Charlotte, please, at least when we're alone."

"Normally, we cannot be alone. I thought we might come to an agreement, and then it wouldn't be so terribly irresponsible for us to be caught together. Although it could still damage your reputation."

Abruptly, he reached out and took her hand and drew her into the space directly in front of him, between his outstretched legs. With him on the stool and her standing, her head was above his, and he had to look up to her.

"You are a puzzling female," he said. "If I'd started my proposal to any other, I am certain she would have let me finish at the very least. You do like me, don't you?"

She couldn't help smiling. "I do."

"Then tell me what you want," he implored.

It was an unusual view, looking down on a man. They always stood until one sat down and then they stood the moment one rose again. She'd always thought it was some sort of chivalric custom, but now, realizing how differently she felt seeing him below her, Charlotte couldn't help wondering if men did it to maintain a perspective of power and authority. She must remember to ask her sisters what they thought of her notion.

Taking stock of his brown hair and eyebrows and the bridge of his fine nose, thinking it might be quite wonderful to gaze upon him every day for a lifetime, finally, she sighed.

"I want what anyone wants, and I think you can figure it out on your own." She started to step back, but he kept hold of her hand.

"Do you think I can give it to you, Charlotte?"

She caught her lower lip between her teeth. Hearing him say her name gave her a shivery feeling. She understood why men and women didn't go around saying each other's given names. It was an intimate thing, and the wrong person doing so would be too familiar.

But Charles Jeffcoat was not the wrong person.

"Yes."

"That was the answer I was hoping for earlier," he teased.

"Now you have it. I think you will figure out what I'm saying, but only time will tell for sure."

He tugged slightly, trying to get her to close the space between them, to lean down and either kiss him or let herself be kissed. That wasn't going to change anything, nice as it would be. To her detriment, though, it might make him think her a little loose for stopping a proposal but not a kiss.

"Do you know what I would like to do?" she asked.

His smiled widened, and since they were inches apart, she could see the interest sparkling in his eyes.

"I would like to move all the empty tins from the front of the shop—the ones on the shelves—to the upstairs."

He drew back.

"Will you help me?" she persisted, wondering if a viscount would consider himself above such things.

"Of course," he said immediately, but his gaze dropped to her mouth. "But I had hoped—"

"For a sweet first?" she asked innocently. "Perhaps a chocolate or a piece of my marzipan rather than the toffee. It seems extra sticky tonight."

At last, he let her slip her hand out of his grasp.

"Actually, I would enjoy another piece of your marzipan."

She froze. *What if he hated it?* Suddenly, it meant more to her than anything else that this man like what she crafted every day. She didn't have to go to the display case. She and Edward had moved all the remaining confectionery into the back to go to deliveries in the morning, making sure none of it would become contaminated by sawdust.

Reaching past him to a covered tray, she lifted the lid and picked up a small marzipan faux cherry. At its center, she'd put a dollop of Amity's chocolate fondant. It was one of her favorite sweets.

"Try this," she said.

Nodding, he sunk his teeth into it, biting it in half, dropping a little onto his pant leg. Unthinkingly, she brushed at it while he chewed. His eyes widened, either at the deliciousness of the treat or the feel of her fingers on the top of his thigh. Withdrawing her hand with haste, she crossed her arms and waited as he popped the remainder into his mouth.

Then he licked his lips, an attractive thing for a man to do if he had just been satisfied by something of one's own creation.

"I loved it. The marzipan was silky soft but also firm. And the surprise of chocolate in the middle was a triumph, particularly the way it paired with the almond flavor. I think I detected a little vanilla, too. Yes?"

"Yes." Charlotte clapped her hands. This man definitely had promise. "Now that you're fortified, will you help?"

"I would have helped even without the bribery."

When he stood again abruptly, he seemed to shrink the size of the room. And she took a step back.

"I know you would have, but it is important you understand what I do here." She wanted him to love every aspect of her, recalling how Lionel not only wouldn't come into the shop but didn't care for her marzipan.

Charles made a sound of dismissal. "I think you do a lot more here than make marzipan pigs and fruit, but I'll admit you do that very well."

He reached for her again, and she ducked away, grabbed the keys to the upstairs and left the room.

"Are you coming?" she called over her shoulder. "These tins won't move themselves, and the builder starts tomorrow."

CHAPTER EIGHTEEN

The builder! Charles wished he'd helped her find one and hoped she had hired a reputable man. She'd said the other night he was related to Edward. That was reassuring, since the boy had a good work ethic.

Holding his arms out in front of him, he let Charlotte pile tins on his forearms before he realized the absurdity of such a precarious way to move them.

"Don't you own any sacks or boxes?"

She paused. "I suppose that would be safer. If these hit the ground, they will dent. I can't sell dented tins even if the contents are perfect." She dashed away, leaving him frozen in place.

After a moment, he called out, "How are you faring, Miss Rare-Foure?"

"Call me Charlotte when we're alone, Charles!"

Her teasing voice made him smile. Most everything about her made him feel like smiling. Somehow, she had avoided his proposal while making him feel good about their future—because she said she believed he could give her what she wanted.

His arms were starting to ache. *What did she want?*

She hadn't let him reach the part of his speech when he told her he had come to care for her. He sighed. *Care* was too tepid a word for the emotions she raised in him anyway. *Should he have declared he loved her?* Doing so seemed premature, and he hadn't wanted to scare her off.

A gentleman did not escort a woman out a few times and then announce he'd fallen in love.

No one in their right mind did that. *Only a lunatic!*

And Charlotte wouldn't want a lunatic. Given her upbringing, solidly middle class, she would want a slow, steady blossoming relationship with a normal man who said, "Over the past few long and leisurely *months*, I've fallen in love with you."

Otherwise, he would be like one of those crazy poets, Keats or Shelley. Or like Oscar Wilde. Any of those folks who adhered to the pursuit of beauty over goodness, although Charlotte was both.

Did she want one of those wild men? Like the artists Rossetti and Morris, who wrote about self-expression being more important than moral expectations, who rebelled against the restrictions of conformity and vowed their allegiance to the cult of beauty and art for art's sake.

All of that was opposite to the pedantic life of a barrister, which was steeped in rules and laws and practical application. Especially a barrister who was also a viscount, and some might say a *stuffy* viscount.

Finally, she reappeared.

"Sorry for the delay. Edward had folded all the delivery bags and put them away in a new place. Now I know how my mother feels when I rearrange the shelves after she's had them a certain way for a decade."

Placing sacks on the floor, she started to unload his arms of their cargo. When she'd put the last tin into the bags, he flexed his arms and groaned, catching her glance. Now she thought him a weakling.

"They weren't heavy," he explained, "just an awkward position to hold."

"Of course. And you were right," she said. "We have plenty of sacks to hold all these tins, and they can stay in them in the corner upstairs. They'll remain clean and undamaged."

"How will your mother feel about something far greater than rearranging confectionery on a shelf?" he asked her.

Her face grew serious, but she took a breath and picked up two sacks. "Unwieldy but light, as you said. Let's take them up, shall we?" she said and turned toward the door.

When they were walking up the stairs, she added, "I believe my mother will think I've made the best choices for our business in her absence."

He heard her mutter under her breath, "I hope so."

"And you are closing the shop while the staircase is built?"

"It seemed the prudent thing," she said. "What if a customer was hit by a piece of lumber or got sawdust in her toffee?"

"Will this in any way endanger your ability to pay your rent?" He hated to pry but it seemed an important thing to have considered.

They stepped inside the abandoned space. "I hope not. The deliveries will continue, and as long as we have that steady money, we should be fine. It's only for a few days after all."

They set the sacks down at the back, as far from where the builder would cut a hole in the floor as possible.

"Furnishing these rooms will also be expensive," he pointed out.

"I've already started. I was telling Edward, but it was like talking to a bowl of almonds. I found the perfect table and ordered six of them. They're in the Aesthetic mode everyone is going on about these days. At first, I was going to make the upstairs look like the downstairs, but then, when you think about all the wondrous things we can do with color and peacocks—you know how everyone is mad for peacocks!—as long as we use the sapphire blue my mother likes as an accent color."

Dear God! She *was* part of the wild art movement. *How would he, a mundane man, ever satisfy her if she was thinking of Edward Burne-Jones and Albert Moore?* She would indeed respond to grandiose declarations of passion and fanciful promises of undying love. She might expect her beau to threaten to jump off a cliff onto sharp rocks if she withdrew her favor or imagine he might set sail alone to fight in foreign wars like Byron. Charles didn't even like going to a strange club and not getting his favorite type of brandy.

"Peacocks," he repeated, "painted on the walls?"

"Maybe," she said. "I can sketch a few in and think about whether to hire a painter."

"You were taking painting classes, weren't you? Are you skilled enough?"

She shook her head. "Not to put on the wall of Rare Confectionery, no."

"Then perhaps someone from your class," he suggested. "A student might work cheaply."

Her expression clouded over, and he wondered what he'd said wrong. Quickly, he added, "In any case, blue peacocks sound most enchanting."

"But are they timeless?" Charlotte asked him. "Imagine if the trend fades away, and we have to do the walls over again in a year or less."

"There is that risk. Maybe you should go with dark paneling. Everyone likes that."

By the face she made not everyone did, in fact, like that.

"We'll see," she said noncommittally, and he decided not to attempt any further advice on decorating the café.

In the ensuing silence, the realization they were alone again with no agreement between them made him prickly. He wanted to take her in his arms and kiss her.

"I'll get the rest of the tins," he offered and disappeared before she could say anything. When he returned, she was waiting at the top of the stairs, the keys in her hand, ready to lock up.

That was a relief. There would be no more temptation. Passing her, he dropped the bags off with the others, before vacating the suite of rooms. Standing beside her as she locked the door, he detected her soft floral, lemon-and-lime scent in the closed confines of the tight stairwell.

"All set?" he asked.

She turned to him. "Yes."

An instant later, his mouth was upon hers and, after hearing the sound of the keys hit the landing beside him, her fingers were threaded in his hair. Pressing her against the door, her warm curves molded themselves against him, and he held her hips in place, his legs getting lost in her full skirts.

He opened his mouth, and she did the same, their tongues immediately dancing, sliding against one another. She tasted of treacle and butter from the toffee, a heady, delectable sweetness.

He could retrieve the keys and let them back in. The insane notion flit through his desire-soaked brain. He yearned to possess her, this special woman. He wanted all of her in a way he'd never felt before. *How could that be?*

But he wanted to make her his wife, and one didn't take a wife against a door or on the floor of an empty room. That was the disrespectful way one treated a light-skirt.

Charles broke away, stepping back, dragging in a breath as he heard her do the same.

When he looked into her eyes, they were glinting from the light coming up the stairwell and they were not condemning him as he'd feared.

He vowed to do better. He would tame his animal passion because she deserved better than to be mauled every time he got her alone.

Swearing under his breath at his own lack of control, he bent down and picked up the keys.

Offering her his hand, which he was grateful she took when she had every right to shy away from him, he escorted her down the stairs. At the bottom, he halted. "Let me leave first, then wait a few moments before coming out and locking the door."

She shook her head, about to protest.

"Please, do as I ask. I have behaved terribly," he insisted. "Let me try to protect you in this small way."

"All right. Leave and I'll count to ten."

"Charlotte," he said with exasperation, even while acknowledging a secret thrill at freely using her name, and feeling, in his heart and soul, that she was his.

"Twenty, then," she agreed, "but that's all, so you'd best dash like a fox at the hunt."

Her teasing smile was utterly becoming, and he groaned inside.

"Don't forget," she said. "We're going riding on Sunday."

He certainly hadn't forgotten, although he had thought to be showing off his new fiancée. Nodding, he slipped out through as small an opening as he could and hurried down New Bond Street without a backward glance, hoping she counted slowly.

"ZOUNDS!" CHARLOTTE EXCLAIMED WHEN an axe head abruptly came through the ceiling. She'd had a ruder curse word in mind and luckily kept it from crossing her lips since Edward was in the next room.

As promised, his uncle had shown up the following morning. After Charles's hasty departure the day before, she'd spent time dismantling the shelves and storing them upstairs, and then emptying the display cases of the last bibs and bobs. With the sign firmly attached to the front window, she wrote another one for the door, just in case.

With everything ready, she'd been able to enjoy her dinner and her night, thinking of Charles Jeffcoat and how much she enjoyed being with him. Yes, she wanted to become his wife. Her heart was fully engaged. But she had done the right thing in halting his proposal. She wanted him to speak with words the way he kissed with his lips. For if he felt what was in his kisses, then he was half in love with her already. She was with him—more than half.

With her heart pounding as she stared at the axe head, which disappeared in the next instant, leaving debris falling down onto the floor in its wake, she wished Mr. Tufts had laid down floor covering. After all, in a few hours, there would be a good chunk of ceiling on the polished wooden floor of the confectionery. Surely, it would be easier to clean up if he could drag it all out at once.

"Mr. Tufts," she called up to him, just as the axe appeared again. *Shouldn't he be using a saw?*

"Mr. Tufts," she tried again.

"Yes, miss?" he yelled through the ceiling.

"Two things, can you cover the floor down here and will you soon switch from axe to saw?"

Silence met her words. "Mr. Tufts?"

"Yes, well, miss. I shouldn't think you want me to go away now and get what we call a tarpaulin for the debris. It would take up time better spent on my working."

She sighed. He ought to have thought of that at the onset.

"In any case," he added, "dust is going to go everywhere. A tarpaulin isn't going to hold it, and that's no lie."

The axe struck again. "As soon as I get a big enough hole, I'll start sawing," he assured her.

She'd already paid him half his fee, and was simply relieved when he'd actually strode in with his tools to do the job. But she couldn't help wishing he would take a little more care with the existing part of the shop.

"Edward, are you ready to make deliveries?" she called to him.

His head poked through the curtain. "Nearly ready, miss." Then he glanced up at the axe head sticking through the ceiling, rolled his eyes, and retreated. A minute later, he reappeared with two bags.

"I'll stop back for the rest, miss. But I can't find enough sacks."

"Oh, Edward. That's my fault." She handed him the keys, just as the end of a saw appeared and began to move, back and forth. "I used them to carry the tins. Just go take the tins out of a couple of the sacks. I'll think of something else to put them in later to keep them clean."

"Yes, miss." And the boy disappeared out the front door and into the glass front door next to it. She could hear his feet trudging up the stairs.

The stairwell in which she'd again allowed the viscount to kiss her. She really should have let him ask her to marry him since she intended to eventually. Suddenly, she heard raised voices from above. It was such an unfamiliar occurrence since for all the years of her daily working at Rare Confectionery, she'd never heard a peep from upstairs.

"I will not," came filtering through the small hole.

"You will. Not another word, or you know what'll happen."

And then the sawing started up again.

Hm, Charlotte mused. Edward and his uncle were having a quarrel apparently. This time, she knew better than to ask the boy anything, since the more she'd tried lately to find out what was bothering him, the more stoic he became.

"I'll take these that are packed, miss, and fill the rest when I get back."

"All right." Although with little to do besides make enough confectionery for the next day's deliveries, she would surprise him and pack them herself. After that, what task could she set for him? He would be crushed if she had to cut his hours and his pay, but she wasn't sure what she could use him for.

Then she had an idea. She would create a notice announcing their expansion and send him to the printer. Edward could walk around New Bond Street, Old Bond Street, and all over Mayfair and then through Hyde Park handing out the notices.

She opened the door for him and watched him head along the street. An unexpectedly loud crash behind her made her jump. Whirling to face it, her heart racing, Charlotte saw a large chunk of the ceiling had slammed to the floor.

Gracious! Why hadn't the builder warned her?

"You all right, miss?" came his voice from above.

"Yes, a little startled." Good thing she didn't have customers in the shop. Getting struck by plaster would certainly be bad for business.

"More to come," he said. "That tarpaulin wouldn't have been a bad idea after all."

Rolling her eyes, she looked at the fine layer of white dust already covering everything. Maybe that would be Edward's task over the next few days, keeping up with mess in the front of the shop.

"Mr. Tufts," she called out, but he was still sawing the great rectangle for the top of the staircase.

"Mr. Tufts," she said again and the sawing ceased.

"Yes, miss."

"Your nephew and I will clean this up at the end of the day, but please bring a tarpaulin tomorrow. I fear we already may have some scratches or gouges in the floor down here, but we shall carry on."

"Yes, miss," he agreed and resumed the sawing.

"Yes, miss," she muttered and went into the back room to pack up the rest of the deliveries for the day.

CHARLOTTE OPENED HER FRONT DOOR, heart pounding as hard as if Mr. Tufts were dropping plaster behind her. There was Charles, looking incredibly handsome in a tan coat and pants with black riding boots and his crop in his hand, which he raised as he doffed his hat.

"Are you ready, Miss Rare-Foure?"

"I am," she said. She'd been pacing for the last half hour while looking out the front window, eager to get started. She had on her favorite shade of green with a full skirt for draping over the pommel and saddle and a smart-looking, brushed-cotton paletot. With her hat in place, a pretty feather protruding out the back of it and the weather holding up with brilliant sun, she was anticipating a wonderful ride.

He turned around and gestured behind him. Not only did he have two horses but, as promised, he had a footman holding their reins and another one, mounted and holding the other footman's horse. It was quite the gathering—two footmen as chaperones for a ride with the Viscount Jeffcoat. *How could this be happening to her?*

In a few minutes, she'd been helped upon Trudy, a gentle chestnut-colored mare with a pretty white blaze on her forehead. Charles rode a slender gray roan. The horses moved at an ambling pace toward the Marble Arch and Hyde Park's northeast entrance. Despite it being a new experience, Charlotte felt no trepidation, nothing but happiness. Thus, she was surprised when Charles turned to her and told her not to fear.

"If anything happens on the crowded Rotten Row, Trudy will carry you safely through."

"Honestly, I am not worried. I never see the sense in fearing the worst." It was true, and while it kept her from being an anxious or overly cautious person, she knew it sometimes made her act without considering all the consequences. *But what could go wrong during an afternoon ride with Lord Jeffcoat? Or with expanding her mother's confectionery, for that matter?*

They traveled in silence through Portman Square and along Oxford Street. Upon entering the park, Charlotte couldn't help smiling as they took the path south to The Serpentine and the King's Road beyond. She'd never seen it from this vantage, looking over the park from atop a horse.

There were many people out, and every one of them seemed joyful. Children with hoops and sticks and balls, families picnicking, and couples strolling together. And there were many other riders, both on horseback and in carriages as well.

"It seems to be the busiest place in London," Charlotte said, having to raise her voice to be heard over the many park-goers.

He nodded. "Teeming with people, indeed. It is less crowded during the week when all the businesses and factories are open. Then you have only the nobility to contend with and not . . . ," he trailed off.

Charlotte stared at him. He had been going to say something insulting. Of that, there was no doubt. *The riffraff, perhaps?* The regular, working-class people, of whom she was firmly one, were in his lordship's way while he rode his horse on a Sunday.

Plainly, the viscount was a pompous snout-nose, after all, and Charlotte wondered how on earth she could excuse that or even ignore it long enough to fall in love with him.

Perhaps she shouldn't go to the effort.

CHAPTER NINETEEN

A spark of annoyance flashed through her. Beatrice had been lucky to fall for a man who was as ordinary as they came—except for being a strange American and wealthy, to boot. And while Amity had captured the heart of a duke, he had always seemed the most unassuming man. Obviously, he lived in the rarefied world of the aristocrats, and now her oldest sister did, too, but the Duke of Pelham had never made a single conceited comment that Charlotte could recall.

Plainly, she and the viscount were from two different worlds and, undoubtedly, they saw London in vastly dissimilar ways. Today, for instance, Charlotte saw the beauty of all the city's people enjoying the outdoors. How she wished she had a big bag of confectionery to give out.

What if Charles saw them like rats swarming all over his precious park?

"I apologize," he said into her continued silence. "I'm sure that sounded impossibly arrogant."

"It did," she said stiffly. "Although I take your meaning. You wouldn't want to trample over some factory worker on his one day off and soil your horse's hooves."

"Sharp-tongued comments don't suit you," he said. "A sweet kitten howling like a banshee. Anyway, I apologized. Of course, I don't wish to trample anyone. I was only bemoaning the crowds that will prevent us letting the horses have their head for even a minute. Truth be told, I would rather be racing over a field at my country estate than anywhere in London." He glanced around him. "At certain times of the week, depending on the weather, you can trot and gallop without running into anyone. But at my estate, I can run my horse without fear of collision or mishap. And I can wear anything I like rather than being dressed to keep up with my peers."

He gestured to his own clothing.

She couldn't help shaking her head. "You have to dress a certain way in case your peers see you and judge you lacking?"

"In fact, I do," he assured her. "Or there will be whispers my father and I have lost our fortune. Before you know it, my accounts will be closed all over town. People will say we're practically bankrupt. I'll read in the papers that the destitute lords of Bentley will be selling their townhouse any day."

She narrowed her eyes. "All that if your cravat is the wrong color, I suppose."

He shrugged. "Truly, I'm sorry if I offended. It was not well said of me. I don't usually come here on a Sunday. And at this early hour, I was simply surprised by the throng of people."

"People outside of your class don't waste their day off by lying abed," she informed him. "For some, it's the only day they can enjoy some fresh air."

He nodded and a moment later said, "I understand. I am sorry for speaking without thinking first."

They rode on. She never held a grudge, and he had sincerely apologized. Nevertheless, she would be on the watch for any similar statements. She didn't think her parents would be particularly disposed to her saying she'd fallen for a snout-nose.

"I don't come to the park often," Charlotte admitted, "but I must say I like the view from atop a horse." Leaning forward, she patted Trudy's silky neck and ran her fingers through the coarse reddish mane. "It gives one a different perspective. Down on the ground, you can't see past the person in front of you, but up here, I can see all the way to the Carriage Drive."

"I'm glad you like riding. Some people, if they haven't done it much as children, find it frightening."

She wondered if he had someone particular in mind, like a former lady-love, the person who'd caused Charles's heartache to whom the duke had made reference.

"It would make me happy to show you my estate and my horses," he continued. "If you like flowers—"

She laughed. "Who doesn't?"

"Flowers make some people sneeze. Anyway, we have a particularly skillful gardener and our gardens are superb. Visitors drop by unannounced just to stroll through them."

"And you don't mind?" She had a feeling he must be referring to visitors from the aristocratic class, as she couldn't imagine he would welcome *hoi poloi* wandering around his property. Perhaps she was being judgmental.

"I'm not there enough to mind," he said. "Not often enough for my liking, at any rate, but usually three times a year." He cocked his head. "Are you entirely enamored of Town, or would you be happy with extended stays in the country?"

"I would very much like to see your country home," she said, then realized how presumptuous that sounded. She hadn't let him propose but she was already installing herself at—"Where is it again?"

"In Wiltshire, between the mysterious Stonehenge and—"

To her amazement, the viscount's words were unceremoniously cut off when a ball hit him on the side of his head, making him flinch sideways, losing his hat before unseating himself entirely. His roan reared at being suddenly without a rider, and then took off, although it couldn't get too far along the crowded path.

As promised, Trudy gave no more notice than a flick of her ears and kept plodding along as if nothing had happened. It was probably a good thing Charlotte hadn't screamed, but it had happened so quickly, by the time she drew breath in astonishment, the incident was over.

Drawing back on the reins and halting her docile horse, she looked down to see Charles scrambling to his feet and brushing himself off, his face a distinct shade of red.

One of his footmen had dismounted and was rushing after the roan.

"I haven't fallen off my horse since I was four years old," Charles said through gritted teeth. "And now I've done it in front of half of London."

He bent down and retrieved his hat, which was not only dirty but crushed beyond repair.

"Look on the bright side," she said, after ascertaining he was uninjured. "At least most of the people here are not of the nobility and don't know who you are, nor care."

He glanced around for a second to see she was right. Except for a moment's pause when it happened, mostly to discern if they were in danger, the park-goers near them had gone back to their own business unbothered.

"Think how much worse if you'd fallen from your horse on one of the days when this park was cleared of all the low and middle-class workers," she reminded him. "Then you would have performed such a perfectly mortifying dismount before your peers."

The footman had returned Charles's horse to him, and after handing his servant the ruined hat, he remounted with a light, swift movement.

"No," he corrected her. "I wouldn't have because there would not have been some miscreant throwing a ball at my head."

They both looked around, but the child, as most assuredly it was, had long vanished along with his or her ball.

"It's not funny in the least," he protested at the expression on her face.

"No, I know. You could have been injured, but luckily, you weren't."

"If it had happened to you," he said, "you might have been seriously hurt. I shall rethink ever riding here again on a crowded Sunday."

She shrugged. "If you intend to keep company with a middle-class shopkeeper's daughter, my lord, then . . . ," she trailed off. Offering him an ultimatum when he had dirt on his riding pants and had a scandalously uncovered head was probably not well done of her.

"Then we shall wait for rainy Sundays and ride here in only the most dismal of weather when there is no one else about." With those words, she sent him a warm smile. Hopefully, he was not one of those men who nursed a grudge or a slight.

After a moment's pause, he agreed. "Here's to rainy Sundays. Luckily, London provides us with many."

He didn't even turn for home as she'd half-expected given his present state of disarray. Instead, he ran a hand through his hair, which was the worse for wear and undoubtedly unrecognizable to his valet.

Then he asked, "Shall we ride?"

CHARLES CONSIDERED IT TO have been a perfectly blissful Sunday, notwithstanding being unseated from his horse and ruining a perfectly good hat. And despite nearly making a terribly small-minded, patrician remark from which it would have been difficult to recover.

They had continued their ride, returned to her home without further mishap, and dined together with Delia as their chaperone because he thought it inappropriate to invite either of his footmen into Charlotte's home. All in all, a banner day even if tomorrow would be made more trying by the writs of court he hadn't completed.

As he sat sipping brandy in his study, however, he couldn't help feeling he'd missed something important. Besides the obvious when he'd restrained himself from stealing a kiss even though they'd had about thirty seconds alone while Delia went into the hallway to fetch her needlepoint.

Other than not getting to once again taste Charlotte's sweet lips, he'd also missed out on determining what she really wanted from him. She knew he could provide her a townhouse and a country estate, horses, and even flowers. There was no reason not to think he could also provide babies, and that would be an extremely enjoyable task.

She would even have a barrister in the family, always useful.

Then what was Charlotte waiting for?

He heard his father scuffling by. "It's late," he called out to the earl. "Why are you still up?"

After a pause, the earl's head came around the open doorway. "I was reading the papers and the latest acts of Parliament."

"Anything interesting?" Charles asked him.

"I would come in and tell you, but you don't yet have a second comfortable chair. Most inhospitable," he added with a sniff. "I was in the drawing room, but it's like the Pharaoh's tomb down there."

"Which Pharaoh?" Charles teased. In fact, he had meant to get another chair brought in but hadn't realized his father was waiting for him to do so.

"*Bah!* Any of them. No matter. When are you bringing that pleasant young woman over again to visit?"

Charles sat up straighter. "That would be highly inappropriate to have a single young woman of good standing over with us two bachelors.'

His father took a step into the room. "But she did before. And it was splendid. No harm done."

Charles sighed. *Had everyone relaxed their morals but him?*

"That was an aberration, a mistake, a meeting that became a dinner."

"Don't you like the girl?" His father frowned. "What's wrong with you? You probably cannot do better than her. If you face facts, Charlie, you are a little dry and stodgy. She can probably do better than you just about anywhere."

"How kind of you," Charles quipped, but it got him thinking. Maybe Charlotte wanted a less dull man, although he wasn't sure what that meant.

"Should I grow my hair long and spread my seed over many women and then die of a wretched fever in Greece? Then I might be hailed a romantic hero. That sounds fun."

"Are you mocking Byron? Poor chap only lived to see thirty-six."

Charles swallowed. No, he didn't want his life to end in a decade, nor did he want to wander the world with various paramours. He simply wanted Charlotte and a rather subdued life in his beloved London or with his horses at his Wiltshire estate.

"You might want to be more like that American artist everyone's talked about since he sued our stuffy art critic."

"You're talking about Whistler suing Ruskin," Charles clarified. He didn't particularly care about the artist or the critic, but he had attended some phases of the popular trial because it was a singular case.

Ruskin's words about the artist had been oft-repeated until they all knew his insult by heart, "I have never expected to hear a coxcomb ask two hundred guineas for flinging a pot of paint in the public's face."

Moreover, Charles had noted how despite a poor defense, Whistler won in principle but was awarded merely a farthing. Surely, there was a lesson there about the cost of being right, especially with court costs. Last he'd heard, the painter, now impoverished, had gone to Venice.

"I'm no painter," he grumbled, thinking of that transient lifestyle.

"Neither was Whistler," his father said, then laughed, "not if you went by his *Nocturne in Black and Gold*. That was Ruskin's point precisely."

Charles sighed. If Charlotte was looking for a flashy man given to openly passionate actions or words, like one of the popular artists—Rosetti with his wombats and exotic birds, not to mention his exotic models—then Charles did not stand a chance of winning her over. He doubted he would ever do anything flamboyant. He might go out tomorrow wearing his *second*-favorite hat since his favorite was ruined and couldn't be replaced at such short notice, but that was hardly like Whistler painting the Thames during a winter freeze.

Perhaps he could woo her with flowers.

Out of the blue, his father said, "Your mother would have liked those blasted pre-Raphaelites or the Aestheticism everyone is talking about. Bunch of profligate artists!"

Startled at hearing his father make mention of the former countess whom he'd divorced after she'd left for the Continent, Charles was about to offer him a glass of brandy when he turned and walked away.

"Bed," he heard his father mutter. "To sleep, perchance to dream."

Poor man! That was what came of marrying an unsuitable woman whom one couldn't satisfy or please.

And his mother had been given the privilege and honor of being lifted from the level of a viscount's second son's daughter by her sheer beauty alone. Anyone would think becoming a countess would have been a reward unto itself that she wouldn't possibly throw away with her careless infidelity.

Yet she had.

For Charlotte, the elevation in status would be even greater, but he'd learned that could mean nothing. It didn't gain a woman's loyalty, fidelity, or love.

On the other hand, it bode well that despite his being a viscount, and some day in the distant future an earl, neither had not been enough to sway her to accepting his proposal. *Hell's bells, she hadn't even let him finish it!*

She was, thus, no opportunist. She was a middle-class woman of business with whom he was more smitten every time he was with her.

CHAPTER TWENTY

It was a disaster! Without even a day's notice or a friendly face stopping by to discuss the matter, one of the hotels and one of the restaurants had abruptly canceled their standing orders. The messages came by morning post.

Charlotte reread the curt letters and wanted to weep. And at the worst possible time, too when they weren't getting any revenue from shop sales. Moreover, by the look of the mess, Mr. Tufts was going to take longer than three days to build even a rudimentary staircase. There was still nothing but an ugly gaping hole in the ceiling of the confectionery.

At that moment, Mr. Tufts was in the shop, hammering at boards, which he called treads, and attaching them to more boards, which he called risers. But the work was progressing terribly slowly and involved a lot of sawing and swearing on the builder's part.

Edward was already making the deliveries for the day, and now, since the orders had been halted, she wasn't even sure the recipients would pay for them when they were billed.

A tapping on the window drew Charlotte's attention. A woman in a pretty yellow bonnet was standing there.

In a state of shock from receipt of the cancellation letters, Charlotte muttered, "Can't you read?" The notice of closure was right beside the woman's face. Nevertheless, she went to the door, unlocked it, and stuck her head out.

"I'm sorry, but we're closed," Charlotte began and gestured to her handwritten sign.

"Yes, I can see that. Also, I'd heard from another shopkeeper that you are going out of business."

Another shock. *Who was saying such a thing?*

Before Charlotte could ask, the woman continued, "I just wondered what kind of establishment is going in here. I can see some renovations are happening. I'd be pleased to spread the word and tell my friends."

A gossip! Charlotte reminded herself it wasn't this woman's fault that people loved to hear the latest whether about a store or a nobleman, for that matter.

"Rare Confectionery is not going out of business, I assure you, and you may tell that to anyone who wishes to know. We are expanding. There will be a perfectly delightful café upstairs." She would make another sign saying such, but since the café wouldn't be open by the time the shop reopened, she hadn't wanted to confuse the issues.

"Our regular shop will be open just as soon as the staircase is finished."

"Oh."

Was that disappointment in the woman's tone? Charlotte was ready to scream. Instead, she breathed deeply and remained calm.

"I hope you'll come back at that time. Good day." Closing the door firmly, she walked past Mr. Tufts who was hammering a piece of wood which even Charlotte could see was crooked. Going directly into the back room, she put the kettle on. Hot, strong, sweet, milky tea was in order.

When Edward returned, she pounced. "Is anything strange happening during the deliveries?"

His eyes darted all over, but finally he fixed his gaze upon hers.

"Strange how, miss?"

"Anything, Edward. This is important. Perchance did you trip and squash the confectionery? More than once? Or show up late? Or give the wrong order to an establishment?"

He looked pale, to be sure, and she would guess at least one of those things had happened, but he shook his head.

"Why, miss?"

"Because two of the places have cancelled without telling me why except to say unsatisfactory service. I suppose it is entirely possible that their patrons have simply grown tired of our confectionery, but it seems unlikely they would both do so at the same time."

His eyes had grown wide. "Perhaps we can pick up new customers, miss. Could I go to some other restaurants or hotels and try to sell?"

"It is easier to keep old customers than to make new ones, although I agree we shall have to try to make new ones."

Suddenly, Mr. Tufts yelled loudly, and not for the first time. She'd seen him hold up a throbbing thumb. And she'd witnessed one step collapse under his feet as he'd tried it out. *Most unprofessional!*

"But we can't pursue new business, not in this chaos when we don't even have all of our products available. First, we need to get the shop re-opened. I am sorry to say I believe your uncle underestimated the time it would take him."

By day's end, that was confirmed. Mr. Tufts went off, looking cheerful even as Charlotte eyed the shoddy work of just two steps finished and attached to nothing, simply resting on the floor. A wave of despair washed through her.

During the day, she'd gone along to another furniture maker and ordered chairs, giving them a down payment. Rapidly, their account was becoming thin. Tomorrow, first thing after letting Mr. Tufts and Edward into the shop, she was going to pay a visit with the two customers who had cancelled their standing orders and determine if they could be recovered. She had to salvage some income.

If they continued like this, she would be at the bank enquiring about a loan.

"I DON'T UNDERSTAND HOW this could have happened," she told the *maître d'hôtel* at The Grosvenor Hotel the next day. Edward had not shown up that morning, and Charlotte had delivered to their two remaining contracts herself, discovering they, too, had been on the verge of cancelling.

With her assurance and an offer for that day's delivery to be free, she'd managed to keep the hotel, but the other, The Albion restaurant, wasn't sure. He would discuss it with his partner. Then she'd gone to those establishments who'd already cancelled, hoping to recover the Rare-Confectionery reputation.

"I know those orders were complete." She'd packed them herself recently since she had little else to do.

The *maître d'* at The Great-Western Hotel shrugged. "It's no way to do business, young lady. For certain, our customers love everything we sell that comes from Rare Confectionery, but we can't be foxed out of a pound here and another pound there. Eats into our profits." He paused. "Eats into. *Ha!* That's amusing since we're talking of sweets, isn't it?"

Charlotte didn't find it the least bit amusing, but she offered him her best smile.

"I assure you we are not trying to fox you out of anything."

"If it had only happened once or twice, I would have thought it a genuine and honest mistake. But week after week, those pounds add up," he pointed out, "and seems intentional."

"Yes, I agree," she said. "I am very sorry for this, and I will get to the bottom of it. Naturally, the delivery from yesterday will be without charge. But I hope you will reconsider cancelling. How about if I personally count the order, pack it, and deliver it?" Though once the shop got busy again, Charlotte didn't see how she could do such a thing.

In any case, the man was shaking his head. "It's out of my hands now."

"How can that be?" She felt a little desperate and heard it in her tone. "Don't you run this establishment?"

"I run it, but I don't own it. And once you start meddling with the accounts and the profits, then the owner takes a hard look. I'm not risking my job because someone at your sweet shop is fiddling around."

Someone—*Edward!* For sadly, he had to be behind this mess. Fortunately, the manager at The Langham was more understanding. They'd been delivering there since the previous year when Beatrice's now-husband was staying there.

"Why didn't someone tell us?" she asked while sitting in the manager's office.

"Miss Rare-Foure, we are a large hotel. We have many accounts and many vendors, as I am sure you can imagine. I don't have time to be your nanny. If your business is not being overseen correctly and I am being harmed because of it, then I am going to terminate my business with you."

She sighed and drew out a bag of confectionery from her beaded purse. Haphazardly opening it, she offered the manager one. He paused, about to refuse, but then he caught a whiff of chocolate and helped himself.

"Delicious," he proclaimed. "We have never had a problem with the quality. That is for certain. Such a shame."

"Then give me the chance to remedy this," she insisted.

He held up his hand. "For all I know, you might have been the one perpetrating the deceit."

"Sir!" she exclaimed. "My family owns the shop, and I would not make mischief for them or myself. But I am certain I know the culprit."

"I ordered and paid for seven pounds per week," he persisted, "and on more than one occasion, I received a mere five. That's no small matter."

Charlotte recalled packing the latest delivery herself, and then handing it to Edward. Only a child, a relatively honest one with little experience at duplicity, would do something so carelessly stupid it could easily be traced back to him.

"I agree, it's no small matter. Thievery never is. Can you tell me when it began, if you know?"

"I can't say exactly since until we noticed it, we didn't start to examine each delivery. We have more important things to do than to weigh chocolates. But it has definitely occurred over the past couple of months."

"I know I can stop this ever happening again. And we have been providing you with excellent confectionery since last year. You know you cannot find its like elsewhere."

"Strange you should say that," The Langham's manager said, clasping his hands together on his desk. "When I was speaking with one of my staff about your confectionery, she said she'd bought the exact same marzipan pig off a street seller at Covent Garden."

"I am sure others make similar marzipan shapes," Charlotte said, despite not having personally seen any other pigs. But to think it would be on a street cart and not even in a fine confectioner's shop was unsettling.

"Not similar, Miss Rare-Foure, identical in taste and shape. I was going to send someone round there to find out who makes them."

She drew back, shocked.

"Because the same street-seller also had chocolates and toffee, all as good as yours and not as costly."

Naturally, not as costly, Charlotte thought. The person didn't have a New Bond Street rent to pay.

"If you will give us another chance, we won't let you down," she promised.

"You shall have to drop your price," the manager said, and so quickly she knew he'd been waiting for her to beg.

However, she was not that desperate.

"Absolutely not," she told him, clearly hearing her mother's voice reminding her how much The Langham charged for a room, or even for a pot of tea in one of their dining rooms. "If you wish to pin your reputation to your guests on the capriciousness of a Covent Garden street-seller's ability to deliver you pounds of confectionery every week, then I wish you good luck, sir. And even if you look in other London shops for our quality at such good prices, again, I wish you luck."

She stood, refusing to be cowed or broken down.

He rose to his feet. "The Langham will continue selling your confections, as long as you personally reassure me that the matter—or the nefarious person—has been dealt with."

"Of course," she agreed. Meanwhile, she was going to Covent Garden to discover this confectionery seller who could perfectly mimic their sweets.

CHARLES COULDN'T BELIEVE HIS luck when he saw Charlotte crossing the street toward him. Having just finished his midday meal at a pub around the corner from the Italian-style piazza that surrounded Covent Garden marketplace, he'd emerged from the Lamb and Flag. Over a meat pie and chips washed down with a glass of ale, he'd written up notes for court. He always sat in the back by the fireplace, whether it was lit or not, as the tables were larger than in the front by the bar. Even so, he'd scarcely managed to concentrate while his mind wandered to what his lady-friend was up to, imagining her safely tucked behind the counter of Rare Confectionery.

And yet there she was, having just exited a cab.

"Miss Rare-Foure," he called to her.

As her gaze landed upon him, a smile broke out across her face that made his heart race. *What a perfect English rose she was!* He wanted to pluck her from the bush of single females. He nearly laughed at that, the most poetic thought he'd ever had. He wanted to follow it up with something about establishing her in the marital vase but lost the thread, and then they were but a few feet away.

Bowing slightly to her, he received a nod in return.

"What a delight running into you here, my lord," she began, unmindful that he wanted to be the one to say that first. She didn't need to fawn or gush over him. He was lucky such a welcoming, warm, and luscious woman was interested in him, boring as he now feared he was, with an uninviting home to which she'd been privy and a cranky father.

Thank goodness he was a viscount, for he couldn't think of anything else that would recommend him to her.

"The delight is all mine, Miss Rare-Foure." Saying her family name now seemed like a farce, a secret code from a Gothic mystery since in private they were on a first name basis. It made him offer her a silly smile in return.

"What are you doing here, and in the middle of your workday?"

He could see instantly something was wrong, as her expression clouded over.

"I am not on a happy errand, to be sure," she confessed.

"May I assist you in some way?"

She shrugged. Such a delightful movement when she performed it.

"Truly, I don't know. I am looking for a street seller who is somehow selling Rare Confectionery or its exact likeness."

"Indeed. And this person is here?" *Had she truly planned to stroll through the crowds alone until she found a sweet seller? Then what?*

"That's what I've been told. But I don't want to take up your time."

"Don't be silly. I am happy to escort you around the marketplace." Then he recalled the writ he hadn't finished and the court proceedings he ought to be observing later, instantly dismissing both.

"Very well," she said. "I welcome your company."

That sealed it, then. He could no more abandon her now than he could fly off into the sky. While they walked along King Street toward the colonnade area of the marketplace, she told him of her troubles.

"So you can see, it couldn't happen at a worse time, what with the expansion and added expenses of furnishing the upstairs, not to mention having closed the downstairs."

"A staircase shouldn't take too long. It's not Marlborough House, after all," he teased, reminding her of the costume ball they'd both attended the year before at one of the most magnificent residences in London.

"No, it shouldn't," she said, glancing away, not looking pleased, and he figured something more was going wrong in her world. Before he could ask about the staircase, she said, "Over there. That man is selling sweets, I believe."

They wandered toward a rough-looking vendor in festive colors that belied his scowling face.

"Boiled sweets, guvna?" the man offered. "Perhaps a nice sack of 'em for your missus?"

"Thank you, no," he told the man. "Do you have any chocolates?"

"Nah, sir. What do I look like?"

Charles didn't want to tell the man he looked like a grumpy Harlequin. Instead, he merely nodded, and they moved on.

"I don't like to think of you wandering around here, approaching strangers," he said.

Sighing, her head on a swivel as she looked at the crowds and many sellers, she said, "That's nonsense. I deal with strangers most every day."

"From the safety of your shop."

"I had a robber in there last year," she confessed. "I had to chase him off with our cricket bat."

He stopped still, his heart pounding. "You went after a man with a bat?"

She nodded. "He fled, too, although it was my loud whistle that finally roused him from the shop and sent him into the street. He got my favorite green purse, but he was really after Beatrice's."

"Come along," she added when he didn't move. She took a few steps without him, and he hurried to catch up.

"Tell me," he demanded, but she shook her head.

"That's a story for another day," she said. "Let's keep looking or ask someone."

"Who would we ask?" It wasn't as if there was any order in the chaos of the Covent Garden marketplace, or there didn't seem to be. Nevertheless, at that time of day, the market was peaceful compared to earlier. If they'd arrived at six o'clock in the morning, they would have been in the midst of the chaos of vegetable sellers, with cabbages, cauliflower, peas, carrots, turnips, and potatoes.

Women would sit in groups to start shelling peapods by the hundreds. And chasing between the carts and through the stalls were the many street urchins who came to gather what spoils they could. Sometimes, it was their only food. Charles had studied the situation when Parliament was creating the public school laws. Confine some of these children to a classroom and they wouldn't have access to the rotting piles of food that kept them alive.

When the mountains of vegetables had disappeared and every last onion had gone to its destination, whether to a green grocer or a restaurant, the flower and fruit auctions got underway, usually by ten o'clock. Some flowers were destined for florists, but hundreds of women and girls bought carnations, roses, violets, and more, to make bouquets to sell on the streets. And when these auctions ended, on each side of the main avenue the markets continued in the enclosed squares. Charles's friend Pelham, who'd been to the Continent many times, said Covent Garden had the most and best of any market he'd seen in Europe, if not the world. From the commonplace British cherries, apples, and pears to the exotic oranges, Hamburg grapes, French pears, American apples, and more, the variety was astonishing.

Little of this abundance made it out of London's wealthy west end, and even then, there were ragamuffin children sucking on discarded fruit with joy.

Charles couldn't help but think of the recent cholera outbreaks and hoped the fruit would provide sustenance to these waifs rather than illness.

"Let's try over there," Charlotte said, and he walked with her to a watercress stall, where a young woman sold the tender shoots.

"Over 1,600,000 bunches of watercress are sold in Covent Garden alone," he told her, recalling from the last *London Labor and the London Poor* report he'd read.

She stopped in her tracks. "How on earth?" Charlotte began.

"Your young man is right, miss," said the stall's owner. "It's nutritious, delicious, and cheap. Best quality bunches are found right here. Care for a bunch or two?"

Charles couldn't help smiling as Charlotte bought two from the impressive young seller.

"Would you have seen the very opposite of watercress?" Charles asked the woman. "Someone selling confectionery?"

"Someone new?" Charlotte added. "Perhaps in the past few weeks?"

"Over by the sacks of nuts," the watercress woman said. "Go along the colonnade." She pointed in the direction. "I've seen a woman strolling with sweets for sale. She doesn't have a stall, mind you, so no one can vouch for her."

"Thank you," Charlotte said, and Charles doffed his hat. They wandered along to no avail for many minutes.

"I think we should ask someone with children," Charlotte said, looking around at the strolling people.

When a woman—obviously a governess by her clothing—emerged from the crowd with two young charges, Charlotte approached them.

"Excuse me, missus," Charlotte began, "by any chance would you know of a sweet seller hereabouts? I was told there was a good one nearby selling chocolates and toffee, not boiled sweets."

The woman nodded. "Yes, there is. We found her two weeks ago by the flower stalls. She has no cart, just a box with sweets in bags. This lot scented chocolate like hounds with a fox. And they were remarkably good. The chocolates, not these brats," she clarified as the boy started to pull the girl's braids. "Stop that, Samuel."

"Was the chocolate seller dressed in anything identifiable or have a sign?" Charles asked, hoping they wouldn't have to wander up and down the colonnade forever.

"She was by the roses last week, and close by, in front of the carnations the week before. She didn't wear anything special except a pale blue cape, both times we saw her."

"Thank you," Charlotte said. "Good day to you," she added and hurried past toward the first row of flowers.

"I'm surprised you didn't give those children something from your purse," he said.

She gasped. "As am I. On the other hand, the boy was a little terror and the girl looked spoiled, and it sounds as though their governess gets them plenty of sweets. There!" she exclaimed.

A middle-aged woman in a faded blue cape had a wooden box at her side and was soliciting those who walked past.

"Some chocolates, missus? Toffee, sir?"

The man in front of them stopped. The transaction was swift.

"Toffee is tuppence a bag," the seller said.

Charlotte gritted her teeth at the low price that wouldn't even pay for the ingredients, never mind her sister's hours of work.

"How much is in the bag?" the customer asked.

"Quarter pound, give or take. You won't be disappointed."

The coins were exchanged, and the woman handed the man a bleached white bag with the distinctive blue stamp: *Rare Confectionery*.

CHAPTER TWENTY-ONE

Charles glanced at Charlotte. The bloom was off her cheeks to be sure. She marched up to the woman.

"Do you have marzipan, too?"

"Of course, missus." The woman said, glancing at Charles, then back to Charlotte. "Would you like a bag of it, assorted shapes?"

"Yes," Charlotte said, her voice barely above a whisper. Her stare was plainly one of fascination as the woman reached down, lifted the crude lid of a plain wooden box and drew out a bag. "Hold on, that's all chocolates." Dropping it, the woman grabbed up another. "That's the one, missus. *Marchpane*, as my mother called it. And this is the most delicious you'll ever taste."

"How much for the bag?" Charlotte asked, her tone soft and quiet, making Charles more worried.

"It's dearer than toffee, to be sure. Made with almonds, which ain't cheap," the woman added. "A farthing for the bag. There are cute shapes in there. Three pieces. Sometimes a fruit shape, sometimes a pig—"

Charlotte snatched the bag from her and opened it, releasing a soft gasp as she did.

"Here now. That ain't free," complained the street seller.

Charles quickly dug into his pocket and pulled out some coins, paying the woman, which made Charlotte scowl. Then she smoothed out the bag, and he could see the sapphire blue words with a little arching design over it and squiggly bits on either side. *Artistic*, he thought, but hardly the point.

"Rare Confectionery?" Charlotte prompted the woman, as if reading the bag.

"Yes, missus. I call it that because the sweets are so delicious as to be rare around these parts."

"Indeed," Charlotte said, and her tone was becoming harsher with each word.

Charles considered the situation and made a decision. "How long will you be here today? We might want more after we've done our shopping."

The woman glanced at the clock tower visible above the stalls. "I'll be here for a few hours longer, sir. Got to put food on my table. I have three young ones to feed."

At those words, he saw the anger drain out of Charlotte. Nodding, he turned away, but when she didn't accompany him, he took hold of her forearm and drew her with him.

"But—" she began.

"Let's talk first," he murmured into her ear, leading her farther away. "Come along, be sensible."

She let him take her to the end of the row of flowers, but then she yanked her arm free.

"Be sensible? I find my own confectionery being sold at less than half price by a stranger—and you paid her for it instead of denouncing her! Now you are telling me to be sensible."

"I know you felt sorry for her when she mentioned her children."

Again, he saw her righteous anger leave her like air from a deflating balloon. "You cannot be angry at a mother," she agreed.

"Did you recognize her?"

"Edward's mother by the resemblance," she murmured. "Undoubtedly. She looked like him about the eyes and mouth." Putting a hand to her forehead, she sighed. "Goodness, what a mess!"

"I thought perhaps we should discuss what you want to do. Call the police or simply confront her. Does Edward know you know about this?"

"No, but I questioned him about the deliveries being off. We had two of our steady contracts cancel yesterday. I was depending upon that money while the shop is closed." She clasped her hands together. "Edward didn't show up today. It was the first time he's missed work since I hired him. I made the deliveries myself and found we'd nearly lost the other contracts, too. Then the manager at The Langham told me someone was selling confectionery exactly like ours, and he was right."

"Since Edward knows he's been found out, he will probably tell his mother tonight. I doubt she'll be back tomorrow, either." Charles hoped that made Charlotte feel better. "In any case, he won't be able to steal any more sweets to give to her."

"Stealing! How could I have misjudged so terribly? I am an idiot. I treated Edward like family."

"That was good of you. You're a kind, decent woman, but ultimately, he had his own family to whom he owed more allegiance."

"What do you think I should do about . . . ?" and she gestured back toward the woman in the blue cape.

"That's up to you." He had a feeling he knew what she would do. "She'll run out soon."

Charlotte nodded. "Especially at those prices." Sighing, she said, "I'm going to let her finish."

"I knew you would." He began walking toward the road where there would be a Hackney available.

"She did say it was the best marchpane," Charlotte quipped, making him love her more.

Charles almost tripped. *He loved her!* She was the best person he knew, and he wanted her to be beside him for the rest of their lives.

"If Edward shows up for work tomorrow, at least I'll get to talk to him," she continued, unaware of his astounding revelation.

He flagged down a cab, helped her in, and got in, too. Open air, they could easily talk to the driver.

"Where to, guvna?"

Charlotte suddenly looked at Charles as if surprised to find herself seated in the cab, next to him.

"Well, Miss Rare-Foure? Are you going back to your shop or home?"

She groaned. "Edward's uncle is still working. I must return and see how he's faring. It hasn't gone well thus far. In any case, I have to lock up."

"You left the builder there alone?"

"I had no choice," she told him.

Charles gave the driver the address.

As soon as they arrived, Charles could see there was a problem. By Charlotte's cry of dismay, she could, too. He helped her down before she jumped. While he paid the driver, she ran to the door, which was ajar, and dashed inside.

CHARLOTE FELL ILL. SHE was staring at disaster. Inside the shop were a few people wandering around. There were four makeshift steps lying uselessly sideways on the floor, sawdust and nails all over, and no sign of Edward's uncle.

"The shop is closed," Charlotte told a man and two women who had clearly entered just out of curiosity, and one was behind the counter.

That woman's face turned red with embarrassment. "I was hoping there were some samples back here," she said. "I wasn't stealing." She hurried between the counters and dashed out of the store.

The other two were gawking up at the hole, and Charlotte was grateful when Charles helped to usher them out. Then she heard a noise in the back room.

"Edward," she called out. Parting the curtain, Charlotte found a stranger staring back at her. He was crouched down, rummaging through the drawers that held their towels and some supplies. The candy-making supplies on the shelves had also been moved. Some were missing.

He stood, a sack in his hand, probably holding their spoons and pots.

"Set that down," she ordered.

A nasty smile appeared on the man's face, then vanished at the same time that Charlotte felt someone behind her. Smelling Charles's familiar scent, she knew he was right there, supporting her. *How fortunate she was!*

"You heard the lady," he ground out.

Slowly, the man set down the bag, one of their own delivery sacks, and held out his hands to show they were empty.

"I thought you'd gone out of business and was given everything away. Seemed like it."

Charlotte felt close to tears. "You shouldn't be back here," she said, when she wanted to scream at him to get out. The man moved toward her and the only exit. Taking a step back, she bumped into Charles, who then dragged her to the side, clearing the way for the stranger to exit. Charles saw him out of the shop and locked the door.

Before she knew what she was doing, she sagged against the counter, put her head into her hands and let the tears fall. After a moment, she felt his warm hand on her back, first patting and then rubbing gently until she stopped crying.

"What a mess!"

"I cannot believe your builder left your shop unsupervised and open. It's unconscionable. We're lucky there's anything left at all."

She doubted one particular thing remained. Looking behind the counter, she saw the glaringly empty space.

"Someone filched the cashbox. Luckily, it was nearly empty since we haven't been serving customers."

Charles's hand stilled on her back. Then perhaps realizing the impropriety, he moved away a few feet. "I suppose your builder has finished for the day?"

"He ought to be here," she said, and they both looked at the mess he'd left. "Do you think he's coming back?"

Charles's grim face was her answer. They walked over to the mess of wood that would never be proper stairs.

"Has he already been paid?" He picked up a split piece of lumber.

"Some of it. Half to start, then a little extra for more supplies."

She heard Charles sigh and knew what he was thinking. Then he asked, "What is his name?"

She told him.

"And do you know where his office is?"

Office? She doubted the man had any such. "No."

"How about where he lives? Or Edward for that matter. Perhaps it's the same place."

She shook her head feeling ever stupider. *What must Charles think of her?*

Groaning, Charlotte gazed around her and thought how just a couple of weeks ago, Rare Confectionery was bustling. Not only did they have many customers until the terrible newspaper review, they also had good contracts, and no hole in the ceiling.

Now they had double the rent, someone selling their sweets at Covent Garden, they were down two contracts, maybe three, they had no customers at all, and a massive hole in the ceiling.

Feeling lightheaded with worry, she knew she must be pale for Charles stared at her a second before saying, "Let's make tea and discuss what to do next."

Following him into the back room, she began to remove the pilfered things from the sack on the floor while Charles lit the stove and put the kettle on.

"I did it!" he exclaimed as she righted Amity's bottles of raspberry and orange essence that had been knocked over.

Glancing at him, and at his pleased expression, her heart lightened a little.

"I suppose you don't have to make your own tea at home," she realized aloud. "Or anywhere for that matter. Well done."

"Are you making fun of me?" he asked, taking a toffee tray from her hands and setting it on the shelf where she was reaching to put it back.

"Oh, no, Charles. I am speaking in earnest. You lit the stove, filled the kettle, and put it on as if you knew what you were about."

He grinned. "That was the extent of my kitchen abilities, I assure you. I would starve to death even with a well-stocked pantry if I didn't have a cook."

"I doubt that. You are a capable person who would figure it out. You would probably buy a recipe book and be a chef in no time. You have sense and you think ahead. You are never rash, not that I've seen." She felt the tears well up as she compared him to herself. "And you would never pay a man to build you a staircase without knowing if he truly could do it."

The tears flowed down her cheeks, and he embraced her. Disappointed in herself and in Edward, and especially in Edward's uncle, Charlotte couldn't even enjoy being in Charles's arms, despite trying to find comfort there.

If only she wasn't so angry at herself.

"Maybe the boy will return tomorrow," he said, "and you can find out where his uncle lives."

"And if he doesn't?" she said against his coat.

"Then I shall help you find him anyway. Edward Percy and Mr. Tufts both. I know some detectives at Whitehall who can help."

"Oh, how embarrassing!"

"You are not the first to be duped by the unscrupulous. Tufts probably did as much as he could and then, when he couldn't continue with the farce, he decided he'd take what he'd already got from you. Obviously, he wasn't going to be able to finish and collect the balance."

"I need to find a new builder, and quickly, but the place I went into treated me like a silly woman. I guess the clerk was right."

"I'll take you back there—" he began with a scowl.

"They were too expensive anyway."

Charles paused a minute. "I feel rather ineffectual myself. I've never had to hire a laborer and wouldn't know where to find one. When our home needs repairs, I just tell . . . That's it! My butler knows everything!" he exclaimed.

Surprisingly, his declaration made her smile. "Does he?"

"He seems to. I should have thought of that before. I'll ask him about a builder, and we'll get your stairs started again in no time.

She looked up at him. "I was thinking how fun it would be to have a blue ribbon tied across the bottom step with a sign that said, 'Come upstairs soon.'"

"And you shall," he said as if soothing a child.

Rolling her eyes, she did in fact feel better. "As soon as those stairs are done, then I can reopen the shop. I'll need to hire someone to replace Edward. All that training in making confectionery—wasted! Not to mention how much I liked the boy."

He squeezed her shoulders reassuringly, and it was almost as nice as sharing a kiss, knowing Charles cared enough to comfort her. She sniffed his spicy scent.

"I do hope Edward returns tomorrow, yet I don't believe he will," she added. And she had to think beyond the boy and his bewildering betrayal to the well-being of her family's shop.

"Rare Confectionery will recover, and then I'll find a reporter to come interview me about the shop and our expansion. He or she will love everything, and our customers will come flocking back, eager to enjoy the upstairs, too."

"That's my girl," he said. "It all seems bleak, but it won't be so hard to fix."

His girl!

She craned her neck to look up at him at the same time as he glanced down at her. And her thoughts returned to their kisses, because although being comforted was *almost as nice*, there was nothing quite like sharing a sensual kiss. When he put his hand under her chin, she parted her lips.

"Charlotte," he began.

"Charlotte!" echoed another voice, not softly but making her heart beat just as hard. *Actually harder!*

And then raised a little louder, the voice came again. "Charlotte Rare-Foure, you come out here this instant!"

"Mother," she exclaimed.

CHAPTER TWENTY-TWO

When Charles released her, the sickening feeling returned instantly. The haven of his arms had made everything seem all right for a few minutes. Straightening her shoulders, she parted the curtains and walked through to the front.

Both her parents stood next to the pile of debris, still in their traveling clothes. Her father was looking up at the hole, while her mother, hands on her hips, fixed her instantly with her piercing brown stare.

"What on earth?" Felicity asked.

And then, as Charlotte knew he would, Charles stepped through the blue velvet curtain behind her.

That got her father's undivided attention.

"Well, well," Armand said. "The viscount. In the back room, Mrs. Rare-Foure." He exchanged a veiled look with Charlotte's mother—or what he thought was veiled.

Felicity's expression softened measurably. "Well, at least we have some good news."

Instantly, Charlotte thought her mother was referring to her father's health.

"Father is doing much better. I can see by the color in his cheeks."

"Yes, of course," her mother said, "but to *your* good news."

"Mine?" Charlotte asked. *How could her mother think there was anything good in the disaster in which they all stood?*

"I assume you have come to an agreement. Otherwise why would Lord Jeffcoat be in the back room?"

"Oh!" Charlotte said.

Charles, who had remained silent up until that moment, stepped forward and shook Armand Foure's hand before nodding to Felicity.

"I must apologize if we gave the wrong appearance. You see, we'd just discovered some rather disturbing events, and therefore, I was making tea," he trailed off at the bemused expressions on both her parents' faces.

"Were you about to don your apron, as well?" Armand asked, then laughed heartily at his own jest. "Perhaps you were going to put on the frying pan and make some eggs and bangers."

"Father!" Charlotte scolded. "The viscount was kind enough to see I was in some distress and attempt to—*oh! the kettle!*" She left them to go turn off the stove. "Shall I make the tea anyway?"

"Of course," her mother said. "No need to waste boiled water. Then come out here and hug us."

Charlotte poured the water over the tea leaves, quickly put the cozy over the teapot, and ran back to face her parents in case Charles was being further insulted or pressured.

Her mother opened her arms, and Charlotte ran into her comforting embrace. She'd always considered it to be the very best place in the whole wide world. Warmth and rosewater fragrance surrounded her. And then after feeling her mother's kiss upon her temple, she was handed off to the other best place to be, enfolded in her father's strong arms. Having missed his familiar tobacco scent, she was glad he was home.

"Are you truly feeling better?"

"Yes, dear girl. Nothing some sea air and glasses of port couldn't cure."

She sighed, relaxing until he said, "You had best tell us what's happened to the shop before your mother has a fit. I know she's contained herself as best she can, but an explanation is in order."

He set her away from him, and she almost moved toward Charles. After all, his embrace had become another of her favorite places. Glancing at him, he nodded with encouragement.

Charlotte took a breath. "Surprise! I'm expanding Rare Confectionery upstairs. That's double the space for customers. With room for a café to sell coffee, hot chocolate, and tea, as well as our confectionery, and maybe some biscuits or even patisserie?" She wished she hadn't ended on an uncertain, questioning note, but she was feeling impossibly unsure of her actions.

Her mother frowned. "Didn't we discuss a café before I went away?"

"Yes, Mother. But it would be right here." Charlotte gestured to the gaping, ugly hole. "And I had to say yes to Mr. Richardson as he had some loud tenants waiting for the space."

"What do you mean you said yes?" Felicity asked.

Charlotte had to confess. "I mean I signed a lease, for three years."

Her father barked out a laugh. "You've raised a miniature you, Mrs. Rare-Foure, except *you* would have demanded five years at a fixed monthly rate."

"Indeed I would," her mother said. "I shall speak to the landlord at once for trying to fox my daughter when we have been good tenants all these years."

"Then you're not angry?" Charlotte asked.

"I can see you were caught in a difficult position. Naturally, I would rather you had contacted me—"

"I would have if he'd given me more time."

Her mother pursed her lips. "Again, I shall have words with him. He knew what he was about in pressuring you."

"Lord Jeffcoat looked over the lease to make sure nothing was amiss."

"Did he now?" remarked her father.

Charlotte rolled her eyes. Her parents had them at the altar exchanging vows already.

"Finish up, Charlotte," her mother prompted. "We're going to Amity's next to see how she's feeling."

"She's feeling rotund and exhausted," Charlotte told her. "And Beatrice has gone to Scotland."

"I know. And poor timing. But what possessed you to try to build stairs on your own?"

"Is that your handiwork, too, Jeffcoat?" her father asked good naturedly. "Making tea, reading contracts, hammering and sawing—all for the sake of my youngest daughter?"

Charlotte watched Charles's cheeks grow ruddy, and then she answered for him.

"Unfortunately, the stairs, or lack thereof, are the work of a builder whom I fear has taken off with our money."

For the first time, her father looked truly annoyed. "He did, did he? Well, that won't stand, I can tell you. I'll hunt him down, make no mistake."

Her mother patted his shoulder. "Don't get worked up, my love. There is no clean sea air here to restore you." Then she looked at Charlotte. "Is there anything else? Tell us everything, and then we'll leave you two . . . to have your tea."

Charlotte felt her own cheeks grow warm. That her parents would consider allowing her and the viscount to remain alone after discovering them was incredibly improper. Perhaps it was a test.

As if sensing the same thing, Charles said, "Now that you are here to . . . support Miss Rare-Foure, I shall take my leave. I have writs of court to work on. It was good to see you both again," he added.

Turning to Charlotte, he took her hand and formally bent over it as if they were at a ball instead of in the midst of a ruined shop.

"I hope to see you again soon." Their gazes locked, and all the feelings growing between them seemed to be apparent in the depths of his blue eyes.

"Yes," she said, then coughed at her breathy tone in front of her parents, almost giving away how she longed for a kiss goodbye.

She could see Charles knew her thoughts when his glance went to her lips, then back to her eyes. He smiled, his dimple appearing. "I'll send an invitation to your home."

She nodded. "Thank you for all your help, especially at Covent Garden."

"Covent Garden?" her mother asked.

With that, his lordship took his leave, knowing she had a lot to tell her parents. After the door closed behind him, Charlotte considered the situation.

"Perhaps you should stay for tea after all, for it will take a little while to catch you up. Or we could abandon it and go to Amity's. I can explain it as easily to you there."

"Wasting a pot of tea," her mother said. Then she brightened. "We'll take it with us."

Charlotte's father laughed until he was crying. "As if anyone would ever want to be in their carriage with a hot beverage."

Her mother glared at him. "We have most definitely had chocolate in mugs while in a sleigh. I remember that Christmas in France on your father's farm."

"And Beatrice spilled hers all over the blanket. It sounds good, but I for one don't want scalding tea spilling on my lap. It's uncivilized."

"Very well," Felicity said. "We shall have a cup here and then go to Amity's. Hurry along," she ordered Charlotte.

"Go find three mugs and pour. As long as you have milk. We are not savages, after all."

Charlotte dashed into the back room. "Cannot waste a pot of tea," she heard her mother add.

Felicity was frugal but never cheap. How she would take the income losses, Charlotte couldn't guess, but soothing her with strong, milky tea was a good start.

"Where's Edward?" she called out.

It was going to be a long afternoon of explanations, but hopefully Amity and her duke would put a good dinner on the table and have some smooth brandy after. They were all going to need it.

THE NEXT MORNING, NEITHER Edward nor his uncle appeared for work, and Charlotte felt truly heartsick. She had let her family down at least twice.

Fortunately, her mother was excited about the upstairs expansion, and when Charlotte drew her a sketch of the tables she'd ordered, Felicity approved.

It was tense over breakfast, however, when her mother insisted on reading the article disparaging the confectionery. Armand had to talk her out of going to the publisher's offices in search of the reporter. Her mother wished to give the woman a stern talking to.

That would solve nothing. What they needed was to get up and running, and have good publicity outweigh the bad.

"We ought to sue her for defamation," Felicity said, "now that we have a lawyer practically in the family."

Charlotte ignored her words. She'd said something similar three years earlier when Amity was engaged to a solicitor, and that had come to naught. Thank goodness! A duke was infinitely better than a solicitor. But a viscount who was also a barrister—he was a fish of a different scale!

"We ought to sue that charlatan masquerading as a builder," her father chimed in instead of calming her mother further.

Charlotte knew she'd best get a plan of action before her parents started litigation against everyone. They had not taken kindly to the loss of the Great-Western Hotel account either, but at least that wasn't a prosecutable offense. She hoped.

"Everything depends upon us getting the shop reopened," Charlotte pointed out.

"Our daughter is correct," Armand said. "I know where to find a professional carpenter, but good ones aren't usually available upon short notice. We'll see what we can do."

"If Lord Jeffcoat remembered," Charlotte told them, "then he was going to ask his butler about getting a builder."

Silence blanketed the table. Then her parents laughed.

"He's going to ask his butler!" her father exclaimed.

Charlotte frowned. "It was nice of him to offer. After all, if a nobleman needs work done, he asks his butler to find someone to do it, and they probably find people falling all over themselves to do so."

"Our daughter is correct again," Felicity said. "But I think you should look, too, my love," she told her husband. "Just in case, the viscount doesn't follow through."

"If he's trying to win Charlotte's heart, I'm sure he will," Armand declared.

Both her parents turned to her for confirmation. She merely shrugged, unable to keep the smile from her lips.

"*Ha!* I knew it," her mother said. "What have I told you all about that back room?"

The romantic back room in which she'd nearly become engaged.

"You're sighing," her mother said.

"Am I?" she asked.

A sudden knocking noise from down the hall had her father on his feet. After a moment, she heard him say, "Not at all. Come in, do come in." The prickling at the back of her neck left her in no doubt who it was, even before Lord Jeffcoat appeared behind her father.

Their eyes met, and for a moment, it was as if they were alone. In the next instant, she felt the strangest sense of belonging, as if Charles was already her man, her beloved, her intended. She wanted to rise to her feet and let him take hold of her hands, as if greeting her own husband.

As proper, he greeted her mother first and then Charlotte, wishing them each a good morning, before her father gestured for him to take a vacant seat at their table. Charles declined.

"As I said to Mr. Foure, I apologize for intruding before polite visiting hours, but I wanted to offer my services in seeking out Edward and his uncle. Also, my butler gave me the name of a reputable builder."

She and her parents eyed one another, and her mother nodded meaningfully to her father as if this sealed the impending wedding nuptials.

Then Charles slid his calling card onto the table with a name scrawled upon it. "The carpenter's availability is, naturally, unknown, but I would be perfectly happy to lend my name if it will speed up the building of your staircase."

"That's very kind of you," Felicity said.

Charles made a wry face. "As you may be aware, even in this day and age, after two great nations have had revolutions for freedom, it is still the case that here in Britain, a nobleman is given preferential treatment by the exact class that ought to seek out equality."

Charlotte blinked. "How self-aware of you, my lord. My sister Beatrice would approve."

"And what about you, Miss Rare-Foure?" He fixed his rich blue gaze upon her.

"I am simply grateful for your help. I fear I've made a mess of things—"

"No, not at all," three voices said at once.

"You did well under the burden of having neither of your sisters to help and a pushy landlord pressuring you." Her mother said this with obvious pride.

"And she could not have known that young Percy, who seemed to be top notch, would prove to be a scalawag," Charles said.

It hurt Charlotte's heart to believe the worst of Edward. She stood.

"If he is a scalawag, as you say, then what is the point of seeking out him or his uncle?"

"Satisfaction," Charles said.

"Too right," her father agreed. "Why don't you go with his lordship and see if you can hunt down the boy and even his uncle. That is, if the barrister here thinks we can get any restitution. And your mother and I will pay a visit to this builder."

She turned to her parents. "I am terribly sorry I forced us into this predicament."

"But she may have regained The Langham account," Charles pointed out on her behalf. *Bless him!*

"Gather your maid as chaperone, Miss Rare-Foure, and we shall venture eastward in search of the Percy family."

CHAPTER TWENTY-THREE

A few minutes later, Charlotte found herself in the viscount's plush carriage, with Delia at her side passing The Worshipful Company of Carpenters on the London Wall Road. With regret, she peered down Throgmorton Avenue to its entrance before it disappeared from view. That was where she should have gone first to find a reputable builder. All she knew, though, was that Edward was within "spitting distance" of the Aldgate water pump, as she'd told Charles.

"There is a police station that handles that end of town," he said. "We can start there and ask for his family name and that of his uncle's."

Which is what they did. Inside a cramped two rooms, bobbies milled about. Two cells were in plain sight, one holding women in various stages of undress who'd been picked up during the previous few hours, and the other holding men for various infractions.

"You can wait in the carriage if you like," Charles said to her for the second time in under a minute. In fact, they'd convinced Delia to stay inside doing her knitting, as Charlotte couldn't possibly come to any harm in a police station.

"I'm sure I can handle whatever I may encounter here," Charlotte said. "I am not one of your noblewomen who swoon at stray dogs and hold their scented handkerchiefs over their faces at the first sign of a poor person."

She wished she hadn't sounded sharp, but she was galled that the viscount's name alone would gain her family a good builder and in short order. She ought to have been able to accomplish that herself.

"Have you come to pay me fine, luv?" a woman called out, startling Charlotte, even though she knew it was Charles who was being addressed. "I'll make it worth yer while."

Most of the women laughed, but some just looked hopeless, and Charlotte wished this part of London— Edward's world—didn't exist. Or if it had to, then she wished she understood why the wealthiest Londoners didn't take better care of the most unfortunate. It seemed as if the poor laws were all designed to punish people for the sin of being poor, and the punishment meant workhouses or worse, jail.

"I know it's hard to witness," Charles said as if reading her thoughts, "but my peers in Parliament, good men like the Duke of Pelham, are working to better their lives."

Nodding, she stayed close beside him as they approached one of the policemen working at a desk.

"I am Lord Jeffcoat," Charles began, getting the man's attention as well as that of those around them within hearing distance.

Charlotte had seen it occur with Amity's husband. There was something magical about the reaction to a nobleman, especially in a place where he didn't belong, such as a police station or a confectionery. She was sure her father had experienced the same just by handing a builder the viscount's card.

"Yes, my lord. How can I help you?"

"I am looking for a family who live near the Aldgate pump by the name of Percy or Tufts."

The bobby frowned. "I don't know any Percys, but we regularly keep an eye on Archie Tufts. A bad one there, always seems to have someone else's stuff or caught selling it. He's been brought in more times than I can count, but he's never had the same address twice."

Charlotte shuddered at the notion she'd been alone in the shop with a "bad one."

"And you've never heard of a family in the area by the name of Percy?" Charles persisted.

"No, my lord. Maybe you can find an address for them at the Census Office."

Charles had already told her he thought it far more likely a family member had ended up encountering the police than having answered a census. Most people in the poorer districts of London were wary of the goal of head-counting, fearing it meant further taxation.

"Since the last census was in April of 1871, officer, I doubt that will help us much. As you know, the poorer among us do not keep the same dwelling for long. Would you mind taking a look in your records first, my good man? Just in case you've forgotten the name."

"'Course, my lord." He wrote down *Percy* on a piece of paper and called over another man with a shock of red hair. "Head to the basement, Nigel, and see if you can come up with an address. Also for Tufts."

"Ol' Archie?" asked the red-head.

The officer shrugged. But when the man called Nigel sighed, the officer added, "For his *lordship*, here."

Red-headed Nigel straightened and with a bit more enthusiasm said, "Yes, sir."

"Within spitting distance of Aldgate pump," Charlotte offered.

Both policemen stared at her, before Nigel added, "I'll do my best, my lady."

She felt a little foolish, especially when Charles didn't correct him. Obviously, the information about the pump wasn't helpful. Either they had an address or they didn't.

"How long do you think it will take?" she asked the seated officer.

"Long enough that you and his lordship might want to leave and come back," the man said. "Nigel will do his best."

Charles escorted her out, and they took his carriage, with Delia still knitting, to the pump with its crowning lantern.

"Now what do we do?" she asked, as they stood staring at what had been the water supply for a whole neighborhood until a mere three years earlier.

"Life-giving water," the viscount muttered. "Or death."

"Indeed." Not a soul in London hadn't heard the egregious tale of the contaminated sixteenth-century well beneath the pump. At first, the East Enders had praised the taste of the water until it grew foul, and the high mineral content turned out to be leeched human remains from nearby cemeteries.

Charlotte shuddered as even then, a man was drinking from it, no longer by pumping the wrought iron handle, but using a tin cup hooked to a chain and pressing a brass button installed by the New River Company that had rerouted clean water to the Aldgate landmark. Watching him, she had difficulty swallowing at the memory of the hundreds who'd died from drinking the well water.

With a smile, the man doffed his hat to her and ambled up Fenchurch Street. The next in line, a stocky, ancient woman, filled two earthenware jugs, and Charlotte imagined she'd probably used it when it was pumping well water, and probably for all her life.

"Nothing wrong with it," the old woman exclaimed, seeing Charlotte eyeing the brass wolf head spigot. The old lady caressed it fondly and shuffled down Leadenhall Street. It purportedly represented the last wolf killed in greater London.

"Perhaps we should go back to Covent Garden," Charlotte said. "Maybe Edward's mother will be there again."

"Without confectionery to sell, unlikely." Charles was eyeing the surrounding area. "Within spitting distance, the boy said."

"He did." She followed his gaze around the intersection. Behind them was a bank, on the other corner was a small grocer, a tobacco shop, and a printer. Above the bank, she could tell were other serious businesses with dark shades drawn down. However, above the shops across the street, the windows looking over the square could contain small flats. They had flowery curtains or ratty sheets, depending upon the occupant's financial means.

And then she saw Charles startle. "Isn't that the woman from Covent Gardens? And Edward with her?"

Charlotte whirled around. At first, she didn't see where he meant. Then the flash of a blue cape caught her eye on the opposite side of the street coming in their direction. Edward was walking beside the woman, and two younger children were in front of them.

"You have very good eyes for a man who wears glasses," she told Charles.

"I need them solely for reading. For distance, I have eyes like a hawk's."

"Indeed you do," she agreed, keeping her gaze on the small family. "He hasn't spotted us yet. What should we do?"

"I suppose we can approach them. I think I can protect you from a mother and her three children."

The teasing tone made her look at him. "Maybe so, my lord, but I wouldn't fancy your chances against my own mother if she were protecting me and my sisters."

His face shadowed. "Not all mothers are like yours, Miss Rare-Foure."

And then they crossed the road between horses and carriages and other pedestrians. Calmly, they intercepted the four Percys in front of a cozy pub that had clearly been there since the previous century.

"Mrs. Percy," Charlotte said, "May I have a word with you?" She ignored Edward's widening eyes and the way his glance darted from her to Charles to his mother. Clearly, he was flummoxed by their appearance and didn't know whether to stay or run.

And Charlotte saw the moment his mother recalled her as well. She probably wouldn't have if Charlotte had been alone, but she stood beside the handsome viscount, who was undoubtedly unforgettable. The woman's face paled.

"You bought sweets off me the other day."

"Yes," Charlotte said. "They were my own. I'm Miss Rare-Foure."

"Rare Confectionery," Mrs. Percy whispered.

Charlotte nodded.

The woman looked at Edward. "Is *she* your boss?"

"Yes, mum." He had hold of one of his siblings by the hand, a little girl with a patched dress. In front of them was a young boy, also in well-worn clothing, probably wearing Edward's hand-me-downs.

"What are you going to do?" the woman asked, and for the first time she glanced around. "Have you called the police?"

Charlotte could almost smell her fear. "No, we came to speak to you and to Edward, and if possible, to your brother."

"My brother?" she exclaimed. "I don't know what you're on about. I ain't got no brother."

"Mr. Tufts," Charlotte said, glancing at Edward and holding his gaze. He looked ashamed, chagrinned, embarrassed, and frightened—all at once. "You said he was your uncle."

"Blimey!" his mother said. For a moment, Charlotte thought the woman would crumble or start to wail, but she straightened, hefting the grocery bag on her hip as if it were a baby.

"We live upstairs," she gestured to The Three Brooms pub. "Two flights up if you want to come in and talk."

"Mum," Edward said in a warning tone.

"It's all right, love. He won't be back for hours."

Charlotte imagined the "he" was Archie Tufts, and she was awfully glad to have Charles with her. Glancing at him now, he nodded, and just like that, they had decided to enter an East End dwelling. *What an adventure!*

"It's the second door," Mrs. Percy indicated.

Just then, Charlotte heard her name and realized it was Delia.

"Here now, miss, where are you going?" Delia, who'd been waiting by the carriage, hurried over, obviously not about to let the youngest Rare-Foure disappear from her sight. After all, this was no police station. There were loud shouts and laughter coming from inside the pub, and even then, a man stumbled out followed by scantily dressed woman.

Receiving a questioning glance from Mrs. Percy, Delia held her head up. "I'm her chaperone," she declared with a sense of importance entirely unwarranted in Charlotte's opinion. In fact, it was a little mortifying.

"I'll be fine," she told Delia, "I am perfectly safe."

"Of course, she is," Mrs. Percy said with a huff, probably unable to imagine what Delia's purpose was.

Thinking the room or rooms upstairs must be small—and the subject of thievery and dishonesty might bring some heated words, Charlotte decided to keep her maid out of it.

"Please go back to the carriage, Delia. We'll return shortly."

Her maid pursed her lips, but eventually nodded. Charles, acting as a doorman, opened it and gestured them all inside. Behind the door was a steep staircase, reminding Charlotte of the one next to Rare Confectionery, except at the landing, they kept going up another flight.

It was slow going with the small children in the lead.

"Hurry along, Emma. Come on, Albert," Edward urged his younger siblings, sounding anxious.

"Leave them be," his mother said. "It's been a long day, and it ain't over yet."

CHAPTER TWENTY-FOUR

Just before Charles closed the door behind him, he caught his coachman's gaze, giving him a nod. He wanted to be certain the man knew where he was in case there was trouble.

As soon as they entered the flat, the Percys' dismal situation became apparent—a lone floor lamp, no heat, no carpets. Serving as a kitchen was a small chipped sink with a single tap and a small stove like the pillow woman's with no oven. A table looked to be used both for preparing food and for eating it. There were chairs enough for four. The only other thing in the small room was a pile of piecework, spread on a cloth in one corner, presumably to keep the fabric clean.

Through an open doorway with no door on the hinges, Charles could see there were mattresses on the floor.

And this family was one of the lucky ones, having a separate room for sleeping, a sink with running water, if it did, in fact, run from the tap, and apparently just one family for two rooms. These were luxuries few could afford. In a heartbeat, he could see why Edward had done what he'd done.

"Go on, you two," Mrs. Percy said, sending her littles ones into the bedroom. "Play quietly and don't come out until I tell you."

Charles wondered what they had to play with and tried to swallow the lump from his throat. It was one thing to be in Parliament, privy to reports concerning the poor. It was another to know someone like Edward, and go into his home.

"We're hungry," said the one called Albert, probably named for the Prince Consort as many young boys had been over the past two decades since his untimely death.

Not surprisingly, Charlotte dug in her purse for a bag of sweets, drew it out and handed the entire thing over to Edward to dole out to his younger siblings.

"I'm sorry. I should have asked first," she said when she noticed Mrs. Percy staring.

"No, it's not that," their mother said. "But I could have sold those and had enough to buy bread for a week."

Charlotte's cheeks turned pink, and again, she muttered, "I'm sorry."

"That's all right. They haven't tasted any of it before, except what Edward bought at Easter." She set down a crocheted bag on the table, and Charles could see through the netting it had potatoes and onions in it. And hopefully something fortifying from the butcher's shop wrapped in the white paper he could see. He wondered if she ever bought watercress.

Edward took his younger brother and sister into the next room, and the grown-ups, waiting in silence for his return, could hear the squeals of joy from the littlest Percys. By the look on Charlotte's face, she wished she had more to give them.

"Would you care to sit?" Mrs. Percy asked. "I can't offer tea as we ran out, but you don't have to stand like you're waiting for the omnibus."

Not wishing to offend, Charles pulled out a chair for Charlotte, which she graciously took, then he went to do the same for Mrs. Percy, but she looked affronted. He waited for her to sit. When she didn't but only stared at him, hard, against all common courtesy, he finally took a seat.

Now what?

Thankfully, Edward returned and took the chair across from Charlotte, so the explanations could commence. "I'm sorry, miss, I truly am," he began.

"Don't say nothing," his mother warned him.

"Mrs. Percy," Charles began, "we are not the police, but we do already know that Edward stole sweets from Miss Rare-Foure and turned them over to you. There's no point denying the obvious."

"I didn't steal from Miss Rare-Foure," Edward protested. "I . . . I just kept some confectionery back from my deliveries. But I gave you *all* the money," he said looking at Charlotte. "I didn't keep a ha'penny nor a farthing."

"You stole from the hotels and restaurants," Charles said, thinking Charlotte might have too soft of a heart to say the obvious.

"Yes, sir," Edward agreed, "but . . . not money. I would never steal money."

Charlotte sighed. "In a way, you did. I cannot get some of those contracts back, so that money is lost to the shop. And it was revenue I was counting upon."

Edward hung his head. His mother had said nothing, simply looking between her two unexpected guests and her son. Now, she sat down heavily in the last chair and fixed Charlotte with a desperate stare.

"Are you pressing charges against my son?" she demanded.

Charles thought she was going to be belligerent, but her voice broke on the last word. Then Mrs. Percy added, "Remember, he's done good by you, miss, working like someone twice his age. I know how dependable my boy is." Her words ended on a quiver of emotion.

"No," Charlotte said without hesitation. "I am not going to press charges against *him*."

"Oh!" the woman said, sitting back. "Against *me*, then? You'd rip a mother away from her three children? I work hard as a shirt-finisher for 3 shillings a week. If I could afford a machine," she trailed off sounding more desperate. "But you can't send me to Newgate."

Edward jumped to her defense. "No, Mum, Miss Charlotte never would."

"He's right," Charlotte assured the woman.

Charles felt the whole scene was like something from a Dickens' novel. Too clichéd by far, too trite, and far too sad when it happened to be real life.

"Then why did you come here?" Mrs. Percy demanded.

"Edward didn't show up for work, and neither did Mr. Tufts," Charlotte pointed out.

Mother and son exchanged a glance. For a moment, Charles wondered what it would be like to have such a close relationship with his own mother that they could communicate with a quick look.

"Who is this Tufts really?" he asked.

Edward looked down at the table. His mother took a deep breath and sighed. "Mr. Percy, my husband went into the workhouse last year for unpaid bills. Separated us as if we were cattle, they did." Then she sat up straighter.

"Cholera took my husband, or so they told me. Mr. Tufts was there, too, in the same ward as my Richard. When Mr. Tufts got out, he found me and the little ones beyond hope, living in a single room with another family, up the Whitechapel Road. He said my husband had asked him to take care of us, and he moved us in here."

"They were friends?" Charles asked.

The woman shrugged, looking weary. It was Edward who spoke next.

"Mr. Tufts told me to tell everyone he was my uncle. I'm sorry, miss."

"Was it his idea for you to keep some of the confectionery meant to be delivered?" Charlotte asked the boy.

"Yes, miss," Edward said, his voice hardly above a whisper.

"He was right about selling it at Covent Garden. Easy as falling off a log," Mrs. Percy said.

"Is he really a builder?" Charles asked, wondering at the audacity of the woman crowing about how easily she'd sold stolen sweets.

Mother and son again exchanged a look. "We don't know what he did before," Mrs. Percy said. "He wanted whatever I still had of my husband's. Said my Richard had promised it all to him."

"But he's *not* a builder," Edward added. "He stole the tools from somewhere after I came home and told my mum about the shop expanding. He was listening and said I had to introduce him."

Charles looked at Charlotte's face. She was calm and accepting, not hysterical or angry at the deception perpetrated upon her.

Then she asked, "Did you know he would make a hash of it?"

Edward's cheeks grew pink. "I wasn't sure, miss. I hoped he knew what he was doing."

Charles looked at the pale face of Mrs. Percy and the embarrassed one of her son. "Why are you both helping him?"

"He lets us live here," Mrs. Percy said. "If he didn't, we'd be in the street or the poorhouse, and my children would end up God-knows-where."

"And he has a temper," Edward said quietly, making Charles stomach flip. The idea of a grown man committing violence upon a family—and it was another man's family at that—sickened him.

"He's not all that bad," Mrs. Percy said. "We're not living in constant fear as some I know, and he's not keeping us here. We could leave if we wanted to."

"If you had somewhere to go, but he knows you don't," Charlotte pointed out.

"I have no way to make money excepting the piecework," she said nodding toward the stack of fabric. "Shirt finishing," she added, looking at Charles as if it were his fault she needed to sew. "It's the beast to do and pays worse than hop-picking, but Edward's money and mine pays for the food and some of the rent."

"And how does Mr. Tufts make his living when he's not pretending to be a builder?" Charlotte asked.

"He's no shirkster," Edward said. "He never sits idle. Sometimes he does a scaldrum dodge down by—"

"A what?" Charlotte asked.

"He pretends to be injured so he can beg," Charles told her.

"Right, my lord," Edward said, looking impressed.

"A lord!" Mrs. Percy exclaimed, pushing her chair back. "Why, I never!"

"He's a viscount, Mum," Edward said, looking more like his old self, now that he knew neither he nor his mother was going to be charged.

Charles didn't want to become the topic of conversation. "Tufts begs to help support you. Is that correct?"

"He's also a smatter, a sneeze-lurker, and a snidesman," Edward continued, "not to mention a wipe-hauler, a dragsman, and a speeler using weighted tatts."

"None of that sounds good," Charlotte said, looking to Charles for the meaning, but this time he was as lost as she was.

"Tatts are dice," he offered lamely.

The boy nodded, as did his mother, who added, "He's got a lot of swank in any case for someone with no steady job except for being a skilled tooler. A pickpocket, you understand?"

Charles nodded. Of all the people whom Charlotte could have chosen to build a staircase!

"He said you were the perfect pigeon," Edward added, staring at Charlotte.

"A pigeon?" she repeated.

"A victim," Charles explained, having heard the term many times around the courts.

"Oh." At that, Charlotte rose to her feet, forcing Charles to do the same. She paced the small room. "I'm not particularly pleased with being a pigeon," she said. Then she looked at Edward. "And I've promised the manager at The Langham that I would handle the problem with the deliveries coming up short. How do you think I should do that, Edward?"

He swallowed, looking less talkative again. Charles felt sorry for the boy, and they both waited for Charlotte to fire him on the spot.

"I will tell you how," she added. "I think you should work extra hard for me and my family, and even put in a few hours for free to make up for it. In return, I won't let you go. But you must never compromise the good name of Rare Confectionery again. If you can't promise me that, then you must say so and leave my employ."

Charles was impressed by her generosity, as was Mrs. Percy.

"Thank you, miss. He was only doing as he was forced to do. But my boy won't let you down again, will you?" She turned to her son.

"No," Edward said, his voice a little firmer.

"What happens when Mr. Tufts returns," Charles asked, looking at Edward's mother, "and expects your boy to continue providing sweets for you to sell?"

"I already told him I was found out," Edward said.

"I suppose that was why he abandoned the ruse," Charlotte said. She was staring at Mrs. Percy with a thoughtful expression. "I've had a thought or two during this enlightening discussion."

They all stared at her. Charles hoped she would get on with disclosing her ideas, since they'd pushed their luck in staying as long as they had. While he had no doubt he could defeat Archie Tufts in a duel of fisticuffs, he had no wish to bring danger upon this family or Charlotte.

But she shook her head. "My parents have returned from a brief trip, and the shop is really my mother's. Thus, I cannot say any more without speaking to her first. In any case, nothing can be done as long as you are associated with Mr. Tufts. While I don't wish him ill or even for him to end up at Newgate, I don't intend to be his pigeon again."

"Have you nowhere else to live?" Charles asked Mrs. Percy, wondering if the woman had formed a romantic relationship with the aforementioned snidesman.

"We wouldn't be here if we had," she said with a lift of her chin, then added, "your lordship." Frowning, she asked, "Or it is *my* lordship?"

Before he could answer, she said, "To the best of my knowledge, I've never spoken to a member of the nobility before, and I cannot believe my eyes that one is in my own home. Honest to God, you look like a regular person."

Charles felt like a zoological specimen. "That's quite all right. Let me speak plainly. Are you intent or compelled for any reason to stay with Tufts?" He hoped that was clear enough. *Did the woman want to get away from the charlatan or not?*

"I see no way to leave, but if I could, I would. I have no—" she glanced at Edward, who wore his normal earnest expression. "I have no particular feelings for the man."

"Very well. I sit on the council of the Society for Organizing Charitable Relief and Repressing Mendicity. They may be able to help."

"Mendicity?" Mrs. Percy asked.

"Begging," Charles said.

She drew back, affronted. "Mr. Tufts gets up to all sorts of things, most I don't ask about, and it's true, he's forced us to do his bidding in some things we ought not to have done," she glanced at Charlotte, then back at him, "or we'd have faced his nasty temper, your lordness."

Charles nearly corrected her but wisely held his tongue, as the woman was working her way into high dander.

"But I am no beggar, nor was my husband, God rest his soul. He was in the shoeblack brigade when he was younger up the old York Road at King's Cross, and even went to school four nights a week. When he was sixteen and too old to be in the brigade, he got a job as a cobbler with my own father, God rest his soul, too. Last year, we lost the shop," Mrs. Percy said, her tone thick with emotion. "Then we lost it all."

"I'm very sorry," Charlotte said, sounding overwrought, and Charles, too, felt the lump in his throat.

Many of London's lower classes lived insidiously close to the edge of ruin and poverty. They might work all their lives and still end up dying in the workhouse, as Mr. Percy had. Charles had known this fact all of his life, but knowing it was entirely removed from spending time with Edward, and also seeing his two younger siblings with very little chance for their lives to come to anything.

"I was going to send my Edward to the same shoeblack brigade after Easter." Mrs. Percy reached over and touched her son's hand. "He would have had to be declared homeless and destitute and live with the other dozens of boys there, and I would have sorely missed my son." She sighed, and Charles again was touched by the look they exchanged. She would have done what was right for him even if it meant having to send him away.

"Then he found work with you, Miss Rare-Foure. Learning to make sweets seemed far more promising and safer than being out on the street cleaning and blacking men's shoes. Some boys ain't given a good pitch—you know, a station—and they don't make much. And sometimes, the gentlemen don't pay after having their shoes done. Now, that's a tooler for you!" She nodded emphatically. Then looking directly at Charles, she said, "No offense to you, my lordship."

"None taken, I assure you." His valet always polished his shoes, so Charles knew he'd never bilked a young shoeblack out of his pay. "As I was saying—or I think I was, at any rate—I sit on the council of a society that helps people. There are about thirty-two members doing the work of hundreds, but they do succeed in finding affordable housing. Moreover, they usually raise enough money each month to get someone back upon their feet. It's considered temporary assistance, but it can get you out of a bad situation."

"How quickly?" Charlotte asked him. "I mean, if Mr. Tufts has a temper, I wouldn't want to wait one day too many."

"Don't worry about that, miss," Edward said. "I can protect my mum."

Mrs. Percy sniffed at her boy's courage. "I can protect my children," she insisted, "but I would welcome the help. When my husband died, no one at the workhouse could tell me where to go or what to do."

Charles knew that was one of the problems. The charitable society could have the best of intentions, but if they didn't get out into the poorest communities and offer assistance, what good would they do.

"I will go to the society's headquarters directly," he said, thinking of the tidy suite of rooms on Buckingham Street in the Adelphi neighborhood. "With their help, I'm sure we can find you a place to live." And if he couldn't, he would put them up in his own townhouse until he could.

"Edward can come back to work tomorrow," Charlotte said. "He will have to apologize to my mother and to the places where he made deliveries, but I won't make him pay for all the stolen confectionery. We'll call it a lesson learned, and I shall be glad to have him back."

Edward's face had gone through a myriad of emotions, but at the end of it, he said simply, "Thank you."

"I thank you too, miss," his mother said. "And I'm sorry for selling your chocolates and such."

"I understand why you did it," Charlotte said.

Admiring her generosity, Charles thought he'd fallen in love with her just a little more at that moment. "We'd best be going. I need to get to the society before four."

"I'll see you first thing," Charlotte said to Edward. "Mrs. Percy, you've raised a good boy."

"He gets his smarts from his father," she said, looking sad.

"Do you have enough food for your family tonight?" Charles couldn't help asking.

"Yes." Her voice was tight, and he figured she was holding back tears. He wanted to get out before they were shed.

"Come along, Miss Rare-Foure. My driver will think we've fallen asleep up here."

"Delia!" she exclaimed. "I'm shocked she didn't come in here and try to forcibly remove me."

But when they returned to his carriage, they found Delia sitting on the dickey beside his coachman, so lost in laughter and chatting, neither noticed their master or mistress's arrival.

"Perhaps a new romance has sprung up between our households," Charlotte mused.

Charles wanted to tell her one certainly had, but it was not the time to try again to make her his own.

"Bertie, help Miss Rare-Foure's maid down and let's get going. You both must be sick of the view of the Aldgate pump."

"Aye, sir."

CHAPTER TWENTY-FIVE

Charlotte was certain she would never recover the money she'd paid Mr. Tufts, but she was relieved that Edward and his mother were not dishonest people, merely desperate.

"Will you tell me the idea you want to discuss with your mother?" Charles asked, as they headed back along Fenchurch Street.

"Of course." Charles had become practically her dearest friend, next to her sisters. "I think Rare Confectionery should have a permanent place at Covent Garden, either a stall or a cart, and Mrs. Percy can run it."

She appreciated how he considered it, rather than dismissing it out of hand, but after a moment, he shook his head.

"I believe she does piecework at home in order to look after her little ones."

He was right. She'd forgotten about that. Obviously, they were too young for school.

"I wonder where the children were when she was at Covent Garden before?"

"If she left them here alone, that's dangerous, and you wouldn't want to encourage such a thing," he pointed out.

Charlotte didn't want to let that stop her from helping Edward's mother out of poverty and give her the ability to stand on her own two feet without relying on the duplicitous Mr. Tufts.

"We shall figure it out," she vowed. "If you can find her a place to live, hopefully a bit farther west of the pump, we can think of a place her children can stay while she works There must be many a mother in a similar situation."

He nodded. "I've sat on that council for two years and felt useless. They always have a member of the nobility on the board to help with fundraising. But this will be the first time I've been able to help someone directly."

"You've already helped me and my family," Charlotte pointed out to him. She didn't know how she would have managed without all his assistance. Moreover, without him knowing, he'd mended her wounded heart, too. It had happened almost without her realizing it, and now, she had a bright, brilliant love in her heart.

"You are a different case altogether," he said, his tone soft, but then his gaze flicked to Delia, leaning in the corner with her eyes closed, and he smiled instead of saying more.

When his adorable single dimple showed, Charlotte smiled back. *What a truly decent man!* She admired everything about him, and seeing his expression, her heart opened like a rose in the sunshine.

Wishing they could have a moment alone—no, that wasn't true! She was now wishing for a lifetime with Lord Charles Jeffcoat. However, she needed privacy to tell him she'd fallen in love with his intriguing nature—alternately calm and serious and then excitingly passionate.

"You seem thoughtful," he said.

She shrugged. "It has been an interesting few days, to say the least. Who knows what tomorrow will bring?"

"Hopefully a new carpenter," he joked.

"When you say something in jest, you seem about a decade younger."

He looked taken aback. "Am I usually so stern and off-putting?"

"You are often reflective and intent," she said, hoping those words soothed him.

"Thus, a serious, grim-faced toad. Is that what you mean?"

She couldn't help laughing. "Absolutely not, my lord. Your steady, sincere manner is a wonderful trait. One knows what you are about and where one stands."

After a moment, he nodded. "I think I know what you mean."

She wished Delia wasn't leaning against her arm. She wanted to tell Charles she wouldn't trade him and his earnest, dependable ways for anything, certainly not for the flamboyant and fickle manner of Lionel Evans. She cringed at previously thinking Lionel admirable for being sometimes loud and joyful, other times sullen and even cruel. She'd considered him to have an artistic disposition, and thought his immersion in the Aesthetic movement to be interesting and exciting.

In comparison to Charles, he was a willful child.

THE FOLLOWING DAY, CHARLOTTE intended to be first in the shop as usual, but when she approached, she could see the door was ajar and the noise from inside told her someone was at work.

Pushing the door wider, she witnessed a miracle. Her father stood by the counter, which was draped in a tarpaulin as was the floor. He was chatting with Charles! The two looked up at her entrance, both smiling, although only one had the devastating dimple that made her stomach do a queer little flip.

Over to the right were two men with heavy aprons and caps, tidy toolboxes at their sides, crafting a staircase.

Shaking her head in wonder, she approached her father and gave him a kiss on the cheek. Then she wished the viscount good day before giving voice to all her questions.

"How long have they been working? When did you both get here? I wondered where you were when you missed breakfast." She paused. "Are you sure this is a healthy environment for you, Father, what with the sawdust and all?"

"It's probably not a healthy place for anyone," he said looking cheerful. "But I'm fine. Don't fuss like your mother. His lordship wanted to meet me here early to make sure the men he referred were on the up and up."

Beaming at the workers who hadn't even lifted their heads from their tasks, Armand Foure added, "They were waiting at the door ready to work an hour ago."

She smiled at Charles. "Thank you, my lord."

"No thanks necessary. I was remiss in not helping you find a builder before."

"I wouldn't have listened," she confessed, "not when I thought I could help Edward's uncle."

"I think you and your father should pursue legal action against the man. After all, he is not related to the Percys and as soon as we get them away from him, he won't be any threat."

"His lordship is right," her father said. "You know I'm not a litigious man, but what's right is right, and apparently, we have some furnishings to purchase." He nodded to the ceiling. "That money he stole from you could come in handy. Besides, we have a lawyer practically in the family. You won't charge us, will you, my lord?"

"Father!" she exclaimed but Charles looked unbothered.

"I would not charge you, Mr. Foure," he insisted. "That is one of the advantages of being already in possession of a fortune. I cannot be bribed, nor can I be forced to take cases in which I do not believe, nor must I represent only those who can pay me."

"Ideal!" her father said, rubbing his hands together. "Not that we can't afford to pay, of course, but it would feel like being scammed twice."

Charlotte shook her head at her father's audacity. Before she could remind him that Charles's fee would not be a scam at all but well-deserved payment, Armand Foure continued, "When we win—as I'm sure we would by the smart glint in your eye—then you can charge that Tufts person for your fees and any court ones, too. What cheek! Taking advantage of my girl."

"I doubt Mr. Tufts will have the money for court fees," Charlotte protested. "He's probably spent what I gave him so I doubt he'll even have that to give back. He'll assuredly go to Newgate. And then his lordship will be stuck with court costs, too."

Her father shrugged. "The price of being a barrister, I suppose, and falling for my perfect Charlotte."

She gasped. He was truly beyond the pale. *How could he say such a thing when nothing had been declared?* Her cheeks felt as if they were burning. She and Charles had no understanding, no agreement.

With exasperation, she lifted her gaze to the viscount who stared back at her, and then, against all expectations, he smiled again.

"I suppose you are right," he said to her father.

He was practically confessing his feelings about her— and to her father! They must talk privately, and soon. But first, to the other matter at hand.

"How did you fare at the . . . what was it called? The Mendicity Society?"

"I spoke with Mr. Loch, the council's secretary, and he had immediate good news. He knows of housing for those who are not destitute but have means of an income, like Mrs. Percy. He works with Miss Octavia Hill. You may have heard of her. She has done much good work, and thanks to her association with Mr. Ruskin—"

"The art critic?" Charlotte wondered. For her, Mr. Ruskin was the nasty art critic who had spoken unkindly about Whistler's Nocturne paintings at the Grosvenor Gallery show. Lionel's dander had reached a high level during a lengthy discussion in art class.

"The same," Charles said, "but he is also a man of philanthropy, producing the monthly *Fors Clavigera* for the working class. Also known as 'Letters to the Workmen and Laborers of Great Britain.'"

"Good stuff," her father interjected. "I've read a few of those letters. Lots of interesting articles on the man's social vision."

"He gave Miss Hill one of the first properties she manages for the poor," Charles continued. "She now has about eighteen places to put families and over three thousand tenants. She is particularly interested in the well-being of children." He looked at Charlotte. "Our hope has been answered for the littlest Percys as there is a common area with care for the young ones."

"That's perfect! And there is a place for them?"

"Mr. Loch says there is a vacancy in Marylebone," Charles informed her.

"That is quite a bit west of the Aldgate pump," Charlotte said, thinking how pleased Edward would be. "You've done a wonderful thing."

"One of Miss Hill's associates will go to the East End today and collect Mrs. Percy and her little ones and whatever she wants to bring from that flat."

Charlotte was once again astounded at the power of the nobility. All she could say was, "Thank you."

"We did it together, I would say." Charles's blue eyes held her gaze for a moment, until her father coughed, nearly as loudly as the sawing going on in the background.

"I need to get the deliveries ready for Edward," she said.

"Do you think he will show up?" Charles asked her.

"I do."

After raising a friendly eyebrow, he declared he must be off to court. "I shall send you an invitation," he told her, "if you're amenable."

"I am," she said. "Very much so." And she watched him leave. She had Perrault's godmother on her side after all, in the guise of a viscount.

"I'm leaving, too, my girl," her father said. "You have everything under control as usual. I'll be back to review the progress at any time, though," he said loudly enough for the workers to hear, as if that dire threat would keep them in line.

Rolling her eyes, Charlotte went into the back room to get started. Barely ten minutes later, Edward arrived ready for work.

"We didn't tell Mr. Tufts anything about your visit, miss," he said, lingering between the two rooms, glancing over his shoulder at the workers.

"Probably wise," she agreed. "I think you and your family will be moved soon. Are you ready to make deliveries?"

"Yes," he took another step into the back room as if unsure of his welcome. "And I will apologize, too, miss."

"Good. Then let's get to work."

"A DINNER PARTY!" CHARLOTTE exclaimed aloud to Delia when the thick piece of stationery arrived with Lord Jeffcoat's seal. "With dancing."

"Just like last Season," her maid reminisced.

Charlotte thought it was nothing at all like the previous year. Although she'd enjoyed attending balls with Beatrice and sometimes with then already-married Amity, Charlotte hadn't cared a whit for any of the men. While thrilled at the venues and the gowns, she'd felt unmoved by her dining and dancing partners. This time, she would be escorted by the man she loved. And the thought of being in his arms on the dance floor caused a delightful fluttering inside her.

Excited anticipation mingled with tension, thinking of how she might dazzle or fail on the arm of the Viscount Jeffcoat. It was fun to be nervous over a man.

Before she knew it, his arrival was mere minutes away. Dressed in a saffron-colored silk gown with a shimmery, silver-beaded neckline and silver lace at the sleeve hems, Charlotte felt confident in her appearance. Matching dancing slippers and a frivolous, absolutely adorable turquoise feather tucked into her up-swept hair completed her look.

"Mr. Finley's just called up the stairs to say your viscount is here, miss," Delia said.

"Yes, I heard him," Charlotte said, wanting to laugh. Her father's man servant was hardly ever in the right place, not like a real butler, and it was something of a miracle when he was actually able to announce a visitor. The fact that he'd yelled it up through the stairwell instead of coming upstairs with dignity only made her fonder of the man.

A sudden thought occurred to her.

"Delia, are you interested in Mr. Finley?"

"Interested," her maid asked, tugging on her own simple, brushed cotton cream-colored gown. "How do you mean, my girl?"

Charlotte suddenly wished she hadn't pried, but Delia caught on to her meaning a moment later.

"Don't be daft," she said irreverently. "He's in love with Lydia."

"Is he?" Charlotte wondered how such things could happen under her nose without her awareness. *Their butler and their cook?* "And does Lydia love Mr. Finley back?"

"Yes, miss."

"And what about you?" Charlotte asked, seeing how Delia didn't seem offended. "Do you . . . like anyone?"

"I enjoyed chatting with Lord Jeffcoat's driver the few times I've met him. Nice chap. Has good accommodations at his lordship's home and a pension coming when he sees fit to retire."

"Would you leave us if you married?" Charlotte wondered, trying to imagine Baker Street without Delia.

"Well, if *you* married, too, miss, each of us to the right person, then we might stay together, if you see what I mean."

Goodness! Delia was planning on marrying Charles's coachman and moving with her. Rather presumptuous but also . . . sweet!

Descending the stairs and seeing Charles awaiting her at the bottom, the flutter in Charlotte's stomach seemed to become a tumult of birds' wings. *What on earth was wrong with her?*

His expression, the warm admiration in his eyes, did nothing to quell her nerves. She wanted to please him, to be the woman he deserved for a wife. As long as he had fallen in love with her, she could see no impediment to a future together.

"You look astonishingly beautiful," he said when her feet touched the foyer floor. He took her gloved hand in his, bent over it, and brushed his lips across the back.

She almost giggled at the wicked shiver that tickled down her spine since she could feel the heat of his breath through the thin silk. Giggling was *not* the behavior of a future viscountess so she pressed her lips together and looked at his lovely dark hair until he straightened and their gazes locked.

"As do you," she murmured. Behind her Delia made a sound, and Charlotte's gaze snapped to Charles's surprised expression.

"I mean, of course, that you look extremely handsome, my lord."

"Thank you," he said, showing his dimple. "I knew what you meant. All I need is a jeweled tiara and I would rival the queen."

This time, she did giggle. *How had she ever thought him too stuffy?*

"Are you ladies ready?"

CHAPTER TWENTY-SIX

Charles intended to get Charlotte alone even if he had to dunk Delia in the punch bowl after dinner or lock her in the water-closet while he absconded with her silk-clad charge. They arrived at the Fitzwilliams' dinner party, and not only couldn't he take his gaze from his companion, neither could the other single men in the room.

Charlotte was the embodiment of any man's desire in her fetching fiery-orange gown that set off her deep-brown hair, giving it streaks of fire. More than that—it molded to her curves as if she were gilded in the brilliantly colored silk. Short sleeves showed off her shapely arms, and the artful décolletage gave a hint of the creamy swell of her generous bosom. Not so much as to appear wanton. In fact, her dressmaker had done an admirable job. His confectioner looked as well-turned out as any woman in the nobility.

And more than anything, he wanted to elevate her into the nobility as his wife. Recalling his last thwarted attempt, he intended a vastly different approach from the dry and detached way he'd asked for her hand. Knowing her warm heart as he did, it was plain to him—she wanted a passionate pronouncement of his love, and absolutely, he was ready to give it.

After partaking of wine in the Fitzwilliams' drawing room, he and Charlotte were among some of the guests spilling over into the adjoining parlor since there were about forty. He'd dined there before and knew the dining room would seat everyone, not in a spacious manner as if they were at a palace dinner, but well enough. Besides, he didn't mind close quarters in this situation.

Adding to his glee, the chaperones had already been taken downstairs for a separate dining experience, and would return for the dancing portion of the evening. Charles felt like a schoolboy whose stern headmaster had retired right before an assembly. Naturally, some of the guests would take advantage and be on their worst behavior, those who most desperately needed a chaperone. He and Charlotte had a healthy dose of respect for one another, and while he would love to steal her away and claim her full lips, he would do nothing to compromise her, and he knew she would do nothing to entrap him.

Truthfully, he wouldn't mind her trying to trap him into a hasty marriage. A little adventure with Charlotte sounded grand except for how her reputation might suffer.

Watching her chatting with Baron and Baroness Winslow, he vowed never to cause her a moment of heartache. She was bubbling with joy, sipping white wine, talking animatedly about the concert they'd seen together, and then . . . *Oddsbodkins!* She started talking about the Aldgate pump and the horrors that seeing it in person had brought up.

Dear God! As her tone and words turned serious, the baron began to frown and his wife's lips pursed in disapproval. *Hardly the light chitchat acceptable at one of these gatherings.*

"Miss Rare-Foure," Charles interrupted before it got any worse, "did you tell the Winslows about—?" His usually quick mind flailed. Don't talk about her making marzipan or running a shop, as neither would go over well. Don't mention Covent Garden, as the Winslows would certainly not have gone there but sent their servants. Then he recalled something. "—About your various trips to the Continent? I once ran into the baron and his wife in Paris. I think they share a love of that city with you. Didn't you say you'd been to the Louvre?"

And Charlotte, bless her heart, nodded to him, a sparkle in her eyes. After a brief discourse on her own experiences, she asked the couple many questions. Once steered on the right path, she made trifling conversation seem effortless as well as genuine. Truly another one of her gifts, undoubtedly gleaned from years of helping customers.

And then he had the pleasure of escorting her in to dinner. The dining room was as he'd envisioned. The table with all its leaves stretched out to the size of a small room. Lace, candles, and flowers adorned the center, and footmen surrounded the perimeter.

After pulling out Charlotte's chair for her, Charles was settled snugly as he'd hoped, next to the most wonderful woman in the world. Their arms were practically touching.

"The Winslows were very nice, my lord," she said as she stripped off her gloves, placed them in her lap, and then put her napkin atop them, while all the ladies around them did similarly. "Everyone is extremely kind."

He didn't disabuse her of her rose-colored notions. But he'd seen two couples talking about her, although probably just wondering whom he'd brought to the party. More than one man had ogled her, and he'd overheard some female sniff loudly and disparage the loud color of Charlotte's fabulous gown. The woman, dressed in dull tan, looked like a stick insect compared to his love's curvy form and vibrant coloring. He couldn't be happier.

"As soon as Lord Fitzwilliam invited me," he told her, "I knew you would enjoy it."

She glowed, radiating pleasure, and his insides tightened. *How easy it was to make her happy!* He wanted to be the one to bring that smile to her face for the rest of their lives.

And thus, when Charlotte's happiness dissipated with the unexpected conversation that occurred during dessert, Charles felt helpless to do anything. *A terrible and unusual sensation!*

"Normally, as many of you know," Lady Fitzwilliam began, "I serve confectionery along with cake and tarts and whatnot." She gestured to the desserts that had been lined up in the middle of the table after the last course had been cleared.

"However, you also may have heard in our midst, right in the heart of Mayfair, we are losing our favorite confectionery."

Charles felt Charlotte stiffen beside him.

"Many of you probably read the review indicating their slip in quality right before they closed their doors. Such a shame. I don't know how it could have happened. We have always had the most delicious chocolates from that shop."

"And toffee," Lord Fitzwilliam called out from the other end of the table.

Charles heard Charlotte rustling beside him, seeing her bosom rise as she took a deep breath, undoubtedly to speak. To interrupt the hosts would be a *faux pas* from which she would not easily recover. Where her hand rested upon the white tablecloth, he reached up and brushed it discreetly with the back of his own, feeling her jump. She glanced at him, and he shook his head slightly to warn her.

She frowned, an expression of dismay that pained him, but she would have her chance to rebut the rumors, just not right at that moment.

"And of course," Lady Fitzwilliam added, "Rare Confectionery had the creamiest marzipan." Her ladyship sighed. "Due to mismanagement, inferior ingredients, and the like, apparently they went to the dogs, as the expression goes. A pity!" she finished.

Charles felt the young woman beside him go from simmering to a decided boil and clasped her hand, not caring who saw him while he still hoped to stave off the inevitable. He'd once seen Charlotte publicly give an earl's daughter a severe dressing down at Pelham's house. That, too, had been in defense of Amity and also the quality of Rare Confectionery—and she'd been wonderful. Jeffcoat, along with other guests, had watched open-mouthed, and Waverly had been unable to stop remarking on the "saucy shopgirl" for a month of Sundays.

But this assembly was not being hosted by someone as tolerant as the Duke of Pelham.

Abruptly, Charlotte wrenched her hand out from under his quelling grasp.

"No, we most certainly did not go to the dogs!" All eyes in their immediate vicinity turned toward her.

"Who said that?" Lord Fitzwilliam asked from the other end of the table, attempting to see who was speaking, causing all the heads to swivel toward their host.

Apparently taking it as an invitation to introduce herself, Charlotte stood up. Charles shook his head before he could stop himself, wishing he could yank her hand and drag her back down into her chair. As it was, he and every man at the table made a motion to stand with her.

"I did," she said. "Please, sirs, remain seated. I am Miss Rare-Foure of Rare Confectionery."

A collective gasp rushed around the long table like the whisper of wildfire as it caught dry grass.

"How did you get in here?" Lord Fitzwilliam asked as if she'd wandered in from the street and taken an uninvited seat at his table.

"Why, I . . . ," she glanced uncertainly down at Charles. Before he could say anything, Lady Fitzwilliam jumped in.

"You own a confectionery, at your tender years?" The heads turned to their hostess.

Charles thought it might not go badly unless she confessed to—

"No, my parents own it. I work in the shop, and I make the marzipan. The creamy one you mentioned." The guests' attention was firmly back upon Charlotte.

"My word!" exclaimed her ladyship. "Why on earth would you confess to such a thing?"

"True, true," voices muttered.

"Because I am proud of my family and our shop. And most proud of our confectionery. I hate to be contradictory, your ladyship, but Rare Confectionery has not slipped in quality."

"How did she get in here?" Lord Fitzwilliam asked again, this time directing it to his wife while he slapped the table.

Charles sighed and rose to his feet. "I brought her as my guest."

"Well that was ill-advised of you," his lordship said. "She a pretty thing to be sure, Jeffcoat, but rather common. Like inviting our butcher just because we're serving a roast," he added.

Her ladyship gasped since her reputation as a gracious hostess was in terrible danger. Not to mention the fact that her husband had insulted a viscount by insulting his companion.

"My lord," Lady Fitzwilliam called down to the other end of the table, "surely any guest of Lord Jeffcoat's is welcome in our home. Besides, it is not the same at all since we are not serving her roast. I mean, her confectionery. They are going out of business."

"No," Charlotte insisted, and all heads turned to her again. "We are not. In fact, we are expanding. There will be a delightful café upstairs above our shop."

Lady Fitzwilliam liked being the first to know things and definitely didn't enjoy being gainsaid at her own dining room table.

"Young woman, I read the article," she insisted.

"What article?" his lordship called out, then he added, "More wine," and gestured to a nearby footman.

Lady Fitzwilliam ignored her husband. "The writer stated some egregious faults that would indicate—"

"A series of unfortunate occurrences," Charlotte interrupted. "That's all it was. A rainy day, a mix-up of sweets—"

"Burned toffee," someone else interrupted. All heads turned to the new informant. "I read it, too," said a woman with heavy jowls like one of the bulldogs on Charles's country estate.

"Indeed!" said her ladyship. "*Burned.* And that is why I didn't order anything for tonight."

"You couldn't order anything, my lady," Charlotte corrected her. "We are closed."

Exasperated, Lady Fitzwilliam gestured for more wine, too. Charles hoped that would be the end of it, but then her ladyship added, "And thus, you admit it."

"I assure you, the closure is temporary," Charlotte insisted. "Rare Confectionery has always served the finest sweets and will continue to do so. You are all welcome to come to our grand reopening."

"For burned toffee," someone said, and a few snickered.

Charles had had enough. There was no salvaging the evening. He was not going to take Charlotte into the ballroom and dance with her while all eyes stared at the girl who made marzipan and whose shop sold questionable confectionery.

How had he not foreseen any of this?

"We shall take our leave," he said tightly.

However, it was Charlotte who rounded on him with her eyes flashing. "We are not leaving on account of this discussion, are we? Is that how the nobility behaves? I discredit some untruths, and then we don't get to stay and dance because of a silly article in the papers. Surely, these clever people—your *friends*—believe me rather than something they've read in the newspaper. Why, that would be like believing nonsense about themselves that they've read in the gossip columns."

Charles glanced around the table. Some people looked interested, some uncomfortable, but no one seemed particularly hostile, not even Lord and Lady Fitzwilliam who were happily drinking wine at either end of the table.

Still standing in their midst, Charlotte looked around the table. "I happen to enjoy dancing very much, you understand. I've been to balls at Devonshire House, Marlborough House, and Clarendon House. I have danced on the same floor as Their Highnesses, the Prince and Princess of Wales. My companion here was Robin Hood."

Charles winced. "At the fancy dress ball, last year," he clarified in case any of their dining companions thought she meant he had been up to something ridiculous.

In any case, she was doing well to justify her presence at Lord and Lady Fitzwilliam's home. Not that he thought she needed to prove her worth, but these people, born to the aristocratic class looked at things differently. He did, too, for that matter, or he had until he became a barrister. Dealing with real people of all classes and their problems had changed him. He hoped for the better.

Looking around the room, he suddenly had a notion few of them had been at Marlborough House on that extraordinary night. In fact, those tickets had been hard to get, exclusive to the top echelon of society. Charles was fairly certain despite being a viscount, he had attended only because the Duke of Pelham had got him in as his guest. These folks, therefore, had no cause to look down their noses at Charlotte.

For her part, she seemed to understand that the Fitzwilliams' guests would respond well to her having matched them at the game of being well-connected. And she hadn't even mentioned her best connection of all.

"If Miss Rare-Foure, wishes to leave," he said, "we shall go have an after-dinner glass of wine with her brother-in-law, the Duke of Pelham, and her sister, the Duchess. Yet if she wishes to stay, then we shall be happy to dance with you in your quaint ballroom."

He would let the choice be hers.

CHARLOTTE LOOKED AROUND THE room, gauging the friendliness of those who stared back at her. It had been a dodgy few minutes, but she hoped they understood how special Rare Confectionery was.

"Oh, I should like to stay. I am sure Lord and Lady Fitzwilliam will provide us with excellent music since their taste in confectionery is so fine."

Then she regained her seat since footmen had moved forward to start serving from the various bowls, plates, and platters.

When Charles sat beside her once again and the normal level of conversation had resumed, she looked up from her sponge-cake with cream and strawberries to see him watching her.

"Is everything all right?" she asked.

"You handled yourself with such grace. You defended your family's shop forcefully, but in a way that did not cause us to have to leave in a huff. Although I would have gladly left if you had not wanted to dance."

"You are as sweet as this cake. And I am looking forward to dancing with you," she told him. "Honestly, I cannot wait to be in your arms."

His pleased expression told her she hadn't erred in speaking frankly.

"In that case," he said, his tone low, "I hope everyone eats quickly."

She glanced around the table and sighed. "If there is one thing I learned during last year's Season, it is how excruciatingly long a meal can be."

With a thoughtful look, Charles nodded, then he turned away. "Lord Fitzwilliam," he addressed their host. "Do we have time for a quick smoke before we dance?"

And then, he stood up.

Even Charlotte knew he was behaving badly. Standing before ones' hosts stood was quite the break in decorum. Apparently, her words had spurred him to drastic actions.

Lord Fitzwilliam glanced around the table, looking taken aback, but then he shrugged and stood, causing the other men to follow suit. "I would, indeed, like to have a cigar, Lord Jeffcoat, but I fear my wife would thrash me for it later. Let us head into the ballroom, *quaint* though it may be," he added sardonically.

With half the dinner guests standing, the ladies put their napkins on the table, retrieved their gloves from their laps, and slipped them on swiftly. Then they rose to their feet as the gentlemen drew back their chairs. Charlotte thought this looked as much like a dance as anything that happened on the polished floor of a ballroom. Finally, each female took the man's right arm and let their hosts lead the way.

In truth, the Fitzwilliams' ballroom was perfectly adequate, and the next two hours flew by. With Delia keeping watch nearby, Charlotte danced twice with Charles, as was allowed, and also enjoyed the attention of other men who were perfectly adequate dancers. No one spoke cheekily to her despite her speech at dinner. However, each time a dance ended and she reconvened with her beloved escort, Charles met them with a scowl by way of greeting.

"Stop making that face at every one of my dance partners," she ordered, but secretly found it charming.

"That one held you too close," Charles muttered.

"I thought I might have to pry him off of you," he said about another.

"He was no gentleman," he fumed over a third. "He was blatantly looking down your décolletage."

"The musicians are playing so beautifully," Charlotte soothed.

"They are," Delia agreed, tapping her toe happily.

Charles gave her chaperone a withering look, and Charlotte almost laughed. Delia hadn't made society's rules, and there was no point in blaming her for being in their midst.

Nevertheless, Charlotte wanted a private moment with him.

"If you come to my home tomorrow," she informed him, "my parents will have no problem with us visiting."

"Truly?" he asked, even though Delia made tut-tut noises. The glee returned to his glance, and a smile crossed his lips bringing out his dimple.

"I shall be with you in the parlor, miss," Delia protested.

Charlotte shook her head. "Even if a certain coachman is on the other side of the front door?"

Her maid's cheeks went rosy. "Well, I . . . well!"

"My coachman?" Charles exclaimed.

Charlotte bit back a laugh. "It's nearly time for the last dance. I assume you have reserved it for me."

"Yes," he said.

"Three dances," muttered Delia, as if the fate of all things civilized hung by a thin thread and their dancing at the end of a lovely evening might snap it entirely.

"Three is allowed," Charlotte protested, knowing it was the absolute maximum before their names would be linked.

"Oh, good," Charles said. "A waltz!"

As soon as they began to whirl around the dance floor, she sighed. She was right where she wanted to be.

He leaned in close as his hand pressed the small of her back. "My coachman?" he whispered.

This time, Charlotte couldn't refrain from laughing as they danced past the stroke of midnight.

CHAPTER TWENTY-SEVEN

As she expected, her parents were more than happy for Charlotte to host Lord Jeffcoat in their home when she mentioned it over breakfast.

"Your father can come to the shop with me," Felicity said. "While he chats with the builder, I'll get the deliveries ready for Edward."

"What am I chatting with them about?" her father asked, although at that moment, while contentedly munching on a piece of bacon and sipping tea, he seemed perfectly happy to do whatever was asked of him.

"I am considering a dumb-waiter," her mother said, "from the back room up to the café."

They all called the upstairs *the café* now, giving Charlotte a little thrill each time she heard it.

Charlotte clapped her hands. "A wonderful idea, but I hope we will be able to put in a small kitchen upstairs because making confectionery and beverages all in the back room might prove difficult, if the upstairs gets busy."

"*When* it gets busy," Felicity corrected.

Thank goodness her mother had embraced the expansion whole-heartedly!

An hour later, her parents had left, and Charlotte strolled around the drawing room, wishing she could concentrate on anything except the man who any moment—

"You're here!" she said because Charles was standing in the doorway clearing his throat to get her attention.

"I am. And as usual, there was no Finley to greet me. Honestly Charlotte, I knocked, but anyone could have strolled in."

"It's really too bad," she said. "We are very lax." But she didn't really care. Their neighborhood was safe, and normally one of them remembered to lock the front door.

"My parents are out," she declared as he started toward her.

He froze in his tracks.

"They have gone to the shop together. We may have a dumb-waiter. Isn't it wonderful?"

"Is it?" he asked, looking around. "Where's that infernal maid of yours who is always jabbering on when I'm trying to speak with you? The one who has her eye upon my perfectly happy coachman?" He sighed.

"Why aren't you happy for them?" Charlotte asked. *Didn't he think servants should have love, too?*

He shrugged. "What if she breaks his heart, and he decides to retire tomorrow?"

Rolling her eyes—because she knew Delia would never break anyone's heart but was as caring as any person she'd ever met—Charlotte went to the door.

"Delia," she called out. When there was no response, she gave a short, sharp whistle.

"Good God!" Charles exclaimed behind her. "We really must try that out at my country estate and see how many dogs you can round up."

Delia came downstairs, and Charlotte addressed her.

"Lord Jeffcoat's coachman is outside, and I have been told he's very lonely."

"Oh, we can't have that. I'll go see if he wants to come in for a cuppa or stay outside and chat." Hefting her shawl around her, Delia disappeared out the front door.

When Charlotte turned, Charles was shaking her head. "That woman has no sense of duty. She didn't even stick her head in here to give me a stern look and put me in my place. What if I had already removed my coat and even my cravat and was dancing a jig? Without my shoes!"

Clapping a hand to her mouth, Charlotte laughed hard. Still chuckling at the image of the viscount in such a silly state of undress, she sat on the sofa.

"Sit, Charles."

"You said that as if I were a dog," he complained. But he obeyed, and as she'd hoped, he gave up on the prim notion of sitting opposite and instead took a seat beside her.

And then, all laughter was whisked from her throat when he leaned closer and kissed her, entirely without warning or preamble.

Slanting his mouth, he firmly claimed hers beneath his. Raising her arms, she clasped her fingers behind his neck and let him push her back on the sofa.

"Charlotte," he murmured against her mouth.

"Charles," she said back.

"I've been going mad wanting to kiss you again." He nibbled the edge of her mouth, making her body sizzle. "Having you in my arms last night with no way to hold you close was torture. Dancing was nothing less than a teasing torment." And then the kiss deepened again.

Her stomach tightened, low between her hips when he swept his tongue between her lips.

"*Mm,*" she said, the way she would when eating a delectable sweet, for he was the most delectable man.

"*Mm,*" he repeated, and before he pulled back, he gently tugged her lower lip with his teeth.

"*Oh,*" she breathed as her stomach flipped again and her heart thumped a rapid beat. When he tried to draw away, she clasped her fingers in his soft, thick hair at the nape of his neck.

"Again," she demanded.

And he did.

A LITTLE WHILE LATER, she sat primly and properly at one end of the sofa while he sat at the other, grinning at her like a fool. Charles couldn't help himself.

"Miss Rare-Foure . . . Charlotte . . . I should make some pretty speech," he began.

She shook her head. "Not needed or expected."

He halted, not having expected her comment. Then he went over in his mind what he'd rehearsed before his mirror and decided to leap ahead to the best, most pertinent part. "I confess my heart is overflowing with love for you. Will you be my wife?"

He didn't expect her to laugh in his face, but she did. He swallowed, his mouth suddenly dry, and a thousand fears raced through his veins.

"Oh dear!" she said at once, probably because he'd gone pale. Reaching out, she took hold of his hand, which he ought to have done in the first place, not to mention going down on bended knee. He would have done both if he hadn't been distracted by their heated kiss. More than that—he was truly nervous to learn her answer.

"No, please," she said, "don't look offended. It's only that I didn't expect such a short declaration any more than I had expected a pretty speech. After all, you are a barrister. I suppose I anticipated a long persuasive argument, designed to quell any misgivings I might have."

"Do you have any?" he asked, hoping this wasn't going to end badly. He wasn't sure he would have the fortitude to try a third time. Waverly would have a field day making fun of him if a viscount couldn't secure the hand of a shopgirl. Even the most spectacular shopgirl who ever existed.

"No," she confessed.

He'd nearly forgotten the question. "No? Oh, you mean *no*, you don't have any misgivings." He blew out a breath of relief. "Preparing any such argument seemed a waste of time, as I hoped I knew your thoughts on the matter. May I dare to believe my feelings are reciprocated?"

"Yes, and in the strongest measure," she agreed, wrinkling her nose in a sweet fashion and treating him to a generous smile of her full lips.

The strength left his body along with the tension he hadn't realized was holding his muscles taut. He put his head back and closed his eyes, all the while feeling her squeeze his hand which she continued to hold.

"Charles?" she asked uncertainly.

"I'm simply immensely relieved and happy." Then he realized what a besotted noodle he must appear to this vivacious woman. Sitting up, he did right by her and dropped to his knees next to the sofa.

"Charlotte, will you make me the happiest man alive and marry me?" He realized belatedly he was still staring at their joined hands. Lifting his gaze to her face, he looked into her eyes, the color of rich chocolate and saw a few tears glistening there. His heart clenched.

"Oh, no," he said at once. "Don't cry. Please. I want you to feel solely happiness at the thought of being my wife."

An uneasy thought flitted across his brain. *Had his own mother held in reserve her hopes and dreams for a life of travel and fun when she became a countess with all the dreary duties and expectations?* It seemed to him, if she had truly loved his father, she would have created the life she wanted within the boundaries of their marriage.

"I am extraordinarily happy," Charlotte said, putting all his doubts to rest. "Make no mistake. As long as you truly love me."

"Dear lady," he murmured, "you have entirely captured my heart. I think from the first time I went in the back room of your shop and—"

He stopped when she gasped. "That's exactly what my mother always says. I have long thought the shop had a magical power," she trailed off. "You're frowning."

"I assure you it was not your shop. It was you, Charlotte. You made it impossible for me not to love you. Your sweetness and caring manner, the way you laugh and see fun in everything, even dancing with a bunch of pompous folks who tried to insult you."

She shrugged. "I like to dance, especially with you."

"Especially? I should hope so, too. I would rather you never danced with another man again," he declared.

"I would be considered terribly rude and never invited to any dances. And how could I be your viscountess and host parties if I refuse to dance with anyone except my dashing husband?"

"Dashing? Who are you marrying again?"

She giggled, but then her expression turned serious as she rested a palm on his cheek. "I'm marrying a barrister who rides to the defense of strangers without being asked."

"Or paid," he reminded her.

"You are dashing in every way, even with your lopsided smile."

"My lopsided . . . ?" he trailed off. "Do I smile crookedly? Is it noticeable? Have you got a looking-glass handy?" He scanned the room and saw one hanging on the wall behind a lamp.

Rising to his feet, he went over to it, immediately peering at himself in the mirror.

"My mouth doesn't look lopsided."

He felt her arms go around his middle. *How familiar! How wifely and wonderful!*

"Smile," she ordered him, and he did, looking to himself like a dog baring its teeth. And sure enough . . .

"Dear God! Is that preposterous buffoon with his grimace askew really me?"

He felt her laughter as he heard it. Her body jiggled against his back, and he grabbed hold of her hands where they were laced across his waistcoat.

"Do you see the dimple, my lord? It is, I promise you, a dashing one."

He smiled again and saw the dip in his cheek. "If you say so."

"I promise you. Every woman loves a man with a dimple."

He turned in the circle of her arms and held her close. "I bet women prefer a man with two dimples even more."

"Nonsense. A single dimple is quite . . . ," she trailed off, and her cheeks turned delightfully pink.

"What?" he prompted.

"Sensual. It invites one—namely me—to salty and steamy thoughts," she finished.

His own thoughts went instantly to steamy ones, too. "I had no idea a dimple was all that. What do you think about a short engagement?"

She laughed until tears sprang to her eyes again.

"I'm not speaking in jest," Charles protested. "If you are amenable, I think three months. Perhaps I can hang on through four months, but—"

"Three would be perfect," she agreed. *Such an amiable woman!*

"I shall go with you to the shop at once and ask your father's blessing."

She smiled. "Do not be alarmed if my parents behave as if we're already engaged, or as if they thought we were at any rate. I swear, they have been far ahead of each of my sisters and the men who became their husbands."

"All the better. I won't need to rehearse a persuasive argument. And we'll get our families together soon. Not that I have many on my side. My father has a sister in Scotland, but I've only met her twice. She probably won't come, and it's too far to bother going to see her." Charles realized he was babbling like a brook but couldn't stop himself.

"We'll have your parents over to meet my father by week's end. And your sisters and their husbands must come, too, of course." It would be good to have Pelham there to smooth out any rough patches. "Naturally, Pelham has met my father on many occasions, but I don't think your sister, the duchess, has."

Charles felt a bit of anxiety thinking of his tetchy father together with the sunny Foure family, but as to nervousness about becoming engaged, he had absolutely no doubt Charlotte Rare-Foure was the woman for him.

BEATRICE WAS BACK, AND just in time for dinner at the Earl of Bentley's and the Viscount Jeffcoat's home, soon to be Charlotte's, too. Letting Delia fiddle an extra twenty minutes with her hair, Charlotte waited while her maid set another ringlet on the right, an extra curl down her back, and then a peacock feather tucked into the small braided bun on top.

"I think that's good," Charlotte said at last.

"Good? We want splendid. You're going to dine with your future father-in-law."

Charlotte kept it to herself how the man had thought her a light-skirt the last time she was there.

"I love this dress you chose," Charlotte said, standing and twirling in front of the full-length mirror in the corner of her room. "It is an unusual shade of greenish-blue. Or is it bluish-green, would you say?"

"Neither," Delia said. "It's jade." She made sure the white lace at the neckline was lying flat, and gave a tug on the bodice.

"*Oof,*" Charlotte said. "Not too low."

Delia smirked. "Have I ever dressed you in any way that wasn't decent? But now, you've got the viscount, you can dress a little more adventuresome. It will ensure you *keep* the viscount."

"Delia!"

Her maid took no notice of her tone. "Turn," Delia said, before making sure the folds and pleats of the gown's tournure were perfect.

"It will all be mucked up after the ride over there anyway," Charlotte reminded her.

"Perish the thought. Have one of your sisters go into the water-closet with you and you can all take turns making sure you're tidied and arranged after you get there."

"Yes, Delia," she agreed, but Charlotte had no intention of fussing. After all, sitting at dinner or in the drawing room would mess up the perfect folds of her bustle again anyway. Therefore, the best she could do was to keep facing forward. In any case, she was far more interested in being with Amity and Beatrice once more.

As expected, they congregated in the drawing room, which looked vaguely better than the last time Charlotte had seen it, simply because more lamps had been brought in and a fire burned brightly in the hearth.

Her mother and sisters glanced around the room with the same discerning eye, undoubtedly thinking what she thought about the need for a brighter carpet, fresh paint and wallpaper, and some pretty vases with flowers. Her father, on the other hand, and her sisters' husbands, Mr. Carson and His Grace, the Duke of Pelham, didn't seem to notice the drab appearance at all.

The Earl of Bentley was fully dressed, hair combed, and greeting his guests. "So this is the one who snagged a duke, eh?" he said when meeting Amity.

Charlotte hoped her sister didn't take offense, but Amity was distracted by her heavy condition and merely offered her lovely smile before taking the first available seat. As for the duke, he was well-used to his friend's father's irascible ways.

"She did indeed bag me, sir," he said, shaking the earl's hand, "like I was a prize stag."

When he turned, Charlotte noticed he exchanged a look with Jeffcoat, tolerant and fond.

"And you are?" the earl asked Beatrice and her husband. After Charles introduced them, his father made little comment except to say, "American! Really?"

Charlotte dragged them away from him, a little afraid of her middle sister's quick temper when she thought she was being snubbed.

Her parents skated through without incident, too, and then Charlotte went up to her future father-in-law and bypassed the hand he stuck out to her. Instead, she leaned in and kissed his cheek.

"I'm very grateful for Charles," she murmured so he alone could hear.

"You smell good," the earl returned, which everyone heard, causing them all to laugh, and they were done with introductions.

With champagne in hand, except for Amity who presently enjoyed nothing but a little glass of stout occasionally as advised by the midwife, they all took seats. The sofa was hard as Charlotte recalled, and she winced when Amity reclined awkwardly, looking blatantly uncomfortable.

Charles made the announcement of their engagement, which wasn't news to anyone, and he said it as if she were doing him a favor. *What a dear man!* He could have any woman he wanted, but Charlotte was confident she would love him best of anyone—from his crooked smile to his, hopefully, not crooked toes, although that would be fine, too. She looked forward to seeing his bare feet and his bare—

"I cannot believe we shall be related at last, Jeffcoat," the duke said raising his glass. "You couldn't be marrying into a better family."

"Agreed," said Mr. Carson, whom Charlotte thought a wonderfully pleasant person with whom she had spent the better part of the previous Season while he courted Bea.

"All three of our girls, Mrs. Rare-Foure," their father proclaimed, "engaged within three years. Rather remarkable."

"The magic of Rare Confectionery," Felicity mused, placing a hand on her husband's arm.

"I knew it!" the duke said, his voice teasing. "Something grabbed a hold of me when I went in there, and wouldn't let me go. I thought it was solely my wife's delectable chocolate, but perhaps it was magic."

"All I know is something was thrown at me," Mr. Carson joked, giving Beatrice a loving smile, "and yet I returned in order to receive many *magical* tongue lashings along with a goodly amount of toffee."

Beatrice didn't look bothered one bit at having her sharp tongue brought up in mixed company. She shrugged and sipped her champagne before asking, "And what magic brought Lady Marzipan and Lord Jeffcoat together? Will you tell us or will we have to read about it in the gossip rags?"

"Lady Marzipan?" Charlotte repeated, looking past her sister's stomach to see Beatrice grinning like a cat.

"Well, you labelled me a *treacle toffee heiress* before all of London's nobility," she pointed out. "But you, you shall be a titled lady."

They all laughed, except Amity, whose face was unusually pale and whose mouth looked pinched. Charlotte was about to ask Charles if he thought their cook had some ginger tea to soothe her sister when, over the laughter, Amity groaned. It was a loud and strange sound that made the room fall instantly silent as they all stared at her.

The duke rushed from a winged chair toward his wife, and Beatrice scattered to the side to give him access.

"Are you . . . do you . . . that is, can I . . . ?" he asked.

Charlotte had never seen the Duke of Pelham look more helpless.

Amity could do little more than shake her head, which told them all nothing, and then she closed her eyes and groaned again.

Charlotte took hold of her sister's hand and felt her give a reassuringly strong squeeze. Amity had the strength of ten men, and Charlotte had a feeling she would need every ounce of it.

After a pause, Felicity Rare-Foure, sounding calm, said, "I believe we shall have to postpone the dinner party. My daughter, the Duchess of Chocolate, has gone into labor."

CHAPTER TWENTY-EIGHT

Charlotte didn't mind the abrupt ending of the dinner party because she was suddenly an aunt, which was practically the best thing in the world next to being a mother herself. Without going home first, she went with her family straight to her sister's grand home at St. James's Place. A doctor arrived shortly after, as well as a midwife because the duke said he was taking no chances.

When he wondered aloud if he ought to also summon the best veterinarian in London, Felicity ushered him from the bedroom and shut the door on the anxious duke, Charlotte had joined her mother and Beatrice to sit with Amity.

"There's really nothing to do but wait and possibly eat something," their mother said, after making sure her eldest daughter was as comfortable as possible. "I was looking forward to trying out the skills of your future cook," she added, looking at Charlotte.

They sent Amity's maid to fetch a pot of tea, another of hot chocolate, and whatever was in the pantry since the Pelham's kitchen staff hadn't expected to feed guests that night.

"It's a shame," Amity said between contractions, "because you all look perfectly lovely tonight, especially Charlotte."

"Leave it to you to be so amiable," Beatrice remarked. "Wishing your labor hadn't started in order for the rest of us to have a nice dinner party."

"Besides," Charlotte said, "my fiancé got to see me in this dress." She looked down at her now-wrinkled evening gown. "And that is really the point, isn't it? Besides I'll have the opportunity to wear it again. By then, I will be an auntie." She clapped her hands. "How exciting!"

She noticed her mother exchange a glance with the midwife, and then Felicity shrugged. "This won't be all strawberries and cream. You girls understand that, don't you?"

"Mother," Bea said. "We're not children. We're married women." She glanced at Charlotte. "And engaged. Anyway, the point is, we've all either had a friend go through this or read about it."

Charlotte nodded, as did Amity, who looked a little frightened. Charlotte couldn't blame her but thought the best thing was if they kept her mind occupied as long as she wanted them.

"Would you be put out," she asked her mother, "if I took Delia with me?" And then she told them all about their maid's growing *tendre* for Charles's coachman. "It's utterly romantic, isn't it?"

Bea laughed. "Not as romantic as Lord Jeffcoat, who has known you for years, if I may point out, unexpectedly realizing you are his heart's desire."

"And he for me," Charlotte pointed out.

"Even more remarkable," Amity said from her bed, "as he is your first love and will be your only."

Charlotte decided there was no purpose in mentioning Lionel Evans. On the other hand, she didn't want them to think she'd fallen for the first man to come along and show an interest in her. Charles would have won her over even if she'd had a long list of suitors.

"I've had my eye on another man before. I'm not entirely green, as they say."

"Ha!" Beatrice said. "We knew it. Didn't we?" She glanced at the bed.

"We wondered," Amity said.

Charlotte didn't expand upon who, nor ask what her sisters thought they knew.

"It was a silly infatuation compared to how I feel about Lord Jeffcoat." Lionel had faded into insignificance entirely. More than that, Charlotte was actually relieved he'd left when he had. She might have done something imprudent that would have ensured she had to marry him. And now that she'd experienced the meeting of the minds with Charles—not to mention the lips—she knew being with Lionel would have been a dreadful disappointment and ended badly.

Amity moaned. Charlotte sighed. There was nothing to do but wait.

BECOMING AN AUNT AFTER Amity had been delivered of a beautiful boy was the first of Charlotte's blessings. Secondly, the staircase was finished to everyone's satisfaction and the shop was set to reopen. Life was good.

And not only for her and her family.

"You should see the size of the place, miss," Edward said after he and his mother and siblings had moved into their new flat in Marylebone. "Mum feels like a queen."

Charlotte's heart felt full, almost to bursting. And although she hadn't seen the place, she had been told they were well-cared for by Miss Hill. Despite what Edward said, the flats were small by any standards except for having lived as a family of four in an East End flat. Definitely not a palace, but the Percys' new Marylebone home would be safe and cheap.

"We didn't even tell Mr. Tufts where we were going."

"I think he'll be too busy with my parents' lawsuit to worry about finding you and your family," Charlotte said.

Her mother had agreed that expanding to Covent Garden, if the license for having a small stall there wasn't too expensive, would be a grand idea.

"Think of all those customers," Felicity had said, "who don't come to New Bond Street, but who wander through or near the marketplace every day."

As soon as they reopened and were back to full steam, as her father put it, then they were going to pursue the notion with Mrs. Percy.

In the midst of it all, Charlotte had her wedding to look forward to. Charles had already chosen St. George's Church, unless she had any misgivings. She had none. However, having never been inside it, she decided to stroll over and peruse the interior instead of eating a midday meal in the back room.

It was a short walk from the shop on a sunny day with just a few white clouds. Charlotte popped a piece of toffee into her mouth as she walked, wondering how her life had become so blessed. To think that she'd been working just a street away from the centuries-old church where she would marry seemed yet another miracle. Built after a parliamentary act called for fifty new churches in London and Westminster, the grand old building momentarily stopped her in her tracks.

The ringing of its single bell had been a familiar sound in her life, and she'd seen St. George's many times, but never with the eyes of a bride. Passing through the six Corinthian columns at the front, the sole adornment to an otherwise plain exterior, she encountered no one else inside in the middle of the day. Free to wander into the nave, her gaze was instantly riveted to the stained glass above the altar in the apse at the other end. With the sun shining through, every color of the rainbow breathtakingly sparkled back at her. It was better than any painting she'd ever seen.

Passing between the box pews on either side of her, their height having been lowered eight years earlier allowing worshippers to see over them, she imagined her family seated there witnessing her wedding.

Glancing up at the arched ceiling, supported by pillars that mimicked the exterior columns, she breathed in the scent of the old building—not musty, simply . . . rarefied. There was something special there, to be sure. It reminded her of being in a museum in which she'd felt compelled to speak in hushed tones while taking in the magic of great art with her eyes.

Shrugging at her silly notions, Charlotte took a last look at the polished gold leaf of the Corinthian tops and the gilded bands striping the ceiling. How fitting that the most expensive decoration had been placed closest to Heaven.

How incredible she, a shopkeeper's daughter, would marry there!

Leaving the church, being as it was such a lovely day—rare for London, no matter the time of year—she headed north two minutes to Hanover Square, intending to enjoy a bit of greenery in the shade of the old trees.

Crossing the square, determined to find a place in the middle to sit for five minutes, suddenly, she spied Viola Evans, whom she hadn't seen for months. And with her was . . . Lionel.

Lionel! Her heart nearly stopped. He looked the same yet different. His hair was shorter, his clothing different, more reserved than he'd worn to art class. Less a flamboyant continental traveler and more . . . ordinary.

Viola saw her next, dropped hold of her brother's arm, and ran toward her. In the next instant, she'd clasped Charlotte's gloved hands.

"It's good to see you," Viola declared.

Was it? It was the first communication they'd had since Viola had asked her for money. If Viola had written again with simply a few words of friendship, Charlotte would have responded in kind.

Lionel came to a stop in front of her. She realized she was trembling. A year and a half she'd devoted to watching him, hanging on his every word, letting him kiss her, waiting for the time when he would claim her publicly, as he'd hinted. When the time was right . . .

"Good day, Miss Rare-Foure," were his first words. "I'm pleased to see you looking well." And his gaze took her in from head to foot before offering his charming smile.

Scarcely able to breathe from the shock, she couldn't speak.

"Won't you greet my brother?" Viola said, her tone thin. "I hope you do not hold a grudge against him for not saying goodbye."

Viola had conveniently forgotten her own grudge against him when he had fled with just a note to her parents. Apparently, all his subsequent letters had won over his sister.

Recalling a time when she would have melted if he'd told her she looked well and smiled benignly upon her like the sun in the sky, Charlotte found she no longer gave a fig.

"I am well, thank you." Her thoughts flew to Charles. Without a hint of selfishness, he'd helped her, and then he'd kissed her, and all her troubles had faded. He hadn't asked her for anything in return. Unlike Lionel.

Shading her eyes against the afternoon sun, she looked up at Lionel. "Are you recently back from your trip?"

Brother and sister glanced at one another. "Yes," he said. "Just a couple days ago."

"We were heading to Gunter's for ices. Will you join us?" Viola asked. "Lionel was going to tell me in detail about the sights he saw."

The sights! Viola spoke as if the trip had been a sanctioned journey instead of a sneaky, slippery escape with a young woman's whose reputation was now ruined.

Feeling a little ill at the thought of hearing Lionel prattle on about places she'd seen with her own family, Charlotte shook her head emphatically. Then she recalled her manners.

"No, thank you. I have just been . . . on an errand." *What a banal way to describe touring the church where she would be married to the most wonderful man in the world.*

However, the engagement announcement hadn't yet been made, although she knew it would appear in the papers that very day. But the Evans were not her first choice of people to tell outside of her family, and to disclose such a thing out of the blue on the street seemed vulgar and boastful.

Charlotte excused herself. "I must get back to the shop."

Viola released her hand. "All right. Another time. I'm sorry we lost touch, but now that my brother is back, perhaps we can return to our former friendship, the three of us."

It had become blatantly clear over the course of the past few months that they had no common interests outside of the art academy. Not only had Lionel behaved reprehensibly, Viola had become peevish when Charlotte had expressed dismay at his departure, and then petulant when she no longer took an interest in his conceited letters. And that was before the request for money.

Nevertheless, there was no reason to be rude.

"Are you going back to art class?" Charlotte asked Viola, but her glance took in Lionel, too, and it was he who answered.

"If my sister still wants lessons, I can now instruct her, after all I've seen and done." He gave a superior smile. "I've painted with some great artists in an atelier in Paris, and I would not go back to our old teacher, regardless. I don't think any of us gained much from him."

Lionel had gained a pretty blonde traveling companion, and Charlotte vaguely wondered what had happened to the model by the time they'd reached Rome. She couldn't bring herself to care enough to pry, even if that had been an acceptable topic.

"I shall bid you both good day, then," she told them. "Enjoy your ices." That was if Lionel thought British ice could hold a candle to the French *cream ice* in Paris. After all, a few short months had apparently turned him into the next Delacroix if not Botticelli.

"Charlotte," Viola said, halting her departure. "I hope you will forgive Lionel his former ill manners and abrupt departure."

Viola didn't know the half of it unless she included stolen kisses in those "ill manners."

Because she no longer cared a wit, she said, "There is nothing to forgive, I promise you." And she meant it. That aside, it would be impossible to return to any semblance of friendship with Viola alone, not with Lionel constantly being mentioned, or worse, lingering about with his smug expression. It was unseemly.

"Good day, Viola. I wish you well." She hoped that sounded as final as she intended. Then her glance flickered to Lionel. "Good day to you, Mr. Evans."

Again, he took her measure, head to toe. It caused her cheeks to warm with shame for him, and she didn't care for the sensation.

"Good day to you, Miss Rare-Foure. I hope we shall meet again."

Lionel's eyes, which she'd always thought flawlessly exciting, sparkling with interest, now looked wild with inappropriate thoughts in comparison to Charles's intelligent and loving gaze.

Hurrying away, Charlotte felt rattled. It was the only way she could describe the unsettled feeling at unexpectedly seeing him again despite no longer having an ounce of affection for him.

THE SPRAY OF STONES upon her window and the wall beside it had her throwing up the sash in the wee hours of the morning.

As soon as she opened it, she recognized the perpetrator. Lionel appeared to be reaching for even bigger rocks in her parents' garden and was swaying like a ship in choppy seas.

"Charlotte, Charlotte. I dream of you and you alone. My muse of fire! Let me paint you in the nude."

Rolling her eyes at the drunken fool, she called down to him, "Mr. Evans, be quiet."

"Your cruelty knows no bounds. Am I truly now 'Mr. Evans' to you when I have claimed those perfect lips?"

Sweet mother! Did he care nothing for her reputation?

"I have returned," he added unnecessarily, "to claim the rest of you." With those words, he held his hands up and spread his arms wide as if he would catch her should she jump from the second floor.

His behavior was indefensible. Delia had probably popped awake at the first shouted words and had heard everything. Her parents, whose room was on the other side of the house, hopefully had not roused from their slumber. But Mr. Finley and Lydia may also have awakened. Not that she thought their household help were disloyal gossip-birds, but anyone with a cup of tea in one hand and a biscuit in the other was liable to start gabbing about something this irreverent.

"Go away, Lionel," she said, hoping by using his name he would calm down and retreat.

"Oh, yes! She loves me still. Look at yonder window how Charlotte outshines the sun," he said loudly, mangling a Shakespeare quote that even she knew by heart.

"What will make you leave this instant?"

"A promise, dear Juliet," he insisted. "Meet me today at the paradise in miniature."

His meaning was clear. Duck Island in St. James's Park. He'd painted a crude rendition of it once, and when she had not immediately recognized what it was, Lionel had scrawled those very words along the bottom: *Duck Island, Paradise in Miniature.*

"I will come if I may bring my sister or my maid."

"Absolutely not. What fun would there be in that?" Suddenly, he plonked himself down on the edge of the small garden, not even bothering with the stone bench. "You must come alone or I . . . ," he trailed off.

She waited, but when he said nothing more, she wondered if he'd fallen asleep in a drunken stupor.

"Lionel?" she prompted, about to shut the window.

"Or I shall tell everyone how ill you used me" he finally finished.

CHAPTER TWENTY-NINE

Lionel *was* mad! Perhaps he'd been eating some of his oil paint. Charlotte had heard it could drive a painter as batty as a march hare.

"What on earth do you mean?" she demanded.

"Your feminine wiles were more than I could handle," he pouted.

He'd had no problem leaving her and her wiles behind. When she started to say as much, he rose to his feet again.

"Meet me at . . . at noon," he said in a more demanding tone.

"That's impossible. I must work today." She hoped that would put him off. Besides, he would be sound asleep before noon, she had a feeling, and that would be the end of it. *But what if he returned with his loud voice and menacing words?*

"Then when you close up shop," he amended. "I will await you on the island amongst the water fowl."

Something was foul, all right, and not merely the ducks. Charlotte clenched her fists. *What did he hope to accomplish?*

"Promise," he added. "Or I will stay here until forever. And also return daily."

If he stayed, how could he return? He was truly a terrible drunk.

"All right. I will be there by six o'clock." She shuddered at the notion of doing something so sly as to illicitly meet a man who wasn't her fiancé.

"But you must promise me after that, you will never come here again," she insisted. "You will leave me alone."

"If you wish," he said softly, sounding less inebriated than before. "It will be hard to wait until I see you again." And he walked away without teetering or stumbling.

CHARLES SAW THE ANNOUNCEMENT in the paper, which he read with his morning pot of tea—a day late as often happened, since he hadn't had a spare moment for newspapers or tea the day before. The effect of seeing his name linked with Charlotte's was a welcome one, and he gave a sigh of relief. Somehow, seeing their engagement in black and white made it real, irrevocable. Charlotte Rare-Foure was going to be his capable, warm, loving wife. They would have many babies and many happy years together.

He had to spend the day in court on a case he didn't expect to win but hoped to see his fiancée later, making any potential legal loss fade into utter irrelevance.

Fiancée! He realized he was smiling to himself for the umpteenth time simply by thinking of the word. It wasn't as if he hadn't expected one day to have one. But to suddenly be able to acknowledge he'd bound himself to someone, to the impossibly wonderful Charlotte, had elevated his happiness.

His *betrothed*—Charles smiled again, another good word—she had told him the stairs were finished and the shop was close to reopening. She and her mother had started working on the upstairs ahead of schedule. With her insight into what people liked, Charlotte's new café would be a resounding success.

And he was determined to support her in whatever way he could. For one thing, Pelham had taught him how to live with a wife who worked, and how to steer the conversation away from that very fact when necessary, under certain circumstances. He wasn't ashamed of her middle-class status and didn't mind at all that she couldn't play piano or sing. If they needed entertainment, he would hire it, not expect Charlotte to provide it.

It was rather insulting when one thought of it that way—prancing out one's wife to amuse people in his drawing room the way one brought out the winning horse at the Ascot racecourse or even a prize pointer at one of those newfangled dog shows in Newcastle-upon-Tyne.

And for those times when he could safely sing her praises without embarrassing her or inviting censure, then he would do that, too. To the right group of his friends, he would proudly tell them his wife was a confectioner who made the creamiest, smoothest marzipan.

Perhaps he could increase the Rare-Foures' business simply by patronizing it, just like Pelham. Maybe Charlotte would even name something after him.

The Jeffcoat marzipan. He grimaced at the silly notion. *Maybe not.*

As long as he could make her happy for the rest of their lives, he didn't care if anyone ever ate a Jeffcoat sweet.

CHARLOTTE TUGGED AT HER trim cotton jacket. She had been pleased it was warm enough not to need a cloak until she realized the benefits of a hood giving her a degree of anonymity. Instead, she had on a vivid cream-and-pink striped skirt and fitted matching striped paletot. She loved the outfit for its whimsy, making her feel like a sweet confection. However, now that she was going to meet Lionel, she feared she had the appearance of a walking barber pole—far too conspicuous.

Leaving Rare Confectionery, she considered going on foot but decided the twenty-minute walk would take too long. Her nerves would be frayed. Thus, after debating with herself for half a block, she hailed a Hackney that was, all of a sudden, right in front of her. *How fortuitous!*

The trip to St. James's Park was short, hardly time to arrange her skirts on the worn leather seat before they'd crossed The Mall and had arrived.

"There you go, miss."

She considered asking the driver to wait, but there were many cabbies at the park's entrance, making it an unnecessary request.

Hurrying past other strollers on the various path, she headed toward the lake. In another minute, she clambered through the half-destroyed fence that had seen better days, barring the footpath to Duck Island, which was actually a peninsula. It certainly no longer kept the city cats out as the fence was first intended to protect the various species of birds, nor did it keep out people determined to go on the island.

Passing a man with a pole, she glanced into his bucket. Having read about the stagnant water, she couldn't imagine eating anything caught in St. James's Park lake.

She slipped past the bird-keeper's house, also in a sorry state of disrepair, and hurried halfway around the small island to a scraggy tree. There he was. Lionel Evans.

He didn't interest her in the least, and now, she had to convince him to get on with his life. If he was infatuated with her in some newfound obsession, she would insist it cease at once. She would even tell him of her engagement if necessary to ward him off. Surely, he wouldn't want to tangle with a viscount, especially one who was also a barrister.

Lionel turned and smiled. "There's my girl," he said, giving her pause. He seemed alarmingly sure and smug.

"Actually, I am not," Charlotte affirmed, wanting him to know at once where they stood, "and that's why I came."

Crossing his arms, he looked her up and down in that insolent way he had. She recalled he'd always done so, but it used to excite her. Now, she felt insulted.

"Are you saying you came to meet me secretly in order to tell me you don't still have feelings for me?"

She faltered. It hurt to know he'd seen how much she'd previously cared for him, and he had left her anyway. She'd rather hoped he'd been an oblivious fool, not a cold, heartless man, who'd callously dismissed her feelings.

"I came here because you forced me to," Charlotte reminded him. "Although you were rather far in your cups, and I wasn't absolutely certain you would remember."

"I wouldn't miss a meeting with you, the future Viscountess Jeffcoat."

She took a shocked step back. "How did you know?"

"It was in the papers yesterday. I noticed it after my sister and I ran into you," he said, sounding casual. "Congratulations are in order."

Pausing, she knew she was on unfamiliar territory. *What did he want?*

"Thank you," she said softly, continuing to study him. "But you said you . . . you wanted to claim the rest of me."

"And so you rushed here to see if it were true." He shook his head.

Anger arose in her. "No, I came to—"

"I do think you're a pretty girl, Charlotte. Maybe not quite lovely enough to capture a wealthy viscount unless," he paused, "unless you let him unwrap the wedding night present ahead of time and trapped him."

"What?" *Was he saying what she imagined?*

Turning on her heel, she began to walk away. She'd come because he'd threatened her, thinking she could talk sense into someone who plainly had none.

"Or does he think you are yet an innocent?" His mocking words came after her.

She stopped as her cheeks heated. Without turning, she said, "I am," and took another step away from him.

"But you did let me kiss you. More than once."

"I cared for you, Lionel," she said, facing him again. Recalling his words at her window, threatening to tell everyone she had ill-used him, she asked, "What do you want?"

"While I do think you're a special bit of stuff, you are more useful as a viscountess since I find myself in some debt. The Continent was not good to me."

"Can't you sell some of your paintings to raise money?" she asked, trying not to follow his words to their natural conclusion—he was going to ask her for money, just as Viola had done.

His face turned sour. "I am not appreciated as I will be eventually. Sometimes, that doesn't happen until after an artist dies, but I'm not willing to wait that long. I need to live. And after an incident in Italy, it turns out the best place for me to live is right here in boring old England."

To her bad luck. "What about your family?"

"What about them?" he asked angrily. "My parents didn't approve of my going in the first place. I had to . . . borrow money from them. I had to!"

It sounded as though he'd stolen from his family, and now they didn't trust him.

"Surely they will at least let you live at home until—"

He interrupted her. "Only Viola has stood by me, sending me money when she could. I hoped you, too, would be a good friend. For what we once meant to each other."

Charlotte shook her head. "I will not give you anything. I wouldn't when Viola asked me to, and I won't now."

"You will," Lionel said, looking down at his glove, giving it a tug, and then back at her. "Or I will ruin you."

A shard of fear sliced through her, but then she pictured Charles's intelligent face.

"My fiancé won't believe you," she declared, revolted by Lionel's behavior. "No one who knows me will believe anything you say."

"No?" Lionel cocked his head. "I think you are as naïve about the world as ever. Men don't like to think they've been made a fool of, not even a hint of it. And we did meet alone. How many times? Who's to say what we did or what you might have done with me?"

She didn't know exactly what he meant, but she could certainly guess some of what he intimated. Nevertheless, the one thing she was sure of was that Charles loved her.

"I'll tell him you're blackmailing me for money," she said, even though she would have to confess to having had a *tendre* for this odious man. *How mortifying!*

"Viola will tell the world you were my lover." His words came out coldly, assuredly, and without mercy.

Gasping, she felt lightheaded. *Would Viola?* Charlotte feared she would. This time, she took a step toward him, her hands held out beseechingly.

"Lionel, why would you do this to me? I cared about you, I did. You know that. But I have fallen in love with someone else. And I don't have money to give you."

"You will, and plenty of it."

"I cannot give you Lord Jeffcoat's money! If he discovered it, what would he think of me? I would never betray him like that."

"Oh, Charlotte, you've already made a terrible mistake coming here today, don't you think? If he ever found out, your engagement would be over. Why would you meet me unless you thought I had something to hold over your pretty head? That's what he'll think. Or worse, that you wanted to pick up where last we left off?"

He reached out and drew her toward him.

"We kissed," she said, looking up at him, wanting him to admit the truth. "Nothing more. That's all we ever did."

And then, out of the corner of her eye, she saw movement. At the same time, Lionel looked past her and his eyes widened, his face going pale.

Turning swiftly, she saw Charles nearly upon them. His manner was calm, his visage like stone. It terrified her more than anything that had happened yet.

Yanking herself free, which was easy since Lionel had turned to putty, she faced the man she loved.

"How did you find me?" she began, struggling to feel relieved for he had always helped her, but this time . . .

His first words left her cold. "I *trusted* you."

Trusted? In the past but no longer? She worried that Lionel—curse the man—was correct. It would take a lot of explanation to turn this burgeoning nightmare back into the gorgeous day it was earlier.

Before Charlotte could say anything more, Charles pushed past her and planted his fist in the middle of Lionel's face.

CHARLES FLEXED HIS FINGERS, then shook the discomfort from his hand. He wished he'd started with a blow to the blackguard's stomach and then an uppercut to his face. He had little satisfaction in seeing the stranger sprawled on the ground, blood spurting from his nose, already defeated.

Who was this man who'd ruined everything? In the next instant, he didn't care to find out. Ultimately, the stranger was entirely insignificant.

Turning to Charlotte, Charles thought she looked . . . different. Same big brown eyes, her lustrous hair artfully arranged for work so it didn't hang in her eyes—but her expression was one he'd never seen before. *Was it guilt? Fear?*

He wasn't sure, but he didn't like it. And her soft, full lips were tight with worry over having been discovered in some sordid mess.

Anger raced through him again, except this time, he didn't have a man's face to release it upon. He'd been approaching Rare Confectionery when he saw her come out, a delicious pretty pink-and-white vision, reminding him of a present to be unwrapped. Before he could hail her, she'd jumped into a cab. His heart set on spending time with her, Charles had followed her all the way to the park and then onto the island, wondering at her whimsical adventure. *Only to discover she was meeting with a man!*

It had been hard for his eyes to believe, even harder for his brain to accept as the first wash of fury flowed through him.

"Charles, may I explain?"

"Do you know him?" His voice sounded hollow and strange to his ears. Moreover, he wasn't sure why he asked that question first. Yet if this had been a chance meeting somehow, if she'd been taking an innocent stroll and the man had surprised her, they might salvage everything. Then, she would have to forgive his terrible assumptions.

"Yes, we used to—"

He held up his hand to stop her. He had no interest in what they used to do or mean to each other.

He'd unexpectedly won the court case that day. And even more unexpectedly had his heart broken. His worst fears were realized—he'd fallen for a woman just like his own duplicitous, disloyal mother.

"Come with me," he said. Even if she could no longer be in his life—as, from that day onward, Charlotte would mean absolutely nothing to him—yet he could not leave her alone on that wretched island. It wasn't safe.

At his words, she brightened. Her relief was palpable. She truly thought he would give her another chance to deceive him.

He reached out his arm to her, and her smile settled on her face as she placed her hand through his.

"We won't be able to stay this way," she chattered. "The path narrows too many times."

He nodded, gutted at her knowledge of the island to which he'd never been before. Obviously, she had. As she correctly predicted, they had to separate when bushes and trees crowded the narrow trail, and he let her lead the way.

Once they were back on the park's main path, she turned to take his arm, but he didn't give it to her.

Shaking his head, he started to walk away. She was safe enough now by herself. The sun wouldn't set for hours, and there were plenty of cabbies at the park's various entrances.

"Charles?"

He turned to her and her questioning expression. In his mind, he saw his father, doubled over with grief and was grateful for the small blessing of having found out before he made the mistake of marrying her.

"Miss Rare-Foure, we are finished. It may be too much for me to hope that I'll never see you again, but that is my ardent wish."

Turning on his heel, he walked away.

"Charles," she shouted after him, unbothered that there were other people on the paths. "How can you say that? Don't you love me?"

Inside, he didn't hesitate. His heart screamed *yes*, echoing futilely in his brain. Instantly he was anguished and bone-weary. However, she hadn't asked the correct question. She should have asked if he trusted her. And the answer to that was a resounding *no*!

CHAPTER THIRTY

Luckily, Amity's house was nearby, or Charlotte might have sat in the park and cried for hours. As it was, after watching Charles's broad-shouldered figure storming away from her, she quickly reached her sister's door and sobbed her heart out in private. Or, at least, as private as could be in Amity's drawing room with a new baby and a nursemaid and her sister's diligent husband hovering every few moments.

As it turned out, the duke was more helpful than Amity. While Charlotte's sister kept trying to soothe her and explain how everything would be all right, her husband wanted details, seeming determined to "repair" whatever damage had been done.

"You shouldn't have met with the man," he said, after Charlotte had got a hold of her emotions for the second or third time with the help of multiple cups of chocolate and some handkerchiefs.

"He gave me no choice. Or so I thought. Mr. Evans certainly didn't want us to be discovered. He wanted to hold it over my head until I married and then blackmail me into paying him."

"The scoundrel," Amity said. The word was strange from the lips of a nursing mother, dressed all in pale-blue, soft cotton. Charlotte felt almost as if she'd brought harshness and filth into their home.

"Nevertheless," the duke protested, "we are family. You should have come to me or, at the very least, to your own father."

"No," Charlotte disagreed. "I should have spoken to Charles first."

She thought Henry would agree at once, but he didn't. "My dear friend is a little prickly when it comes to the fidelity of women."

"Of course I am faithful!" Charlotte protested. "And I always will be. I have no interest in Lionel Evans or in any other man. I have given Charles my entire heart, and now I am lost without him." She started to cry again, recalling the tone of his voice and the harshness of his words, not to mention the quelling look in his beautiful blue eyes, icy cold when they had last looked at her.

"We believe you," Amity said, then glared at her husband.

"Of course," the duke said. "But Jeffcoat has old wounds, and they are opened every time he looks at his father." He sighed, absently picking up a cup of chocolate from which Amity had been drinking and downing it in two gulps. Then he looked at it, surprised, and licked his lips before gazing fondly at the mother of his newborn.

"Will you tell me about his wounds?" Charlotte asked, wishing she could hear the story from her fiancé. But if it would cause him more pain, then all the better it should come from the duke instead.

Henry frowned. "It's not a long story, but it is an ugly one that Jeffcoat perhaps wished to spare you."

"Whatever you are willing to tell me," Charlotte said, "I would appreciate. It is unfair for Charles and I to lose everything over someone else's wrongdoing."

"Agreed," the duke said. "The bare bones of it is that his mother was unfaithful to his father, and when she eventually moved out and went abroad, she left a great deal of damage in her wake, including a distraught husband and a scarred boy. Neither of them ever heard from her again."

Charlotte tried to imagine a young Charles with those cornflower blue eyes. *How could a mother leave him?*

Tears started to trickle down her cheeks again. "Is she still alive, do you know?"

The duke shrugged. "I don't know. But if you think somehow, after all this time, there could be a happy reunion, please don't give that a second thought. That countess needs to stay in the past."

She dabbed at her eyes with the handkerchief. The duke was probably correct. What she needed to focus on was convincing the man she loved that she was not like his mother.

"Does he not trust any women?"

The duke shrugged. "I feel a little disloyal discussing this further with you."

"Discussing what further?" came a voice from the doorway.

Charlotte recognized Lord Waverly from previous gatherings. A little mortified to be caught with her tears barely dry, she rose to her feet, having decided to make a hasty escape. With a quick nod in his direction, head down and her face practically hidden behind the damp handkerchief, she wandered toward the other door that led out of the spacious drawing room and into a smaller parlor.

"If it's about Jeffcoat," Lord Waverly called after her, "I've just seen him."

Charlotte spun about and faced him. "Where?"

"At our club," he said, his tone measured. "He is halfway to being Lord Lushington already."

"Lord Lushington?" Amity asked.

"To put it plainly, Duchess, our friend cannot see a hole in a ladder."

"That isn't plain speaking at all," the duke admonished him. "Nor is it kind."

"I tried to get him to come with me to see you—not knowing she would be here," he explained, looking at Charlotte with nearly as chilly a gaze as Charles's. "But our friend is determined to be full up to the knocker by bedtime."

"If all your babbling words mean Charles is becoming inebriated, then you should have stayed with him." Charlotte hadn't meant her words to come out harshly, but of all the three friends, Lord Waverly had always seemed the most devil-may-care. He was also known, at least in the gossip columns, as a womanizer, which to her way of thinking was a reprehensible trait.

He blinked, then narrowed his eyes. "Miss Rare-Foure, I am not Jeffcoat's nanny. What's more, after he told me a sad story of treachery," Lord Waverly added, seeming to weigh each word, "he needed some time alone. I think on top of it all, he felt slightly humiliated to have fallen at the hands of a shopkeeper's daughter."

"Waverly!" the duke scolded him. "I will ask you to hold your tongue. Recall my wife, please, is that same shopkeeper's daughter, and you are in her home."

Lord Waverly had the grace to look shamefaced at the duchess. "My apologies, Your Grace."

As expected, Amity was all graciousness and light. "That's quite all right. I know you are speaking out of great friendship for Lord Jeffcoat. But you must understand that this terribly sad and treacherous story you mentioned has befallen my sister, as well. And you must also know, if you don't already, my sister is very much in love with your friend."

"Is she?" he demanded, not ready to let go of someone to blame, or it seemed that way to Charlotte.

"I can answer for myself," she said. "I love Charles with all my heart. I was tricked into meeting an old . . . acquaintance. He has fallen on difficult times and thought he could use my engagement as a windfall. I had just disabused him of such a notion when Charles showed up."

Lord Waverly lifted his head, looking down his nose at her, one eyebrow raising and then the other. She knew it for an imperious stare, often given by the nobility she'd encountered. She didn't let it bother her one bit but stared right back at him. After a few seconds, the man lowered his chin and openly considered her.

"You truly love Jeffcoat?"

"I do." She started to lower her gaze at discussing something so personal with practically a stranger.

"No," he said, "look at me right here. For I like to think I am a good judge of character, and most people's show plainly in their eyes."

"My sister doesn't need to be interrogated by you," Amity said. Her tone was soft but with a heart of pure iron. Unfamiliar as it was, Charlotte shivered.

"That's all right. I can look Lord Waverly or anyone in the eyes and declare my love and my fidelity. Charles didn't give me the chance, but I am determined he will."

Another long moment, and then Lord Waverly nodded, looking satisfied. "I am at your service if I can help. But if I were you, I would wait until at least noon tomorrow before you seek him out. Otherwise you might find him at his worst, and nothing makes a man quicker to temper and poor judgment like a pounding head and a sour stomach."

CHARLES SAT IN HIS STUDY and considered his future. Waverly had tried to dissuade him from drinking too much. Naturally, he'd failed. Regardless, no matter how many glasses of brandy, Charles felt as sober as a priest. Eventually, he'd given up trying to drive Charlotte out of his heart with liquor and had headed home.

On the carriage ride, he'd realized what he needed to do. It was his turn to leave.

Not forever, but for the time being, until he didn't feel . . . anything. Not for Charlotte. He didn't want to go to Pelham's baby's christening and see her there. He didn't want to drop by Pelham's house and run into her. He didn't want to go into a restaurant and be offered a Rare Confectionery.

By the time he'd vacated his carriage—annoyingly realizing that even his own driver reminded him of Charlotte, or at least her maid—he'd decided to go for a tour of the Continent. He'd missed out on such a whimsical thing, what with studying to be a barrister and taking care of his father.

He grimaced into the glass of plain water he was now nursing in order to avoid a headache in the morning. And he would drink at least two more before bed, a trick he'd learned while spending too many nights at one pub or another with Waverly when they were at school together. All the more helpful a trick when exams loomed the following day.

His father, who would abhor thinking he'd ever been "taken care of," was the singular impediment. How could Charles up and leave him? Or he should say, how could he leave him *too*?

If he thought for one moment the earl would go with him, he would welcome him as a traveling companion, but his father had made his feelings quite clear on ever leaving the isle of Britain. "Not on your life."

The few times Charles had been away, just for a week to France or Spain, he'd been with Waverly, always looking for women, or with Pelham, always searching out the best cup of coffee. Or with both.

Actually, he didn't mind going alone. Charles would talk to the earl in the morning, making certain his father knew, despite his intent to stay away for an extended period, that it was temporary. At the end of that time, he would return as the dutiful son he'd always been. Tomorrow, he would turn over his court cases to one of his associates and then depart from the coast with all due haste.

And quite a bit of haste was due as far as he was concerned.

Before he weakened and changed his mind.

Before he gave in to the desire to see her face again and let her lie to him so sweetly.

To punish himself for such weakness, he dredged up the image of Charlotte moving into the circle of the stranger's arms just before Charles had made his presence known to them. *If he hadn't, would he have had to watch her kiss another man?*

Feeling his stomach turn, he drank down the water and lifted the glass to hurl it at the wall. His hand was trembling and his heart pounding. After a moment, he breathed a calm, steadying breath, set the glass down, and refilled it from the pitcher his butler had left. He had let her unexpected betrayal rob him of his civilized nature once that day. He wouldn't let it happen again.

"DEPARTED?" CHARLOTTE REPEATED THE word. The startling information had come from her mother's lips, making it even stranger. "Lord Jeffcoat has departed? For where? And how do you know this?"

Charlotte had simply gone into work as usual, intending to go to Charles's home later in the day, as Lord Waverly had advised. At that moment, she held a piece of lacy, cream-colored fabric, shot with small blue flowers in one hand and a peacock feather in the other, as they designed the curtains and the interior of the café.

As casually as possible, she'd said, "I'm sorry to say Lord Jeffcoat and I had a . . . a falling out yesterday, but I intend to see him and sort it all out." Armed with the knowledge from the duke, she thought she could get to the heart of the issue of Charles's trust and make him understand she was not like his mother.

And then her mother had said those puzzling words indicating Charles would not be found at home. Felicity stared at her.

"Now that the police are holding Mr. Tufts in jail, your father wanted to discuss the lawsuit with Lord Jeffcoat. He went to Lincoln's Inn this morning but was told your viscount had turned over all his cases, including ours, to other barristers and taken a leave of absence."

It was already noon. "Why didn't you tell me as soon as you came in?"

Her mother blinked. "Naturally, I thought you knew."

Charlotte snapped her mouth closed. Of course her parents would assume she knew where he was going. But she didn't. All she knew was he was no longer her betrothed, and if she didn't hurry, he might slip away from her forever thinking she'd betrayed him.

"How can I find him?" she asked out loud, not caring what her mother thought of her youngest daughter's carelessness in losing her brand-new fiancé.

"You could ask his father. If anyone knows, it will be the earl."

NOT HALF AN HOUR later, Charlotte, with her mother at her side, stood in the cheerless parlor when the Earl of Bentley entered. He had agreed to see her immediately. In the next instant, she knew why.

"What have you done?" he demanded in lieu of a greeting, obviously prepared to berate her.

She took a step back at his intensity, and then realized his words were born from pain, dredged up from the past. Moreover, just as she was losing her heart's desire, he feared he was losing his son, and by her actions.

"It was a terrible misunderstanding," she began.

Charles's father waved her words away. "That's what my wife said at first, until there could be no misunderstanding anymore. Then there was only the sickening truth."

"I am not that woman!" Charlotte declared, feeling her mother bristle at her side. Felicity had been clear she would not interfere, but Charlotte also knew her mother would not stay silent if her daughter were unjustly attacked.

"No, and you shall not be my son's wife, either. He saw through you in time."

"Please, my lord, there was nothing to see through. I love your son."

"Do you?" he asked, his tone bitter.

"The question is, does your son love my daughter?" her mother asked, drawing the earl's attention. "I think it rather unbecoming of him to turn tail at the first bump in the road."

"Mother, please," Charlotte began, but the earl drew himself up even taller than he already was.

"Are you disparaging my son?"

Felicity sniffed in a way she had that managed to convey a "take it as you will" message. Charlotte didn't think it would go over well.

"Madam, how dare you?"

"How dare you to point fingers at my daughter without even knowing the facts. These young people should work it out for themselves without the ghost of your own past interfering. But they cannot do that when one of them has run away."

"Run away!" the earl looked as though he were going to pop a button. "I'll have you know, madam, that my son has worked hard all his life, even though he didn't need to, while his peers were lazing about doing very little with their God-given talents. Charlie has earned the right to spend a year traipsing about the Continent."

Charlotte gasped. *A year!* First Lionel and now Charles. She was beginning to think she drove men to cross the blasted Channel!

"He should be doing that on his wedding trip," her mother pointed out.

The earl sighed as if he were deflating along with his anger. "It's true that I do not know the details of their falling out," he glanced at Charlotte with less anger, "but something severe occurred."

"Honestly, my lord," Charlotte spoke up before her mother could rile him again, "Charles misinterpreted something he saw because . . . because—oh dear!" she didn't want to say it.

"Because?" the earl prompted.

"Because he was hurt by your countess—by his mother's departure."

Charles's father paled, and he shook his head, looking lost in his own painful thoughts.

Charlotte reminded him, "Think of how hurt that young boy was, with a mother who didn't want him."

"Of course she wanted him!" the earl exclaimed. "But I wouldn't let her have him. She would have taken him from me, and I had to punish her."

Felicity grabbed hold of Charlotte's hand as if someone were trying to separate them, so fierce was the older man's tone.

"You punished your son along with your wife?" The words were in Charlotte's heart, but they were spoken by her mother. "I understand you were the victim of a terrible betrayal," Felicity continued. "And I can tell you loved the countess a great deal. However, when one becomes a parent, one must put the child first. You would have done better, sir, to make sure your son knew his mother was not a monster."

The earl backed up a step at the notion, making it plain he hadn't been able to be that generous.

"Did she try to contact him?" Charlotte asked, wishing her tone didn't sound small and sad, but her heart was breaking all over again.

The earl nodded. "I stopped her," he admitted. "I blocked her every attempt and destroyed every letter."

"Surely, when he was older you could have allowed it without fear of losing him," Felicity said.

"The missives stopped years ago. She may be dead for all I know."

Or care. The unspoken words hung in the air between the three of them.

"Don't let him think I don't love him. Don't let him leave with such pain," Charlotte begged. "Please tell me where he is going, and I will go after him."

"Yes," her mother agreed. "She will."

CHAPTER THIRTY-ONE

Charlotte could see his tall form over the heads of the others in the crowd at the Dover ferry dock. Charles was ascending the gangplank, about to steam out of her life. Tears were streaming down her cheeks, causing people to stare and, at the desperate look upon her face, to move out of her way as she fought to reach him through the throng of travelers.

Sailors were untying the lines holding the steamship to the dock. She would be too late. She'd spent the morning first at the harbormaster's office and then at the Channel Steamship Company's ticket office trying to determine the correct vessel, and thus, had almost missed him entirely.

"Charles," she called out, but she knew at once it was pointless. There was a good breeze that in earlier years would have carried a ship swiftly, if perhaps choppily, across the Channel. Currently, it was sending her words uselessly in all directions except toward the man she most desperately wanted to touch again.

For a moment, he seemed to turn in her direction, perhaps taking a last look at England for the next year, but she couldn't hope that he would notice her plain green hat in the sea of people milling about. Some waited for another steamship, some for a sailboat, and some surged forward to board the Empress with the man Charlotte loved.

Anguish, strong and terrifying, filled her and she nearly collapsed to her knees, carpetbag and all, but for the fear she would be trampled.

"Charles," she yelled, causing a few people around her turn to stare. But he had already reached the ship's railing and was speaking with someone at his elbow, whom she thought might be his valet.

Delia, by her side, as she had been for the past day and night, grabbed her by the waist to comfort her.

Without thinking how unladylike she would sound or how her mother would strongly disapprove, Charlotte whistled, long and loud. The shrill sound sliced through the blustery wind that whipped at her cape, and made those near her cringe. She didn't care about any of that, only noticing that Charles lifted his head and glanced again over the throng on the dock.

A spark of hope lit in her.

Whistling again, she raised her arms, waving them wildly.

"I think he's spotted you, miss," Delia said.

While unable to see his delightful dimple from that distance, Charlotte hoped he was smiling. After all, he couldn't doubt her love when she'd come after him all that way across the southeast of England.

Assuredly, he'd seen her for he started to lift his hand, a little hesitantly. But to her amazement, he rested it back upon the railing and didn't do anything more. He didn't try to disembark or reach her, and her heart began to pound like a soldier's drum.

"Don't despair," she said aloud to bolster herself. After all, at that moment, they were still within yards of each other, and he was finally within sight.

Continuing forward, she made little headway as she fought through the crowd continuing to board the vessel, as well as those who'd stayed to say farewell.

"Over there, miss," Delia said, pointing to the ship's bow. Another gangplank was in use by the hustling crew, carrying last-minute cargo and supplies, perhaps even mail heading to France.

Charlotte found it just as difficult at first to fight against the tide of people as to push through it. But after a few yards, she'd cleared the worst of the throng, and, suddenly, she had reached the gangplank.

About to set her foot on the rough wooden board, a sailor grabbed her arm. "Here, now, you can't go that way. If you have a ticket, you have to board at the other end."

"I don't have a ticket," she confessed, trying to wrench her arm free. "I need to speak to my fiancé. He's already on board."

"You can't board without a ticket, miss. Move along." He released her, then crossed his arms and blocked the gangplank.

Glancing up, she could see that Charles was now leaning over the railing, trying to discern what she was doing.

"You see," she said, pointing up at him. "He's right there." She waved at him, but to her consternation, he didn't wave back.

"He doesn't look interested in seeing you, miss."

"I just want to speak with him for a moment," she persisted. "I promise I won't cause you any trouble. If I could just dash up there and talk to him, then I'll come right back down again. Just like the Grand Old Duke of York."

"From the nursery rhyme, miss?" he asked, scratching his head.

"Yes indeed." And it must have been her nervousness at how everything might go terribly wrong that caused Charlotte to start reciting:

"Oh, the grand old Duke of York,
He had ten thousand men.

He marched them up to the top of the hill,
And he marched them down again."

The sailor was taken aback, and even Delia laughed nervously at her side.

"She just wants to see her fiancé," her maid explained.

"Then her fiancé should have bought her a ticket." He looked Charlotte up and down. "Maybe he can't afford a wife, and you'd do better to look elsewhere. Pretty girl such as yourself.

"He's a viscount," Delia protested, obviously not appreciating the sailor's forward manner with her charge. "And he'll be most annoyed that she can't get to him. You know how the nobility are. One minute you're a seaman and the next, it's off with your head."

When Delia made a slicing motion across her throat to illustrate her meaning, Charlotte decided the stress must be getting to her maid, too. After all, Charles was hardly a ruthless tyrant.

Then inspiration struck her as it always did in the shop. "I have something for you," she said, thinking perhaps the sailor didn't have easy access to confectionery. "A tin of sweets if you will accept it."

Naturally, she hadn't traveled without something sugary and soothing. Although she and Delia had eaten a few on the train journey, there were many left. Without waiting for an answer, she fished the Rare Confectionery tin out of the carpetbag she carried.

"You can have whatever is left—chocolates, toffee, and marzipan—if you'll just let me up the plank to speak with Lord Jeffcoat. Please."

The sailor looked from her to the outstretched tin, which he took so slowly she wanted to scream. But eventually, with eyes narrowed, he opened it.

"*Ah,"* he said after breathing in the aromas of chocolate, butter, sugar, and almonds—all combined to smell like heaven. He chose a piece of toffee, popped it into his mouth and closed his eyes.

A whistle sounded on board, barely louder than hers, indicating the ship's imminent departure.

"Please," she said. "I'll come back directly."

Nodding while sucking the sweet, he stepped aside. However, when Delia went to follow, he barred her and said to Charlotte, "Just you, miss, the *fiancée*." He said it as if he still doubted her. "This one stays with me."

"This one!" Delia repeated, sounding outraged.

The sailor shrugged, again addressing Charlotte. "That way I know you'll return."

"As if I'm a hostage," her maid muttered.

"I'll be back shortly," Charlotte promised. And finally, she set her foot upon the gangplank.

CHARLES THOUGHT HIS EYES might pop out of his head. Charlotte was bounding up the plank. *Was she insane?* He watched her board the vessel, but hemmed in from both sides by passengers standing at the rail, he couldn't rush to intercept her and send her back down as he wished. Instead, slowly, he moved in her direction, annoyed that she was going to force them into a public display.

When they did finally get near one another, she didn't stop at a civilized distance. As carelessly as she'd performed her unseemly whistle on the dock, she now did the unthinkable—she collided with him so he had to sweep his arms around her in front of the other passengers or be bowled over by her.

As soon as he had her against him, the noises of the vessel and the dock fell away, as did all thought of who might be watching. His familiar Charlotte had dropped her carpet bag upon his shoes and was holding on to him tightly.

"Charles," she said, looking up into his face. "I caught you in time. Please come off the ship with me."

"I'm going to France," he said, thinking his words sounded a little lame and tepid in comparison to her grand gesture.

"If you go to France, then I will, too."

He shook his head. She had no idea what she was saying. "Why?" he demanded.

"Because I love you," she declared, and not quietly but as though they were alone and could speak frankly.

He sighed. Maybe she thought she did at that moment, but she might not tomorrow or the week after.

"I will leave the shop and go wherever you wish," she insisted, the tears falling from her eyes, "because you are the most important person in the world to me."

He was taken aback by her vehemence. After all, he knew how she adored her family.

"And because I won't let you believe for another moment you're not wanted."

With those words, cutting to the heart of the anguish he'd felt for as long as he could remember, Charles set her from him. When she dashed at her tears, he produced a handkerchief and wiped her wet cheeks gently, then handed it to her to hold.

"Charlotte, I cannot forget what I saw."

"You saw me telling a man how much I loved you and that I wouldn't be blackmailed into giving him money. He wanted to tell you untruths about me, but I wasn't scared for a moment. I know deep inside you trust me. You must, elsewise how could you love me as you do?"

Tears pricked his own eyes. He did love her with his whole heart and until that terrible moment in the park, he had trusted her implicitly. *Why had he stopped?* He should have given her a chance to explain.

"Now that I've told you," she continued, "he cannot blackmail me. And after you clobbered him like that, I believe he understood you were not a man with whom he should trifle. After all, you are a barrister, and he is only an artist, and not a very good one at that."

An artist! The passionate, poetic, dashing creature he'd imagined women admired. But not someone who could take a punch—that was certain.

"I shouldn't have jumped to a conclusion that flew in the face of everything I know about you." It was a miracle she had come after him.

"Dear Charles," she said, blinking up at him. "I'm so glad I caught you. I would have followed you to the ends of the earth to make you understand how much I adore you."

Reaching for her, he drew her once more into his embrace, bent down, and kissed her. Ignoring someone clearing his throat and another person exclaiming about her sensitivities, Charles felt Charlotte's warmth race through him, easing his pain as she thawed his heart.

"*Oh!*" she exclaimed when he lifted his head. "I can feel your love tingling down to my toes."

Her artless words eased the bands that had been squeezing his heart for days. Besides he felt the same way, except it was more of a sizzle. Glancing down to see if his toes really were on fire, he realized the deck was tilting under his feet. They had departed the dock, and the people around them had moved to the railing on the other side of the ship.

At the same time, Charlotte let out a slight squeal before exclaiming, "Gracious! I don't have a ticket. I gave the sailor confectionery."

"Of course you did." His delightful fiancée, for he had never stopped thinking of her as his, naturally paid people in sweets. "I will pay your passage."

"And what about Delia?" she asked, her brown eyes filled with worry.

"I'll pay her passage, too."

"No," Charlotte said, shaking her head and peering back the way they had come. "I left her on the dock."

He couldn't help laughing at her morose tone. Nothing seemed sad anymore. He couldn't dredge up an ounce of worry or fear. He had the woman he loved at his side, and they were going to France.

Dear God! They were going to France, unmarried, having just kissed in front of a ship full of people. And she had no chaperone. What's more, they would have to spend the night in a hotel and return via the morning's vessel. Her reputation would suffer no matter what they said or did on the Continent. Unless . . .

"Charlotte, will you marry me?"

She giggled. "I already told you I would." She reached up and stroked his cheek. "Have you been in the seaside sun too long?"

"I mean will you marry me when we get to France. You have family there as I recall, and then we can return to England as husband and wife."

For a moment, she sunk her teeth into her full lower lip that he loved to nibble on. *What were her thoughts? Did she have doubts?*

"I suppose my parents have had the enjoyment of two church weddings for my sisters. As long as we have a splendid party when we return, then I see no reason why not."

Then she frowned. "But what of your father? Won't he be disappointed not to witness the marriage of his only child?"

Charles couldn't help grimacing. "My father will definitely not be sorry to miss a wedding. They are among his least preferred events. In fact, we will be doing him a favor by getting it over with."

"Then, my dear viscount, I say yes to France. We must go directly to my grandparents. They have a large apartment in Paris. Also, a farm that my father inherited when his older brother died last year, but I doubt we shall go there. Unless you want to. Oh, you will love the Foures, such warm people."

Charles didn't mind as she continued telling him about the French side of her family, and how she'd become The Honorable Miss Rare-Foure the previous year when her father also inherited the barony.

In fact, as they faced forward toward the distant horizon, he was so wrapped in their love, he could no longer feel even a hint of the gusting breeze. And despite the pungent sea air that had filled his nostrils all morning, now all he could smell was her delicate aroma of flowers and citrus.

"Good Lord!" she suddenly declared. "We're eloping. How exciting!"

He grinned at her.

"Your dimple," she exclaimed. "I have missed it dreadfully."

"I have missed *you* dreadfully," he told her. "Up until now, I've been a rather boring person, but I hope this is just the first of a lifetime of adventures."

"I don't see why not," she said, her utterly practical words making him laugh again.

"No, I don't see why not either," he agreed.

EPILOGUE

Charlotte had been incorrect in her assumption her parents wouldn't mind missing their youngest daughter's wedding. As soon as a telegram was sent from Paris to London and delivered to the Rare-Foure home on Baker Street, one was sent in return and delivered to her grandparents' home on the Boulevard des Capucines.

"Wait for us! We are coming. Love, Mother." Charlotte read the short message aloud over dinner to her father's parents and to Charles, who then slipped on his glasses to reread it.

"I guess we are not marrying tomorrow after all," he said.

Instead, they went through the formality of banns being published at the mayoralty of the city in preparation for their civil wedding at City Hall.

Meanwhile, both her grandparents were delighted to chaperone the engaged couple wherever they wished to go. Their first stop was Boucicaut's multi-floored emporium, Le Bon Marché, since Charlotte had nothing with her except her small traveling bag. In the spacious department store,

Charles insisted she let him buy her a new wardrobe, not simply for the duration of their stay before the wedding, but also a trousseau befitting a viscountess for their wedding trip.

Naturally, they couldn't do all that at the ready-to-wear department of a single shop. Once her parents arrived—surprising her with Beatrice and her husband, too, as well as Waverly as best man—the shopping and eating began in earnest. For the sheer excess of it, they strolled three arcades in one day. Since it was sunny out, the covered shopping malls were not crowded. The sunlight streamed down through the glass overhead onto the flagstones of the oldest of them, the Passage des Panorama.

When they came out, they crossed the Boulevard Montmartre directly into the next row of covered shops at the Passage Jouffroy. After they'd enjoyed every type of shop imaginable, from books to tiny teacups to parasols, Felicity declared herself famished.

Leading them in a lively debate over whether to eat at Le Grand Véfour or her favorite, Le Procope, Charlotte's mother settled for the former as it was closer to the last arcade they intended to visit. Yet immediately after the sumptuous meal, they couldn't resume shopping without a stop at Stohrer's.

"Mother's beloved patisserie," Charlotte told Charles, leaning in as she often did, just to breathe in his beloved scent. "It's supposed to be the oldest one in Paris, too. If we decide to serve anything other than beverages and our sweets upstairs at Rare Confectionery, we will want to find someone who can make pastries like these."

Then she paused before adding, "If you try to order anything other than a rum baba, Mother will make you also get a rum baba. Everyone must have one who goes to Stohrer's, or so she thinks."

"What do you think?" he asked her.

"My favorite are the eclairs, which I may get, as well as a—"

"Rum baba," he supplied.

"Precisely. You will get along well with my family."

They ended their day at the third arcade, the Passage Verdeau with its magnificent pitched glass ceiling and timber shopfronts.

"This was the perfect day," Charlotte proclaimed later when they had returned to her grandparents' spacious apartment on the wide, tree-lined boulevard. Sitting in the garden behind it, she added, "The only thing that would have made it better was the presence of Amity and her duke."

"Do you think you can have *more* than perfect?" Beatrice asked.

Charlotte looked at Charles who smiled back, showing his dimple. "Definitely," she said.

A week later, Charles and Charlotte were married at the Hotel de Ville, still undergoing its finishing touches after being burned in 1871, but already looking extremely majestic.

"Even the name sounds much grander than calling it merely City Hall," Charlotte whispered as they stood on the gorgeous red carpet before Monsieur Moreau, mayor of the 19th arrondissement in Paris.

Naturally, officiating in French, he read from a book, while bureaucrats remained seated on either side of him. As witnesses, she supposed. Behind her, her family and Lord Waverly were seated, and behind them were her grandparents' friends, standing between the mural-clad walls depicting the countryside, reminding Charlotte of her grandparents' farm outside the city.

"I hope you're not disappointed," she said. "It's not St. George's, but it's a fine building nonetheless."

Charles cocked his head. "If you think this government building is fine, I cannot wait for you to see my country home of which you will be its mistress. Another minute and you shall be my wife."

She nearly slapped a hand to her forehead as a thought dawned on her. She had run away to the Continent with a man without telling her family—the exact thing she'd thought was too selfish to ever do. Granted, crossing the Channel had been unintentional, but if Charles had gone ahead of her, she would have pursued him without care for her own ignominy by the very next steamship. Luckily, she had caught him.

They were holding hands, facing one another, and she squeezed his gently.

"I love you," she whispered.

"I love you," he said loudly enough for everyone to hear.

There was an approving murmur in the room, and she knew there was nothing selfish about what she'd done. For she would spend all the days of her life loving this man with all her heart.

When the mayor declared them married, Charlotte turned to see her parents, certain she could see joy shimmering in the room.

A MONTH AND A half later, having seen everything they wanted to see of France, Switzerland, Italy, and Germany, Charles sat beside his viscountess on a train from Dover to London in a private carriage. Taking hold of her gloved hand, there were times when he still couldn't believe they were together. He should never have doubted her.

It was strange then to hear her suddenly doubt herself over the clackety-clack of the train wheels. "I don't know anything about running a nobleman's household. What if I make a hash of it?" she asked as they approached the outskirts.

He grinned down at the capable woman who could accomplish more than most men he knew.

"You shall make a welcoming hostess," he vowed. "But as your older sister will tell you, it is not all parties. Or rather, it can be too many parties. Hosting becomes a duty and a job, as demanding as being a confectioner. And the stakes are higher."

"Higher than my almost ruining my family's shop with a few hasty decisions?"

Shrugging, he brought her hand to his mouth and nuzzled it through the thin cotton, making her laugh.

"You didn't almost ruin anything. However, a misstep in the wrong place, such as at a royal event, for instance, or a word in the wrong ear can have monumental consequences, international ones even. On top of being a viscountess, you are the wife of a barrister."

"Meaning what exactly?" she asked, trying to keep her face solemn and failing. Abruptly, she flashed him a smile.

"What do you find amusing?" he asked.

"Every time you use the word *wife* and refer to me, it feels as if you're tickling my ribs."

"I enjoy tickling you," he said, then thought of the past few weeks in various inns, especially their nights together. "I've enjoyed everything I've had the pleasure to do with you," he added, making her cheeks turn pink.

And since they were alone, he yanked off his gloves and trailed his finger down the sweet curve of her cheek.

"As the wife of a barrister," he said, trying to sound grave, "you must not seem perverse or depraved in any way."

She clamped her hand to her mouth, but her shoulders began to shake. Finally, she let loose her laughter, spilling out like water from a broken dam.

"Oh, Charles," she said when she could speak again. "You are so dear to me, even when you are too serious. Do I seem as if I might have a tendency toward some perversion I cannot even imagine or depravity that might get you thrown from the bench or disbarred?"

"No," he said, glad she hadn't been insulted because he was, in fact, only joking. "In summation, as the wife of a peer of the realm and a barrister's wife to boot, you must behave with decorum and dignity, demonstrating good judgment and . . . you're grinning again," he pointed out.

"You said *wife* again." She tapped her lap with her free hand. "I don't wish to gainsay you, for you know better than I, to be sure, but I have read the papers, including the scandal sheets. A bad habit, I know. Nevertheless, it seems you are discussing standards that are broken daily by men and women of the nobility."

She was right, but he wanted to do better. Moreover, he wanted her to do better. He didn't want anyone to ever whisper about her as they had his mother.

"I don't want to be in the gossip rags," he insisted. "I don't want people reading how you were dancing too closely with another man or how I slept with my cook or with Lord So-and-So's wife."

She drew back. "Would you sleep with our cook?" Her tone was appalled.

"Of course not," he said quickly. "Thus, I will behave in a manner that precludes my having to worry about seeing such a story in the paper. But I also don't want to read about my wife with another man."

"*Oh,*" she said, her tone soft. "Whether nobility or not, no one wants such a thing to happen. I cannot imagine the heartbreak of my mother or my father were either to find the other had been untrue."

"Exactly. Heartbreak and humiliation," he added, thinking the latter destroyed his father nearly as much as the former. "But your parents wouldn't have to read about it in the morning, afternoon, and evening standard, or hear it whispered every time they walked into a room, or even in the chambers of Parliament."

Charlotte nodded. "I wouldn't treat my beloved husband in such a fashion no matter if anyone ever found out. Even if one could get away with it in perfect secrecy, one would know it deep down and feel its sting the rest of one's life. Don't you think? I don't know how anyone lives with the guilt."

"Nor I," he agreed, staring into her eyes.

He leaned down and kissed her, relishing the way she turned in her seat and lifted her arms to clasp her fingers behind his neck. Already, they were acting with impropriety, but it wasn't the type of thing that would get into the scandal sheets. The gossipmongers feasted on the type of unseemliness that hurt. It was a blood sport amongst the *ton*, and if someone didn't go away wounded and bleeding from the scandal, then they didn't consider it a proper disgrace!

How could he make her understand how it would crush him?

When he drew back and they both could breathe again, she fixed him with her deep-brown gaze.

"I would never do to you or our children what your mother did." Her quiet words reached him in the space of a heartbeat and across the span of years from the time he was a child, watching his father's despair.

Charles gasped, raising his eyes to hers. He didn't need to make her understand. She already did.

"We would win the flitch of bacon," he vowed. "Be it a year and a day or a hundred years that go by, I shall have no regrets marrying you."

"We would win the whole pig," she agreed.

AS SOON AS CHARLOTTE awakened in her husband's arms, in her new home, she was ready to tumble out of bed and rush to New Bond Street.

However, Charles stirred and dragged her back against him for early morning kisses . . . and more. A long while later, she stretched and proclaimed herself famished.

"After breakfast, I shall go see how everything is progressing." Arising, she wandered to the window to see what her morning view would be. Amazingly, Hyde Park stretched out across the street westward into the distance, with Kensington Gardens at its far end. In her mind though, she was already at Rare Confectionery.

"What if the stairs collapsed or the tables don't look right, or someone has painted the peacocks in the wrong colors?" She wasn't truly worried. Life was too good to borrow trouble. She simply missed the shop and her family.

"We arrived on British soil yesterday," Charles protested. "Must you go to work today?"

"I've been idle too long. You didn't marry an upper-class sluggard."

"Watch your words, woman. Not all upper-class people are sluggards." Jumping out of bed, he chased her as far as her new dressing room, where he let her figure out her clothing in peace. Soon, she hoped Delia would be there, too.

"Will your father be at breakfast?" she asked through the closed door.

Her new father-in-law had welcomed them back the night before. They'd been too exhausted from the past days of travel to do more than enjoy a celebratory glass of brandy while he toasted their nuptials before they'd retired.

"I don't know," Charles confessed. "You'll get used to his ways, sometimes crabby, sometimes . . . well, if not exactly cheerful, then at least wryly humorous."

"That's fine, my love. He is your father, and I will love him." She hadn't told Charles about her meeting with the earl before she'd raced to Dover tracking her fiancé like a dog at the hunt. She hoped to get her father-in-law alone before she left for New Bond Street and urge him to confess to her husband that his own mother had not abandoned him.

It was the best wedding present she could think of.

An hour later, having kissed Charles goodbye, she was in her husband's carriage, being driven to New Bond Street. The coachman's cheery face reminded Charlotte she must speak with Delia later that day, not only to apologize for abandoning her on the dock but also to do a little matchmaking.

And then she sent a fervent prayer that all went well in the townhouse behind her. She'd left the two tall men, father and son, talking quietly. When she got home that evening, she hoped a most important disclosure had been made and Charles's heart could start to heal.

The familiar bell tinkled as she pushed the door open. Charlotte couldn't help the loud whistle of happiness that escaped her at seeing Rare Confectionery re-opened, with customers already at the counter. Every head turned at her loud entrance.

Her mother didn't have the heart to look annoyed at her uncivilized youngest daughter. Felicity had written to Charlotte while she was away, telling her they'd had a visit from a *Herald* reporter, who had praised the confectionery and the décor of the café, and so enthusiastically that Londoners were chomping at the bit for it to open.

Even then, her mother was filling a white bag. Beatrice, who a moment before looked sour at being in the front of the store, grinned at Charlotte and nodded toward the staircase. White lacquer with sapphire blue curlicues painted down its skirtboard, it was whimsical and magnificent.

Edward came down the stairs carrying some tins, giving her a happy smile and nod by way of greeting. He had to duck under a blue satin ribbon that blocked anyone from going up to the second level. They'd been as good as their word, promising not to open the café without her.

She went through the opening between the counters.

"Greetings, My Lady Marzipan," Beatrice exclaimed. "We're so glad to have you back."

All Charlotte could do was smile as she hurried behind the curtain and into the familiar room that seemed to have sparked true love for her and both of her sisters.

Hanging her jacket on a hook, she took a clean apron from the drawer and quickly pinned it onto her blouse before tying the bow behind.

It was good to be home!

Finis

AUTHOR'S NOTE

In this story, I've made mention of the popular Aesthetic mode or movement that flourished in Britain in the late-nineteenth century. As best I understand, it grew naturally out of the pre-Raphaelite Brotherhood, which started about 1848, blossoming into a collective of likeminded, rather privileged artists and poets who believed in *art for art's sake* and in depicting the natural world sensually and colorfully. Most of us are aware of Rossetti's luscious-lipped, red-headed models from which he created the epitome of a pre-Raphaelite painting.

Strangely, while art critic and philanthropist John Ruskin vigorously defended and championed them, he took great offense at Whistler's looser, impressionistic paintings that came later, particularly, as mentioned in this book, his *nocturnes*. The Aesthetic movement, with Whistler and Moore, among others, was greatly influenced by Japanese art and culture, especially in the furnishings using lacquer and bamboo. And Charlotte's beloved peacocks were a great favorite of the era.

While artists were living a somewhat rarefied, esoteric life, many in the Victorian era were struggling simply to survive, with art far from their minds. The Aldgate pump, mentioned in this story, also called *The Pump of Death*, was not the only water pump to poison people in the Victorian age. Much closer to Mayfair and Rare Confectionery's New

Bond Street was a cholera outbreak in 1854. It was traced to a water pump at the intersection of Broad and Cambridge Streets (now Broadwick and Lexington Streets). This occurred during the greater pandemic of cholera between 1846 and 1860.

In that area, however, the illness rate plummeted drastically when they closed down the pump after famed physician John Snow created a map of dots to show the prevalence of illness near the pump. Finally, he proved his theory that cholera came from water not from particles in the air, something he'd been trying to verify since at least 1849. (Fun fact: He is also the doctor who first administered anesthetic to Queen Victoria for birthing two of her children.)

Another danger in this period, and indeed through much of the eighteenth century, was thievery, scam artists, and pickpockets. As Edward and his mother started to mention, there are numerous words for criminals, particularly thieves in Victorian slang, particularly cockney rhyming slang. Here are just a few more than I mentioned in the story: *cracksman* (burglar or safe cracker), *mug-hunter* (street robber, like a modern-day *mugger*), *dragsman* (steals from carriages), *gonoph* (minor thief), *roller* or *mutcher* (steals from the inebriated and from prostitutes), *sneeze-lurker* (throws snuff at one's face then robs while the victim is sneezing), *snoozer* (steals from hotel rooms while guests are sleeping), and many more crime-related words: *area diving, babbling brook, barkers, beak-hunting, bearer up, betty, bit faker, blag, bludger, buster, cly faking* (or *to fake a cly*), *crack a crib,* or *ply the crooked cross.* (I cannot even get through the letter *C.*) This didn't necessarily mean it was a more dangerous society than today. Perhaps only that they had a more colorful and descriptive vocabulary.

On a lighter note, I found a photo of a woman who had spread almonds on a piece of cloth, covered them with another, and whacked them with a rolling pin. Reputedly, the almonds came out to be the perfect consistency for making marzipan, as if they had been put through the grinder. Nevertheless, I decided Charlotte probably wouldn't do that in the front room of Rare Confectionery, so I gave her the gentler method of grinding. If you decide to try making marzipan and you don't have a grinder, you can still find some satisfaction using this alternate method.

ABOUT THE AUTHOR

USA Today bestselling author Sydney Jane Baily writes heartfelt historical romance with engaging characters and attention to period detail.

A first-generation American daughter of Brits from either end of London, Sydney resides in New England with her family—human, feline, and canine. The rest of her extended family live in the U.K. where she spent many happy childhood summers. She loves shandies, Maltesers, Cadbury chocolate, fish and chips, and anything from Harrod's food hall or in a Fortnum and Mason's basket.

You can learn more about her books, read her blog, sign up for her newsletter (and receive a free book), and contact her via her website at SydneyJaneBaily.com.